PRAISE FOR

Suzanne Redfearn and *Hush Little Baby*

"This psychologically astute, swiftly paced story will leave you wondering 'what if' even after the last page is turned."

—Christina Schwarz, *New York Times* bestselling author

"Chillingly realistic and pulsating with suspense, this deftly told story will leave you breathless."

—Heather Gudenkauf, *New York Times* bestselling author

"This snappily paced, cinematic novel about the dysfunctional modern American family from architect and first-time author Redfearn contains heavy doses of violence, danger, and fear. Events hurtle along with great urgency to a rousing climax. A smart, suspenseful debut."

—*Publishers Weekly*

"A compelling tale of the deceit, violation, and anguish that undergird the myth of suburbia. Redfearn's debut ratchets up the tension page by page, as husband and wife try to inflict the most damage on each other without harming the kids. Every character hides something, and each surprising revelation torques the plot further. The emotional and physical injuries mount, driving inexorably toward a surprising climax."

—*Kirkus Reviews*

"Having recently read *Gone Girl* by Gillian Flynn and *Lie Still* by Julie Heaberlin, I was thinking that the chance of finding another book that would have me sitting on the edge of my seat, practically holding my breath, was pretty close to nil. I am pleased to say I was wrong. *Hush Little Baby* is the type of book that you don't put down."

—BookBinge.com

"Top Pick! 4 1/2 Stars! With clear, efficient dialogue and authentic scenes, this story rings universal. Equal parts suspenseful and moving, Redfearn's skillfully told, candid story flows easily within a well-defined plot, making this novel a stunning and captivating read."

—*RT Book Reviews*

Also by Suzanne Redfearn

Hush Little Baby

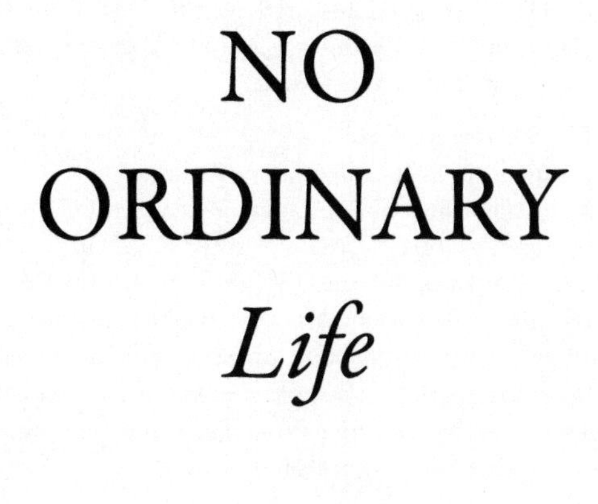

Suzanne Redfearn

GRAND CENTRAL
PUBLISHING

NEW YORK BOSTON

This book is a work of fiction. Names, characters, places, and incidents are the product of the author's imagination or are used fictitiously. Any resemblance to actual events, locales, or persons, living or dead, is coincidental.

Grand Central Publishing
Hachette Book Group
1290 Avenue of the Americas
New York, NY 10104

www.HachetteBookGroup.com

Printed in the United States of America

RRD-C

First Edition: February 2016
10 9 8 7 6 5 4 3 2 1

Grand Central Publishing is a division of Hachette Book Group, Inc.
The Grand Central Publishing name and logo is a trademark of Hachette Book Group, Inc.

Library of Congress Cataloging-in-Publication Data has been applied for.

ISBN: 978-1-4555-3390-9 (paperback)

For Joe

"Fame is a dangerous drug and should be kept out of the reach of children."

—Paul Petersen, child actor

1

Molly and I sit outside the principal's office, my eyes staring at my hands in my lap like a defendant awaiting a verdict. Molly's pudgy legs stick off the plastic seat, her pink Crocs bouncing up and down in rhythm with the beat of the class singing in the auditorium beside the office.

The rubber of the soles are too short for her feet, her heels extending a quarter inch beyond the edges. She needs new shoes. *Why haven't I bought her new shoes?* Suddenly embarrassed, I want her to stop bouncing her legs and drawing attention to the evidence of my maternal failing. My eyes shoot to the school secretary. Mercifully, the woman types on her computer, completely oblivious to Molly's too-small shoes and my parental incompetence.

The door on the other side of the room opens, and Tom walks through, his eyes on the ground as he shuffles shamefully forward. The school counselor walks two feet behind, her face turned up haughtily. She's the one who called an hour ago to tell me Tom had gone missing after lunch, which in turn sent the entire campus into lockdown. Half an hour later he was found in an empty classroom, sitting on the floor reading, entirely unaware of the commotion he had caused.

I pull Tom to me, and he buries his face against my hip. Smoothing his honey hair, I open my mouth to make excuses, but already the counselor has turned and is walking back toward the door.

I lift Tom's face so he is looking at me, his blue eyes so sorry that it makes my heart hurt. "Darn cat," I say, our secret code for the anxiety that wraps around his vocal cords like a serpent whenever he's confronted with a new or difficult social situation, an expression coined from the saying *Cat got your tongue?*

He nods and again buries his face against my jeans, his desire to disappear so palpable that I wish I were a magician and could make the wish come true, zap him onto the couch at home and put a mug of steaming hot cocoa in his hands.

The social anxiety disorder Tom suffers from is called selective mutism, an insipid label suggesting he chooses to be silent. Which is ridiculous. No eight-year-old would choose to be a freak other kids make fun of, an outcast unable to voice his opinions or defend himself when he is called stupid, crazy, or a scaredy-cat. Tom is none of those things, and he certainly doesn't choose to be silent so he can be thought of that way. It should be called something more like verbal abandonment, his voice literally deserting him as soon as he steps from our van as if his tongue has been cut from his throat, his ability to speak ripped away, and no matter how desperately he wants to, he is suddenly, inexplicably rendered mute.

"Mrs. Martin?"

I turn to see the school secretary beside us.

"Dr. Keller will see you now."

"Tom, take Molly and wait for me in the van," I say, dropping a kiss on his head and handing him my keys.

Like a prisoner being released from a stockade, I feel his sigh of relief as he takes Molly by the hand and leads her toward freedom.

"I get to choose the music," Molly says, immune to the worry around her.

I follow the secretary to the principal's office and am surprised when I walk in and find another woman already seated in one of the two chairs across from Dr. Keller's desk.

The woman stands, and I need to crane my neck to greet her. Tall as a man and thin as Gandhi, her height is exaggerated by the two-inch pumps she wears, which are perfectly matched to her navy suit, and I'm amazed she can stay upright on her two spindly legs.

I give her extended hand a weak shake, feeling short and disheveled in my T-shirt, jeans, and worn-out Jack Purcells.

"Elizabeth Glenn," she says, as if it explains her presence.

I look at Dr. Keller in confusion.

"Ms. Glenn is from Children and Family Services," the principal explains.

My heart thumps in my chest then leaps into my throat, where it lodges behind my tonsils, making it impossible to respond.

"I called her because we are concerned about Tom."

"Where is Tom?" Ms. Glenn interrupts, looking around me as if I might be concealing him.

"I sent him to wait in the car," I manage. "With my daughter."

"Your older daughter?"

"No, my younger one."

Ms. Glenn opens the manila folder in her hand and scans it. "Your daughter Molly?"

I nod.

"Your four-year-old?"

I nod again, causing the woman's eyes to bulge. "You sent your eight-year-old with your four-year-old to the car by themselves?"

Heat rises in my face, and the pounding in my chest intensifies until it ricochets like cannon fire in my ears.

Dr. Keller stands from behind her desk and brushes past me. "Candice, please go to the parking lot and bring Tom and his sister back into the office. Then please keep an eye on them until we're finished."

I want to defend myself. The van is parked right outside, in the spot beside the sidewalk. The windows are open. The school is not a dangerous place. Tom and Molly will be more comfortable in the van listening to the radio than sitting in the office doing nothing, with Tom staring at the door aware that we are discussing him. His problems stem from social anxiety associated with the school, and he's phobic about attention being focused on him. I was being a *good* mom.

Of course I say none of these things. The thoughts remain in my head as most of my thoughts do, where I bury them behind the regret that comes from not speaking up when I should. It's not difficult to trace the roots of Tom's shyness. Though I don't have an anxiety disorder, I certainly have anxiety. At the slightest provocation, my tongue grows thick, and at the first sign of conflict, my brain shuts down. And at this moment, I am suffering an acute attack of both afflictions, my pride buried deep beneath my cowardice.

Dr. Keller returns to her seat, and Ms. Glenn smooths her skirt, both women puffing with superiority.

"Faye, please sit," Dr. Keller says.

I don't want to sit. I want to flee. Already I've failed whatever test I needed to pass in order to avoid Family Services infiltrating my life, and I desperately want to avoid whatever repercussions are to follow. I feel like I've been ambushed. The counselor led me to believe I was in for the same lecture I've been given the last three times I was called in to discuss Tom's issues—*Tom is not improving as much as we would like... His issues cannot be ignored... Have you been taking him to therapy as we suggested?... blah, blah, blah. You need to do this, you need to do that... This is all your fault.*

Dr. Keller sighs through her nose, and I manage to stagger into the remaining chair.

"First, I want to say we're on your side. All of us have Tom's best interests in mind."

"May I ask where Mr. Martin is?" Ms. Glenn interrupts again with the annoying habit she has of stopping the flow of conversation to look for missing members of my family. "I had hoped both of you would be here. This is important."

As if I don't know this is important. My son doesn't talk, and he locked himself in a room so he wouldn't have to go to chorus where he would be asked to sing out loud.

"Faye?" Dr. Keller says, making me realize I haven't responded.

"He's on the road," I answer in the voice I call my waitressing voice because it's the voice I use when I work. The voice is strangely flat and staccato, but it's the only voice I can manage when I'm stressed. Sean thinks it's sexy because it's low and sultry. The kids think it's weird, which it is. "He's a truck driver."

This is almost the truth except for the omission about Sean leaving five months ago for a one-week trip and not returning since.

Ms. Glenn frowns, her mouth tight and her nose pinched. "Mrs. Martin, Tom needs help, professional help."

Professional help that costs $120 an hour, and that he needs to go to three times a week to be effective.

I look back at my hands in my lap and mumble, "I'll get him into therapy."

It's a promise I've made from this very spot three times before, and it sounds false even to my own ears. And Ms. Glenn's response is so quick that I know her answer would have been the same regardless of what I said. "While I'm sure your intentions are sincere, it's my job to ensure Tom's welfare. So unfortunately, at this point, we're going to need more than your word. I've opened a case file, and from this point on, I will personally be monitoring the situation. Dr. Keller will keep me apprised of Tom's progress in school, and I'll need to visit your home to get a better understanding of his life outside the classroom."

"That's not necessary," I blurt, my voice spilling out with my panic. "Tom's mutism has nothing to do with his home life. It's like stuttering; it can happen to anyone." I'm quite aware of how I sound, like I'm completely freaked out at the idea of her visit. Which I am. But it's also the truth. I may not have the money for therapy, but I've read every book on selective mutism there is. Tom's issue wasn't triggered by anything we did. It's simply who he is, like a child being born with bad eyesight, except the cure isn't as easy or straightforward as buying him glasses.

Dr. Keller speaks up, her voice sympathetic. "Faye, we know you're a good mom, and we're not saying Tom's issues stem from you or Sean. It's just standard procedure. When a case is opened, the home environment needs to be investigated."

Investigated! The word causes temporary heart stoppage, and I wish she'd go back to using the word "visit." Molly's too-small Crocs irrationally flitter through my brain, blinding me with the thought of how many other deficiencies might be discovered if this woman comes into my home. I don't think we have anything to hide, no more than any other family, but like cramming your mess into a closet, even if you're pretty sure everyone does it, you still don't want anyone opening the door.

"I'd like Mr. Martin to be there as well so I can meet him," Ms. Glenn says. "When will he be returning?"

My mouth skews sideways as I shrug and give a noncommittal answer. "Hard to say. Sometimes he picks up new jobs on the road."

Looking up through my brow, I see Dr. Keller studying me, her mouth in a tight line, her radar for deceit finely tuned from dealing with adolescent delinquents every day.

Ms. Glenn stands and holds out a business card. "Call me when he gets back." Halfway to the door, she stops. "One more thing. An eight-year-old and a four-year-old should never be left in a car alone."

She continues on, her condescension trailing behind her like a bad odor, and when the door clicks closed, Dr. Keller says, "Faye, I know you're doing your best, but three kids is a lot to deal with on your own, especially when one has special needs."

The words "special needs" stick like a burr in my chest. Tom is perfect, *was* perfect. Until he started school, he was my perfect little boy—shy and perhaps a bit reticent, but sweet, loving, and happy, blissfully oblivious to the world beyond his own and how difficult and cruel it could be.

"Sean seems to be gone a lot. Maybe you need some help. Is there family nearby who can give you a hand?"

I give a thin smile and nod. Another lie, but who's counting?

2

Family Services, whooee," Bo says, looking up from the awl he's using to make a new hole in the harness on his lap.

Bo, owner of Bojangles Stables, is my unlikely best friend. Five foot six on a tall day, a day when his arthritis isn't acting up and crimping him at the waist, he's black and wrinkled as an overripe raisin, has an opinion about everything, and isn't afraid to share it. He was the first person I met when Sean and I moved to Yucaipa twelve years ago and has been part of my life ever since.

"Ain't those the people they call on *Law and Order* when they find kids chained to their beds and eating cat food?"

"You're not helping."

"Sure I am. I'm telling you that going to live with your mom to avoid Family Services is a good idea. Your mom is good people."

It's been two days since my meeting at the school, the threat of Ms. Glenn's visit compelling me to finally make the decision I've been putting off for months.

"My mom and I can't survive five minutes together. How am I going to live with her?"

"Because there ain't no other choice. Sean ain't coming back, and you in a pickle. That's life, full of more pickles than cucumbers, but that's the way it is."

"He called last night."

Bo's hairless brows rise, his black eyes looking straight into the back of my brain. "You talk to him?"

I shake my head. "I hung up."

Bo nods his approval and returns to his work.

I smooth the muzzle of the horse in the stall beside me and bite back the tears that have threatened every other second since Sean's call.

Hey, beautiful, he said when I answered, the greeting slow and gravelly, thick with drink and emotion. In the background, there was traffic, and instinctively I wondered where he was. It had been a favorite game of ours, me guessing where he was calling from. Before he would leave for a trip, I would memorize his route, tracing it with my finger in our old atlas and reciting the names of the towns he'd be driving through so, when he called, my guess would be close.

Last night I didn't guess. I said nothing, the whoosh of cars and trucks behind him filling the silence.

How are they? he said finally, and that's when I hung up.

"You tell him you was leaving?" Bo asks, working another hole through the tough leather, his hands impressively deft and strong for a man so old.

"I told you, I hung up," I snap.

A smile plays on his thick lips. "Finally getting some fire in your belly. That's good."

I sneer at him, and his smile grows.

"Mom, wlook," Molly says, waddling into the barn, the bib of her overalls stuffed with apricots, grinning like she just scored a touchdown in the Super Bowl. Gus, our mangy mutt, stands beside her, his tail wagging as if he had something to do with the accomplishment.

"Theyw're for Mischief," she says proudly, sticking out her lumpy belly.

Mischief is a horse that doesn't belong to Emily, my oldest, but who Emily thinks of as hers.

"Awre Em and Tom awlmost home?" Molly asks, toddling forward awkwardly, her arms wrapped around her stash.

I look at my watch. "A few more minutes. Should we wait for them by the road?"

"Okey dokey, jokey smokey," she says, spinning around to change direction, the extra weight throwing off her center of gravity and pulling her around quicker than she expects, causing her to topple over and lose her load.

She busts up laughing as Gus leaps around, barking with delight. Bo and I laugh with her. The kid is downright hilarious.

Molly frowns when she puts the last apricot back in her bib and it causes another to pop out. She does it again with the same result, then again and again, making herself smile with the game. I swear the kid can make fun out of anything.

"How about we give this one to Mitsy?" I say, snatching the one that just plopped on the ground.

"Sounds wlike a pwlan, Stan."

I hold the apricot out to the mare beside me, and the horse gobbles it up, and again I need to pinch my nose to stop the emotions. In two days we will be gone—no more apricots, no more horses, no more Bo.

"It's not forever," Bo says, reading my thoughts.

"What's not fowrevewr?" Molly asks.

"Nothing, baby," I say quickly, painting on a smile. "Let's go wait for Em and Tom."

I have yet to tell the kids we're leaving. I thought about breaking the news last night but decided to give it one more day. Today is Friday, our favorite day, the day Emily gets to ride Mischief and the day the neighbors come to the stables when the sun goes down for a weekly cookout. Tomorrow is soon enough to tell them we're leaving the only life they've ever known.

We get to the corner as the bus wheezes to a stop. The door opens and Tom ambles down first, his head bent so his gold hair drapes across his face. His backpack dangles from his narrow shoulder, his hands shoved in the pockets of his jeans.

"Hey, buddy," I say.

He lifts his head and smiles but doesn't answer. I don't expect him to. His voice won't return until the bus is out of sight.

"Wlook, Tom," Molly says. "I got apwricots for Mischief."

He gives her a thumbs-up.

Emily bounds down behind him, her colt legs and amber hair flying. A boy taunts her from an open window, and she sticks her tongue out at him. Then one of her best girlfriends yells, "Love you."

"Love you more," Emily says back, the two of them declaring their BFF status openly in the way only eleven-year-old girls can do.

The bus rolls away, and Emily skips to where we are. "Hey, Itch. What you got there?"

Itch is Emily's nickname for Molly. On account of Molly's oversized eyes, Molly has been called Bug since she was born. I call her Love Bug or Herbie. Tom has stuck with Bug. And Emily alternates between Itch or Pest depending on her mood.

"I got these fowr Mischief," Molly announces proudly.

"Good job," Emily says, patting Molly's apricot belly. "How about we put them in my backpack?"

"Good idea," Molly says, undoing her bib so the apricots tumble to the ground.

As the three of us squat to put the apricots in Emily's backpack, Tom throws a stick for Gus, laughing as Gus, uncertain of his target, attempts to retrieve the root of a tree instead of the stick, tugging at it with all his might.

"Mom, look," Tom says, pointing to the comedy, his first words since he got home, totally unaware he said them.

Like a switch, his voice has returned, and relief floods my heart as it does every day when those first blessed words escape. I'm so worried that one day his ability to talk will dry up altogether, not only at school but at home as well.

Beside me, Emily fills me in on her day. I call her the queen of Ridgeview Elementary School, little miss popular, a kazillion friends, captain of every team, class president. Today they dissected worms in science. None of the girls in her group would touch it, so she got to do the cutting. She tells me about the small stomach called a gizzard, and how the intestine was filled with dirt because that's what earthworms eat, and how Willy Jones tried to freak her out by wiping worm guts on her arm, but that she got him back by putting her dissected worm in his lunch.

In the distance, a big rig rumbles toward the freeway, causing Emily to stop her monologue and snap her head toward the sound. She squints down the road and I squint with her, both of us straining to see if the cab is yellow with black stripes.

It's not, and my heart resumes its pulse, my jaw sliding forward as I pretend to be glad it was someone else's truck, that I didn't want it to be Sean.

Emily looks at the dirt, not concealing her disappointment at all.

I put my arm around her and kiss the top of her head, the air heavier as the reality of our life slogs back into focus. He is gone, and unless a miracle occurs, in two days, we'll be gone as well.

3

Emily is riding Mischief, and Molly, Tom, and I are in the barn with Bo. Molly clambers onto Bo's lap and rests her hand on his shoulder. Bo doesn't look up, but simply adjusts his position to accommodate her weight and threads his right arm around her so he can continue his work.

Tom shifts from foot to foot like he needs to go potty, but I know his restlessness has nothing to do with his bladder.

When Bo finishes punching the last hole in the harness, he says, "What you got?"

Tom puffs out his chest and says with great theatrics, "*I* challenge *you*..." He points from himself to Bo for added effect. "To a throwdown."

"Motown thwrowdown," Molly squeals, leaping off Bo's knee and clapping her hands.

Bo's left eyebrow lifts. "You sure?" he says. "If I remember right, last time you challenge me to a throwdown, you and your sister got your lily white heinies whooped, and the two of you ended up mucking out stalls for the rest of the day."

Molly's brow furrows as she listens. Bo's thick-tongued words make him difficult to understand even if you're older than four and have mastered the English language.

I feel Tom's heart pick up its pace. A Motown throwdown is a dance challenge. Loser pays. If Bo loses, which isn't often, he shells out five bucks each to Tom and Molly. If Tom and Molly lose, they need to clean five stalls. To even the playing field, only one of the two kids needs to beat Bo, and they each get three mess-ups before they're out.

Tom nods. He's ready. He's been practicing every day for a week. I know his motivation. The Croon just released a new album, and he's hoping to earn enough money to buy their new songs for his iPod shuffle. Molly's motivation is always the same, money for chocolate ice cream from the Baskin-Robbins downtown.

Bo stands and stretches his arms over his head, his body creaking as he forces his ancient bones to unfurl.

"Time for a hoedown Motown thwrowdown showdown," Molly says.

Bo is the one who turned Molly onto rhyming, and since she could string two words together, she's been Dr. Seussing her comments. Each time they're together, he gives her new rhyming phrases to add to her repertoire.

Like now, he answers with, "Slow down, Motown, old Bo need to go down for a few lowdowns before he's ready for a throwdown."

Molly grins ear to ear, her eyes flicking back and forth as she catalogues the new rhymes for later use. Bo bends over to touch his toes, straightens, then whirls his hips around a few times.

Before Bo went into the horse boarding business, he had been a dancer, and when he got too old to dance, a choreographer. He's too bent to do any professional boogying these days, but whenever he and Tom are together, he teaches Tom what he knows. And like Molly does with everything, she just joins right in.

"Okay, honkers, let's get this on," he says.

He starts off with a simple shuffle-hop-step that Molly easily imitates then tops with a toe-heel scuffle. Tom goes next, adding a three-beat tap.

On and on they go, round after round, each adding a step or two until they're tapping and kicking and twirling a routine worthy of Fred Astaire. Molly messes up way more than three times, but Bo generously only notices every third one, causing Molly to nearly squeak each time she gets away with her blunder unnoticed.

Bo finally calls Molly on her third miss right after Tom gets his second. "Aw," she says, really believing she had a shot at it. She shuffles over to where I sit on a bucket and plops to the dirt beside me.

"Could still call it off," Bo offers Tom.

"You scared?" Tom taunts.

"Whooee, boy. Fine, have it your way. Them stalls calling your name. Your turn."

Tom nails the routine that Molly just missed then tacks on a move I've never seen before, a bizarre hip thrust that makes it look like his legs have left their sockets.

Because Bo is a fossil, ground flopping, head spinning, and gymnastics are off-limits. But this isn't any of those things. It's just a bizarre move that seems to require the suspension of gravity and the liquefaction of muscle and bones.

Tom grins like a Cheshire cat. He planned this as his kill move.

Bo cracks up, a cackling laugh that shakes his whole body. "You think you gonna beat me with that?" he says. "I taught Michael that move."

And sure enough, Bo not only matches the routine and Tom's kill move; he performs the move better than Tom did, his chicken legs literally rubberizing as he thrusts out first the left then the right.

Tom's face deflates, his features melting with his disappointment.

"Shoot," Bo says, scratching his bald head. "Dang it, I lose."

Tom's brow furrows, then his eyes bulge and he shouts, "You lose. You didn't add a move. You lose. I win."

"I win too," Molly says, leaping to her feet.

"Mmm, mmm," Bo says, shaking his head. "Must be losin' my touch."

From his front pocket, he fishes out a money clip and peels off a five for each of them.

"Now let me show you how to do that move right. Shake out them vanilla genes and pour in a little smokin' hot chocolate."

Molly giggles. I don't think she understood a word he said, but the way he said it was worth a laugh.

4

It's an emotional good-bye, Emily taking it the hardest. She's the oldest and therefore leaving the most behind. Since I told her we were leaving, she hasn't spoken a word to me, her hateful glare telling me all she cares to say. *How could you let this happen to us? To me?*

I'm trying, I want to scream. *I'm doing the best I can.*

Molly's most upset about leaving Gus behind. She doesn't fully grasp the concept of us living somewhere else and for that I'm thankful.

Tom pretends to be sad, but a glimmer of hope radiates from his feigned malaise, an anxiousness to get on the road, driven by a thin optimism that things might be different for him in LA, better for him there.

"What about Dad?" Molly asks just before we set off.

"Don't worry, baby, he'll find us," I say as I pray like hell that Sean shows up and doesn't have a clue where we went, getting a healthy dose of his own medicine and feeling firsthand the decimating hurt of being abandoned and left behind.

I look in the rearview mirror to find Molly's saucer eyes filled with concern, and my hate softens, my daughter's love for her father reducing the vengeful spite to a longing for the truth to be different than it is, for Sean to be a different man than he is, for life to not be so hard, for him to have stayed, and for none of this to have happened in the first place.

We merge onto the 10 freeway, a direct artery from our old life to our new, seventy-five miles of asphalt that might as well be a thousand for how different the world we're going to is from the one we're leaving behind.

"Wiwll Mr. Bo tewll him whewre we went?"

"Yes, baby," I answer, adding to the long list of lies I've told the kids since Sean left, protective instinct or cowardice stopping me from telling them the truth.

The kids know we are on our own, recognize that I've been working more, understand that money has grown more precious, but there was no blowout fight or emotional family gathering where Sean and I sat the kids down and told them we were separating or getting a divorce, and for the most part we have gone about our lives as if nothing has changed. Their dad left for a trip, but instead of returning a week or two later like he usually does, he hasn't come back. To their questions about when he's coming home, I've given noncommittal answers like, *He's on a really long trip this time* or *I'm not sure*. I've considered telling them a big lie, like he joined the military and is fighting in some faraway land, or even telling them he's dead. But that would only simplify things until the day he shows up very much alive.

And he will show up. I know Sean. It's only a matter of time before he comes back looking for us, either to beg forgiveness and return to the fold or to check in on his progeny while passing through.

I should probably tell the kids the truth, but the truth seems impossible to explain: *Your dad wasn't cut out for this life. He never wanted to get married or have kids—he never wanted you. I tricked him into it by getting pregnant, and he ended up loving you, so he tried, but then it got too hard—you got too hard—so he left.*

I hit the brakes to slow down for traffic, and the van sputters and coughs like it has a chronic case of bronchitis. The mechanic explained the problem is a cracked head, which made me imagine him wrapping gauze around the engine and giving it some Advil. Unfortunately the fix is not that simple, and the cost to repair it is more than the van is worth. So each day, I top off the radiator and pray it lives another day, knowing we're living on borrowed time, and that at some point, the head is going to split open, and its brain matter will explode all over the road.

"Wlook," Molly says, causing me to turn where she is pointing.

On the other side of the freeway, a mother duck waddles across the road, four ducklings waddling behind her as cars swerve and blare their horns to avoid them. Bravely the mother does not take flight. Her feathers ruffle with fear and she honks, but valiantly she continues on, leading her tiny family through the gauntlet. And I wonder if, when she chose her path, she realized the danger or if, like me, she was oblivious, but now she's in it, halfway across the road and with no choice but to trudge on, to lead them as best she can, hoping and praying they make it to the other side.

5

My mom and I are in the hallway outside her condo. She's been going at me nonstop for the past twenty minutes.

"...so you stick your head in the sand and pretend it's all okay?" she says.

I haven't seen her in a year, but the woman doesn't age—not a thread of silver in her blond hair, her light skin lineless. At some point, I'm certain I will catch up to her, and we will look more like sisters than mother-daughter—her, the older, stronger, more competent, better-endowed sister—me, the younger, less capable sister whose body and life never filled out the way everyone thought it would.

"Did you even try to track him down, get him to give you some money, garnish his wages? You know there are groups that do that, track down deadbeat dads..."

The kids are inside catatonically plugged into the television. No dog, no orchard, no yard, nothing to do. We've been here half an hour, and already they're bored out of their minds.

I focus on my breathing, in and out, reminding myself of the sacrifice my mom is making by taking us in. And when that no longer works, I tell myself that this is for my kids and that I would walk over red-hot coals for my kids, that I can do this.

"Have you even filed for divorce? Or what, Faye, are you still pining away for him, waiting for him to come back and take care of you? What were you going to do if he showed up, welcome him back with open arms?"

No. No. No. No.

No, I did not try to track Sean down because I know exactly where he is. He's shacked up with Regina, a woman he met in Albuquerque. No, I did not try to get him to give me money. I didn't feel like wasting my breath. No, I did not have his wages garnished. He owns his own rig, good luck with that. No, I have not filed for divorce. Divorce is for people who can afford a lawyer.

Yes and yes.

Pathetic as it is, yes, for months after he left, I prayed he would come back, and, yes, I would have welcomed him home.

My mom can't understand this. She never had to go it alone, went straight from husband one to husband two to husband three, then she had me and her marriage to my dad stuck. She has no idea how overwhelming and scary it is to be on your own with three kids to support.

At first you think your anger will sustain you, but it doesn't. It wears out quick, and you get tired, the kind of tired that makes your bones hurt and your mind numb until you feel like you're a hundred instead of only thirty-two—so done in that you can't imagine continuing the way you're going. And that's when the fear sets in: *What happens if I don't hang in there or if something goes wrong? I'm all they've got, just me, and there's no way I can do this. I'm going to fail. Then what?*

So, yes, you start to miss him…*him*, the one who caused this, but also the one who created this. The one who made promises you believed, words you staked your life on, vows to love and cherish—a dream faint but remembered. The one who looked at you adoringly when you delivered his first child, his lips grazing your forehead as he whispered, *Well done, we'll name her Emily because the name is as beautiful as her mother.*

My mom continues on with no sign of slowing, the rant saved up since I confessed to her two months ago that Sean had been gone three months. "For whose sake?" she says. "The sake of appearances? Who are you trying to impress—your neighbors, the school, me? You think we're all sitting around judging you? Or is it because you still want to be right, too stubborn to admit that Sean turned out to be exactly the loser I knew he was? I knew it the moment I met him, spineless, worthless. How you ended up with him…"

Perhaps walking over red-hot coals would be preferable to standing here like a five-year-old being scolded by my mother. At least it would be quicker. I return to counting my breaths, silently congratulating myself after each one I manage without detonation, wondering what sin I committed in some past life that condemned me to such harsh penance, because being forced to live with my mom is certainly too severe a punishment for anything I've done in this life.

"Or maybe that's not it at all, and instead it's exactly what it's always been with you, you're just muddling your way through the way you always do. No plan, just bebopping along whichever way the wind takes you, things always happening to you instead of you making things happen. It's not like how you end up pregnant is a mystery, yet you're surprised every time..."

I nod. I married Sean at nineteen because I was pregnant with Emily. Three years later, life already hard, I got pregnant with Tom. Then four years after that, Sean, who was already taking more trips and staying away longer each time, came home vowing to make things right, a promise that fell apart almost immediately but lasted long enough for me to end up pregnant.

She's right, I'm an idiot.

6

We survived the night, and this morning I'm determined to take control of my life. And to do that, I need money.

"Come on, kids," I say after a quick breakfast of Cheerios, the only breakfast food in the house. Food has never been high on my mom's priority list, and if I don't get a job quick, I'm a little concerned we might starve.

"Whewre we going?" Molly says, sliding off her chair and pulling on her Crocs, clearly excited to be leaving the confines of the condo.

Tom stands as well but looks less than enthused. New experiences don't suit him well, and meeting new people doesn't suit him at all. Bo taught him to think of it like a throwdown, one move at a time, don't get too ahead of yourself. I see him doing that now. Stand up. That's all. One move.

Emily remains in her chair, her arms crossed.

"Coming?" I ask, challenging her, my sympathy used up. My fault or not, she's being a little skunk, and for all I care, she can stay home and brood.

"Come on," Molly says, yanking on Emily's crossed arms.

Emily allows her sister to pull her from the chair. The truth is, she's as antsy to get out of the condo as the rest of us, and Molly just gave her the excuse to give in.

As if releasing the strings of a corset, the moment we're back in the van, I exhale. If I keep this up, I'll die of asphyxiation before the first week is through. The van is like a haven, the closest thing to a home we still have. If I could afford the gas, I'd simply drive around, enjoying the reprieve, but the tank hovers near empty, and if I don't get a job, it's going to stay that way.

My prospects for employment are limited. I have no degree and no experience outside waitressing. The problem with this occupation in LA is that every out-of-work actor is a server or bartender, making restaurant jobs as rare as openings for a bugle player at the racetrack.

I drive to the place where I have the most chance of success, the Third Street Promenade in Santa Monica, the highest density of restaurants per square foot in the city. Plus, it's an outside mall that doesn't allow cars, so the kids can wait safely outside while I apply for work.

"Great," Emily says when I tell her where we're going, "we're going to a mall where we have no money to buy anything."

"Would you rather we turn around and stare at the television all day? I promise this is going to be fun. There are street performers—singers, dancers, clowns, magicians—usually a band or two."

"A freak show," she scowls. "That's what Grandma says."

"Your grandmother doesn't know everything."

Neither Molly nor Tom participate, already wisely choosing the stance of Switzerland, both remaining silent as Emily launches barbs and I bat them away.

Parking is a nightmare and costs a small fortune. The parking structure is full, so we park in a metered spot on the street that costs two dollars an hour. I deposit four dollars and check my watch. We have until 12:02.

Despite Emily's determination to be a grouch, her sour mood lightens the moment our feet hit the promenade. Like the circus or an amusement park, there's a carnival atmosphere and a sense of adventure, the unexpected lurking in front of us—music, voices, chimes, cotton candy, churros, ice cream—all of it floating in the air, all of it only moments away.

We've just started when Tom tugs at my shirt and points. My heart clenches knowing his voice has disappeared, but I brush away the feeling, determined not to let the "cat" interfere with our day. Following his finger, I see a man sitting on a box in front of a trash can holding two bushy branches in front of him. He blends into the background and is so still that, had Tom not pointed him out, I would have missed him completely.

It doesn't surprise me that Tom saw him. Tom notices details the way a blind man compensates for lack of sight with highly attuned hearing. The rest of us are so busy talking or thinking about what we're going to say that we miss things, but Tom sees and hears it all.

I hold the kids back, allowing two girls in their twenties to walk ahead of us. One texts as the other window-shops, each of them carrying a shopping bag swinging at their side.

When they're a foot away, the man extends the branch in his left arm into their path. Cell-Phone Girl screeches, and her phone flies from her hand. Window-Shopping Girl jumps nearly a foot, and her hand shoots to her heart, causing her shopping bag to fly up and smack her in the face.

Both bust up laughing when they realize they were ambushed by the famous Third Street Promenade bushman, and Window-Shopping Girl fishes into her purse and hands the man a dollar.

Molly claps with delight and says, "I want to be scawred."

Tom grins ear to ear, and Emily's face is lit up. It's the first happy moment of our new life, and I savor it. *We can make happy out of anything.* It's a phrase my dad used to say.

I give Tom a high-five for spotting the stalker. Not only would I have hated being scared, but I would have hated giving up a dollar for the privilege.

~

We've canvassed nearly two-thirds of the promenade, and I'm starting to feel desperate. There are no jobs. Things may improve in a few weeks when it's closer to summer and the busy season, but right now is slow and no one is hiring.

I check my watch. Twenty-two minutes remain before our meter runs out. We need ten minutes to walk back, leaving twelve minutes, enough time for one more rejection.

"Last one," I say. The kids don't even acknowledge my departure. Emily is looking at bracelets on a jewelry cart. Tom stands beside her watching the people. Molly is doing little he-man dance squats to the beat of a band playing nearby.

I walk through the door of a restaurant called Namaka, Exotic Cuisine, and as soon as I walk in, I know this isn't the place for me. Cumin and curry—the overwhelming smell of the Indian spices makes me want to gag.

Growing up, I ate all kinds of food. My dad loved to cook. We didn't have money to go to fancy restaurants, so he made fancy food at home. I liked all of it except for Indian food.

I pivot to leave when a voice stops me. "Welcome," it says in a nasally tone that makes me want to run instead of walk out the door. Painting on a smile, I turn back.

The man is dark and little and wears a false smile too big for his face.

"I was wondering if you have any job openings," I say, hoping for a quick rejection so I can squeeze in one more restaurant before our meter runs out.

"You experience?" It isn't said with so much an accent as an abruptness, as if he doesn't have the patience for verbs.

I nod.

He runs me over with his eyes. "Fine. Table nine." With the back of his hand, he gestures toward the patio where two lone customers sit with closed menus in front of them and looks of impatience on their faces.

I blink several times, unsure I heard him. "You're hiring me?"

He squints like now he's not so sure.

"I mean, I'm glad you're hiring me," I say quickly, "but I can't start right now. Can I start tomorrow?"

He harrumphs, and I swallow at the thought of having just lost the one job I was offered. "Eleven," he says, then walks past me, his oversized smile beaming as he greets a family of four that has just walked through the door.

"It smells wonderful in here," the woman says, and her husband dutifully nods.

My new boss walks the family to the patio to join the hungry couple, and I return outside, relieved but unenthused. I do not like Indian food, and I do not like the man who hired me, but it's a job and I start tomorrow. I check my watch. We have two minutes before we need to start walking back to the car.

Emily and Tom are still beside the cart where I left them, absorbed in some sort of puzzle cube, each of them holding one and trying to unravel it.

"Where's Molly?" I ask when I walk up and realize she's not beside them.

Emily looks up from her puzzle, her eyes scanning side to side before swelling in panic. "She was right here."

Emily and Tom drop the toys on the cart and chase after me as I run person-to-person asking if anyone has seen a little girl in overalls, my heart scatter-firing in panic, the absolute worst feeling in the world. Thousands of people now crowd the walkway, the foot traffic having picked up with the lunch hour. In and out I weave, my eyes searching wildly.

A crowd is gathered around a street performer, a mime. I burst through the huddle mumbling excuse-mes. No Molly. Pushing my way back out, I run toward another group gathered around a band, music thrumming from the center.

A wide black lady with a purse the size of a suitcase shoves me back when I try to push to the front, so I scoot around her to another part of the crowd.

This audience is denser and deeper than the one clustered around the mime, a press of at least sixty people laughing and clapping and making it impossible for me to get through.

"Please," I cry, "I'm looking for my little girl."

My voice is tiny in the din of the music, but one man turns. Perhaps fifty with pink skin and a purple golf shirt stretched over a large belly, he smiles then presses his impressive weight against the crowd to create an opening. "That her?" he says, pointing.

Tears spring to my eyes when I see Molly in the center of the crowd, relief flooding my system and nearly sending me to my knees. The man braces my elbow, keeping me upright.

"She's quite a performer," he drawls.

And sure enough, there she is, center stage, dancing with a very tall black man who is playing a guitar and singing. Actually she's having a throwdown with the man. He does a simple two-step or slide then Molly mimics it.

I have no idea how it started, but the audience is loving it. It's very amusing, a six-and-a-half-foot-tall black dude with beaded dreadlocks laying down smooth dance moves that then a small, pudgy white girl with gold curls imitates. And watching it, it's impossible not to smile. My heart radiates with pride. That's my girl, *my* girl.

Tom and Emily sidle up beside me and are proud as well, all of us beaming as we watch Molly do her Molly thing. Several people in the crowd have their phones out and are taking pictures. I pull out my own antique flip phone and snap a shot as well.

The big man stops playing the guitar and starts clapping his hands over his head, encouraging the audience to join in, and the entire street explodes in unison to sing the ending. Then he pulls the microphone from its stand, holds it down to Molly, and Molly leads the audience in the finale, "...Jowhnny B. Goode."

The crowd erupts in applause, and the big man gives Molly a high-five. Then Molly skips to the guy playing the drums and they knock knuckles.

She is skipping back when a woman steps forward and hands her something. I rush toward them, but the woman disappears into the crowd before I get there.

"What'd she give you?" Emily asks, hugging Molly against her hip, clearly relieved that Molly was found and clearly feeling bad about losing her in the first place.

Molly opens her hand to reveal a twenty-dollar bill.

"Why she give me money?" Molly asks.

"She must have liked the way you danced," I say, my heart swollen to bursting.

We race back to the car and arrive to another fabulous relief, no ticket. In a splurge of celebration, I drop another two dollars in the meter, and Molly treats us to ice cream with her twenty dollars. We carry our cones to the beach and for the next hour play in the sand.

Today might just be our lucky day.

7

We've been in LA a month and have settled into a routine, not miserable but a good measure shy of content, a sustainable existence that borders on normal.

My mom and I barely see each other, which is perhaps the reason the precarious peace exists. My four shifts at Namaka keep me out until after the rest of the house is asleep, and my mom works the other three days, two as a volunteer at the local library and the third at *Star Gazer*, a weekly tabloid devoted to stalking celebrities, snapping photos of them, then making up stories to go along with those photos.

Prior to her retirement, my mom had been a middle school English teacher. Now she uses her writing skills and her obsession with the famous to write an astrology column on celebrities, divining their futures from the position of the sun and the moon, the exact moment of their birth, and their current location on the globe. It's all very scientific hogwash, but the readers love it, and her column is one of the most popular in the magazine.

School ends in a week, and I'm stressed about the summer routine, or rather lack of routine. Since we moved here, my mom has homeschooled Tom, sparing him from starting in a new school, so he and Molly have been home, but blessedly Emily's been gone five days a week, sparing us all from her spite.

Emily hates her new school, hates LA, and hates me. And I hate to admit it, but I'm glad she's not around on the days I'm home so I don't have to deal with it. The only saving grace is the soccer team she joined. Other than that, she's miserable and miserable to be around, and when school ends, she's going to be like a caged elephant with a stubbed toe.

I'm surprised when I walk into the condo after my shift to find my mom still awake. I look at the clock. 10:15.

"What are you doing up?" I ask, my tongue thick from exhaustion and boredom. The new rhythm of my life—working, cooking, cleaning, doing laundry—is like elevator music, droning on endlessly without enough differentiation to tell one day from the next.

My mom springs from the couch, her face lit up in a way that scares me. It's the same look she had on her face when I was eleven and she announced we were going on a celebrity cruise where we would mingle with the famous. A total disaster. Even my mom didn't recognize the has-beens that were billed as the stars on the cruise, and my dad and I spent the vacation leaning over the railing green with seasickness.

"You're not going to believe what happened today," she says.

"You won the lottery."

"Better."

"Better than winning the lottery? Tom got up in front of Congress and gave a speech on the injustice of banning peanut butter from school lunches."

"Better."

Nothing could be better than that. "What?" I say, tired of the game.

She holds out a business card. "Look who came by the condo today."

Monique Braxton, Braxton Talent Agency, a Wilshire Boulevard address, a phone number, a website, an email, a Facebook page, a Twitter account.

I shrug.

"Don't you know who that is? *Monique Braxton.* She's like the biggest talent agent on the planet. She reps anyone who's anyone. Not adults, only kids, but if you're a someone under eighteen, you're a Monique Braxton kid." My mom is so excited that the words spit and sputter like machine-gun fire.

"So?"

"So, look at this."

Grabbing me by the wrist, she pulls me to her laptop on the kitchen table and wiggles the mouse to wake it. The screen opens to a YouTube page. She clicks the play button and the video starts... a video of Molly!

I watch in disbelief. The video is from our day on the promenade. It starts abruptly, the big man strumming the beginning riff of "Johnny B. Goode," his body bobbing with the beat. Behind him, off to the side, Molly does little he-man squats in sync with the big man's big he-man squats. It's very funny to watch.

The big man does a hip thrust and a leg kick, and Molly follows with a hilarious mini–hip thrust and leg kick that causes a burst of giggles from the audience. The big man looks confused by the reaction and repeats the move. Molly mimics him again, and again the audience cracks up, then the big man whirls, spots his miniature impersonator, wiggles his finger for her to come toward him, and that's when the throwdown begins.

The video is three minutes and fifty-two seconds long and ends with Molly knocking knuckles with the drummer. In the final seconds I see us—Emily, Tom, and me standing in the background, matching grins on our faces.

"So, the thing is," my mom says, "this video's gone viral. Look at the number of hits."

I blink at the number, certain it can't be right. 7,867,672.

"Did you hear me?" my mom nearly screeches.

"Huh?"

"The Gap wants Molly for a commercial."

"What?"

"The Gap, you know, the clothes store."

"Yeah, what about them?"

"They want Molly to be in one of their commercials. They hired Monique Braxton to track Molly down, and Monique Braxton did. Not some assistant but her. Monique Braxton, in the flesh. Here. In *my* condo."

She's so giddy that I can almost imagine her as the little girl she must have been, a little like Molly but with a penchant for the stars. I bet she was one of those girls who collected princess paraphernalia and, when she outgrew that, plastered her wall with movie posters—her passion carried into adulthood, a fascination with the famous that borders on obsessive.

My mom can tell you more about most stars than she can about me. She knows how old they are, where they were born, who they've dated, what movies they've starred in, what tragedies have befallen them, the addictions they have, who they're related to, who supposedly likes them and who loathes them. She subscribes to every tabloid in print, has sat in at least a hundred studio audiences, and regularly signs up for Hollywood tours that drive past celebrities' houses.

"And she absolutely loved Molly," she says. "Of course what's not to love? Did you see that video?"

I glance at Molly snoring on the pull-out couch.

"Can you believe it? Molly. Our Molly."

"How'd she find us?" I ask.

"A private investigator. He asked around on the promenade, and one of the managers at one of the restaurants remembered you and pulled out your application. Simple as that."

Simple as that. My skin prickles, and my stomach knots—millions of strangers watching Molly, private investigators asking around about us, famous talent agents showing up uninvited on our doorstep—it feels like a punch to the solar plexus, a strange mixture of exhilaration and horror, a sickly stew of pride and violation.

"So all you need to do is call her tomorrow to set up an appointment."

My head shakes, causing my mom to squint and say in a much slower voice, "What do you mean, no?"

"Molly's not...We're not...I'm...We're just normal people. We're not..." I gesture to the frozen image of Molly on the screen. "That."

My mom's face literally changes color, transforming from pale peach to so crimson I feel the heat radiating from her skin. Then she blows, "Jesus criminy Christ, Faye. Bad enough you haven't an ounce of gumption to go out and do something with your life, but now this amazing opportunity literally lands in your lap, and you're just going to let it slip right through your fingers. You're just like your father. A pot of gold could have dropped from the sky with his name on it, and he'd have walked around it, complaining it was raining gold when what we really needed was a bit of rain."

8

I assumed the whole Monique Braxton incident was over.

I was wrong.

"Your appointment is at ten," my mom says, as if our conversation two nights ago didn't happen, and as if I'm still fourteen and she's reminding me about an orthodontist appointment. "The card is on the table. Molly needs to go with you. I've made arrangements for Mrs. Owen to watch Tom while you're gone." Without waiting for my response, she walks out the door.

I storm toward the table, determined to rip Monique Braxton's card into a million little pieces and sprinkle them on my mom's bed.

"How do I wlook?" Molly says before I get there. She stands in the bathroom door, fully dressed, her hair pulled into two sloppy pigtails. "Gwrandma says it's bettewr if I weawr my haiwr up so I wlook pwrofessionawl."

I suppress a snicker. "You look very professional."

Sitting at one of the kitchen chairs, I pat my lap for her to climb aboard.

Heavy and solid, like a sack of potatoes she molds against me. I kiss her temple and breathe her in. The slightest trace of baby remains—pink flesh and Johnson's baby shampoo. I hope she never stops using that shampoo, though I know she will. Already Tom and Emily have switched to using my Suave, still sweet but not as soft.

"Love Bug, you want to do this? Act in a commercial?"

She tilts her head. "Ms. Bwraxton says she wants me to dance."

"Oh, she did, did she? What else did Ms. Braxton say?"

"She asked if I wlike dancing, and when I towld hewr I did, she asked if I wanted to get paid to dance, and that's when I wreawlly said yes."

I smile because I know Molly is thinking about chocolate ice cream.

"Well, then," I say, lifting her off my lap and standing, "I guess we'd better go see Ms. Braxton about getting you a job."

The offices of Braxton Talent Agency are sprawled across the top floor of a modern glass and steel building on the corner of Wilshire and Western. Before we left the condo, I Googled Monique Braxton and was duly impressed. She's exactly as my mom said, a mega-mogul showbiz giant who represents hundreds of famous child stars.

Molly and I wait in the lobby for the elevator. Standing beside us is a beefy man with no hair on his head and lots of hair everywhere else. Tufts of it sprout from his collar, his cuffs, and his ears. He wears a tool belt and a mechanic's shirt with a patch on the pocket that says Hector.

"Headin' up to the Braxton Agency?" he asks, sizing up Molly. "She's a cute one all right."

I give a polite smile.

"Pimpin' out the pooty, that's the way to do it. Wish my kids had an ounce of cutes. You bet I'd be cashin' in on that action. Get me a big old house, a nice car, maybe a yacht, definitely a Harley."

I say nothing, wishing for the elevator to hurry up.

"Ridin' on easy street. Do me some of that. You should hear the kids that come in here, whinin' and complainin' 'cause they're tired or 'cause the burger they needed to eat for some commercial was cold. If they was my kids, let me tell you, I'd tell them to stop their damn snivelin' and suck it up, to eat the damn burger, imaginin' it's lettuce, green lettuce, the kind a cabbage that pays for a Mercedes and a house with a big-ass Jacuzzi and season seats to the Lakers."

Finally the elevator dings and the doors open. We wait for it to unload, and Hector steps on and politely holds it open.

"We'll take the next one," I say, gripping Molly's hand tighter than necessary.

"We'wre not going up?" Molly asks when the door closes.

"Yes, baby, we're going up. We're just going to wait for the next one."

Ding. The next elevator arrives, and Molly pulls me on board.

"Which button?" she asks, clearly excited by so many bright white prospects.

"Twenty."

"That's the top one," she squeals.

We fly upward so quickly that I'm certain we're going to shoot right through the ceiling and be launched into the sky like in *Charlie and the Chocolate Factory*. But remarkably, at the twentieth floor, we glide smoothly to a stop, and the doors swoosh open to reveal a gleaming reception area with a gleaming young receptionist.

"Hello, may I help you?" the woman singsongs.

Molly beats me to the response. "We'wre hewre to see Ms. Bwraxton. She wants me to dance in a commewrcial. My name is Mowlly Mawrtin."

"Well, aren't you the cutest? I'll let Ms. Braxton know you're here."

She skips off, and Molly and I take a seat on the white suede sofa, both of us sitting on the edge, certain our very proximity will soil it. Surrounding us are dozens of posters for television shows and movies, past and present, all featuring megastar kids, so many that it's hard to believe one agency is responsible for so much success.

"Hey, it's Caleb," Molly says, pointing to a poster for the hit show *The Foster Band*, our favorite show on television.

Caleb is a boy around Emily's age, and both Molly and Emily have mad crushes on him. His larger-than-life face mischievously grins at us, his hands held out in a shrug. And I agree with my girls, he's very cute.

The receptionist reappears. "Ms. Braxton will see you now."

We follow her down a corridor lined with glass-walled offices filled with important-looking people who look like they just stepped out of a Hugo Boss or Anne Klein catalog, depending on whether they are men or women, and as we pass, each head lifts, sizing us up like we are sushi on a conveyor belt being judged for delectability and consumption.

The receptionist raps lightly on a mahogany door at the end of the hall then opens it to reveal a large office with a sweeping view of the city.

Monique Braxton stands from behind a marble topped desk, and I'm so taken by surprise that my nerves run out of me. Funny how the internet can distort things. She's tiny, not a midget but certainly a head shorter than normal. Looking at her photos on the web, I thought she was tall, a formidable woman of substance, but seeing her now, it's as though she's been run through a Shrinky Dinks machine. She's six inches shorter than me and only a foot taller than Molly.

Despite her diminutive size, she's attractive—brown hair cropped precisely at her chin, almond eyes, skin stretched unnaturally smooth over high cheekbones, and an aerobicized body, thin everywhere except a slight bulge at her tummy.

"Mrs. Martin, it's nice to meet you." She extends a French-manicured hand. "And Molly, nice to see you again."

"Faye," I correct as Molly says, "Do you stiwll want me to dance in youwr commewrcial?"

"A gold mine," Monique Braxton mumbles under her breath as her eyes roam over Molly, drinking in her adorableness. Then she smiles wide, showing a set of perfect veneers, and says, "Absolutely. But right now do you mind having a few photos taken?" She looks at me. "With your permission of course. Just a few headshots."

I nod, then as if planned, the door opens and a gorgeous man enters. Six feet tall, day-old beard, chiseled body, ringless left hand.

"Miss Molly and Miss Molly's mom, I presume," he says with no shortage of flair, reaffirming the fact that all gorgeous men over the age of thirty are either married or gay.

When Molly and the photographer are gone, Monique Braxton and I get down to business. It's not a negotiation, nor is she asking whether we want to do this. It is assumed, by the fact that we are here, that we are on board. Which I suppose we are. Now that it is actually happening, it is very exciting.

After explaining her role as an agent and that she gets ten percent of what Molly earns, she says, "The Gap wants her. It's national and has the potential to run like crazy. They'll offer five, but we'll get ten."

"Excuse me," I say, interrupting. "Ten what?"

"Ten thousand for the shoot. It's top end for a noncelebrity, but I'll argue Molly's worth it because of the video. They won't blink. They'll be glad I'm not hijacking them for more. I could, but it's best to keep it friendly. Should pan out to fifty-plus over the year..."

She's still talking, but I'm not listening. *Fifty-plus, fifty thousand dollars or more for a commercial? One commercial?*

That's a lot of chocolate ice cream. My heart and brain pulse in equal measure as I attempt to calculate what that kind of money could do for our family. Therapy for Tom blazes in the forefront. Pay off our enormous debt. Repair the van's cracked head.

"Are you married?" Monique Braxton says, breaking my distraction.

"Huh?"

"Married? Do you have a husband?"

It's a simple question.

I nod, a simple answer. She smiles approvingly, and I reflect the grin back, the answer and my expression suggesting a loving partnership of stability and parenting and conjuring up images of white picket fences, family barbeques, and weekend trips to the zoo.

"How long?"

"Eleven...I mean, twelve years."

She nods, impressed, and I wonder how many trips she's taken down the aisle. There's no evidence of a family—no ring, family portrait, or clay-coiled mug proclaiming World's Greatest Mom. Her desk is stacked with papers, manila folders, a laptop, and a lipstick-stained Starbucks cup.

"Will he be involved?" she asks.

"Who?"

Her head tilts slightly, and her finely teased brow puckers. "Your husband."

"No. Only me." A more accurate summary of my twelve-year union to Sean.

"That's fine. It's better that way. Too many hands in the cookie jar complicates things."

Her words are sharp and concise like the rest of her. Her clothes, her hair, her office—all of it direct and tidy. Monique Braxton is a woman in control of her life, the kind of woman I would like to be though know I never will. Like a beagle being envious of a fox, I can try, but at the end of the day, only one of us is going to end up dinner for the mountain lions, and chances are it's not going to be the fox.

On the wall behind Monique are her claims to fame, over a hundred framed eight-by-ten black-and-white headshots of the children she's discovered and turned into household names, everyone from the megahit band Colorwand to Lloyd Stevens, the actor who plays the adorable Axel on the hit series *The Hamptons*.

My eyes catch on a portrait toward the bottom left, a boy in a striped shirt, his dark bangs draped across slashed eyebrows and smoldering eyes. I stare at his lips, remembering how I used to fantasize about kissing them when I was eleven. Brian Raffo, my first crush. He played Mike Sloan in the movie *The Inside Job*—the tough, street-smart kid who gave a lawyer a dollar to defend him against the police who were trying to bully him into testifying against the mob.

For years, I kept that same photo pasted inside my closet door, until the day Brian got busted for drugs. When I heard the news, I took the picture down and threw it away. It pissed me off, like what he had done was personal. Which in a way it was, four years is a long time to love someone when you're only fifteen.

"I miss him," Monique Braxton says, following my stare to look with me at Brian's immortalized eleven-year-old image. "He was one of my first clients." Her voice cracks with emotion, and suddenly I remember he's dead. Dead a long time. I don't remember how long, but long enough that I read about it in the newspaper instead of online. I remember there were two photos beneath the headline, one of him from the movie and the other, a recent one of him as an adult.

Monique Braxton pulls her shoulders back to recompose her flawless veneer, but she does a poor job of it, a glassiness remains in her eyes that wasn't there before, and I know I was right; Monique Braxton doesn't have children of her own. Behind her are her children, a hundred of them, and she cares about them as much as any mother does.

I glance again at the picture of Brian and realize with a shudder that my tastes didn't change much from when I was a girl to when I was a young woman. Sean looks a lot like Brian, same intense eyes and wiseass smirk. He ended up being a disappointment as well, and I wonder if I was predestined to be attracted to great-looking, sweet-talking losers who lie.

9

Molly is ready. We're in nearly the exact spot where it all started, the Third Street Promenade, half a block from where Molly and the big man had their famous throwdown.

The sun has yet to rise, and though it's the middle of June, it's cold as winter, the air brittle, patent gusts from the ocean piercing my clothes and turning my skin blue.

I sit on a bench with Molly asleep in my arms. The big man, whose name is Leroy, sits beside us—six and a half feet of gentle, sweet teddy bear. He keeps thanking Molly and me for getting him this gig, and I keep telling him we had nothing to do with it, but no matter what I say, he won't be convinced. Like a dog rescued from the pound, he hangs around us like a loyal mutt whose life has been spared.

In front of us, the crew dresses the set, dozens of people bustling around, hanging lights, positioning props, cleaning windows, readying the street for the big dance number. The promenade is taped off for the entire block, security guards posted at either end. It's both thrilling and stressful. We have until nine to get the shots we need, then the promenade will be reopened.

The crew has been here since two this morning preparing, and nervous energy buzzes in the air. At least a hundred people mill around—grips, sound technicians, cameramen, dancers, choreographers, directors, producers, ad people, editors. It's mind-boggling the amount of money, talent, and effort that goes into making a single thirty-second commercial. The Gap is going to need to sell a lot of overalls to pay for all this.

Though the sun has yet to rise, the set is noon bright, illuminated by a thousand lights shining on the hundred-foot strip of promenade, and you would never know it's actually a sunless, chilly morning. I pull the beach towel I grabbed from the van tighter around Molly as I shudder away my own chills.

Molly has her part down, and I'm proud to the point of bursting. The days leading up to this have been both long and hard. Yesterday and the day before, we needed to be up at five to begin our workday at six, and we didn't return home until after nine.

Officially we only worked four hours plus a half hour for lunch, which is the maximum allowed for a four-year-old. The rest of our day was logged as "dance lessons," which were offsite and therefore didn't count as "work."

I asked Monique Braxton if I should be concerned about the rules being bent, and she encouraged me to be flexible, so that's what I've been. But I understand why the rules are in place—four-year-olds aren't built for endurance, and the long days have taken their toll.

The first day Molly was fine, adrenaline kept her awake. The second she faded in the afternoon, falling asleep in my arms during the breaks. And today she's pooped. I could barely get her out of bed this morning, and she's been out since her makeup and hair were finished an hour ago.

The commercial is a direct knockoff of the YouTube video. Molly and Leroy are the stars, and the dance starts off with Leroy dancing to "Johnny B. Goode," then he and Molly get into a throwdown that evolves into an awesome routine with a dozen professional dancers around them.

From where I sit, I can see the yellow awning of Namaka. The manager fired me when I told him I needed a few days off, and I've never been so relieved to lose a job in my life. The next job I get won't have cumin or curry or little men with big teeth who leer at me.

The only sour note of the experience is that Emily missed her soccer playoff. She was supposed to play the evening of our first day of rehearsals, and I was certain I'd be home in time to take her, but that was before I realized how flexible we needed to be.

I shudder at the memory of our conversation.

I'm sorry you missed the game, I said, as I sat on the bed beside her and smoothed her hair. She had been crying, her eyes red. *You'll make it to the next one.*

She whirled and sat up so quickly that she sent me stumbling off the mattress. *There won't be a next one*, she screamed, her hate lancing me. *It was a playoff game, and we lost. You don't even listen to me.*

I opened my mouth to defend myself, but she was right. I had no idea that game was the last one if they lost. She might have told me, but the moment she starts talking soccer, my brain numbs over, detouring to all the other more important things I need to think about.

The AD, assistant director, walks toward us, and I tense. She's a sweet woman unless you piss her off, then she'll rip your head off and display it on a stake for the rest of the cast to see, and Molly and I have learned to be very careful around her.

"It's time," she says, and I feel her stress, her already short fuse nipped to a nub with the pressure of how important this morning is.

Leroy feels it too and shifts to sit up straighter.

"Love Bug," I coo, "time to wake up."

Molly snorts once then resumes snoring.

I jostle her and rub her shoulder. "Come on, Bugabaloo, ups-a-daisy."

Molly flops over, her carefully made-up face swiping across my sweatshirt and leaving a peach smudge.

Makeup is not going to be happy. Neither is Molly. Molly despises primping in general—hates taking a bath, hates having her hair brushed—and she has not enjoyed the makeup and hair portion of this experience. Like a dog at the groomers, she moans and groans each time she's forced into the chair.

The AD's shoulders hitch, and I feel her instant impatience. Her fists clench and the vein on the side of her head pulses—Mount Fuji about to blow. Her mouth opens...

Leroy stands and slides between us and the woman. He lifts Molly from my arms, and she slumps against him, her head collapsing on his massive shoulder. "Hey, Lil' Jive," he whispers in her ear, "it's time to dance."

Molly nods her head against him then wiggles to get down.

Showtime.

10

It's been two weeks since we finished the commercial, and life has never been better. The kids are off for summer break, and I've almost repaired things with Emily. I signed her up for a costly club soccer team that she desperately wanted to be a part of, and that has kept her busy and happy four mornings a week.

Rather than immediately looking for another job, I decided to take a couple of weeks off, and every day has been spent at the beach, except for the days we spent taking care of all the things we've put off taking care of for a year—doctor and dentist appointments, shoe shopping, clothes shopping, and best of all…present shopping.

Today is Emily's twelfth birthday, and I'm so excited I can barely contain myself.

The celebration began this morning at Emily's soccer game. First off, Emily was amazing. Competitive sports are not my thing, my shyness prohibiting such a spectacle, but Emily thrives in that arena. A natural leader, she led her team in a charge of victory, scoring two of the three goals and assisting in the other.

I brought my special pumpkin cream cheese cupcakes for after the game, and her team sang "Happy Birthday." Several of the girls pronounced the cupcakes the best they ever had, and I blushed with pride. I do make darn good pumpkin cream cheese cupcakes. And for the first time in a long time, I felt like a good mom.

Now we're in the van and on our way to the next surprise of the day.

"Mom, you turned the wrong way," Tom says.

"We're not going home," I answer, nearly squealing with excitement.

"We're not?"

"Whewre we going?"

"You'll see."

"Can I give Emiwly my pwresent now?" Molly asks. It's the sixth time she's asked since we woke.

"Yes," I say. "Now's the perfect time."

"It's fwrom me and Mom but mostwly me," Molly says proudly, pulling a wrapped box from the side of her car seat. "I got it 'cause I danced wreal good on the commewrciawl."

It's true. As a thank-you present to Molly for doing such a great job, the project manager gave Molly an iPhone—a ridiculous gift for a four-year-old but thoughtful just the same.

Emily couldn't care less who the gift is mostly from or that it's a regift. It's as if a nugget of gold fell from heaven. Every girl on her team has a cell phone, and only a handful of those don't have an iPhone.

"Do you wlike it?" Molly asks, confused by Emily's silence.

All Emily can manage is a nod.

The mystical device transports the kids into a virtual world of apps and games and music and videos, keeping all three so occupied that none of them realize we've been driving over an hour.

When Tom finally looks up and realizes where we are, he shouts, "Yucaipa!"

Emily and Molly look up as well, then all three are clapping. I lower all the windows so the familiar smell of horses and green fills the car, and we drive the rest of the way in reverent silence, a palpable longing for our old life weighting the air.

When we pass our house, my breath catches as I realize it's been rented. A Volvo station wagon is parked in the driveway, my flower garden brown and wilting.

I swallow and blink against the sudden realization that when we return, it won't be to our home. I should have known this, understood that when you leave, things don't stay the same. But I didn't, and it strikes me as an unexpected blow. Until this moment, I viewed our time in LA as a hiccup, a jostle in our path, and that when we returned, it would be back on the course we had been on when we left. It never occurred to me that things would be permanently altered.

11

The four of us slept curled together like a litter of kittens on the king-size bed of Bo's guest room, our stomachs full of homemade tamales and birthday cake, our dreams full of music, friends, and stories.

Emily disappeared at dawn to go riding, and at nine, I woke long enough to scrub the marshmallow residue from Molly's cheeks then release her into the wild with Tom before collapsing back to the bed to sleep some more.

⁂

I startle awake, blink in the bright light streaming through the window, and look around frantically for the clock.

Crap!

I run for the door.

"Everyone, now," I scream like a madwoman. "The living room. Hurry."

I look at the clock again. Three minutes to go. *Crap, crap, crap.*

"NOW!"

My screech gets Bo's attention, and he gives an ear-piercing wolf whistle while he windmills his arms, signaling everyone to come quickly. The ranch hands drop what they're doing. Emily and her two friends tether their horses and race toward me, Emily grabbing Molly's hand as she runs. Tom sprints from the barn.

He gets to me first. "What is it?" he yelps, panic in his eyes.

I don't answer, just push him forward into the house, then herd everyone else in after him, practically shoving them into the living room.

When everyone is crammed in tight, breathless and worried, looking around for the fire, I shush them and click on the television, then shush them again as I zap to channel eleven and turn up the volume.

On the screen is a commercial for Tide detergent. Everyone starts talking again.

"Quiet!" I snap, causing them to look at me in surprise but also getting them to shut up.

The commercial starts off without music, the screen white except for Leroy doing a quiet soft-shoe in the center. There's no shadow, and he looks like he's dancing on air. His funky clothes—mustard-colored, drop-crotch skinny jeans, an argyle hoodie, and green high-top sneakers—are startling against the starkness and the definition of cool.

"It's Wleewroy," Molly squeals, not realizing this is *the* commercial, *her* commercial, which I can understand. It's so surreal that it looks nothing like the shoot.

"It's me!" she yells as she emerges from the whiteness like a spirit.

Everyone in the room gasps, then claps, then whoops and hollers—surprised, stunned, thrilled—exactly the reaction I was hoping for.

"Shush," I bark in order to silence them again, my attention glued to the screen.

Leroy does a jig, and Molly mimics him, and our little audience bursts out in giggles.

"Well, I'll be," Bo says, "Molly throwing down with a big fella. I hope you showed him how it's done."

And boy did she.

The choreographer was brilliant, capitalizing on every ounce of Molly's abilities and cuteness to make her look like a dancing prodigy.

Within seconds, she and Leroy are dancing together, a syncopated routine that, though flawless, appears spontaneous, as if she and Leroy are making it up on the spot.

As they dance, the white morphs to color, the music escalates, and the other dancers appear, the street transforming into a carnival of noise, acrobatics, and hip-hop in front of the Gap store. Then the mannequins in the windows come alive, a street band joins in, and the entire troupe starts clapping, singing, dancing, and grooving in a performance as impressive as Michael Jackson's "Thriller."

My heart nearly explodes with joy, excitement, and pride. Molly is on television, tearing it up, being her amazing, wonderful Molly self for the whole world to see.

The music and color and dancers fade, and again the scene pales to white except for Leroy and Molly. A final two-step that Molly mimics, a high-five, and the two part ways, leaving the screen empty until the Gap logo appears, and a voice-over says, "Gap. Get funky."

The living room bursts into applause, and one of the ranch hands picks Molly up and twirls her around. "Well, I'll be," he says. "Look at that, our Molly, a star. Tell me, when you get rich and famous, you still gonna remember the little people?"

"I am a wlittle pewrson," Molly answers, causing everyone to crack up.

"Come on, superstar," the woman who does the cooking for Bo says. "Let's see about you and me making those peanut butter drop cookies. Tom, you want to help?"

"I'm going fishing," Tom says, trotting off ahead of them, entirely unaware that he just spoke in front of a dozen people, something he hasn't done since we left Yucaipa.

Emily and her friends follow him, each giving Molly a high-five as they pass. Emily drops a kiss on top of Molly's head. "Good job, Itch."

"Super cool," one of the girls says. "I wish I could be on a commercial. Em, you think you'll be on a commercial?"

Emily shrugs and continues leading her posse away.

I look back at the television. The Wimbledon quarterfinals are back on. I'm tempted to scan every channel searching for the commercial so I can see it again. I could watch it over and over. I think I could watch it a thousand times and not grow tired of it.

Unfortunately the premiere was the only time and channel Monique Braxton was given, so I have no idea when it will be on again.

"Well, well," Bo says, taking the remote from my hand and turning off the television.

"Amazing, don't you think?" I say, my smile so wide that my cheeks hurt.

"Sure is," Bo says, setting the remote out of my reach, sensing my desire to turn it back on. "Take a walk?"

I force myself to leave the temptation and follow him outside. We head toward the creek. There's a pregnant mare Bo is keeping an eye on, and she likes to graze down by the water. As we walk, I tell him about the YouTube video and Monique Braxton and how the whole wonderful adventure came about.

He's quiet, nods several times, and offers a few "uh-huhs" but not much more. And by the time we reach the water, his lack of enthusiasm is pissing me off. After all, *Molly* was in a commercial. She was *the star* of a commercial. She made *a lot of money* to be in a commercial. He should be more excited. This is damn exciting.

The mare stands fat and happy in the shade of an oak tree. Bo takes a seat on a stump nearby, and I lean against a fallen trunk across from him.

"Can you believe it?" I say, my smile exaggerated to ignite his enthusiasm.

"Careful, Faye," he says, refusing to get on board. "Hollywood have a way of sneaking up on people, of making them think they won the lottery, when all they really won is a whole lot of grief."

"We did win the lottery. You should have been there. It was amazing."

"I have been there. I was there for a lot of years."

"Yeah, well you weren't there with us. Molly was incredible..."

"They made her appear incredible," he corrects. "The choreographer, the director, the editor, the makeup artist, the hairstylist, the lights..."

"No. *She* was incredible."

He shakes his head at the ground, and I feel heat rising in my cheeks. "You don't know, you weren't there. Making that commercial was the greatest thing I've ever done..."

"Making a commercial to sell overalls is the greatest thing you've ever done?" he challenges.

"Yes," I shoot back. "Making a commercial, a national commercial."

Bo frowns.

"Fine. It's not like I discovered a cure for cancer, but it was hard work, and I had a ton of responsibility, and I was good at it, and so was Molly. Frown all you want, but it was a hell of a lot more important than waiting tables, and a hell of a lot more profitable. I made more money in those three days than I would have made working three months at the diner…"

"You mean Molly made more."

I huff through my nose. "Yes, Molly made more. But she liked it."

"I'm sure she did. It's damn exciting being treated like a star, all the hoopla and the attention. What four-year-old wouldn't like that? All I'm saying is that you need to be careful. It's a tough business."

"And the horse business is better?"

He shrugs. "There shit in every business, but at least here, the shit is right in front of you. You can walk around it or shovel it out of the way. The thing about Hollywood is, they're all actors, every one of them, from the producers down to the accountants, and you have no idea you about to step into a big pile of steaming cow dung until it's too late."

The analogy softens my irritation and makes me smile, but Bo doesn't smile back. He looks me square in the eye as serious as I've ever seen him. "Faye, I'm telling you how it is. Molly's special. You don't see it because you're her mom, but she is, and other people, they gonna see that commercial and they gonna realize it as well, and they gonna want a piece of her."

"It's just a commercial."

"So this is where it ends? You gonna say no when fame comes knocking?"

"Fame's not going to come knocking, but I'll tell you this, if someone wants Molly to do another commercial, you can bet your sweet bejeebers I'm going to say yes. Did you see that commercial?"

He shakes his head like I've given the wrong answer. "Tell me this, Faye, would you let Molly smoke?"

"Of course not."

"Why?"

I roll my eyes. "You know why."

"Because it's dangerous. Because it might kill her prematurely. Well, acting's no different, probably worse. Them contracts should come with a surgeon general's warning telling parents that child stardom has been proven to cause misery and early death."

I roll my eyes again.

"Roll your eyes all you want, but I'm telling you how it is. Acting pays well, but it don't pay well enough for forever."

12

Emily's not talking to me. I've ruined her life.

We've been driving nearly an hour, and everyone is miserable.

I thought going home was a good idea; now I realize it was a mistake. When it was time to leave, Emily pleaded with me to let her stay, to let her live with one of her friends or with Bo. The answer was no, and since my refusal, she hasn't said a word. She blames me, and I can't help but rile at her twisted perspective as to which parent she should be angry with.

Molly and Tom sit silent and tense in the middle seat, upset both about leaving Yucaipa and about their sister's despair.

The sun is nearly gone, pink and orange streaking the sky as the day melts into dusk. The van lurches and nearly stalls, and I step on the gas hoping that will fix it, but it falters again and my heart falters with it. I turn on the hazards, and we limp to the shoulder then pitch and roll to the next exit, making it halfway down the ramp before the van sighs a final gasp then comes to rest on the side of the road.

"Mom?" Tom says, his voice concerned. Already he's begun taking on the role of the man of the house, and this situation is out of his depth.

"We're okay," I say, though we're not. In front of us is an unpromising-looking neighborhood, desperation scrawled in graffiti on the overpass and coiled in the barbed wire that surrounds the salvage yard to our right.

This is the part of being on my own I hate most, the utter aloneness when things go wrong. A year ago had this happened, I would have called Sean, and though most likely he would have been on the road, he would have told me what to do. He would have calmed me down, asked where

I was, then he would have called a tow truck to get us. He would have assured me we were okay and would have felt terrible that the van had broken down, feeling responsible for not maintaining it or for not earning enough to buy me a better car. This is what would have happened a year ago.

"Mom?" Tom says again, breaking me out of my frozen stupor.

"Yeah, baby, I just need to call a tow truck, and I'm trying to figure out how to do that."

With no idea how you find a tow truck, I call 411.

"City and state, please."

I don't know what city we're in. I hang up. Beneath the overpass, a shadow moves or maybe it's my imagination. All sorts of bad headlines about abduction and rape flash in my mind.

Why did I pull off the freeway? A bad choice, the story of my life.

I call my mom. No answer.

"I cowld," Molly says.

It is cold. Despite it being summer, the sun is now gone, and a frigid wind rattles through the windows.

Tears fill my eyes, and I hate that I'm so pathetic. I hate that I'm scared and that I can't even figure out how to call for a stupid tow truck when my car breaks down. I bite my lower lip to stifle the emotions, to keep them from pouring out and freaking out the kids.

"911. What's your emergency?"

I mutter my distress, and the woman instructs me to calm down, then she tells me to stay on the line so she can track my location. Within minutes, a highway patrol car pulls up behind us. A few minutes after that, a tow truck arrives.

13

It's after nine when we stumble through the door of the condo. Taking pity on us, the highway patrolman offered to drive us home after our van was hauled away. The kids found it thrilling to ride in a police car; I found it humiliating. He assured me I did the right thing calling 911, but my breakdown preceding the drive home and my incoherent mumblings during it were what had me stammering apologies when he finally dropped us at the curb. The culmination of emotions did me in. Between Bo's terse words, Emily's sob-fest, leaving Yucaipa for a second time, and the van dying, I just couldn't take it.

Too much, I want to scream. *You win!* I'm not entirely certain what God I'm screaming at, but I imagine some supreme Buddha sitting on a cloud holding his fat belly and laughing as he sharpens his lightning bolts and contemplates what diabolical blow he's going to deliver next.

Uncle. Mercy. I give up. Please, just stop.

"What happened to you?" my mom says. "You were supposed to be back hours ago."

"Ouwr van died," Molly says, sounding almost as sad as me about our loss.

"I told you not to go to Yucaipa," my mom says, as if she divined our car's death.

She told me not to go to Yucaipa because she wanted us to stay here and have a party with her friends when Molly's commercial aired.

With the name of her longing pronounced, Emily remembers her despair, drops her load on the floor, and runs into the bedroom, slamming the door behind her.

"I see you two are getting along well," my mom says, with a look that plainly says this is all my fault. Then she kneels with her arms open for Molly to walk into. "I'm so proud of you. That commercial was wonderful, and I bet every kid in America is going to be asking their moms for overalls."

"I hope they get the ones fwrom Wawlmawrt," Molly says. "They'wre way mowre comfowrtabwle."

"And guess what?" my mom says, holding Molly by her shoulders so she's pinned in place.

"What?"

"Your agent called. A casting director saw your commercial, and she wants you to come to an audition."

"Really?" I say, my emotions reversing course at the thought of doing another commercial and earning another boatload of money that could possibly buy us a new car.

"What's an audition?" Molly asks.

"It's where you try out for a part on a show, and if they like you best, you get the part."

"And the othewr kids get the othewr pawrts?"

"And the other kids go home until their agent calls for them to try out for a different part. But this is a really good part, so I really hope you get it. It's an audition for *The Foster Band*."

The words electrify the air.

"I wlove *The Fostewr Band*," Molly says.

Everyone loves *The Foster Band*.

"With Cawleb?" Molly says.

"With Caleb. And they want you," my mom says.

"Want me fowr what?" Molly asks, confused.

"To be another Foster kid, to join the band."

Molly's face tilts, and I can tell the idea is too abstract to get her head around. To her, the show is real and so are the Fosters, and you can't just join a family. It's like telling her Santa Claus isn't real. At this age, she simply wouldn't believe you.

"You don't worry about it," my mom says, tapping Molly on the nose.

"You just show up tomorrow and be your cute, adorable self, and they're going to love you. Okey dokey?"

"Okey dokey, jokey smokey," Molly says, skipping off to sit beside Tom on the couch where he is playing on Emily's iPhone.

My mom stands, a slight groan emitted with the effort, making me realize, not for the first time since I've returned, that she is older than when I left, and a pang of unexpected concern prickles me.

"You need to be at Fox Studios at ten thirty," she says. "Monique sent the details in an email. We think it would be best if Molly wears the dress the Gap gave her, the one with the stripes. I went out and bought a pair of Mary Janes that match. Monique also thinks it would be best if she wears her hair in braids, since the show is set on a farm."

My concern for my mom's aging evaporates with my annoyance. *Monique this, Monique that.* My mom flings the name around like she and Monique Braxton are pals. Monique Braxton has never even seen the striped dress the Gap gave Molly.

"I haven't decided if we're going," I say, just to assert my authority and piss her off.

"Well, of course you're going. You can take my car."

And though *of course we're going*, I refuse to give her the satisfaction of saying so. Instead I shrug and plop myself on the couch beside the kids, flick on the television, and scan through the channels, pretending to look for something interesting to watch, while secretly hoping I'll land on the Gap commercial so I can watch my little star.

14

The tickle in the back of my brain has a voice that sounds distinctly like Bo. I try to swat it away, and when that doesn't work, I turn up the radio to drown it out. *Buzz, buzz, buzz.*

"Get lost," I say out loud.

"Who you tawlking to?" Molly asks from her car seat.

"Mr. Bo. He's in my head, and I want him to leave."

"You'wre funny."

Sometimes I am.

Bo quiets, but seconds later, my brain is ambushed again, this time by the flash of the insidious tabloid my mom works for, *Star Gazer*. This morning, the current issue was on the counter as I poured my coffee, the face of Zeke Aaron splashed on the front page, the latest teen idol to fall from fame into shame. *Zeke Aaron Enters Rehab Again!!!*

"Mom, tewll me again what I do fowr the audition?" Molly asks.

My eyes move to the rearview mirror to find my baby, her curls sticking up every which way around her saucer eyes.

"Are you nervous?" I ask, sensing more than curiosity in the question.

"A wlittle. I want to do good. Gwrandma says it's impowrtant."

I force my own desire from my voice. "Love Bug, this is no more important than picking apricots from the orchard. You're going to meet some of the people who help put *The Foster Band* on television and pretend you're a Foster kid like Caleb. Doesn't that sound like fun?"

Not entirely convinced, she says, "But if they wlike me, I get the job, wright?"

I swallow at the word "job." "Sweetie, you're four, you don't need a job. But yes, if they like you, you would get the part."

"And I'wll get paid wlots of money?"

"I don't know how much, but yes, you would get paid."

"And then we could get a new cawr, and you won't have to wowrk, and Em can go to hewr soccewr games?"

This morning, I needed to break the news to Emily that, on top of everything else, she would miss her game because of the audition. I needed my mom's car, so there was no way to get her to the field. It was an ugly scene, replete with screaming and door slamming, and a dozen I-hate-yous.

"Bug, this isn't about that," I try to reassure, though I know it's impossible for Molly to see beyond the tumultuous emotions of the past day. "This is about doing something we've never done before and having fun. Tomorrow I'll get a new job, then we'll get a new car, and then Emily can go to her games."

"But Gwrandma says if I get the job, we can get a wreawlly good cawr. She says we could pwrobabwly even hiwre someone to dwrive Emiwly to hewr games if you and Gwrandma awre busy."

I grit my teeth and don't answer. I should have known there was a reason my mom volunteered to give Molly her bath this morning.

A few minutes later, when I glance in the mirror again, Molly is turned toward the window playing her own quiet game of Sweet or Sour, grinning at the drivers beside us and trying to get them to grin back. If they smile, they are sweet. If they don't, they are sour.

I imagine her in fifteen years and wonder, if she gets the part, if it will change her. I picture a curly-haired young woman with saucer eyes beneath the *Star Gazer*'s banner and the headline *Molly Martin Enters Rehab Again!!!*

I shake my head to clear away the image. Molly is not Zeke Aaron, and his fate is not hers. Bo is wrong—a bazillion kids who aren't famous get into trouble with drugs and alcohol every day. We only think of it as prevalent in show business because it's splashed all over the news.

Molly's not the one I need to worry about, Emily is. It's hard to believe that, in such a short time, a chasm has grown so wide between us that I have no idea how to bridge it.

Things will get better after today. I will get another job and get us back on our feet, then we'll go back to Yucaipa and things will return to normal.

I sigh at the thought, surprised at my sudden apathy to the idea, when yesterday, all I wanted was for things to return to what they were. But today, things are different than they were before. Yesterday, Yucaipa was our certain fate, while today another possibility exists. It's a long shot, but that doesn't stop my mind from imagining a future different from the one of which I had been so certain, my thoughts churning with the possibility of something more, something beyond the impossible struggle that is less difficult and more fun. And in a single day, Yucaipa has been reduced to a consolation prize, the choice we will make if the dream doesn't come true.

15

We pull into Fox Studios, and a security guard directs us to the parking area. A man and a woman cross in front of us, and my eyes follow them, wondering if they are famous. They look familiar, but I don't watch much television, so they could be and I probably wouldn't know. I decide they are famous and try to memorize their faces so I can search for them in the *Star Gazer* when we get home.

In the past day, the weather has transformed from cool to stifling hot, and as we walk toward the warehouse-looking building with a giant number six painted on its side, sweat pools beneath my shirt and my hair sticks to my neck.

Molly seems immune. Taking my hand, she pulls me toward the building. Despite my pleading for her to wear the Gap dress, she insisted on wearing her Walmart overalls over her frayed white tank top and refused to let me braid her hair, and as we hurry toward the door, I bristle with self-consciousness.

Molly can be very obstinate, and this morning she was in a fit. Emily's meltdown over missing her soccer game stressed Molly to the point of refusing to even go to the audition. This in turn broke Emily, who then convinced Molly that the audition was more important.

Emily might hate me, but her love for Molly is absolute and vice versa.

By the time all this came around, we were running perilously close to being late, so I gave in on the clothes and hair and let Molly have her way. But now, looking at her—her hair a mop of haphazard curls and her overalls rolled at the cuffs revealing a battered pair of red cowboy boots—

she looks like a country bumpkin plucked off a farm, and I can't believe I brought her to something as important as this looking the way she does.

Handwritten signs with arrows direct us through the building to the casting room, and as we hurry through the littered corridors, I'm surprised how industrial and drab the building is. I'm not sure what I was expecting, but I think I assumed a soundstage would be more glamorous, at the very least charming and romantic. This is none of those things. Dark and cluttered, it is a parceled-off warehouse with exposed trusses, concrete walls, and buzzing fluorescent lights.

We reach the casting room, and when we step inside, I nearly laugh out loud. The room is filled with at least two dozen little girls sitting beside their moms, almost all of them dressed in denim overalls and white T-shirts, and almost all of them with curls worn in loose ringlets. Without knowing it, Molly insisted on dressing perfect for the part.

I sign the clipboard beside the entry, take a script from the stack beside the door, and as Molly and I make our way toward two empty chairs toward the back, all the eyes in the room follow. It feels like we've just entered a gladiator arena for a fight to the death and the other contenders are sizing us up. I offer an I-mean-you-no-harm smile to each pair we pass, but the gesture isn't returned.

A woman on the opposite side of the room stares particularly hard then turns and whispers something to the mom beside her. The other woman lifts her head to look at us, then her mouth forms into a pout. Her voice is not as hushed as the first woman, and the words "Gap commercial" cut through the mumbles around us.

My pride swells as I realize they recognize us, and that these veterans are actually intimidated. *Way to go, Molly.*

We take our seats, and I look at the script, giddy with the privilege of being allowed to read a scene from one of the future episodes. The season finale of *The Foster Band* was a huge cliffhanger. The youngest Foster kid, Birch, a boy who literally grew up on the show from the age of five to eight, was taken away by his birth mom, an on-again, off-again junkie. The Fosters fought to keep him but ultimately lost the battle, and in the final scene, Birch waved good-bye to his foster family, then he and his mom drove away.

All the Fosters were on the porch, Mrs. Foster crying against Mr. Foster, all of them watching as the car picked up speed, began to weave, then lost control, flipping into the ditch beside the road. The Fosters ran toward it, and the season ended, no one knowing whether Birch survived.

Looking at the script, I'm guessing he didn't, and though I know the show is pretend, a knot forms in my throat at the thought of Birch not making it. I really like Birch. He's a tough little guy, a troublemaker who lends a healthy dose of humor and mischief to the show.

The two new characters, Annie and Ben, are four and seven, and the scene Molly needs to memorize is fairly short, two pages total—eight lines for Annie, ten for Ben.

"Ready to try this?" I whisper to Molly, who is attempting to befriend the girl across from her with a smile and a wave. The girl turns away, clearly not interested.

Molly looks at me, her brow furrowed in an expression that says, *What's up with that?*

I shrug. "What do you say, Bug, should we give this a try?"

She doesn't answer, her attention returning to the room and the kids around us. It's hard not to be distracted. There's a lot going on. Each mother-daughter pair has their own approach to the process, and while all the girls are similar in size and cuteness, the moms vary quite a bit in size and cuteness. And attitude. Some try the sweet-talk approach, doling out incessant compliments and incentives to get their daughters to perform... *Sweetie, that was wonderful... Oh baby, you're the best... Let's do a good job, then we'll go to the mall after this... Did you see the cupcake store we passed? Just practice a few more times.* Others take a hard-line approach, harsh and relentless... *Again... Don't fidget... This is important. Do you know how important this is?*

"Baby," I say, trying not to fall into either extreme, "do you want to do this?"

Molly looks up at me with her big saucer eyes and nods.

"Okay then. I'll read it to you first, then we'll see if you remember it."

She curls her legs beneath her and snuggles against me the way she does when I read her a story.

Before I can start, the door on the other side of the room opens and a young woman with a clipboard steps through. "Janine Jones," she announces, causing my heart to leap into my throat. The auditions are beginning, and we have yet to even read the script.

A pair two rows from where Molly and I sit jump to their feet, and the pudgy mom pushes her pudgy daughter forward. A foot from the door, the mother makes the sign of the cross, then with a deep breath, she and her daughter follow the young woman into the room.

Everyone quiets, and we all lean slightly toward the door as if a strong wind is blowing us that way, our ears straining to hear through the wood for a clue as to how it's going, listening for a giggle, a sigh, applause—some sign of whether the woman's prayers were answered.

The door is beside the two women who hissed about us earlier, and I realize those are the prize seats, those nearest the casting room where they can hear what's going on inside. After a minute, I realize not only am I being ridiculous, but I am wasting precious time. The door could reopen at any moment, and we could be called next.

"Mols, we need to go over this," I say, my voice tight.

I read her the script. Ben is asking Annie to sneak into the neighbor's yard to take some carrots from the man's garden, and Annie doesn't want to because she's scared.

"Then what happens?" Molly asks when I finish.

"It doesn't matter. They just want you to know this part."

Her nose wrinkles. "But I want to know the stowry."

I stare with fear at the closed door on the other side of the room as if it has claws and teeth, certain that at any second, it's going to open and swallow us whole. "Baby, let's just memorize this part."

"But why is the giwrl scrawred and why awre they going to steawl the cawrrots? Why not just go to the stowre owr ask the neighbowr fowr some cawrrots?"

I smile. I can't help it. Despite my terror that we're going to make total fools of ourselves when we walk through the rabbit hole on the other side of the room, Molly's right: without context, the script makes no sense. So with a deep breath, I set down the pages and tell her a story to go with the script. I explain that the neighbor is an old man who lives by himself. He doesn't talk to the neighbors, and he keeps a gun on his porch. His leg is twisted, so he doesn't walk right, and sometimes at night, he hobbles around his backyard carrying his gun and making strange noises.

Because of this, everyone thinks he's mean and crazy. But the truth is, he's just old and his leg hurts when it gets cold, so he walks around to ease the pain, sometimes grunting because it hurts so bad.

He carries the gun, which is actually only a BB gun, to scare off the raccoons that like to eat from his garden.

"That's sad," Molly says. "He's awll awlone."

"He is," I say, "but I think it's going to turn out okay because I think Ben talks Annie into sneaking into the garden, and then the old man catches her, but he doesn't get mad and they become great friends."

"And I bet he's going to give hewr the cawrrots so she doesn't need to steawl them."

"I bet you're right."

"Why's she and Ben need the cawrrots?"

The door opens, and Janine Jones and her mom walk out. Judging by their expressions—Janine's stunned, her mom's long and lined—I'm guessing it didn't go well.

"Dana Kincaid," the clipboard girl calls.

My pulse beats a little harder. If they're calling the girls in alphabetical order, we might be next.

"Bug, we need to memorize this."

"Why they need the cawrrots?" she asks again, her face set in the stubborn look she has that's difficult to override.

I force myself not to panic and scream, *What the hell difference does it make? We just need to memorize these two pages before they call your name and we go into that room and they ask you to recite your lines. These lines. These eight lines that, at this moment, you don't know!*

"Because they're taking care of a bunny with a hurt paw, and their mom told them they couldn't keep any wild animals, so they have to get food for the bunny without their mom knowing," I say in an amazingly calm voice.

"Oh," Molly says, mercifully satisfied. "Wread it again."

I do, then I show her which parts are hers.

The door opens surprisingly quick, and Dana Kincaid bursts through in tears, her mother racing after her. Satisfied smirks cross the faces of the two women beside the door.

"Marley Harkin," the woman in the doorway announces.

My heart bounces around like a pinball in my chest, until I realize she said Marley not Molly, and Harkin not Martin. Which means there's no rhyme or reason to the order in which the kids are called. It isn't alphabetical, and it doesn't follow the sign-in list. Somehow this adds to my anxiety, the uncertainty of when we might be called.

Molly and I run through the script again, this time with her saying her parts. She doesn't get every word exact, but the gist is close and I hope that's good enough.

"Should we go over it one more time?" I ask, knowing we should, since every other pair in the room is huddled in deep concentration, rehearsing again and again.

Molly shakes her head. "I got it."

She bounces her legs and smiles at a girl a row away, and the girl returns the grin, giving me back some of my faith in humanity until her mom snaps at her, "Becka, focus. Now remember, you're supposed to be scared. And on the last line make your eyes well up with tears. Don't cry, but make them like you're about to cry. Let's go over it again."

I pull Molly closer to me, and Molly doesn't look at the girl again.

Marley walks out, and everyone in the room watches. Marley is very pretty, petite and fairylike. She has blue eyes and rosebud lips, and I could imagine her on television. I listened to her and her mom rehearsing, and she was very good. America would fall in love with her.

Bodies straighten and eyes study Marley's and her mom's faces for smirks of triumph or frowns of defeat, but as they walk through the room, their faces reveal nothing, not giving hide nor hair as to whether the rest of us still have a chance.

Another girl is called, then another, and another, and with each audition, the nervous energy builds—nails are chewed, wedding bands are twisted, and the air grows thick like a pressurized chamber. At one point, laughter drifts through the door and everyone freezes—a good sign for whoever's inside, a bad one for those of us still waiting our turn.

I don't want to get caught up in it, but as the moments tick by, it's impossible not to. Like being in a race or a tug of war, you can't help but want to win. And the longer we wait, the more the desire builds.

"Maybe we should practice again," I blurt.

Molly glances at me like I've lost my marbles. Which I have. I feel like my brain is going to explode.

"Say it with more urgency," one of the remaining moms snaps at her daughter.

We should practice. Everyone else is practicing.

Another pair walk from the room.

"You did so good," the mom beams. "You were the best."

The girl gives a weak smile, betraying the mom's attempt to make it seem better than it was and completely undermining her mom's lame attempt to deflate the hopes of those of us who remain.

"You're my special girl. I love you so much. You're such a star." She swings the girl's hand back and forth between them. "How about ribs for dinner? Your favorite."

The group has been winnowed from thirty pairs down to six, the two women beside the door still among the remaining few. A willowy blonde wearing a too-small sundress over her too-large breasts walks from the casting room, pushing her little girl forward, her disappointment and irritation barely concealed, and the moms beside the door perk up. It's obvious the little girl was a front-runner and that she failed.

"Molly Martin."

16

I leap from my seat, and Molly slides off beside me.

Suddenly I'm nothing but nerves, and I realize this was a terrible idea. Molly's not an actress. She doesn't…We don't belong here. We're not prepared for this. She's going to make a fool of herself, and I'm setting her up to do just that.

What was I thinking? I wasn't thinking. I was blinded by the idea of my daughter being a star. Insanity, temporary insanity caused by staring into the bright light of possibility too long.

I consider grabbing Molly's hand and fleeing, but I can't because Molly has already grabbed my hand and is pulling me toward the door. I stagger behind her, and to my baffled amazement, as we pass the remaining contenders, the resentment around us grows, those that remain glaring at us. And I realize when we reach the door, it's because Molly is the real deal and they know it. Unlike the others who went before us, Molly is the genuine article—a precocious four-year-old who prefers to wear overalls and who hates to brush her curly hair—something no amount of hot curlers, rouge, hissing, or bribing can transform their little darlings into.

We step into the room, and the woman with the clipboard directs me to a seat against the wall. Molly is told to go to the middle of the room and stand on a red X. Already standing on a blue X is a boy a few years older. Skinny as a beanpole and dark-skinned, he looks like he might be African American but could also be Indian.

Across from me, on the other side of the room, a woman with the same color skin and waist-length black hair sits in a chair identical to mine. She looks nervous, and I assume she's the boy's mother.

Molly and the boy face a table of three people, a woman and two men. Behind them is a camera and a cameraman. Other than that, the room is empty.

The woman at the table is petite and has hair so blond that it is nearly white. In front of her is a stack of files, and I take her for the casting director. From the top folder, she removes two copies of Molly's resume and hands one to each of the men. The page is nearly blank—Molly's photo in the upper-left corner, a few lines beneath. A very sparse, single-commercial resume.

The man in the middle has an intensity that makes me nervous, his dark eyes boring into Molly and the boy. The man on the right is heavyset and bald, his eyes small and squinty. He wears a shiny black button-down shirt with gold cuff links and looks slightly bored.

"Hello," the woman says.

The boy mutters hello, and Molly waves.

"Okay, Shariq, you go first," the woman says, looking at her notes for the boy's name. "Tell us your name, how old you are, and who your agent is."

"My name is Shariq Jobe. I am eight. And my agent is Monique Braxton," he recites stiffly, the words memorized.

"Hey, that's my agent too," Molly says, holding up her hand for Shariq to give her a high-five. He hesitates then reluctantly raises his hand, and Molly smacks it.

"Your turn," the woman says to Molly.

"I'm Mowlly Mawrtin, and I'm fouwr."

"Very good," the woman says sweetly. "Ready to read?"

Shariq nods, and Molly looks at me confused.

"She's asking if you're ready to say your lines," I clarify.

Molly's face breaks into a grin, and she nods.

"Does she read?" the woman asks, Molly's reaction concerning her.

"A little," I say. "She's only four, so it's limited, but she has a real good memory." I'm horribly aware that I sound like a street vendor hawking my wares and want to stop, but for some inexplicable reason, I keep right on going. "Her brother's in second grade, and she does his homework with him and gets most of it right."

When I stop, I'm so mortified that I wish I could tap my heels three times and magically disappear to Kansas.

"Okay," the woman says, seemingly immune to stage moms' puffed-up elucidations. She turns back to the kids. "Ready, kids. And action."

Shariq has the first line. It's simple: *We need to go now.* That's all he needs to say, but his eyes grow large and flick back and forth, his expression frozen as he searches his brain for the words lost somewhere in its coils.

"We need to go now," Molly whispers.

"We need to go now," Shariq repeats a little too loud.

Molly looks down at the ground. "I can't," she says. "What if he comes back?"

I nearly cheer with how perfect she did it, the line delivered with genuine reluctance and fear.

"He left," Shariq says. "I saw him get in his car. He's not going to be back for a while."

The line is supposed to be: *He's gone. We need to do it now before he gets back.*

Molly hesitates but barely. "But what if he comes back soonewr than you think?"

She added the "sooner than you think" part, causing Shariq to realize he made a mistake.

His eyes bulge again, and his lip trembles. Across from me, his mom sits rigid, her hands clenched in her lap. The room has grown deathly quiet, all of us holding our breath, a united willing for Shariq to remember his next line.

"Then we'll hide behind the shed!" he blurts, his face lit up with relief as all of us let out a collective sigh.

"That's fine," the woman at the table announces, stopping them from continuing. "Thank you, Shariq. We'll be in touch."

Shariq walks away, his eyes averted as his mom falls in behind him and nearly pushes him out the door.

"Behind the *garden* shed, baby," she says before the door closes, her voice shrill. "You forgot the word 'garden.'"

He forgot more than that, but perhaps her memory is as bad as her son's.

When the door closes, the man in the center leans back in his chair and peers at Molly over steepled fingers. "Do you sing?" he asks.

The man is not particularly handsome, his nose slightly large for his face, his chin slightly small, but he has a magnetism that causes the room to swirl around him. The others are glued to his words, and I find myself drawn to him as well. Even the heavy man beside him pays attention, looking up from his boredom as if suddenly Molly is interesting.

"Evewryone sings," Molly answers.

"Will you sing something for us?" the woman says. "Anything you like."

Molly tilts her head, and her mouth skews to the side, then she starts tapping her foot, and I know what's coming, and it's all I can do to control my snicker.

"Hey…ey…ey. Uh. Yeah, hey…ey…"

The three at the table blink rapidly, unsure what Molly's singing, and even the heavy man smiles when Molly breaks into the chorus for "Play That Funky Music."

When she finishes the chorus, the man in the center holds up his hand to stop her, a smile still on his face.

My heart bursts with joy and panic in equal measure. The competitive spirit in me applauds because I know Molly nailed it, while the annoying buzz from this morning returns, blaring at full volume because I'm uncertain what exactly it is we've won.

"Thank you, Molly," the woman says. "We'll be in touch."

"You'wre wewlcome," Molly says with a small bow like Bo taught her to do after a performance.

I take her by the hand to lead her from the room.

"One more question," the man in the center says, stopping us. He is looking at Molly's sheet. "It says here you're 53 inches, but that can't be right. How tall are you?"

I swallow, frozen by the question. I have no idea how tall Molly is. I'm five-two, that's sixty-two inches. Molly's at least two feet shorter. Sixty-two minus twenty-four...I try to do the math in my head, but my brain won't function. A mother should know this. What mother doesn't know how tall her child is?

Molly saves me. She puts her hand on top of her head and drags it out to the air in front of her. "This tawll," she says, then she turns and pulls me out the door.

The man's voice reaches my ears before it closes. "We just found ourselves a star."

17

My certainty that Molly got the part has ebbed.

It's been three days without a word.

I try not to be disappointed, reminding myself that it was a long shot.

The other little girl, the adorable one with the blue eyes and rosebud lips, probably got it. Perhaps they found her cuter or maybe she sang better than Molly.

C'est la vie, it wasn't meant to be. Everything happens for a reason.

But no matter how many clichés I recite, I'm horribly disappointed, the future I dreamed of since we left the audition dissolved into the dismal reality of the present—no car, no job, a daughter who hates me, a son who doesn't speak and whose therapy I can't afford.

Though the Gap commercial is doing well, we won't see any royalties for months, and the money from the shoot is nearly gone. So it's time to face the facts: I need to get another job.

Walking distance from my mom's condo are a handful of restaurants. I decide to start with those.

Tying on my sneakers, I tell the kids to do the same.

"No," Emily says.

"Em, come on, get your shoes on."

"No. I don't want you to get another stupid job in this stupid place."

"Yeah, well, tough. I don't want to get another stupid job in this stupid place either, but there's no choice. We need money to eat, to live, to pay for your iPhone."

She throws her iPhone at me, and it lands on the carpet at my feet.

"Take the stupid iPhone. You do have a choice. You can send *me* back to Yucaipa."

I sigh through my nose to rein in my anger. "Em, we're a family. And like it or not, you're my daughter, and that means you're stuck with me as your mom. So get your shoes on so I can get a job and earn enough money so eventually *we* can go back to Yucaipa."

"Pwlease, Em," Molly says, her lip trembling.

Emily closes her eyes tight, inhales the tears that are on the brink of eruption, then reluctantly slides on her Cons. She stands, arms crossed, eyes on the ground, then shuffles past me out the door.

"Hewre, Em," Molly says, handing Emily her iPhone.

"Thanks, Itch," Emily says.

We are waiting for the elevator when my phone buzzes. I answer it, expecting it to be the mechanic asking again for payment for the towing service of the van to the junkyard, a bill at the bottom of my priorities.

"She got it."

It takes a minute for the voice to register.

"Ms. Braxton?"

"Yeah," Monique Braxton says, then repeats, "She got it."

"She got it?" I say dumbly, not trusting my ears.

The elevator opens, but I signal to the kids to let it go.

"Yeah, they loved her."

"They loved her?" I repeat, my disbelief reducing me to a parrot.

I stumble back into the condo, and the kids follow, Emily rolling her eyes in annoyance as she herds Molly and Tom back through the door.

"Belinda, the casting director, said Chris was so over the moon about Molly that he didn't even audition the remaining girls. After Molly left, he sent them all home."

I think of the two women beside the door, and gloating satisfaction washes over me. Then I remember their little girls, one blonde, the other a redhead, and I think they didn't deserve to not even be given a chance.

"Chris is who?" I ask, knowing he was the man sitting in the middle but unsure of his role.

"Chris Cantor, the executive producer of the show, the boss."

I smile at the idea of Molly working for him.

"Molly did her part," Monique Braxton says. "Now it's my turn. Give me a few days and let me see what I can get. You'll be designated as her manager, standard fee of fifteen percent. Good?"

"Yeah, great."

"Perfect. Molly won't start until the details are ironed out, but I told them you'd go in for a fitting so they can get started on her wardrobe. So you need to be there tomorrow."

She rattles off the details, and I scrawl them with a crayon into a coloring book Molly left on the table, my hand shaking with excitement.

"Get ready," Monique Braxton says. "It's going to be a wild ride."

18

The disturbing buzz in my head won't go away. I clean the refrigerator and the oven. I dust. I do laundry. I go to the grocery store. I make a nice dinner.

I'm excited, euphoric, thrilled, "over the moon," as Monique Braxton says, except for the damn buzz that relentlessly vibrates in the frontal lobe of my brain and which is giving me a pounding headache, making it impossible for me to fully enjoy the moment.

Our execution has been stayed; we've been spared. In the eleventh hour, an angel of mercy (Monique Braxton) has swooped down from heaven and lifted us on her golden wings from the gallows of wretchedness. Okay, it wasn't quite that dramatic, but almost.

Fame, money, prestige, excitement. Molly's going to be on *The Foster Band*!

This is the greatest moment of my…of *our* lives.

Everyone should be celebrating, popping the champagne, dancing and singing. But that's the problem. In our little world, other than my mom, who is out tonight with friends, I'm the only one excited.

The issue is Emily. Her response to the news was an eager, *So now we can go home?* And when I explained it actually meant the opposite, that making a television show was full-time work, so we would need to live near the studio, it sucked all the happiness from the moment, and Emily stormed away, locked herself in her room, and hasn't come out since. Then Molly started to cry and said she didn't want to be on the show. And Tom, sensitive to both sides, showed no emotion at all.

I finish washing the dishes, dry them, and put them in the cupboards, then sit beside Molly on the couch, where she is blankly staring at an episode of *The Backyardigans*, a show I loathe but that seems utterly mesmerizing to four-year-olds.

Tom is in my mom's room practicing the exercises he's supposed to do daily to help with his anxiety. Through the door I hear him speaking into a recorder then playing the recording back so he can get used to hearing his voice. It seems like a ridiculous exercise, but Tom has done everything the counselors and books suggest, his desire to get better fueling his dedication.

"Hello, I'm Tom," he says. "It's nice to meet you. Do you want to play handball?"

My heart aches. Tom loves handball. He and Emily used to play it for hours against the garage door. The second time I was called to the school, it was recess, and I saw him sitting on the bench enviously watching the other kids playing on the handball court.

"Hey, what's up? How about a game of handball?" he tries, going for a cooler approach.

"Love Bug," I say, turning my attention to my youngest.

She ignores me, her attention fixed on the odd-shaped animal characters on the screen.

I click off the television, breaking her *Backyardigan*-induced trance.

"I watching," she says.

"I know, but I need to talk to you about something important."

She sighs and frowns.

"Bug, did you mean what you said about not wanting to be on the show?"

She shrugs.

"Sweetie, Em's just upset right now. You know that, right? Once things settle down, and we get a new car, and she makes some friends, she'll be just as happy as she was in Yucaipa."

"What about the howrses?"

"Maybe I can get her riding lessons? Do you think she'd like that?"

Another shrug, her focus still on the screen.

"So, what do you say? Do you want to be on television and play the part of Annie?"

"Sure," she says with no great enthusiasm. "Now can I watch?"

I turn the television back on, give her a peck on her curly head, and pretend I feel better. Decision made.

I look at Emily's closed door. She'll get over it. Kids adapt. She'll learn to adapt. Emily can't see it, but things will be different now. We'll have money, and she'll have nice clothes and be able to go to concerts and movies and amusement parks, do all the things we couldn't afford to do before. This is the right choice. It promises us a better present and a brighter future. Therapy for Tom, a new car, and at some point down the road, a house of our own and money for college.

I open the issue of *Star Gazer* and absently page through it, glancing at the faces to see if I spot the couple Molly and I passed in the parking lot. On page twenty is an article about Jeremy, the oldest child on *The Foster Band*, and his new romance with Maya Chin, the star of the show *Mainland*. Someday soon, Molly might be in these pages. Maybe they'll ask her about ice cream or rhyming.

This is going to be amazing. Emily doesn't realize it, but it will be.

She'll be happy. We all will.

19

The studio is less than ten miles away, but nervous about being late, I allow an hour to get there. We turn from the parking garage onto the street, and my eyes slide to a man standing on the corner. Young twenties and average in every way, he is not tall or short, heavy or thin, his hair is brown, his skin medium, his eyes concealed behind wire-rim glasses—he is entirely unremarkable except for the way he watches us and the disturbing notion that he has watched us before. Molly waves, and his face lights up as he waves back.

"Do you know that man?" I ask.

"No, but he's awlays sweet and nevewr souwr."

"He's waved to you before?"

"Uh-huh. He wlikes to stand on that cowrner and sometimes waves at me when I wlook out the window in Gwrandma's wroom. When he's wreawlly being funny, he'wll do the dance wlike Lewroy, not the whowle thing, just the fiwrst pawrt."

The hair on the back of my neck bristles. "Baby, maybe you shouldn't wave at him anymore."

"Why?"

I consider this. *Why?*

Because it's creepy.

But not really. The guy looks harmless. Molly's going to be a star, which means she's going to have fans. My blood warms with the thought. We are going to need to get used to this, people getting excited when they see us.

Traffic moves at a slug's pace, and I'm glad I allowed extra time for the commute. We park in the same lot we did for the audition, then carrying our crayon note, make our way toward Soundstage 19, which it turns out is on the other side of the lot.

Fox Studios is huge, a labyrinth of buildings and streets and sidewalks teeming with people and golf carts and Segways. There are actors dressed in costumes walking from set to set; crew members hanging out, smoking, and eating; construction crews working on sets; and tour groups shuffling along in small herds, snapping photos, and gaping.

I pull Molly along as she staggers wide-eyed behind me. Two gladiators with swords slung from their waists walk past followed by a woman made up like an alien. I'd like to stop and stare as well, but where I thought I had allowed plenty of time, now the minutes are ticking down quickly, and we are dangerously close to being late.

I get turned around and stop a woman with a lanyard around her neck that holds an ID. "Excuse me, we're looking for Soundstage 19."

The woman is in her forties and has the confident look of a person in charge. "*The Foster Band* set?"

"Yes," I say, relieved to have stopped someone who knows the lot. "My daughter is the new Foster kid," I boast.

She glances at Molly then back at me, and instead of the impressed expression I was expecting, her face softens to one that seems to say, *Oh, I'm sorry to hear that.*

Perhaps she heard me wrong. Perhaps she thought I said, "My daughter is a foster kid."

With a thin smile, she directs us to keep going. The soundstage is half a block farther.

"Good luck," she says, and again I sense sympathy in the tone.

I shake off the strange encounter, and we hustle on to our destination, bursting through the door then stopping.

Despite the swelter outside, inside the building it is cool to the point of cold, and the drop in temperature combined with the stark emptiness causes goose bumps to rise on my arms. There's not a soul in sight, and other than the buzz of the fluorescent lights, not a sound.

Taking Molly's hand, we walk forward, unsure where we're going or even if this is the right place, and I wonder if perhaps there was another entrance.

Halfway down the corridor, a sliver of light glows from beneath one of the doors.

I look at my watch. 9:02. We are late and getting later, so with a deep breath, I kick my timidity to the curb and knock.

"Come in."

"It's the guy," Molly says, her face lighting up as she throws open the door to reveal Chris Cantor sitting behind a paper-strewn desk.

"Well, well," he says, leaning back in his chair. "Look who it is, the two loveliest women in the show."

"Hey, mistewr," Molly says. "We'wre hewre 'cause I need to get measuwred."

He smiles, and I can't believe I didn't think he was good-looking. Perhaps not in a *GQ* model way, but undeniably sexy in a Sean Penn or Al Pacino kind of way. Dressed more casually today than he was at the audition, he wears jeans and a surfer T-shirt, and his hair is mussed and his face unshaven.

"Well, I'm not the one who does the measuring, but I know who does. Follow me." He stands and extends his hand. "Hello, Molly's mom. I'm Chris."

"Faye."

"Please tell me you're not as much of a diva as the infamous Ms. Dunaway."

"Just don't piss me off and you'll never have to find out," I say, shocked and a little embarrassed by the flirt in my voice.

The right side of his mouth lifts. "Then I'll try to stay on your good side."

I realize he's still holding my hand, and I pull it away, my skin so warm that the building is no longer cold.

"We're late," I manage.

"Well then, right this way." He leads us back into the hall. "Is Molly your only one?"

I hesitate a flicker before answering, "No, I have two others," my answer instantly deflating the moment.

"Triple the fun," he says, not missing a beat.

His response nearly brings back my hope but not entirely. Chris Cantor, producer of *The Foster Band*, is not looking for a three-kid single mom. I might as well hang an "Undesirable" sign on my forehead.

"Hey, Two-Bits, you passed it," he says to Molly, whose idea of following is to skip ahead.

She pivots and dodges ahead of us through the door Chris is holding open.

I walk into what looks like a massive closet—racks and racks of clothes and dozens of shelves of shoes and accessories stacked to the ceiling. In the center of it all is a massive woman, her forearms crossed over her very large bosom.

"You're late," she bellows in an accent I think is German, adding to her formidableness.

"Go easy on them, Ingrid," Chris says from the doorway. "It's their first day, and I found them lost and wandering the hallways."

"You." She points to Molly. "Come here." She points to Chris. "You. Leave."

"You love me," Chris says. "Admit you love me and I'll go."

She grabs a shoe from a shelf beside her and flings it at him. He pulls the door in front of him as a shield. "You love me," he says as the door continues to close. "You know you do."

He's so darn cute. *Was he wearing a ring?* No, he wasn't. If he was, I would have noticed. No ring and no photos of family on his desk. No silver-framed portrait of a wife, two kids, and a golden retriever sitting on rocks at the beach—the kind of picture designed to make those of us without that silver-framed life miserable with envy.

Ingrid harrumphs with disapproval, knowing my thoughts, which are easy to figure out since my eyes still linger on the door through which Chris just left.

I give an innocent smile that she doesn't return.

"Mom, make yourself useful," she says.

I perk up, excited to start my job as Molly's manager.

"The coffee station is down the hall. Decaf, two creams, one sugar."

If I had the guts, I would harrumph back, but I don't, so instead I walk from the room to fetch her coffee, my mind filled with the image of me and the kids sitting on an outcropping of rocks at the beach, Chris's arm around my waist, Gus in front of us. Gus is a bit mangy for the dream, but we come as a package deal, all or nothing. Plus, I kind of like it. Gus adds a bit of personality.

20

The contract is for so much more than I expected that I can't get my head around the numbers. Molly will be paid $20,000 per episode for the first seven episodes. If her contract is renewed for the rest of the season and the two seasons after that, a three-year contract total, she will get $30,000 an episode for the remaining episodes. For any *Foster Band* merchandise that has solely her image on it, she will receive a ten percent royalty. For merchandise with multiple persons on it, she will get a proportional split of the ten percent royalty. The contract is exclusive of any money Molly receives for concerts, music royalties, endorsement deals, magazine shoots, or appearances.

Twenty thousand an episode for seven episodes is $140,000. Thirty thousand an episode for fifteen more episodes is $450,000. Molly's gross income for the year will be $590,000, not including the money from the Gap commercial or anything else she might do. The years after, she will make $660,000.

I am designated as Molly's manager, and as such, fifteen percent of what she earns will be mine. Fifteen percent of $660,000 is $99,000. I suddenly have a job that pays nearly one hundred grand a year, possibly more, and the job is to take care of my little girl. I can't believe it. I really can't.

I read the contract three times. Some of the legal jargon is a little confusing, and there's a paragraph about breach of contract that is unsettling because it says if we leave without cause we can be sued, and since I've never committed to anything for longer than a day, signing on to do something for three years is a bit out of my comfort zone. But I also can't imagine ever wanting to quit something like this. Why would we? This is the greatest thing that's ever happened to us.

I sign on every line I'm supposed to then grab a sheet of paper and write a list:

Therapy for Tom
Buy car
Start looking at neighborhoods where we might want to live
Look at private schools
Repay Bo
File for divorce

I smile. I kiss my list. I twirl in a circle then sit back down and stare some more at my wonderful, amazing list.

When my eyes grow too heavy to keep them open a moment longer, I crawl onto the sleeper couch beside Molly and continue the silent reverie in the dark, swooning a little with the disbelief of it all. My hand slides across the mattress until the knuckles rest against Molly's forearm, her solid warmth anchoring me. We made it. All the scraping and scrapping we've done to survive is over, and somehow, miraculously, it all worked out. Tears squeeze from my eyes with the sheer relief of it.

It's so wonderful and I'm so overwhelmed by the thought of it that I can hardly believe it's real. Money, that sweet green stuff that makes the world go round, is going to start rolling in. I open my eyes and stare at the ceiling, the little stucco bumps shadowed blue by the moonlight through the window. No more struggle. Incredible.

Molly snorts then resumes her steady snoring, a perfect rhythm of breath I try to match with my own, hoping to settle the erratic pounding in my chest. *It is real*, I assure myself, but the thought only causes my heart to pound harder.

Our new reality seems so fragile that it unnerves me. We only just got here, but already I'm terrified it will be taken away, that as quickly as it arrived, it will disappear—the whole thing amazing and tenuous as a butterfly's life.

I tell myself it's only the newness that has me off balance, that this is the greatest thing that's ever happened to us. A good night's sleep and tomorrow the shadows of doubt will be gone.

21

We pull onto the lot, and Molly yawns awake then climbs from the car without an ounce of urgency, and it's all I can do not to scream at her to hurry up. It's our first day and already we are ten minutes late.

We race to the soundstage then through the corridors toward the sound of voices, and when we find a small crowd, we stop, assuming this is where we are supposed to be. A few people look our way, but no one says anything and I don't recognize a single face. Some chat in small groups, others hang by themselves with cups of coffee and their cell phones, and a few slump against walls with their eyes closed.

"You're late."

I don't know the woman who has stepped in front of us, but by her tone and demeanor, I assume she's in charge. Petite as a pixie, her hair is jet black and her eyes piercing blue. She could be a haggard thirty-year-old or a well-maintained fifty-year-old; it's impossible to tell. She carries a clipboard and wears black jeans, a black sweater, a headset, and a scowl.

"You need to leave," she says. Her voice matches her hairstyle and wardrobe—severe and shrill—like the squawk of a raven.

I blink, not understanding. Are we being fired or is she sending us home as punishment for being late?

"Give me your cell number," she says.

I scrawl the number on her clipboard as I stammer, "I don't understand."

"What don't you understand?"

"You just told us to leave."

She frowns, her mouth pinching so tight that it puckers. "Minutes. Your daughter has 270 of them a day. They are clocked from the moment you arrive on the lot." She looks at her watch. "You pulled in at 7:09. It is now 7:16. Seven minutes are gone and nothing's been accomplished. By the time you pull off of the lot again, another ten minutes will have been wasted. At this rate, we'll finish the first episode in time for the finale. I told Chris he should have cast twins, but no, he insisted your daughter was *the one*, so now I'm stuck dealing with three hours of set time and four and a half hours of lot time. Does he know how difficult that's going to be?"

I pull Molly against my hip to buffer her from the woman's rant.

"From now on, when you're given your call time, it means you'll be waiting somewhere nearby at that time. Seven means seven, not seven-sixteen. You will wait until I call, then you will come onto the lot. Understood?"

I nod.

"Good. Now go."

"But Molly doesn't have a scene until halfway through the first episode. Do you even need her today?"

She runs me up and down and sneers in distaste like I'm a fly that landed in her soup. "You've never done this before?"

I shake my head.

"First, we don't shoot in sequence; that would be incredibly inefficient. Second, today and tomorrow are blocking."

I swallow.

"Christ, you don't know what blocking is? Are you kidding me?" Her voice has reached a glass-shattering octave, and now everyone is looking at us. "I'm going to kill Chris. I don't have time for this."

"She's scawry," Molly says as we hurry back the way we came.

22

Extreme boredom has set in.

We wait at a nearby McDonald's for the woman to call. We've been here five hours.

Molly plays in the play area, rotating friends as previous ones leave to get on with their days.

I've eaten breakfast and lunch, indulged in a chocolate sundae, and am now contemplating an apple pie. If each day is like this, I'll weigh three hundred pounds by the time the season begins.

While I wait, I contemplate what a loser I am at my new job. I don't know the woman's name who sent us away. I didn't get her number. And I have no idea what blocking is or why we're not a part of it.

Reluctant to tie up my phone, I've resisted calling home to check on Emily and Tom, but unable to stand the boredom one more second, I cave.

First, I call home. No answer.

I try to recall if my mom told me her plan for the day. Emily had a soccer game this morning, that I know because her uniform needed to be washed, but after that, the activities of my other two kids are a blank. My mom might have told me, but last night I was distracted. Molly and I needed to memorize her lines, and it was a lot of work. My mom and Emily and Tom were there, but I can't remember if they talked about their day. If they did, I wasn't paying attention.

I try Emily's cell phone, and she answers on the fifth ring.

"Hey, baby, where are you?"

"We're going to Sky Zone for Melissa's birthday party. Didn't Grandma tell you?"

I don't think so, but she might have. Not wanting to incriminate myself, I say nothing, feeling bad for either not listening or not asking. But it doesn't matter because, for the first time since we got back from Bo's, Emily sounds happy, and I grab onto it. "That's terrific. Melissa from your class?"

"My soccer team."

How do I not know this? In Yucaipa I knew every classmate, every teammate, and most of the parents.

"And Tom is going with you?"

"Yep. Melissa's parents are like super rich, so she invited the brothers and sisters too. They rented out the whole place, like the entire Sky Zone."

"That's wonderful. Did you get her a present?"

"Grandma," Emily squeals in alarm, "we didn't buy a present."

"Crap," I hear my mom say in the background.

"Em," I say, trying to get her back on the phone.

My mom's muffled voice says, "We're already late. We'll give her something at the next practice."

"We can't," Emily cries. "I can't not have a present. She's going to open her gifts, and I'm just going to be sitting there."

"Em," I yell louder, hoping she'll hear me. The other customers in the restaurant look over at my screech that Emily still doesn't hear.

How could my mom not have realized that you need to bring a gift to a birthday party?

Because my mom never remembers things like that. My dad was the one who took care of the details of life—cooking, buying toilet paper, making sure I had gifts for birthday parties.

Emily's sobs resonate through the line, and I want to grab Molly and run to her rescue, but there are way too many problems with that idea. First, I have no idea which Sky Zone they're headed toward. Second, by the time I fight my way out of the downtown, the party will be over. Third, we're waiting for a callback so Molly can finish her workday.

"We're here," I hear my mom say. "Emily, stop crying."

Emily continues to sob.

"Em, come on, let's go. Melissa won't care that you don't have a gift."

More hysterics.

Minutes pass.

"Fine. Then we're going home," my mom says, clearly frustrated.

And that's that. No Sky Zone, no birthday party.

"Mom, what's wrwong?" Molly says, appearing in front of me, and I realize tears are rolling down my cheeks.

I wipe them away and click off the phone. "Nothing, baby." I pull her onto my lap and bury my wet face into her soft hug, reining in my frustration and trying not to be angry with my mom, reminding myself that she's doing the best she can. She didn't sign up for this. Until a week ago, she was a part-time volunteer librarian, and now she's a full-time babysitter.

My phone buzzes.

We're needed back on the set.

23

The black-haired pixie's name is Beth, and she is the assistant director, Chris's right-hand woman, but I'm thinking Hitler in drag or Medusa. She walks very fast as she leads us through the backstage area, and Molly needs to run to keep up. We turn a corner and race past a dozen people who lean, sit, and stand in various states of boredom.

"Who are they?" I ask.

"Extras," Beth says. "We always keep a few around just in case."

Spare people—that's something I've never heard of before.

She pushes open a door, and we walk onto the set of Mr. Foster's law office, and a thrill rushes through me. *I'm standing in Mr. Foster's office. How cool is that?*

In front of us is his desk with two photos of his family on it, his beautiful wife and his five foster kids. One of them shows the family posed on the porch; the other is a shot of them performing at a concert. In the corner of the room is his guitar, and on his desk is a baseball that was given to him by a famous baseball player who guest starred on one of the episodes.

Beyond the office is the reception area, and standing in the middle of it is Chris. His easy smile from yesterday is gone, and today he is clean-shaven and all business, wearing tailored pants and a button-down dress shirt rolled at the sleeves.

Standing beside him is a large man with a rusty beard.

Molly skips ahead of Beth and straight through the open door. "I'm hewre," she announces.

Beth runs in behind her. "Sorry, Chris," she says, corralling Molly away from him.

"Hey, Two-Bits," he says. "Take that toosh off my set until I ask for it."

He turns back to the bearded man but not before noticing me and giving a wink.

A wink! My heart triples its pulse. Molly's wardrobe fitting was two weeks ago, and since then, I've obsessed over not obsessing over Chris Cantor, reminding myself that not only am I a mom with three kids who is not remotely in Chris Cantor's league, but that I am also Molly's manager, and as such, I need to be professional.

A wink, the twitch of a muscle, and all that effort has been undone, my eyes sliding sideways to look at him as the sterling-frame image of our future returns in high-definition Technicolor.

Beth leads us into another corridor, this one teeming with people, and directs us to a spot against the wall. "She knows her lines?" she says, more statement than question.

I nod. Molly kind of knows her lines. We ran through them three times last night then she fell asleep. The scenes are long, and she's only four. I hope the expectations aren't too high.

"Stay," she says as if giving a command to a dog. "Not one toe on the set until I tell you."

Molly's mouth tightens, and I'm afraid she's about to say something not very nice. Molly has a temper, and she doesn't like being bossed around. Fortunately she only nods.

In the reception area, Chris still talks to the bearded man.

"Wlook, Mom, thewre's Cawleb and Gabby."

Standing a few feet away, the young heartthrob talks to Gabby, his foster sister on the show.

Gabby is the middle Foster daughter and the one with the most attitude. Her character has a hard edge from a hard life, but beneath the tough veneer is a golden heart and a diva voice that can fill a football stadium. She's beautiful in a different way, her black hair shaved on one side, chin length on the other, the tips dyed indigo. A thick Hispanic girl, she has broad shoulders, strong arms, and dresses in leather and torn jeans.

In real life, it's strange how ordinary she and Caleb are. Caleb is probably Emily's age, maybe a year older, and if he wasn't a mega-sensation whose face was splashed on the cover of every teen magazine, he'd just be a normal kid I wouldn't look at twice—medium build, brown hair, nice dark, almost black eyes, a small nose, and a dimpled chin.

Beth is back, marching toward us with a boy and a large-breasted, blond-haired woman in tow. The boy looks about seven, and I'm guessing he got the role as Molly's brother. The script said his name is Miles.

Because the kids in the cast are also members of *The Foster Band*, which does concerts and has albums outside the show, their real-life first names are used for their characters to avoid confusion. So Kira is Kira, Jeremy is Jeremy, Gabby is Gabby, Caleb is Caleb, and Molly and Miles will be Molly and Miles. Which worked out well for the producers since Molly and Miles sounds cute together.

Beth doesn't bother to introduce us, just barks a reminder about staying off the set then marches away.

"Bossy," the woman says.

We introduce ourselves. Her name is Rhonda.

Miles and Molly go off to check out the craft service cart, which Rhonda explains is a food buffet.

"They feed us?" I say.

"Yep, but be careful. I think I gained thirty pounds from boredom and unlimited access to mac and cheese when Miles was on *Young Riders*."

"You've done this before?"

"Hell, yeah. Miles has been acting since he was born. My daughters gave it a go also but weren't as successful. Miles is the smartest, and the blond hair helps. The other two take after my ex. They don't photograph as well and have absolutely no stamina."

The more we talk, the less I like her. First, she smells like an ashtray, and second, the way she talks about Miles is like she's talking about her car—his features, his performance value, how many miles he has left in him.

"He's small for his age, which is probably why he got the part," Rhonda says. "He just turned nine, so he can work five hours and be on set nine."

Rhonda is still talking, but I'm not listening because Jules Buchner has just walked into the staging area. For nearly four decades, he has been a superstar. I grew up watching him, and my dad was a huge fan. He has won two Academy Awards as well as a CMA for a song he wrote for his daughter when she got married.

He's shorter than I thought, maybe five foot ten. When he was young, his hair was light blond, now it's white. His eyes are brown and slightly watery at the rims, and though I'm thirty feet away, I can smell the alcohol perfuming off his body.

"Let's do this," he bellows as he steps onto the set.

24

Sex, sex, sex, sex.

I should be concentrating on Molly and what she needs to be doing, but my mind is occupied with Chris and what he needs to be doing to me.

The problem is deprivation combined with boredom.

Blocking, it turns out, is absolutely tedious. It's the orchestrating of the scene, figuring out the movements of the actors, the lights, the microphones, and the cameras. To conserve Molly's set time, a stand-in poses as Molly while they figure things out, and Molly only steps in for the final rehearsal.

I feel bad for the little girl who is her stand-in. Her job is even more boring than Molly's. I remember her from the audition; she was the girl who didn't return Molly's smile. And she doesn't smile now. She's almost cute, and perhaps would be if she had more personality, but like a robot, she dutifully follows Beth's instructions with precision and remarkable professionalism but without an ounce of animation. Her mom sits off to the side knitting, and I realize I'm going to need a hobby as well or else I'm going to spend the next three years obsessing on Chris Cantor and sex.

It's not my fault. My involuntary celibacy is entering its eighth month. That's a *really* long time. Combine that with Chris's diabolical wink and the fact that watching blocking is about as entertaining as watching golf, and I'm like a teenage boy, every other thought going rogue on me.

"Molly, you're on," Chris says.

The stand-in walks off, and Molly leaps up from the floor where she had been playing Go Fish with one of the extras. "Sowrry, gotta go," she says.

Molly's done great so far. Though it doesn't seem like she's paying attention, she incorporates all the notes that were given to the stand-in when it's her turn.

The bearded man is named Griff, and he is the director of photography. Between the props, the actors, the lights, the cameras, and the microphones, there's a lot to coordinate. It's like a choreographed dance with a hundred moving parts, and Griff orchestrates it beautifully.

Something about him is familiar. His eyes are the giveaway, a distinct shape and color, gold fanning to bronze, and I'm certain I've seen them before, but I can't place it. *Griff, Griffin?* Perhaps we went to the same elementary school. He catches me looking at him, and his eyes lock on mine, causing me to turn away.

While the crew adjusts the overhead microphones, Chris settles back in his director's chair, giving me a close-up of the back of his head. His hair is slightly thinning, and I see now that there are strands of gray among the brown, making me realize he's older than I originally thought, probably closer to forty-five than forty.

An older man. I mull that over. Sean is only four years older than I am, and the only other guy I've been with was my high school boyfriend.

The boyfriend was nothing special, but sex with Sean was one of our strong points, never too kinky but always interesting. Once he brought home a feather duster he had swiped from a hotel cleaning cart. He said he saw it and thought of me. We had a lot of fun with those feathers. The memory makes me smile.

I look at Chris and wonder if he'd know what to do with a feather duster. Studying his thinning hair and his intensity, I doubt feather dusters are his thing, and it makes me a little sad to think my feather duster days might be over.

"Cute, isn't he?" I look up to see Rhonda talking to me, a knowing smirk on her face. "Most eligible bachelor at Fox, maybe in all of Hollywood. Rich, talented, charming, nothing not to love."

"I wasn't..."

"No, of course not, you were just admiring the scenery. Can't blame you, need to occupy yourself somehow."

I swallow and say nothing.

Griff gives a thumbs-up that the microphone issue is resolved, and Chris says, "Let's move it to the hospital."

Molly shuffles off the set, and I lift her into my arms.

"Hey, Bug. You're doing great."

She nods sleepily, and her head collapses on my shoulder, our early morning catching up with her. I wish I could let her rest for a few minutes, but everyone is moving toward the exit, so carrying my burden, I follow.

Chris leads the pack across the lot toward the soundstage of the hospital, the mom of Molly's stand-in latched to his side. As we walk, her flirtatious laughter floats back to the rest of us, and I realize that's how I would look if I showed my interest, and I resolve to check my attraction for good. Chris Cantor is not in my league, and I'm embarrassed for that woman for mistakenly thinking he's in hers.

25

Fortunately it takes half an hour for the cameras and lights to be positioned for the next scene, and I take the opportunity to find a half-quiet spot around the corner from the hubbub and slide to the floor so Molly can continue to sleep against me.

Molly's four-and-a-half-hour workday has already lasted nine hours—three and a half on the lot and five and a half at McDonald's—and I'm starting to wonder exactly how flexible I should be. Rhonda isn't complaining, and neither is Molly's stand-in's mom.

I look at Beth then at Chris, wondering if perhaps they're unaware how long we've been here and if I should remind them. The thought of saying something causes my stomach to spit and sputter. Speaking up has never really been my thing.

"Let's do this," Chris says then looks at his watch. "Molly has an hour left then she needs to be off the lot, so let's go, people. Let's get this done."

He knows exactly what he's doing.

The set for this scene was originally used for the hit show *9-1-1* and is now used by various Fox shows whenever they need an emergency room, an operating room, a waiting room, an elevator, or a cafeteria.

I rub Molly's back to wake her, and she yawns, rubs her eyes, realizes we're still at work, then sighs. I sigh with her. It's only the first day, but already the excitement has worn off. This is a job and she's expected to work.

"Ready, Bugabaloo?" I say, nuzzling her nose.

She nuzzles my nose back. "Wready, Fwreddy," she says, hopping off my lap and making me feel a little better about the long day.

I push to my feet to follow and stop in my tracks when I find myself looking at Helen Harlow standing beside one of the cameramen.

I am starstruck. Helen Harlow has as many Academy Award nominations as she has fingers. Statuesque, blond, and insistently sexy, she was in the first movie I ever saw, *Odessa*, and has been my idol ever since.

Molly skips over to her. "You'wre Mrs. Fostewr," she says, as if the woman didn't already know that. "My mom wloves you."

Her head tilts slightly as she sizes Molly up, looking her over as if appraising a piece of art she's unsure of, then she says, "So you're the little urchin everyone's making such a fuss about."

"What's an uwrchin?"

"Adorable, quite. So where is this mom of yours? I'd like to meet her."

Molly grabs the star's hand and drags her toward me.

"This is hewr," she announces proudly, as if the introduction were the other way around and Helen Harlow should be the one honored by the meeting.

Forty-eight but still gorgeous, she's a woman who has aged gracefully without silicone or stitches, her hair the color of nectar with wisps of silver woven at the temples and around the widow peak of her forehead. Beneath the heavy powder on her face, faint freckles and fine lines patina her skin, revealing that she is in fact human, a revelation both comforting and crushing, a little like pulling back the curtain to discover the great wizard is a mere mortal like myself.

Introduction complete, Molly skips away.

Helen watches her go. "Charming and quite precocious. We're going to get along fabulously."

When she turns back, her notorious green eyes have transformed to stone and her lips are curled in a bemused smile, as if there's something funny of which only she is aware, and I retract my earlier statement that this woman and I are anything alike.

Others are watching us, the room suddenly quiet, and I shift uncomfortably under her stare.

"Hmmm," she says, "you don't look the part."

"Excuse me?" I say, wondering if perhaps she's confused and thinks I am a cast member.

"Rumpelstiltskin. Quite brilliant indeed. Able to spin straw into gold, a trick few possess. My mother of course was the master. She would have been impressed."

Helen Harlow's mother is nearly as famous as her daughter. A bit actress when she was young, her claim to fame was as the poster child for overzealous stage moms. Nicknamed Mommie Dearest II, all three of her children began acting as babies and two went on to become superstars.

"Rumpelstiltskin?" I say, not following.

"Quite. You do remember the story?"

I nod, vaguely recalling the fairy tale about a girl locked in a room and ordered by the king to spin straw into gold, a task she completes with the help of a magical little man named Rumpelstiltskin.

She continues, "Of course the ending is rather dreadful, the girl married off to the greedy king who only married her for her ability to spin gold, and Rumpelstiltskin torn to shreds because the girl didn't hold up her end of the bargain."

With her words, the ending comes back to me, the girl spying on Rumpelstiltskin to discover his name, thereby avoiding giving him her baby, which she had promised she would do if he helped her change the straw to gold.

Helen Harlow's lips curl into a rueful grin. "But I suppose at least the king got everything he desired—the gold, the girl. Happily ever after." She laughs, a silky chortle. "Someday you'll have to tell me how you managed it. I always wish I had asked my mother before she died, the original Rumpelstiltskin, three of us spun from straw into gold."

I'm entirely caught off-guard, with her words veiled as a compliment, her eyes sparkling and that awful smile on her famous face, in front of everyone, she has nailed me to the cross.

26

A block away, I see Molly's fan standing on the corner. Tom has nicknamed him John Lennon on account of the round glasses he wears. I wonder if he's been out there waiting for us all day, not realizing we left so early.

When we are nearly upon him, his head lifts, and he musters a thin smile and a weary wave, and I feel bad for him. He looks nearly as exhausted as I feel, his thin shoulders slumped, his young face worn and drained of color. Since Molly is dead asleep behind me and unable to offer her normal enthusiastic greeting, I do the honors, forcing my tired mouth into a friendly smile and giving him a wave.

I look at the clock. 7:32. If he arrived at nine this morning as he usually does, that means he waited over ten hours for that small exchange. I hope he realizes that we are leaving early again in the morning.

"Hey, guys," I say when I walk in the door of the condo carrying Molly, who is still sound asleep.

Until this moment, I had completely forgotten about the birthday party fiasco, but one glance at Emily's red-rimmed eyes brings it hurtling back. Tom seems fine, probably relieved that he didn't have to endure the event that certainly would have incited an episode of acute mutism.

"How was the party?" I say, feigning ignorance, my words slurring with exhaustion.

Emily runs into her room, and my mom glares at me as if somehow it's my fault. It's all I can do not to snap at her that this is absolutely not *my* fault. *She's* the one who accepted the invitation. *She's* the one who should have remembered to bring a gift. I didn't even know about the party until this morning. Something about that last statement makes me bite my tongue, a twinge of guilt pulsing through the fatigue.

My mom opens the sleeper couch, and I lay Molly down and tuck the blankets around her.

"Thanks, Mom," I say, remembering my gratitude for everything she's done and everything she's doing.

Dropping a kiss on Tom's head, I continue on to the bedroom to comfort Emily.

"Hey, Em," I say, sitting on the edge of the bed and placing my hand on her back. She lies on her stomach, her face buried in her pillow.

"I hate it here," she says.

"I know, baby. I'm sorry."

She cries quietly, her distress so complete that it breaks my heart. LA is not a place for a girl like Emily. She belongs in a world where her long limbs can stretch out and run, where there are horses and open fields.

"I want to go home," she says. "I'll die if I have to go to middle school here." She rolls her head so she's looking at me. "Seriously, Mom, I'll die. The kids carry weapons; they have metal detectors at the front door to try and catch them."

"I'll look into private schools."

"That'll be worse," she says. "The rich kids around here are horrible. You should see the way Melissa and her friends look at me when Grandma pulls up in her Honda."

"Shhh," I say, hoping for a quick consolation so I can collapse on the bed beside Molly. It's terrible, but my exhaustion is so complete that my eyes are closing even as I sit here.

"Are you even listening?"

Not really. "Yes, baby, I know."

My eyes alight on Emily's soccer clothes that she sloughed off after her game this morning, and I decide to take the easy way out.

"How was your game?" I ask with as much brightness as I can muster.

She sneers at me then turns her head to feel sorry for herself alone.

I should recant, retreat, apologize, tell her that somehow we'll work it out, but I do none of these things, instead stubbornly I plow forward with my boneheaded approach of avoiding the issue completely. "Did you score any points?" I ask.

"Goals," Emily says to the wall. "They're called goals."

27

Molly groans when we walk through the door of "base camp," a two-room building across the alley from the soundstage that serves as the hair and makeup salon for the show.

"Welcome, welcome, welcome," a man standing in front of an empty barber chair says. He has short, spiky hair and heavily lined gold eyes. "Henry O'Henry at your service. Really, that's the name. My parents thought it was cute." He talks very fast, his voice quick and sharp like his movements.

His hair is the color of plums and his lips are so soft that they affirm the theory that sexual orientation is not a choice. He's a small man, his arms and legs chicken-bone thin, though his middle is thick, which almost gives him the appearance of being pregnant, perhaps entering his second trimester.

He circles Molly. "My oh my, that's quite a roost. Find many eggs?"

Molly squints up at him.

"Well, let me work my magic. Mom, be gone with you." He shoos me away with the back of his hand. "When you return, she'll be nothing but bouncing curls. Forty minutes." Then he touches Molly's hair and grimaces. "Make that an hour."

I wander to the staging area of Mr. Foster's law office set and perch on a stool to wait. Though it's only our second day, I have come to the conclusion that most of the time spent making a television show is waiting. It's almost torturous how slow things move. Everyone deals with the tedium differently. Some have idle hobbies like knitting or reading; others are incessantly on their phones. I can't figure out what or who they're interacting with, but their thumbs move constantly, their eyes fixed on the minuscule screens.

Once in a while people chat, but I imagine most of what anyone has to say has already been said since everyone's waking hours are spent here, and almost all of that time is spent standing around, which isn't real interesting.

Most of the primary cast wait in their dressing rooms, a row of trailers parked behind the soundstage. Molly has a dressing room as well, a dinky little space with a fridge and a couch and a television, but since her work hours are so constrained, we have yet to spend five minutes there.

At the moment, the only cast members in sight are the woman who plays the social worker and a few extras.

Bradley Mitten turns the corner, causing heads to lift and eyes to follow. He and his wife are the writers of the show. A short man with a beak nose and heavy frame glasses, his eyes skit side to side over the actors, lingering on some and passing over others.

The social worker steps forward. "Mr. Mitten, good morning," she chirps, all smiles. Asian with silky black hair, she's very pretty and a talented actress—one minute you love her character and the next you don't.

Mitten gives a brief nod as he tries to sidestep her.

She blocks him. "I've been meaning to stop by your office..."

"Save it," Mitten says, cutting her off. "No one wants to watch a bitchy social worker traipsing around LA saving the future thugs of America."

He continues on without the least bit of concern that he just steamrolled over the woman's dreams, and I wince at the harshness. Though he's right—my least favorite episodes are those about her dealing with the drugged-out moms or abusive dads of the foster kids.

Mitten finally spots who he is looking for, a girl around sixteen with thick gold hair. She stands beside a woman who looks like her twin except a generation older.

A toothless grin fills his face. "Rebecca."

"Mr. Mitten, what an honor," the mom says.

Mitten ignores her, his focus entirely on the girl. "Playing an accident victim today, are you?"

The girl nods. "Thank you, Mr. Mitten, for getting me the part."

He waves her off. "All I did was put in a good word; you did the rest. I'm still struggling with the story line about Jeremy's new love interest. You would be perfect, a girl a little young for him, innocent and sweet, with that beautiful hair of yours."

She nods her beautiful-haired head.

"Sorry I didn't get it done in time. But don't worry, I'm still working on it, and I still have you in mind."

The girl's face lights up, and the mother nearly squeaks with excitement.

"Rebecca could help you," the mom suggests. "You know, perhaps stop by your office, give you some inspiration, be your muse."

My stomach turns with the not-so-subtle intimation, and Rebecca's face blanches, though she continues to smile and nod.

"Perhaps she could," Mitten says. "I'll be in my office all afternoon. Stop by anytime."

"She will," the mom says. "She definitely will."

My phone buzzes, letting me know that Molly's hair is done, and I rush past Rebecca and her mom who are hugging each other and bouncing up and down as if Christmas came early.

"Mom, wlook," Molly says when I walk into base camp. She shakes her head back and forth to show how her curls now bounce.

It's nothing short of a miracle. Her hair, which an hour ago was an irrepressible, straw-colored, out-of-control afro, has been tamed into a caramel-gold crown of perfectly coiled ringlets.

"How?" I say, astounded.

"I know, I'm amazing," Henry O'Henry says, causing Molly to knock knuckles with him. "And you, Mom, could use a little Henry amazement yourself. I mean really, girl—blah, blah, blasé." His hands flick toward my blah, blah, blasé waist-length hair.

Molly giggles and flicks her hands at me as well. "Yeah, Mom, bwlah, bwlah, bwlasé."

"Sit," Henry orders.

"Do I have a choice?"

His eyes look through his fine-tweezed brows. "Girlfriend, no one is walking around my set looking like Jan Brady." He whips open a smock like a bullfighter taunting me to charge. "And you, Miss Jolly Molly, will be my assistant."

"Okey dokey, jokey smokey," Molly says, and I know she's found her new rhyming partner.

I laugh and take a seat in his chair. My hair has been the same since high school—long, blond, and wavy. And though I'm nervous, a little change might be exactly what I need.

Snip.

Crap.

He holds out the tail of hair he just cut from my head like a prized scalp, two feet of wavy blond hanging from his fist. "For Locks of Love," he says. "Molly, hold open that baggie for me."

He drops the cascade of hair into the Ziploc and doesn't give it another glance, while I, on the other hand, can't stop staring at it.

"Relax," he says, turning my chair from the mirror. "You're going to look fabulous."

And I pray that by "fabulous," he doesn't mean spiky and purple like his own hair. I touch the back of my bare neck, and he smacks my hand away. "Trust, darling, a little bit of trust."

I force my hand to my lap and try not to wince each time he snips and snaps with his lightning-fast shears, clippings floating past my eyes until I'm certain not a hair remains.

He tells me he's adding highlights and shushes me when I ask what color. Conspiratorially, he and Molly giggle as they work together at the mixing counter, and I get a horrible feeling that he's asking Molly her opinion, which inevitably will be orange.

When he finishes smearing the concoction on my hair, I'm put under the dryer.

"Don't move and don't look," he orders. "We'll be back."

Taking Molly by the hand, they gallop off, and resigned to my destiny, I close my eyes and drift off to the whir of air and heat.

∞

When I startle awake, I have no idea how long it's been. It could have been a minute or an hour. The dream was right there, but now it's fading. I try to reel it back in, my heart pounding. A premonition. No. Just a nightmare. Vague. Drowning or something like drowning. I hate dreams like that, the kind that make your pulse race and your skin crawl, reminding you of how bad the terror was but not giving you any more information than that to figure out what was so chilling so you can rationalize it away and ease the sick feeling of foreboding that lingers.

Molly and Henry walk through the door, both of them with ice cream on their face—Molly's predictably chocolate, Henry's chalky green, probably mint chip.

He laughs when he sees his face in the mirror, and Molly laughs as well. They wipe each other's faces and end up in a towel fight that leaves Molly squealing with delight. I barely know Henry, but already I like him as much as you can like someone you barely know.

"Okay, Faye, let's see if your hair is now as fabulous as your name." He lifts the dryer and moves me back to the barber chair, where again, with my back to the mirror, he whirls around snipping and snapping like Edward Scissorhands.

Finally he stops, arches his brows at Molly in question, and Molly nods her approval.

"Okay. Ready? One, two, three, voila!" With great dramatic flair, the chair is spun to face the mirror.

I gasp, unsure the woman staring back is actually me.

The hair is wispy and short—chin length—the lobes of my ears showing. Just-rolled-out-of-bed sexy—short, sassy, and bold, yet feminine. Meg Ryan, Annette Bening, Halle Berry, women like that have haircuts like this.

My neck is so long it looks like it's been stretched two inches. I reach up and touch it, checking that it's mine.

"You like?" Henry asks.

Molly stands beside him grinning ear to ear.

"I like," I say as my eyes, which now seem larger and more blue, fill with gratitude. "No more blah, blah, blasé. Thank you. This is amazing. You didn't have to do this. It was very generous."

"Generous, my ass," Henry says. "Girl, this is Hollywood. Nothing is for nothing."

My blood ices with his abrupt change in attitude. I have no idea what a haircut like this costs, but I'm certain I can't afford it. We have yet to get our first paycheck, and the new bills are simply piling up on top of the old.

His face lights up in a full-wattage grin. "Pies. You will pay me in pies. Molly says you make a mean pecan pie, and I'm a boy from the South who misses his mama's cooking."

I exhale in relief and extreme gratitude then reach over and take his hand. "I don't know if I bake as well as you cut hair, but I'll try."

28

Molly looks as ridiculous as E.T. did when Drew Barrymore dressed the alien up like a girl. Her skin is painted orange, a makeup trick that keeps the cast from looking sallow, and the dress Ingrid put her in is red-and-white gingham with lace trim. Molly has never worn a dress in her life, and she's certainly never worn frills.

We stand at the edge of the law office set as the crew makes a few last-minute changes to the lights. Chris sits a few feet away directing them. I wait for him to notice my hair. I know I shouldn't be waiting. After all, I've made a solemn vow to no longer be attracted to Chris Cantor, director of stars, the out-of-my-league, most eligible bachelor in Hollywood. Yet my breath catches in anticipation each time he looks my way.

Finally he glances over but only to say, "Two-Bits, you're on."

The words stop my narcissism cold. This is the moment of truth. Molly's first scene. Molly steps from my side and onto the set, and the stand-in walks off.

Beth lifts her fist in the air, and the studio grows quiet. Her fingers pop open: one, two, three, four, five. "Action."

Molly and Miles walk into the law office with their pretend dad, a burly man with a barrel chest and a wide face. The receptionist greets them, then Mr. Foster walks from his office.

"Paul, nice to see you. Who have we here?" he says.

"The two best investments of my life," the dad says. "This is my son, Miles, and my daughter, Molly. Kids, meet Mr. Foster."

"Miles," Mr. Foster says, shaking Miles's hand. Then he bends at the waist and says, "Molly, a pleasure."

I hold my breath. Molly's first line. *Nice to meet you as well.*

"A pwleasuwre I'll twreasuwre fowrevewr," she says, stopping my pulse, her curls whipping as she gives the line proper sass the way Bo taught her.

"Cut," Beth squawks, running onto the set and glowering at Molly, who shifts to hide behind Jules, who is smirking at Molly's improvisation.

"Beth..." Chris's voice smothers the assistant director's screech of "Your line is, 'nice to meet you as well.' "

Beth's mouth snaps shut as she turns red-faced to Chris, who says, "Last I checked, 'cut' was *my* line. Remember that or get off my set."

"I'm sorry, Chris. I was just..."

His scathing look stops her protest, and she slinks away, and though I'm not a big fan of Beth's, I feel bad for her. She was just doing what she thought was her job. Molly's the one who messed up.

"Ingrid," Chris bellows in the general direction of backstage.

The wardrobe woman steps from the shadows.

"What the hell is this?" He gestures to Molly's outfit.

"You said she was wealthy."

"Exactly. I said wealthy, not from the 1950s. We chose her because she's spunky, and you have her dressed like Little Miss Muffet. Fix it. Now."

Ingrid's jaw clenches as she takes Molly by the hand and leads her away.

I'm about to follow, but Chris stops me, causing my heart to halt as well. In the last thirty seconds, he has torn two women to shreds, and now his attention is on me. Molly missed her first line, the line I was responsible for teaching her.

Every eye in the room watches as I turn to face him.

"Does she always do that?" he says, his voice returned to civilized.

"Do what?" I croak.

"Rhyme, rap, give attitude, singsong her lines. She did it at the audition, and she just did it now. Is that something she does?"

I nod. That's Molly.

For a moment, he says nothing, his eyes focused on a point on the ground in front of him.

The set is so quiet that I can hear my breath, and I'm fairly certain this is the point where we get fired.

He lifts his head to look at Griff. “When she comes back, we shoot it from the top and keep rolling. Jules, improvise and try to keep it on point. Let’s see how it goes.”

Griff nods then speaks quietly into his headset to relay the instructions to his crew.

Five minutes later, Molly is back, her outfit a thousand times better—a teal sleeveless shirt over black capri leggings, purple socks, and white Keds—still not totally Molly but cute.

Chris nods his approval, and a minute later, Beth counts down again… “Action.”

“Molly, a pleasure,” Mr. Foster says.

“A twreat to meet you too,” Molly says with a big smile, changing her line again and pleased as punch with her new rhyme.

A genuine smile crosses Mr. Foster’s face, and he pokes her on the nose. Molly pokes him back, causing him to straighten in surprise and chuckle.

“Let’s go into my office and see if we can wrap up this deal for your dad so you can be on your way.”

The four of them take two steps, then the dad stumbles, clutches his heart, and collapses to the floor.

“911 now,” Mr. Foster says to the receptionist as he drops beside the dad who is now gasping for air.

Molly stumbles back against Miles, both kids doing an amazing job of looking terrified.

“And cut,” Chris yells. He looks at Griff, and Molly looks with him.

Griff gives a thumbs-up, and I exhale.

“Molly and Miles, off set,” Chris says. “And, Two-Bits.” Molly turns. “That was good, but don’t ever look directly at the camera. Even when the shot is done, you need to pretend it’s not there.”

Molly nods, taking his advice very seriously, her brow crinkled.

When she gets to me, she says, “Why do I have to pwretend the camewra’s not thewre?”

“Because he’s afraid if you don’t pretend all the time that you might accidentally look at it when you’re shooting.”

Her brow crinkles again as she considers this logic.

I thought they did the scene perfectly, but they run through it again and again, Molly improvising her line each time and Jules somehow making it work.

I feel like I should thank him. He's doing a wonderful job keeping Molly out of trouble.

"Again," Chris says. Molly yawns, and Miles rubs his eyes. Shooting this two-minute scene has taken nearly two hours, the same lines over and over dozens of times.

Griff speaks up. "It's good, Chris. We got it."

Chris considers Griff's opinion then says, "Okay, that's a wrap."

Molly steps forward, looks directly into the lens of the main camera, and with total attitude announces, "Cwlap, cwlap, that's a wrwap." Then she skips over to Chris, sets her hands on his knee, and looks up at him. "See, I wlooked wright at the camewra, and it didn't huwrt anything. I only need to pwretend they'wre not thewre when I'm acting."

Jules and Griff snicker. She's probably the only one in the entire cast or crew who could put Chris Cantor in his place without getting her heinie handed to her.

Chris smirks, shakes his head in defeat, and pats her on the butt. "Off my set, Two-Bits."

Molly skips toward me.

"Beth, how much time does Molly have left?"

Beth shakes her head. "Under the lights she's fine, still over an hour, but she's been here since eight."

It's a lie. We've been here since seven.

Griff turns from what he's doing, his eyes locking on mine. He also knows it's a lie, and his expression challenges me. I offer a small smile and a shrug, sending the message *It's only an hour*, but before my lips finish curling, he turns away.

I rile at his judgment of me. He should mind his own business. He doesn't know my life, Molly's life. It's one stinking hour!

Chris calculates Molly's workday quickly then explodes, "Are you kidding me? Half an hour! We have half a fucking hour left! Please tell me you are *not* saying that the shoot we've been rehearsing all fucking week is going to end at two o'clock in the goddamn afternoon because you can't count to four."

His words spit like daggers, Beth recoiling with each one.

"I'm sorry. I didn't realize..."

"Get your shit together or I'll find someone who can."

My sympathy for Beth grows, and I decide to take more responsibility for Molly's work time, to realize when we have time to leave the lot and to take advantage of it.

Like right now, I hustle Molly from the set, not wanting to waste another minute.

We walk through the parking lot toward the car, and Molly says, "Home?"

"Sorry, Love Bug, we still have one more scene."

"I want to go home."

"I know, baby, me too."

I lift her in my arms to carry her the rest of the way. The past few days have been exhausting and not nearly as much fun as I thought they would be. Molly's job is hard work—long hours that require endurance, patience, and focus far beyond the call of a four-year-old.

"I want to go home," Molly says again into my neck, her arms draped over my shoulders.

My mind spins with how I can pacify her so we can make it through the end of the day, and I hate myself a little when I say, "How about some ice cream?"

"I awlwready had ice cwream."

Crap. I forgot about the ice cream escapade she and Henry went on this morning while I was under the hair dryer. It seems like a week has passed since my reincarnation—that's how long this day has been.

"Okay, Bug, then how about we just drive around and listen to the radio?"

"No. I want to go home."

I don't answer, praying she'll drop it, which is just wishful thinking because one thing Molly is not is forgetful. Her legs kick against me, making it difficult to hold her. "I want to go home," she says louder, her fists joining in on the action and pounding against my back. No longer able to keep her in my arms, I let her slither to the ground, where she collapses with her face in her hands, her heels pounding on the pavement as she screams, "I want to go home. Take me home. I want to go home…"

A passerby looks at her with pity then at me with blame. He must not have children. Someday he will, and someday his child will have a tantrum, and when that happens, I hope he remembers this moment.

"Baby…Bug…Come on. Let's at least get to the car."

"No…no, no, no." Her head shakes back and forth violently. "Home. I want to go home."

"Bug, we can't go home. You know that. I wish we could, but we can't. We still have one more scene."

"I done," she screams. "I want to go home. Home, home, home."

We now have an audience. Two women have stopped beside the man, the three of them watching the spectacle from the sidewalk.

"How about a cupcake?" I say. "One of those fancy ones with the melted frosting?"

This is terrible, outright bribery, the Supernanny and Dr. Spock and every other authority on parenting would frown, but unable to think of an alternative, I resort to the age-old, ever-reliable barter system, a long-standing tradition of motherhood in which parents promise something irresistible in exchange for getting their children to do something they need them to do, a payment extracted through blackmail—toys, treats, a pony traded for compliance.

"A Spwrinkles cupcake?" Molly asks between sobs.

Sprinkles cupcakes are the Rolls-Royce of confectionary delights and cost accordingly, outrageously priced little cakes that I could bake at home for pennies.

"Yes, a Sprinkles cupcake. Any flavor you want."

She nods sleepily.

SOLD!

Her makeup streaked with her tears, she stands, and when I lift her into my arms, I feel our audience suppress their desire to applaud. She slumps against me, worn out, completely unhappy and done but resolved to having no choice but to continue on. And as I carry her to the car, I wonder what I'll negotiate with when cupcakes aren't enough, and then wonder, as Molly gets older, how she'll feel about it, whether she'll resent the idea of having traded her childhood for a few ounces of sugar, an iPhone, a car, or a pony.

29

The rest of the family is enviously asleep, Molly's snores keeping rhythm with my knife as I stand at the cutting board chopping pecans for Henry's pie. As I work, I sip a glass of wine, my thoughts vacillating between Chris and Sean. Cooking always makes me think of Sean, but I don't want to think about Sean, so each time he pops in my mind, I replace him with Chris.

Chris would probably love my cooking. It's one of the few skills I'm sure of, a craft handed down by my dad and honed over the past dozen years with my family. I smile at how many experiments I inflicted on Sean in the early days of our marriage, my brief foray into Asian fusion then my many ill-fated attempts at soufflés. I shake away the rogue nostalgia, my short hair whipping back and forth. Sexy. That's what Chris called it when we left the studio today.

He started with, *Thank you.*

For what? I asked.

For bringing this amazing little person into my very dull life, he answered, his hand on Molly's shoulder.

Ha, I said. *Dull as a circus.*

Wink. *Well, back to the freak show. By the way I like the hair. Sexy.*

Sexy. Chris Cantor thinks my hair is sexy.

I whip it back and forth again, confirming its sexiness, then set my focus back on the pies. Pulling the four balls of dough from the fridge, I roll them out then spread them into the tins. If you are baking one pie, you might as well bake four; the work is nearly the same. One will be for Henry, two will be for the cast and crew, the last will be for us.

Wred wrover, wred wrover, thank goodness that's ovewr, Molly said directly into the lens after Chris announced the last take was a wrap.

I chuckle at Chris's mock anger. *Two-Bits, don't look at the camera.*

Bossy, bossy, Chwrissy Cwrossy.

She is something. I wish Sean could see her—our girl, a star. He and I would laugh over it, do a jig in the kitchen, toast a pair of Heinekens, celebrating the fact that we could afford such premium beer because our daughter is, in fact, amazing. He would dance with me, then with each of the kids, perhaps all three at once—Molly slung over his shoulder, Tom and Emily being whipped around in his hands.

I try to insert Chris into the scene. He and I in the kitchen celebrating something wonderful. I see him lifting Molly, his face lit up, but I can't quite bring Emily and Tom into focus.

Putting the pies in the oven, I set the timer and carry my wine to the table. My head falls onto my folded arms, and I close my eyes. *Could it work? Me, Chris, them?* Exhaustion and the wine create a dangerous state of slightly inebriated, delusional possibility. Mixed with the smell of pecans and sugar, the idea has a seductive quality about it, and I like the way it flits in and out of my mind.

Would they take his name? Would I? Faye Cantor, Molly Cantor, Emily...

A knock at the door startles me from the foolish thoughts.

I look at the clock. 10:12. It's probably our neighbor. I owe her money for watching Emily and Tom on Wednesday when my mom needed to go to the *Star Gazer* offices. Hoping not to wake the others, I hurry to the door, yank it open, and find myself staring at Sean.

"Hey," he says.

My eyes blink, and I stumble back in order to stop myself from falling forward into his arms, which I inexplicably yet undeniably want to do.

He steps toward me, and I stumble back again, then realizing I'm stepping farther into the condo and that he is following, I reverse momentum and push him into the hallway, closing the door behind us.

"What are you doing here?" I hiss, my indignation catching up with my surprise.

He doesn't answer. He can't. His Adam's apple is lodged in his throat as his eyes run me up and down, scanning from my newly cropped hair to my bare feet and back again, the scrutiny so intense and warm that, despite my determination to hate him, the ice on my heart begins to melt.

It doesn't help that he looks terrible. Three days of beard shadows his face, his hair is in need of a cut and stands up on end, and his eyes are red-rimmed with exhaustion—telltale signs that he's been on a long haul and sleeping in his truck. And as if I'm one of Pavlov's damn dogs, the sight of him looking so wretched causes instant worry and concern, the emotions well trained after twelve years of caring.

Finally his eyes come to rest on mine and he manages, "You cut your hair."

You got a new life, I almost retaliate, but instead, say again, "What are you doing here?"

He swallows, runs his hand through his hair, rubs the rough stubble on his chin, looks at the ground then back at me, and says, "Christ, Faye, why didn't you tell me you were leaving?"

I wrap my arms across my chest. "Because it wasn't any of your business. You left, and we couldn't afford to stay. I have three kids..."

"We have three kids," he corrects.

"Right. *We* have three kids, but *I* was the one left taking care of them."

"I called to see if you needed anything, but you hung up."

To this I say nothing because there's nothing to be said. What I needed was for him not to have left in the first place.

"I thought you were doing okay. I heard you picked up more shifts at the diner."

"I did pick up more shifts," I snap. "And if that's why you came back, to tell me I didn't work hard enough..."

"That's not why I came back," he says quickly. "I don't want to upset you. That's the last thing I want to do, but I couldn't...I hate...I went to see you, to settle things between us and explain things to the kids, and when I found out you were gone..." His voice catches, and he stops, looks away, closes his eyes, opens them, and tries again. "I hate that you're...that we're...Yucaipa is our..." A deep breath and a frustrated shake of the head, then finally, "You hate LA."

All I can manage is a nod, my tears on the brink of detonation, the pain of his abandonment returning like a jolt of thousand-watt electricity and decimating me with the same force it did eight months ago.

Since Sean left, I have envisioned this scenario a thousand times, imagining him showing up and what I would do, the various ways I would kill him, smashing him over the head with a skillet or sending his rig, with him in it, over a cliff. But now, with him standing in front of me, looking wretched, completely distraught, and so pitifully like himself, shamefully, all I really want to do is take him by the hand, lead him inside, and wait with him until the timer rings so I can offer him a slice of pie.

"I screwed up," he mumbles. "I shouldn't have left. It was the worst mistake of my life. I knew it as soon as I did, but I didn't know how to come back. You hated me, wouldn't even talk to me."

He's right. I hated him. "Well, you did leave. And we hit a rough patch, so we needed to move, but now we're okay. So you can go, go back to Albuquerque."

His eyes are on the ground, his hands shoved in the pockets of his jeans, his head shaking back and forth. "I don't want to go," he says. "I want to come home."

My heart hiccups then freezes then bursts into flames, a swirl of deadly emotions erupting with his words. My nose pinches against them as I say, "This isn't home. This is my mom's condo. Home was the place you left, and it doesn't exist anymore."

He nods, accepting my fury without protest, knowing this is what he deserves.

Which he does, I remind myself harshly when I feel the bitterness softening.

"Can I at least see them?" he asks.

"They're sleeping."

"Not tonight. I mean at some point? I'm in the middle of a trip, but I can come back when it's done. Maybe we could spend the day together."

He looks like Tom does when he desperately wants something he doesn't think he's going to get, his eyes looking at me through his brow, his body tense with anticipation.

I toe the ground. "I don't know. They're getting used to life without you. I don't think they can handle having you come back then leaving again. Especially Em—this has been really hard on her."

"I won't leave again," he says, his voice lit up with hope. "I mean, I will. I have to work, but I won't desert them...you...again."

My heart pounds so hard that I hear its pulse between my ears.

"Faye, look at me," he says.

I force my eyes to meet his. A mistake. I've always had a weakness for his eyes—swirling green disks that pierce with intense sincerity, a veracity that has proven false but that fools me every time.

"I screwed up," he says. "I know it. But if you give me another chance, I'll spend the rest of my life making it up to you and to them. But even if you never forgive me, I promise, if you let me see them, I won't hurt them. I won't ever do that again."

And like a fool, I believe him.

30

Molly's only scene today is a jam session with her new family. I love this scene and have been looking forward to it all week.

As usual we raced to the set only to wait.

We're in the staging area behind the Fosters' music studio set. The entire Foster family cast is here except for Jules: Helen, Jeremy, Kira, Gabby, Caleb, Miles, and Molly.

Jeremy and Molly stand beside the set playing a game of who can slap whose hand before they pull it away, which is rapidly degenerating into a full-fledged game of tag. Jeremy is my favorite of the Foster kids. He plays the oldest Foster boy, and though he's a troublemaker on the show, in real life he's a happy-go-lucky sweetheart, and he and Molly get along great. I wait for Miles or Gabby or Caleb to join in on the fun, but all three seem very old for their ages, and I have yet to see them act like kids. Gabby and Caleb talk quietly, and Miles is off by himself looking at the script.

As I wait, my mind spins to last night and Sean. In the light of day, without his magnetic eyes pleading for clemency from two feet away, I'm not nearly as forgiving, and I'm fairly certain I made a mistake agreeing to let him see the kids. Despite his promises, a stiff wind and he'll abandon us again, leaving me to pick up the pieces. On the other hand, he is their dad. Is it right to keep their father from them? Or to keep him from his kids? He was there for twelve years. That's not nothing.

"Morning."

I lift my head to see Chris looking at me, a smile on his face.

Normally this is where I get flustered and trip over myself, but today my thoughts are so distracted that I offer a surprisingly composed "Good morning."

"You found my weakness," he says, dimples deepening.

I tilt my head as I try to regain my bearings.

"Pecan pie," he says. "I just had a slice, and I've got to say, I fell a little in love with you at first bite."

His words snap the moment into high definition, the edges vividly sharp, the colors extra bright.

"Do you always bake like that?" he asks.

I manage a nod.

"So rare. And I know it's horribly sexist, but a woman who is beautiful *and* can cook is a dying breed and damn attractive."

My mind races for something clever to say back.

Blank.

His smile widens, and he gives a wink then walks away.

Your cave or mine? Thank God that didn't come out of my mouth.

I lift my head to see Rhonda glaring at me, confirmation that Chris Cantor, producer of *The Foster Band*, most eligible bachelor in Hollywood, did in fact just flirt with me.

Jules saunters past. "Let's do this," he bellows as he always does when he finally chooses to grace the set with his presence, alcohol fumes wafting in his wake.

"Okay, guys," Chris says, "places. We'll shoot once without blocking to see what we've got then finesse it from there. I want it to be raw, so let's make it good. Remember Molly and Miles have never sung with you before. I want to feel their hesitation and everyone else's surprise at their talent. Beth, let's go."

Watching the actors transform into character is one of my favorite parts of the shoots. Some, like Jeremy and Molly, switch to their alter egos the moment their feet hit the set. Others, like Helen and Kira, need a minute. Helen closes her eyes, turns her back to everyone, takes a few deep breaths, and when she turns back around, she's Mrs. Foster, her face and posture softer and less untouchable. Kira rolls her shoulders forward, works out her neck, and flexes her jaw like a prizefighter getting ready to step into the ring. And when they take their places, Helen looks maternal, Kira looks sweet, Jeremy looks like a sex symbol, and Molly looks like Molly.

"Action," Beth says.

Molly holds a maraca in each hand, and Miles holds a tambourine. Behind them is the band, Jeremy and Mr. Foster holding guitars, Helen at the keyboard, Kira standing center stage behind a microphone, Gabby on bass, and Caleb on drums.

"Play along if you like," Mr. Foster says to them.

Miles shakes the tambourine a few times then decides against it. Molly stands unmoving beside him, her eyes on the ground.

The band continues without them, then Mr. Foster steps forward, swings his guitar behind him, takes Molly by her maraca fists, and starts to dance with her, cha-cha-ing to the beat so the maracas play along. Molly breaks into a smile, and when he releases her, she continues to play. After a few notes, Miles joins in as well.

Kira, who is the sweetheart of the show, starts to sing. She has a beautiful voice with just enough gravel in it to make it interesting. On the show she is seventeen. In real life she is twenty-two. On the show she's pretty and sweet. In real life she's gorgeous and a bitch.

When the chorus hits, Kira pulls the mike from the stand and holds it between Molly and Miles so they can sing along. Molly lisps her part, and Miles melodically chirps his, and I know I am witnessing magic. The scene is clumsy, and they will need to shoot it a dozen more times to get it right, but Molly and Miles are irresistible, their voices a perfect blend of adorableness and talent that conjures up memories of a young Michael Jackson or Shirley Temple or, in this case, a strange duo of both those legends at their most iconic moment transported through time into the present to perform together.

A chill shivers my spine as I think of Molly being that kind of megastar, and I can't decide if the shudder is from exhilaration or fear.

31

I'm giddy with excitement. I've never bought my own car. My first car, an old Toyota, I inherited when my dad passed away, and Sean picked out our van.

It's nearly lunchtime, so I decide we'll eat before starting our quest. Feeling rich from my first paycheck as Molly's manager, I decide to treat us to Red Robin.

"Order whatever you like," I say, surprising them. Rarely do we eat out, and when we do, I make us share—Molly and I share one meal, Emily and Tom share another.

I scan the menu, and my mouth waters with the idea of ordering what I want, not a meal suitable to share with a four-year-old.

We're not wealthy...*yet*...but already I feel liberated from my life of frugality.

"Excuse me," a woman says as she approaches our table. She looks near forty, has wide hips and brown hair teased to twice the height of her head. "Aren't you the girl from the Gap commercial?"

I smile as Molly nods.

"Can I have your autograph?" She holds out a napkin and a pen.

"She wants you to write your name," I tell Molly, setting the napkin on the table in front of her.

Very deliberately, Molly carves out the letters, the "y" ending up backward.

"Thank you," the lady says, her face blushing with excitement.

When she leaves, all of us giggle. Our little celebrity signing autographs for her fans.

∞

The car we bought is awesome. It's a three-year-old lemon-yellow Nissan Pathfinder. It has an auxiliary jack for the iPhone, so Emily thinks it's super cool. It's yellow, so Molly loves it. And it has amazing reliability ratings, so Tom thinks it's perfect—he's still shaken about our breakdown in that seedy neighborhood of LA.

And it's mine! Ours! Mine!

I could drive around for hours reveling in that fact.

Technically I don't actually own it. Only a quarter of it is mine. The rest will be mine after three short years of payments.

It has a sunroof and automatic windows and cruise control. It even has seat warmers. The day is broiling hot, but I roast my toosh anyway just because I can.

The thought of how much I spent makes my stomach queasy, but I just need to keep reminding myself that I get paid again in two weeks.

I roll down the automatic windows and open the sunroof. This is what it feels like to have money. I like it. I really, really do, and so long as the money keeps rolling in, we'll be fine.

32

We arrive home to a surprise, a bouquet of two dozen stunning long-stem red roses in a crystal vase beside our front door. My pulse quickens with the thought of either Sean or Chris sending such an extravagant overture of courtship.

"Those awre fowr me?" Molly asks.

It's then that I notice the envelope sticking out above the flowers with the name Molly scrawled on it, and instantly my excitement transforms to alarm, my eyes darting around the hallway.

"Kids, go inside," I say.

Molly reaches for the vase, and I pull her away.

"Leave it."

"But theyw're mine."

"Em, take Molly and Tom inside and send Grandma out."

Emily shepherds Molly and Tom through the door, and when they are safely inside, I pluck the envelope from the plastic stick and pull out the card.

Roses are red and your eyes are the prettiest blue,
Waching you dance made me fall in love with you.
Your smile and laugh takes away my blues.
Someday we will meet and my dreams will come true.

My mom steps into the hallway and reads the card over my shoulder.

"What should I do?" I say.

"Do you think they're from John Lennon?"

Since our first day on the set, John Lennon has figured out that, in order to see us, he needs to be on the corner by six, and each morning, he is dutifully there, waiting for us to pull from the garage so Molly can smile and wave at him. It shows incredible commitment, and I have rewarded it with my own enthusiastic greeting each morning and even an occasional small honk.

But now I wonder if it was a mistake to encourage him, if I should have realized that his starry-eyed devotion might develop into something more, something disturbing and possibly dangerous.

"You think there could be more than one nutcase obsessed with Molly?" I ask.

My mom shrugs. "Could be. Molly's commercial is on all the time, and the YouTube video is up to over thirty million views."

"Thirty million?" I shake my head in disbelief. The video is cute, but it's not *that* cute. "Should I call the police?"

"I don't know. Is sending flowers a crime?"

"Claiming to be in love with a four-year-old should be."

"So should butchering the English language and bad poetry, but I don't think it is."

"Mom, be serious. What should I do?"

"Call Monique. See what she says."

∞

"Throw away the flowers but keep the note in case things escalate," Monique Braxton says. "Ask your building manager to change the security code and hire a security company to install a camera in your hallway."

"But shouldn't I call the police?"

"You could, but you'd be wasting your time. There's really nothing they can do. The guy didn't leave his name, and even if he did, the cops aren't going to chase someone down for sending flowers. It's part of the business. Some fans are weird and some step over the line. If it gets creepy or there's a threat, call the police, otherwise don't worry about it."

33

The day after we got the flowers, John Lennon was on the corner when we pulled from the parking garage in our new car. It took a minute for him to realize it was us, and when he did, his face lit up and he waved.

Molly didn't look at him, and neither did I. We passed with our eyes glued to the road, my hands gripping the steering wheel so tight that my fingers hurt. I glanced in the rearview mirror to see him frowning, his shoulders folded forward as he watched us continue on, clearly confused over what had changed.

Good job, Bug, I said.

I don't undewrstand why I can't wave at him.

Because he's a stranger and we don't know if he's dangerous.

I caught her sad expression in the mirror, and it broke my heart. Immediately suspecting the worst of people instead of the best is a hard lesson to learn.

Today is Friday, the last day of our third full week of working. Three weeks doesn't sound that long, but the time has passed like dog years, the schedule so relentless and tedious that it feels like we've been working for months.

Today the shoot is on location so we can film the final climactic moment of the first episode, a scene in which Molly and Miles are pulled from the burning wreckage of a car that was just T-boned by an ambulance. The site for the shoot is an industrial neighborhood on the outskirts of the city, the storefronts dressed up to look like a bustling street with a restaurant and stores on one side and a hospital on the other.

We park in a vacant lot with dozens of other cars, several trailers, and a food truck, and Molly and I step from the car to the smell of sizzling bacon. One of the most rewarding perks of working on the show is the constant access to food. Between the craft service stations, the cafes and restaurants on the lot, and the on-location food trucks, Molly and I are never hungry.

As we walk past the set, my eyes slide to Chris. He sits in a director's chair staring at his laptop and looks like he's been here for hours, his shirt-sleeves rolled up, a shadow of beard darkening his chin.

His flirtation has not progressed beyond the occasional wink, compliment, and smile, and though my pulse quickens when I see him, the truth is, when I think about it, I'm not certain how I feel about him. Like at this moment, though I'm excited he is here, I also know to steer clear. Coiled like a cheetah, tension pulses off him like he's ready to pounce and tear someone's throat out. That's the thing about Chris, he's a Jekyll and Hyde kind of character, one minute jokey and fun, the next, unrelenting and harsh. The result is greatness. Because of Chris Cantor, *The Foster Band* is the number one show on television, his energy creating a magnificent propulsion that keeps the show in orbit, but that same magnificent force also threatens instant annihilation to anyone who messes up.

We grab a quick breakfast from the food truck, get Molly's hair and makeup done, then return to the car to wait until we are called, the windows down so we can hear what is happening.

I watch as Chris marches toward two extras. "You." He points to one in a business suit. "You cross and go into the building, then the ambulance comes barreling around the corner."

The extra nods enthusiastically, excited to be chosen from the dozens who mill around the hospital entrance. Pulling his shoulders back, he saunters across the street with great noble strides, and Chris rolls his eyes. Beth rushes over to talk to the guy, and I watch his posture deflate as Beth reduces him back to mere mortalness, telling him to just walk across the street like a normal businessman, one who no one will notice or remember.

I sympathize. Every day I watch as the extras and guest stars overplay their roles, turning in a performance worthy of Jack Nicholson in *The*

Shining when their part is to play a bicycle courier dropping off a package or a man in a suit crossing the street.

A fire truck pulls into the lot, and I tense. It's here to put out the flames after the crash. Molly and Miles won't be in the car when the ambulance smashes into it, but they will be placed in the wreckage after and a controlled fire will be lit to make it look like the car and ambulance are on fire, and although I've been assured by a dozen people that Molly will be safe, I'm still not entirely comfortable with it.

The car being used for the crash is a late model Camry, and I can't help but think what a waste it is to destroy such a nice car, not to mention the ambulance. But I've learned that waste and cost is rarely a consideration. Cars, furniture, clothes, electronics, whatever is needed to get the shot is sacrificed without a second thought.

Molly sits beside me watching a movie on the iPad I bought a week ago. There's so much idle time that she needed something to keep her occupied. I need something as well but have yet to figure out what that something is. Maybe I should take up knitting or read all the classics, something productive. So far all I've done is fritter away my time. Several times a day I check in with my mom, and once a week I call Tom's therapist. I make shopping lists for groceries and sometimes I pay bills. But mostly I watch the slow plodding of the show, and when nothing is happening there, I waste time on my new iPhone Googling the cast, fascinated by the stories the reporters make up and the few facts they occasionally get right.

Today, one of the more popular gossip sites reports that Helen is pregnant with Jeremy's child, which is preposterous on so many levels I can't believe it made it to print. Not only is Helen forty-eight, but she's had a well-documented hysterectomy. And Jeremy isn't going to be procreating anytime soon with anyone from the XX chromosome pool. Gorgeous as he is, and despite his publicist doing a fabulous job spreading rumors about him dating the girl from *Mainland*, Jeremy's ship doesn't sail straight.

Another site suggests that Gabby is Jules's illegitimate daughter, that her mother was Jules's housekeeper and lover, and that he turned them out when he discovered she was pregnant. There's always a lot of speculation about Gabby, mostly about her weight and her suspected drug use.

They also love to talk about Kira's weight, that she is too skinny and might have an eating disorder. They've got it wrong about Kira. Kira is obsessed with her weight, but she's too smart and too driven to deal with it in a way that would be counterproductive to her career. Her rocking hot body is achieved the old-fashioned way, through a strict diet monitored by a personal nutritionist and prepared by a personal chef, combined with a brutal body maintenance routine managed by a private trainer, a private yogi, and a personal masseuse.

They might have it right about Gabby. The other day I heard her talking to Caleb about rolling with "Molly," so I eavesdropped thinking she was talking about my Molly, when in fact she was talking about the drug called Molly.

"Let's do this," Chris bellows, interrupting my perusal of an article about Caleb dating his mother's boyfriend's daughter, bookmarking it so I can return to it later.

34

The crash was spectacular. The ambulance barreled into the Camry, sending it hurtling onto the sidewalk, where it careened on its side toward a store dressed to look like a diner. For a heart-stopping second it looked like it was going to smash right through the window and into the extras sitting at the tables, but it skidded to a stop a foot from the glass.

That was two hours ago.

Bored and done reading the latest gossip on the members of the cast, I decide to Google Molly's name to see if there's any buzz about her joining the show. 282,000 hits! The first listing is for the YouTube video, the second is a Wikipedia listing, the third is for the Gap, and the fourth is for a video I'm unfamiliar with. Its title is *Molly Martin Dances Like You've Never Seen Her Before.*

I click on the listing and stare horrified when a video pops up showing Molly's face superimposed on a naked white woman dancing with a black man. The man strums a guitar and belts out "Go, Molly, Go" to the tune of "Johnny B. Goode." I close down the window, my jaw quivering with rage and disgust.

"Molly, on set," Chris says, interrupting my revulsion, and as I stumble from the car, I decide never to Google Molly's name again.

"Ready?" Beth asks.

Molly looks unsure. I'm unsure as well. No matter how many times I've been assured Molly will be safe, it goes against every fiber of my being to let my daughter go anywhere near the tangled, burnt wreckage of metal and glass that lies smoldering on the sidewalk.

I kneel down to her height and take hold of her arms. "Bug, you okay with this?"

"It's just pwretend," she says bravely. "Chwris says it's going to be a piece of cake."

I stop myself from telling her that she shouldn't trust everything a man says, especially when he wants something from you.

"Okay, baby. I'll be right here." I peck her on the nose, and Beth leads her away.

I turn to look at Chris for reassurance, but he is across the street talking…no…arguing with Griff. I can't hear what they're saying, but Chris's shoulders are jacked up high and Griff's expression is fierce. The two seem to get along well most of the time, but at the moment, Griff looks like he wants to tear Chris's head off, and Chris looks like he's challenging him to do just that. Chris gestures with his hands to emphasize his point, and Griff glowers at him, his head shaking back and forth.

I move closer, curious if the argument involves Molly, but before I get near enough to hear what they're saying, Chris whirls and roars, "Places."

"He's drunk," Griff hisses.

Chris ignores him.

"Who's drunk?" I say when I reach Griff.

Griff squints down at me, the pulse in his neck throbbing. "Who do you think?"

Jules. Jules is always drunk.

Jules is supposed to pull Molly and Miles from the car before the ambulance explodes.

"Clear the set," Chris says, causing me to move from the pavement to the sidewalk to stand beside Griff.

Across the street, in front of the hospital, Jules and Helen stand near the exit. In the wrecked car, Molly and Miles are strapped into the backseat, and the woman who plays the social worker is in the driver's seat. The extras are in their places, and the set has fallen silent.

Griff still looks at me, his eyes fierce, challenging me to do something.

My eyes bulge, and my mouth almost opens.

"Action."

Flash—the ambulance lights up, flames flicking from its engine, black smoke billowing from the smashed hood. Molly cries out, screaming for help.

Mr. Foster runs toward the crash, and Mrs. Foster yells, "Frank, stop. There's oxygen in the ambulance. It might explode."

He doesn't listen. A red-blooded American hero, a veteran who has survived two wars, he charges forward. The car is on its side, its smashed windshield facing us. Through it, I see the social worker kicking at the glass to free herself. The window gives, and she drags herself through, the toxic smoke engulfing her as she staggers out, blood dripping down her face.

She takes two steps then her face transforms from pain to panic, and she cranes her head back toward Molly and Miles.

"I've got them," Mr. Foster yells. "Go."

An extra dressed as an orderly runs forward and leads the social worker toward the hospital.

Through the smoke, I see Miles tugging at his seat belt while Molly continues to cry.

Mr. Foster clumsily scrambles onto the car and wrenches open the door. Griff was right—he's drunk, more drunk than usual. He reaches in and grabs hold of Miles, who has managed to free himself.

Awkwardly he pulls Miles out, nearly falling off the car in the process and causing Miles's legs to flail. Molly yelps, a genuine howl of pain, different from her pretend ones. Miles must have kicked her. I step forward, but Griff grabs hold of my arm, stopping me.

Miles falls to the ground, and Mrs. Foster runs forward to pull him to safety.

"Molly," Miles cries, resisting her efforts.

At the same time, Mr. Foster struggles to free Molly from her car seat while Molly continues to sob. The clip releases, and I watch in horror as she tumbles from the seat to the ground, a four-foot drop.

"Cut," I scream with Molly's shriek. "Cut, cut, cut."

I try to wrench free from Griff's hold, but he only strengthens his grip.

Jules climbs inside the car. He's not supposed to do that. The script said he was supposed to release Molly, pull her out, and carry her to safety. *This is wrong. It's all wrong.*

Awkwardly, he pushes Molly up through the door. Tears stream down her face, but she manages to scramble out, her body shaking.

"I've got you," Helen says, reaching up and lifting her down.

Cradling Molly against her chest, she runs the opposite direction of where she was supposed to run, away from the hospital and straight toward me.

Miles runs beside her, and Jules stumbles behind them. When they're ten feet away, the ambulance explodes. Helen shelters Molly from the blast as best she can, shielding her head with her own and covering Molly's ear with her hand, though there's no real danger, the blast entirely contained to within a few feet of the car.

Griff releases my arm, and Helen hands Molly to me, genuine concern in her eyes.

"Paramedic, now," Griff barks, and it's only then that I realize Molly is actually hurt.

Blood covers her shirt and stains her face. I crumble to the sidewalk to scan for the injury. Four inches above her wrist is an inch-long gash.

"It's okay, baby. You're okay. You're going to be okay."

Molly clings to me, blood dripping down her arm. Griff pulls off his flannel shirt and wraps it around the wound.

"Hang in there, kid," he says.

"I fewll," she says through her tears.

"I'm sorry," Jules says, appearing beside us.

Griff whirls on him. "Get your drunken ass out of here."

Jules simpers away, his head hung like a beaten dog.

"She okay?" Chris asks, walking up and crouching beside me.

A paramedic pushes past before I can answer. He peels off Griff's shirt to examine the wound. Molly isn't crying now, only whimpering, her nostrils flaring with her broken inhales of breath. I press her face against me so she won't see the blood.

"She needs stitches," the paramedic says. "Do you want me to call for an ambulance?"

"No," Griff and Chris say together, panic flashing in both men's eyes.

Chris looks at the man and says sharply, "This doesn't get out. You hear me? Leak a word of this and I'll have your hide."

The man nods as he wraps gauze around the wound.

Helen speaks up. "I can take them," she says.

I didn't realize she was still beside us. Her blouse is smeared with blood, her eyes glassy with emotion.

"Thanks, Helen. I appreciate that," Chris says.

I lift Molly, and Griff drapes his shirt over her. I shove it back at him. "No thank you," I say harshly. He should have let me go to Molly when I tried. Him, of all people, with his condescending judgment when *I* don't speak up, but when the time came for *his* job to be compromised, all he cared about was getting his precious shot.

"Give me your keys," he says, the vein in his neck pulsing. "I'll have one of the crew bring your car to the hospital."

I fish my keys from my pocket then, carrying Molly, follow Helen to her Mercedes.

Helen doesn't talk as she drives, her focus intent on the road as we race well past the speed limit to the hospital a few miles away.

The car skids to a stop in front of the emergency room entrance, and Helen runs around the car, opens the door, and takes Molly from my arms so I can get out.

When she hands her back, she stutters, "I would go in with you...if you want me to...if you need me to, I will. It's just...I'm not sure it's the best idea." Her eyes skit around like we've entered enemy territory and there might be snipers. Which I realize is exactly her predicament. She's Helen Harlow, and there might be snipers. Who knows what headlines they would make up about this? *Helen Harlow and Lesbian Lover Rush Love Child to Hospital after Domestic Dispute.*

"It's okay," I say. "I've got it from here. Thanks for the ride."

She hesitates then says, "Griff was doing you a favor. If he had let you interrupt the scene, they would have made her do it again. Maybe not today but at some point. Once it started, he knew it was better to finish it. If you want to blame someone, blame Chris or look in the mirror, but don't blame Griff. He was trying to help."

35

When the doctors asked what happened, I spun the first lie that came into my head, knowing from the warning Chris gave the paramedic that the truth would hurt the show. The doctor didn't believe my story and neither did the nurses. Metal slides went out with eight-track tape players and pet rocks, but cutting her arm on a metal slide at the playground was all I could come up with when I was asked what happened.

The cut required five stitches and a tetanus shot. We were at the hospital almost three hours, and in that time, I think every member of the cast sent flowers or balloons or a stuffed animal.

Jules felt so bad that he sent a teddy bear the size of a car. He also called at least sixteen times in increased states of inebriation to tell me how sorry he was.

Molly took it all in stride. Once the wound was cleaned and bandaged, and we were just waiting for the doctor so he could put in the stitches, she was in good spirits. She watched television, took a nap, and ate apple sauce that the nurse brought her, artfully dodging the woman's probing questions about how she got hurt—intuition or intelligence cautioning her against divulging the truth.

As Griff promised, one of the crew brought our car. I was disappointed and relieved Griff didn't bring it himself. I hate to admit it, but Helen was right; Griff tried to stop it before it happened, and my lame efforts after were too late. Which means I owe him an apology—an apology I want to give, while at the same time I dread the idea of facing him.

∞

There are so many gifts that they won't all fit in the car or in my mom's condo, so Molly and I leave most of them for the nurses to bring to the pediatric ward, including Jules's giant teddy bear.

We're walking toward the parking lot, our arms loaded with loot, when a voice cuts through the night. "Hey, Two-Bits."

I look up to see Chris leaning against a black Porsche.

"Hey, Chwris Cwross," Molly says.

Her jolly greeting seems to bring him enormous relief.

"I thought I could take you two lovely ladies to dinner."

I glance at my watch. It's nearly six. While we were waiting for the doctor, I had called my mom and told her I would make spaghetti when we got home. It's been almost a week since we had dinner as a family.

"Do you like lobster?" Chris asks.

Molly crinkles her nose.

"How about steak instead?" he says, and his warm laugh causes instant amnesia, a sudden forgetfulness about spaghetti and the remainder of my family.

"Now you'wre talking," Molly answers.

36

We walk into Ruth's Chris Steak House hand in hand, Molly between us. I know how we look, and shamelessly I revel in it. We look like a beautiful couple with our adorable child. Chris is handsome, I am pretty, Molly is darling. He drove us here in his Porsche. We will enjoy a nice bottle of wine with our steaks, and after, we will return to our beautiful home in the hills with its manicured lawn, swimming pool, and built-in barbeque. We probably have a dog and maybe a cat. We definitely have a housekeeper, a gardener, and perhaps even a nanny.

At this moment, I do not have an ex-husband who has reappeared after eight months of being gone, another daughter who hates me most of the time, a son who will not talk. I only have perfection.

Dinner is divine. I actually say that to myself, *This dinner is divine, darling*, causing me to chuckle out loud. Molly sleeps on the bench between us, her head on my lap, her feet pressed against Chris's thigh.

Chris looks over and smirks. "Something funny?"

"I feel like I'm playing pretend," I say, fully aware that the wine is making me loose-lipped and loopy. "Like I should have a long cigarette holder, a fur capelet, and should be blowing smoke rings in the air with a pout."

"Why would you be pouting?"

"Because, darling, our server—who is quite lovely by the way, and quite young—is clearly enamored with you, and though I'm not your date, I could be your date, and she doesn't know I'm not your date, and if I were wearing a capelet and smoking a cigarette, I would most certainly be your date, and therefore I would be pouting because that girl is shamelessly flirting with you while I'm sitting right here beside you...as your date!"

His laugh creates deep lines around his eyes that are very sexy.

He cranes his neck in search of our server who stands at the pickup line traying up an order of food. "Quite lovely indeed," he says. "Though not even close to the loveliest lady in the room. And you *are* in fact my date."

I blush and smile, pleased to be his date, while at the same time well aware that there is a four-year-old snoring between us, which prevents this from being an actual date. "Do desperate actresses always fawn over you like that?"

"What makes you assume she's a desperate actress?"

"Because of the way she's fawning over you."

"Ouch. I'm wounded. You don't think it's my rugged handsomeness and charm?"

"The Bounty Man could walk in here, and he wouldn't get that kind of worship. It's like you're a god."

"I am a god, a short, nebbishy, Jewish god whose humble job makes him the gatekeeper of dreams for all the wanton waitresses of Tinseltown."

"Humble, hardly."

"I would have preferred you protested the nebbishy part."

"You don't need any more idolization."

His face gets serious. "But I am humble, at least I am today." He reaches over Molly and takes my hand that rests on her hip, his dark eyes, the color of espresso, holding mine. "I'm sorry about what happened."

Like static electricity, a jolt shocks my cortex, and I flinch and pull my hand away, setting it on the table and out of his reach. His expression is so like Sean's. *If you give me another chance, I'll spend the rest of my life making it up to you and to them. But even if you never forgive me, I promise, if you let me see them, I won't hurt them. I won't ever do that again.*

Do they practice in the mirror, mastering the art of deception? So incredibly earnest, the words smooth and sincere, a honed ability to say exactly what you want to hear the moment before they rip the carpet out from beneath your feet.

He feels bad. Sean feels bad. But the moment I let my guard down, both would do the same damn thing again.

"Everything okay?" he asks.

"Fine."

He lifts Molly's legs to his lap, scoots closer, and takes my hand again, setting it back on top of Molly, the spot it was originally, the spot he wants it to be. I let him, mostly because I don't have the courage to pull it away again.

The waitress delivers our check, and Chris doesn't even glance at her as he pulls a platinum American Express from his pocket and places it on the silver plate.

He sips his port and I sip my wine, and after a moment, his thumb begins to move gently across my hand, almost imperceptible, and the soft tickle short-circuits my brain, making me forget how little I trust him, or more accurately, making me not care. It's been a long time since I've been caressed by a man and even longer since I've experienced the heart-fluttering rush of seduction.

When Chris's drink is gone, he lets go to retrieve his credit card and the receipt from the tray. Discretely he slides both into his coat pocket, but not before I notice the scrawled note at the top that says, *Call me*, with a name and number scribbled beneath.

I glance at our server, who stands at the server station filling a water glass. Her face lifts, and I turn away just in time to see Chris give her a wink.

I pretend not to notice. "I should get Molly home."

Chris carries Molly from the restaurant, and again I feel the eyes of admiration watching us, but already I'm tired of the game. It's been a long day, and all I want to do is go home, curl up on the couch with my three kids, and watch TV.

37

Sean's coming here? You said yes?"

My mom and I are in the hallway and the kids are inside.

"Shhh, they'll hear you," I say.

"You haven't told them?" Her face has progressed from pink to red, steam practically blowing from her nostrils, which flare with a combination of incredulity and outrage.

"I'm going to. I just haven't figured out exactly what to say."

Her arms are crossed, her finger tapping impatiently against her elbow. "How about you tell them the truth, that their no-good, two-timing, runaway dad is popping in for a quickie before he returns to his life with his girlfriend in Albuquerque? Probably so he can claim he didn't actually abandon you and cash in on Molly's success."

"That's not why he's here."

"It's not? Really, Faye? Have you even thought about why he's here? Eight months, nothing, then suddenly he appears out of nowhere, hat in hand, saying he wants back in your life. A coincidence? Are you really that naive?"

"It is a coincidence. He doesn't even know about Molly acting. He came here because he realized we left Yucaipa and he was worried about us."

"Yeah, right. And I'm Mary Poppins. Christ, Faye. You think Sean just realized you moved from Yucaipa? You moved here three months ago. I'd bet my right arm he's here because he saw Molly on the Gap commercial."

"This has nothing to do with that."

"To hell it doesn't. I don't know what it is about that man, but he's had you fooled from the moment you met him. He's here for the same reason he married you. Opportunity."

"Go to hell!" I pivot and storm into the house, racing past Molly and Tom and into the bedroom.

Emily sits on the bed reading a book.

"Please," I say, "go."

"You okay?" she asks as she stands.

I manage an unconvincing nod, and she hesitates, unsure what to do.

"It's okay, baby. I just need a few minutes alone."

With a concerned look that warms my heart, she leaves, and I pull a pillow to my chest and bury my face in it.

My mom's wrong. She's always been wrong about Sean. She doesn't know him, never even gave him a chance. Yes, it fell apart, but that doesn't mean it wasn't real. My breaths wobble with each intake of air as I try to hold in my emotions. Sean didn't say a word about Molly being on television. He probably doesn't even know.

A tickle bristles my brain, and I try to push it away, but it refuses to budge. I don't like to think about it. It was a long time ago. He would have married me anyway. He told me so. Shame blindsides me, and I pray there is not a heaven and that my dad is not looking down. He didn't leave much, but he worked hard for the little he left, and I gave it away to the first man I fell for so he could buy his own rig.

"Mom?" Emily says through the door.

I take a deep breath, set the pillow aside, and straighten my expression. "Yeah, baby?"

"Can I come back in?"

"Sure, sweetie."

Tentatively she steps in and closes the door behind her. "You sure you're okay?"

Her concern nearly causes the floodgates to open. Things have been so awful between us. "I love you, baby. You know that, don't you?"

She shifts uncomfortably and nods.

I pat the bed, and she shuffles over to take the spot beside me, sitting on her hands, her eyes on her lap.

"You're growing so fast," I say, marveling that she's nearly my height.

She winces at the lame statement, barely stopping herself from rolling her eyes, and my heart hitches at how awkward things have become between us. A few months ago, I never would have said anything so stupid, and she wouldn't have even considered being disrespectful.

I brush her thick hair behind her shoulder. "Baby," I say, "I need to tell you something, and I want you to tell me honestly how you feel about it."

She shrugs and looks at me through her long lashes, her green eyes the exact color of Sean's, and I realize my mom is wrong because, no matter why Sean married me, nothing that gave me a daughter as beautiful as Emily could ever be considered a mistake. And I hope with all my heart that there is a heaven and that my dad is looking down because I know, if he could see Emily, he would be smiling.

"What is it?" she asks.

"Your dad is back."

Her face lights up, causing my heart to reverse course and clench in anger. "I'm not sure why he's back," I add with more than a little bitterness in my tone.

She doesn't notice. "He's back. Where? Here? He's here? Why didn't he come see us? Can we go see him?"

Her enthusiasm is like a red-hot poker to my brain.

"He's coming to see you tomorrow," I manage.

A huge smile fills her face. "I knew he'd come back. I just knew it. So is he going to move here? Will Grandma let him move in with us? I'm going to ask her."

She bounces up, and I catch her by the hand.

"Baby, he's back, but I don't know if it's for good."

Her head tilts.

"We need to see how things go, take it one day at a time and not get too ahead of ourselves. Okay?"

Her head shakes. "No. He's back. Don't you see? He needed to go off and make some money, and he did, and now he's back."

"He what?"

"That's what he told me. He said he needed to stay on the road to make enough money so we could live better. And he must have made enough, and so now he's back."

My jaw clenches. "When did he tell you that?"

"Before he left."

Her eyes are so bright, her worship so complete, I know it cannot be diminished by the truth, so I simply nod and allow her to believe that her father is a hero, a brave warrior who left for noble reasons and who has now returned with the bounties of his victories after months of toiling for the sake of his family and home. The thought causes acid to rise in my throat, but I force myself to give a thin smile to her radiant one.

Perhaps her rose-colored perspective is a blessing. We are a product of our parents, or at least we think we are, so perhaps thinking the best of Sean will allow her to think better of herself.

"I haven't told Molly and Tom," I say.

"I'll tell them," she says and skips away to deliver the joyous news.

38

I fidget. My palms sweat. I smooth my shirt then re-rumple it, mad at myself for preening over Sean's visit. My emotions are so worn out that I've lost track of how I feel about his return. Am I angry, hurt? Should I yell, scream, throw something at him, hug him, offer him a piece of pie?

He doesn't deserve pie.

So why do I want so badly to offer him a slice?

Because he would like it. He would love it. His face would light up, and he would be so happy. Because for twelve years all I cared about was his happiness, and it's hard to turn that off.

He doesn't deserve my pie. I will not give him pie.

The kids are antsy with anticipation as well, each in their own way. Emily hasn't stopped smiling since last night. Tom is nervous. Like me he's unsure what to make of this reunion. Since he got the news, he's barely said a word. It's not mutism but rather too many thoughts and emotions swirling in his brain, making him too distracted to talk. Molly is like a kid waiting for Christmas, and it breaks my heart. She's the youngest, and eight months is a long time when you're only four. Even prior to her dad's permanent departure, he wasn't around most of her life. To her, a dad is almost a fictitious character, something you read about in storybooks or see in movies, an abstract, romantic notion like Santa Claus.

When he knocks, I jump, though he's right on time and we are expecting him.

I smooth my shirt as Emily leaps from the couch and runs to the door.

"Daddy!" She throws her arms around his waist and buries her face against his ribs.

"Hey, M&M," he croaks, his emotions barely held in check as he strokes her hair.

With Emily still clinging to him, he steps inside. Tom and Molly stand five feet away, Tom looking at the ground, his hands in fists at his sides, Molly looking at Sean curiously, a stranger who has come to visit.

"Hey, kids," he says, holding open his left arm while still holding on to Emily with his right. "Remember your old man?"

Tom nods, and Molly walks into his open arm.

He holds both girls against him and looks up at me. "Hey, beautiful."

My cheeks flush though I don't want them to.

"What do you kids say to a beach day?"

"I just need to get my swimsuit," Emily says, breaking away and running into the bedroom.

"Me too," Molly says, leaping after her, suddenly caught up in the excitement.

Tom follows, his head hung, his hands still balled at his sides, and I can't figure out if he is angry or ashamed. I hope it's the first but fear it's the latter. What I'm certain of is that his voice is lost. Tom used to be fine talking to his dad, but it's been eight months and things are not what they used to be. I need to keep reminding myself of that or else I'll forget—this is not Yucaipa and we are no longer a family.

"Hey," Sean says, walking farther into the condo, his eyes running over me until they come to rest on my face. "Thanks for this. For letting me come."

I look away, unable to take the intensity of his stare.

"Do you want a slice of pie?" I offer before my brain can stop my mouth.

He sits at the table as I pull the pecan pie I baked last weekend from the fridge. I cut him a slice and walk toward the microwave to heat it then change direction. He will have to eat it cold.

"Mmmm," he says, his eyes closing with the first bite, making me regret not heating it so he could taste how really good it is when it's warm. "God, you're something."

"Something good or something bad?" I ask, the rhythm of our banter returning like an old nursery rhyme.

His eyes open, those damn swirling green disks. "Something amazing," he says.

"We're ready," Emily announces, leading the bathing-suit-clad troupe from the bedroom.

Sean scans the three of them with such satisfaction my heart swells, and I'm tempted to wrap my arms around his shoulders so we can admire them together—Emily, gorgeous; Tom, strapping; Molly, adorable—our three amazing kids, fit, healthy, and beautiful.

"Hey, Bugabaloo, what happened to your arm?" Sean asks, concern on his face as he looks at the gauze wrapped around Molly's forearm.

"I got stitches," she says proudly. "Five of them. I needed to go to the hospitawl, and it huwrt wreal bad, but the doctowr said I was wreal bwrave, and I got wlots of pwresents..."

"We should get going," I say, cutting her off before she discloses anything about her new career or the show. "Sean, can you help me with the towels?"

"Is she okay?" he asks as he follows me toward the bathroom.

I nod and part of me wants to tell him all about it, to tell him how terrified I was and to talk to him the way I would have if one of the kids had been hurt when we were still together. But yesterday, when Molly fell, I was alone, and the hurt of his abandonment returns. And I wonder if this is how it will be between us from now on, a roller coaster of emotions, forgetting then remembering, forgiving, but not really, because every time I'm reminded, pain like an electric shock will cripple me and I'll be blindsided by my anger.

I practically throw the towels at him then grab the sun lotion and storm from the bathroom.

"Can we take the van?" he says. "All I have is my bike."

By bike, he means his Harley.

"Ouwr van died," Molly volunteers, still sad over the old car's demise.

Sean's eyebrows rise in question then his eyes flick away. Shame. Either because he didn't provide for us or because he's relieved that he wasn't around to have had to provide for us.

"But we got a new car," Emily says. "It's awesome, a Nissan Pathfinder."

"And it's yewllow."

"Wow, nice," Sean says, and I see his mind puzzling over how we afforded it. "Well, then how about we take the awesome yellow Nissan Pathfinder to the beach?"

⁂

I drive, which is weird because Sean always drove when we traveled as a family. But we are no longer a family, and the Pathfinder is *my* car, so I climb into the driver's seat and Sean climbs into the passenger seat beside me.

Emily talks a mile a minute as we inch along in the heavy weekend traffic. It's strange listening to her, and I realize her relationship with Sean is different than mine and hers. They share a special bond that we just don't have. Sean laughs at her soccer jokes and cares about her goals and assists. He understands her competitive spirit and relishes her victories. When she talks about the kids at school and one girl in particular, Alicia, who made it her mission to make Emily miserable, Sean says, "Is she a big girl?"

"You mean fat?" Emily asks.

"Em," I reprimand.

"Yeah, is she fat?" Sean says.

"Big as a cow," Emily answers.

"Sugar-free Life Savers," Sean says. "Put them in a regular Life Savers bag and leave them where she can find them. She'll eat the whole bag and be farting up a storm in minutes then have the runs for days."

"Sean," I say, appalled but not really. Alicia was vicious, and my advice of *just steer clear of her* didn't help at all.

They continue talking, Emily the happiest I've seen her in months. There's so much I didn't know about her life, and I realize how distracted I've been. On and on she goes, without a single mention of Molly, the commercial, or *The Foster Band*.

When she's exhausted every story about her life, she turns to music, pulling out her iPhone to show Sean her playlist.

"Wow, an iPhone, nice," he says, his voice tight, revealing his wounded pride that we're doing so well without him.

"Mom got one too," Molly says.

"The nine key on my old phone stopped working altogether," I say in defense of the purchase.

"New phones, a new car, looks like you're doing pretty good without the old man," he says, then adds, "Change lanes, the merge up ahead makes the right lanes congested."

I do as he says, and we move ahead of the cars on the right, inching forward at a pace only slightly faster than walking. And as we putt along, I wonder if money would have changed things, given us a better chance of making it.

"Watch the car on the left. The asshole is texting," Sean says.

I watch the car on my left. *Asshole.* The word rubs. My dad never swore, and my mom rarely did. Since Sean's been gone, the words "shit," "damn," "fuck," and "asshole" have been absent from our lives.

"Move over one more lane and get ahead of that fucking Volvo."

I race in front of the Volvo, my hands gripping the wheel so tight that my knuckles are white.

"Christ, Faye, are you trying to get us killed? Honk at that asshole."

I pull to the shoulder, storm from the car, yank open the passenger door, and hold out the keys. "You drive."

Happily he obliges.

And as I climb into the passenger seat, I know the answer. Money would have changed things if it came from him, but if it came from me, it wouldn't have worked. Sean can't be in the passenger seat. Our life was a struggle, but Sean took pride in his role of taking care of us, and in turn, I took care of him. There was something beautiful in it. Like a trapeze act, a sacred trust existed—part optimistic naivety, part reckless youth, part courageous faith. We were in it together and believed that somehow, despite the odds and the dangers of flying without a net, our love would be enough to see us through.

But then he faltered, stopped believing and let go, and now he's asking me to trust him again, and I'm not sure I can. No longer naive and too scared to be reckless, I've lost my courage and possibly my faith.

39

I watch them playing in the water. Tom is laughing, his mutism mercifully dissolved the moment his toes hit the sand, the pure joy of being at the beach trouncing his anxiety.

Emily hangs from Sean's shoulders, futilely trying to dunk him. He swings her off, sending her flying into the waves. They've been in the water for hours, Sean teaching Emily and Tom to bodysurf while I build sand castles on the beach with Molly.

Molly feels left out, but she doesn't know how to swim and can't get her stitches wet, so the poor thing is beach-bound with me.

Sean looks good, better than when he showed up beleaguered two weeks ago. Today he is well rested, his eyes bright. He turned thirty-six while he was gone, and like most rugged men, age suits him, his boyish charm fermented into a tough manliness. Tall and broad-shouldered, his skin is golden brown with tattoos that cover his forearms and part of his chest.

I notice he has some new etchings—a tribal circle on his back and a serpent coiling over his heart. I bristle with the thought of how expensive tattoos are and the memory of how I struggled to make ends meet after he left.

I shake off the irritation, determined to enjoy the moment—the rare, blessed reprieve from total responsibility, the unencumbered easiness of co-parenting instead of solo parenting—a relaxing day at the beach instead of a stress-plagued ordeal of constant vigilance.

Like slipping into an old robe, it's so comfortable and soft that I never want to take it off. And sitting here, I'm reminded of all the good things we had and how good we used to be at making something wonderful out of nothing.

Molly turns her paper cup over in the sand, creating a perfect-cast cylinder to complete the wall of her castle, and I release the sand crab we captured earlier. The tiny creature scurries sideways to find a way out, instinctively heading for the ocean, its movements becoming frantic when it runs up against the wall.

"Maybe it would be happier if we let it go?" I say.

"But he might get huwrt," she says, her emotions torn between wanting to contain her new pet or release it.

"Maybe, but that's where his home is. He looks like he really wants to go back."

Molly uses her cup to scoop up the little guy, and together we carry it back to the wash and set it free, then we return to our spot in the sand and to building the fortress. I smile at the chocolate smudges on the corners of her mouth. Lunch today was fried clams and French fries from a nearby fish stand followed by ice cream.

We ate our cones while watching the skateboarders at the skate park.

Dad, don't you know how to skateboard? Emily asked, pure adoration in her eyes.

Sean shrugged then borrowed a board from one of the skaters and showed off his moves, the kids watching with reverence they've never held for me and which they never will. I'm just their mom, the ordinary, unremarkable woman who takes care of them. But their dad—he might not be there day in and day out, but boy is he something special.

And he is. As I watch him laughing with Emily and Tom, patiently explaining how to find the right waves, I find myself falling in love again, not only for who he is to me but for who he is to them, and I realize this is the power men have over us. Yes, we want them to love us, but more than that, we desperately need them to love our children.

The three of them bound from the water, and Sean scoops Molly up from the sand, twirls her onto his hip like she weighs no more than a sack of flour, then dumps her upside down. Holding her by her ankles, he swings her back and forth as she squeals with delight, then he spins her upright and plops her back to the sand.

"Come on, kiddo," he says. "Let's you and me build real sand castles with M&M and Tomcat."

She takes his hand, and they skip toward a smooth part of beach perfect for castle making. I move to the blanket, thinking I'm going to close my eyes and rest, but the ringtone of "On the Road Again" distracts me, and I move Sean's shirt to reveal his cell phone. Lit up on the screen is a message from *Regina, Albuquerque, New Mexico*. Without hesitation, I open it. *hey babe bed is lonely without u did u find out how much she is getting for the commercial.*

40

Go and don't come back," I hiss.

We're in the hallway outside the condo. The kids have said their good-byes, Sean promising he will see them soon.

"Faye, what's gotten into you?"

My arms are crossed over my chest, and I'm shaking. For four hours I've held my rage, but I can't hold it any longer.

"Faye..."

"Go!" I screech.

He ignores me. "They're my kids too."

"They're your kids when there's money to be made off them. I can't believe you, Sean. You really think I'm going to give you a penny?"

His face transforms, the pretense of affability dissolved as his face grows dark. "It's not up to you."

"To hell it isn't," I snap as the awful realization hits me that he might be right.

"How much did the Gap pay her?"

"Go to hell."

"I'm sure that's where I'm headed, but I'm not there yet, and like it or not, I intend to ride there in style."

"You goddamn son of a bitch."

Emily runs through the door. "Mom? Dad?"

Sean wraps his arm around her. "It's okay, Em. Your mom and I are just working things out."

"But you're coming back, right?" she asks.

He turns his face to me so I can see the veracity in his eyes as he says, "Yes, baby. This time I'm here to stay."

"Em, go back inside," I seethe.

Reluctantly she obeys.

Sean shrugs, palms out. "They love me. What can I say? I'm irresistible."

My hate is so raw that if I had a gun, I swear I'd use it. But I don't have a gun, so I stand quivering with rage but with no idea of what to do about it.

"We can do this the easy way or the hard way, but one way or the other, I'm back and I'm a part of this."

The elevator dings, the door opens, and my mom steps off.

"Hello, Brenda," Sean says, stepping on. "Thanks for the great day, Faye. I'll be in touch."

My mom looks at him then at me, and my expression must tell her everything because her lips purse then she opens them to speak.

"Don't," I spit. "Just don't."

I whirl from her and storm into the condo.

"When's he coming back?" Emily asks, her face lit up.

Molly and Tom look at me expectantly as well. My nose flares, and I bite down hard on my lip to keep from lashing out at them as I continue to the bedroom.

Collapsing on the mattress, I bury my face in the pillow and try not to hate them for their betrayal. It's not their fault. Sean is like the Pied Piper who appeared from nowhere and granted them a magic day. And though he will lead them to their doom, at the moment, all they hear is his sweet music, and they can't wait for him to appear again.

I reach for a tissue to wipe the rogue tears that have escaped from my eyes, and when I lift the box, something rattles. Moving the tissues aside, I fish out a small red velvet bag. Inside is a heart-shaped silver locket engraved with the letter "M." The clasp is difficult to work but finally opens to reveal a tiny folded note.

My Dear Molly,

I miss your sweet smile. I no your mother told you not to love me anymore but don't worry that won't stop me. I am still waching even thow you don't see me. I wach you every day. God wants us to be together and some day we will be.

Your True Love

"Em," I shout, the harshness of my voice causing her to appear almost instantly. "Where did this come from?" The locket dangles like a pendulum from my fist.

Her face goes white as she glubs for an answer.

"The truth," I roar. "Now."

"That guy, John Lennon," she stammers. "Melissa's mom dropped me off after soccer on Monday, and he walked up and handed it to me."

Since the day we snubbed John Lennon after the flower incident, he has disappeared. I assumed it was for good; obviously I was wrong.

"And you took it?"

Her eyes drop to the ground. "He paid me. Gave me twenty dollars and said all I needed to do was give it to Molly. I didn't figure it was a big deal. It's just a stupid necklace. I didn't even give it to her. He doesn't know the difference. The guy's a whack job."

"Exactly. The guy's a whack job, and you think it's okay to talk to a whack job, take money from a whack job, then not tell me about that whack job giving you money to give a necklace to Molly, your four-year-old sister?" My voice has reached glass-shattering shrill.

"I figured if I told you, you'd freak out and throw it away like you did the flowers. It's real silver. I was going to sell it on eBay."

My vision blurs with my fury.

She continues, "Molly's like a big deal, and once *The Foster Band* season starts, she's going to be a really big deal. I looked up celebrity auction items, and it's crazy how much famous people get for their stuff. Justin Timberlake's half-eaten French toast breakfast sold for over $3,000, and Michael Jackson's underwear sold for a million. I figure if I take a picture of Molly wearing the necklace then post it for sale, we could get like $10,000 for it."

"Get out," I scream.

She rears back. "Does that mean I can't sell it?"

"Out! Now!"

The door closes, and I bury my face in my hands, my emotions raw. Then taking several breaths to calm myself, I sit up and reach for the phone. Emily's right and she's wrong—I am freaking out, but this time I'm not going to throw the gift away.

∞

The officer that shows up is young, cocky, and bored, his sunglasses perched on top of his buzz cut as he takes down the report without expression.

I tell him about John Lennon and where he used to wait for us. I describe him as best I can, and he asks if I took a photo of him, making me feel stupid for not thinking to have done that.

When he's finished taking down all the information, he drops the locket and the note, along with the card that was delivered with the roses, into evidence bags and, with an unconvincing promise that he'll look into it, leaves.

I put the kids to bed, then spend the next three hours driving myself insane, staring out the window, my eyes roving over the sidewalk and peering into the crevices of the neighborhood, wondering where he is, convinced he's out there, hiding in the shadows, staring back, knowing I called the police, knowing the police are gone, watching and waiting, waiting and watching. Out there somewhere.

41

Fortunately the kids and I are on our way out of Los Angeles, away from Sean and any whack jobs who might be stalking us.

Three times a year the entire cast and crew of *The Foster Band* spend a week on location at a farm in the wine country of Temecula to shoot the vineyard scenes, and the families of the cast are invited along. I've been looking forward to this week since we started. Finally I don't have to leave Emily and Tom behind, and my mom gets a well-deserved week off, and I get a well-deserved week off from her.

The Pathfinder bumps from the road onto the driveway of Paddison Farm, and my heart swells. Though we've never been here, it's like going home. On our left, a vineyard rolls to the foothills, and to our right is a pasture with horses, a barn, and several corrals. I open the windows, and the distinct smell of hay steaming in the sun fills the car, verdant and earthy, flooding my mind with thoughts of Bo and Yucaipa.

In front of us is the Foster home, a white Victorian farmhouse with black shutters, a wraparound porch, and window boxes spilling over with red geraniums.

Beyond the house, a thicket of trees conceals a camp of dark brown cabins. We park beside number eleven and carry our bags inside.

The cabin has two bedrooms, a kitchenette, and a spacious bathroom with a claw-foot tub. It is only slightly smaller than our home was in Yucaipa, and I can't believe that it and the dozen others like it are only occupied three weeks out of the year.

As soon as the kids drop their bags, they are out the door to explore.

"Em, keep an eye on your sister," I yell after them.

She doesn't answer, but I know she will. Molly's been traipsing after her since she could walk.

I wander outside to explore as well, reveling in the freedom of being alone. Most of the cast and crew won't arrive until tomorrow, so other than the people who work the farm, hardly anyone is around.

I make my way past the corral to the barn, following the scent of horses. The farm is perfect. Too perfect. No farm looks like this—a split-rail fence precisely spaced; a vegetable garden with exact rows of crisp lettuce, stands of tomatoes, and boxes bursting with herbs; a barn that looks like it was painted yesterday; and a chicken coop with a dozen plump, gorgeous hens—everything you need to represent a quintessential American farm except the evidence of struggle and hard work.

Which is because none of it is real. The fence is laminate, the vegetable garden is filled with plastic plants, the barn was painted yesterday, and the gorgeous hens are stuffed.

But it's nice to look at, and as I walk around, I reminisce about some of the wonderful scenes from past seasons that took place here. I hear the rush of water and remember that there's a river nearby and that Jeremy likes to fish. He and Mr. Foster are always bringing home trout. It's a running joke on the show because Mrs. Foster, originally a city girl, hates cleaning fish.

I walk past the house and smile. Beside the door is the porch swing where dozens of romantic kisses and heart-to-heart conversations have taken place. A wine bottle–shaped sign hangs beside it, "The Fosters" painted on its label. The sign was a gift from the social worker in one of the first episodes.

"Hello."

I turn to see Chris walking from the barn. He wears designer jeans, a black western shirt with pearl buttons, a belt with a silver buckle the size of my hand, and cowboy boots. His face is unshaven, and on his head is a NASCAR hat with the number 88.

"You're an Earnhardt fan?" I ask.

"Dale and I met a few years back. You know NASCAR?"

Of course Chris Cantor is not *just* a fan. Of course he's *met* Dale Earnhardt Jr. Of course they're on a first-name basis. Chris Cantor may be dressed like a cowboy, but he's still Chris Cantor.

"A little," I answer. "My husband..." *Is? Was?* "Was a fan."

"Where's Molly?"

"Off exploring with her brother and sister." I emphasize brother and sister more than necessary, feeling the need to remind him that I have three kids, not just Molly.

"Wow, I actually have you all to myself," he says, completely unaffected by my breeder status.

"Did you call that waitress?" I say, nipping his Don Juan act in the bud. After yesterday with Sean, I'm in no mood for charming actors.

"The waitress from Ruth's Chris?" he asks, all innocence.

"Has more than one waitress slipped you their number in the past two days?"

He smirks and shrugs, a boyish Dennis the Menace expression, innocent and guilty at the same time. "Hazard of the job."

"Not too bad of a hazard. She was pretty."

He shrugs. "I'm single, and she was offering. Until I find something more, that's what I've got."

I wince slightly.

"You find that distasteful?"

"I don't know. Yeah, I guess so. She thinks you're going to help her."

"Ouch. You really know how to stomp on a guy's ego. Did you even consider that she might have been attracted to my stunning good looks, bulging biceps, and charm?"

"Perhaps the biceps," I say, adding a giggle as he strikes a he-man pose, his arms not even coming close to filling out his sleeves. "But even with those massive muscles, your influence might have had a teensy-weensy little bit to do with her giving you her number without any more conversation than 'How's your steak?'"

He nods in agreement. "A fair exchange."

My nose crinkles again, causing him to laugh.

"That offends you even more," he says.

"It's your business."

"But you think it's awful?"

I think about this for a second. *A fair exchange.* Is it? Sex for opportunity? Involuntarily I shudder.

"Wow, I guess so," he says. "Full-on heebie-jeebies."

"It's not that it's wrong," I say, trying to articulate the feeling that is vague yet undeniably distasteful. "It's just so…so…" I search for the word.

"Meaningless," he says.

That wasn't exactly what I was thinking, but I nod because it's kinder than "repulsive," "callous," "ruthless," and "demeaning."

"It's not so bad. Like you said, she was pretty, and she actually had a great personality. We had fun."

"If you say so, then I'm glad for you."

"You're actually feeling sorry for me?"

And I realize I'm looking at him with sympathy.

I wipe the expression from my face and change the subject. "Yeah, well you do look a little pathetic, especially in that outfit. Who dressed you? Garth Brooks?"

He looks down at his clothes. "The shirt too much?"

"Not if you're going line dancing at a gay rodeo."

"Dang, Faye, you're just full of compliments, aren't you? I'll have you know, I'm dressed to go riding."

"On a horse?"

"Yes, on a horse. Do you ride, Miss I-only-wear-worn-out-Wranglers-and-tight-white-T-shirts-that-drive-the-boys-wild?"

"This look happens to be very retro and very functional." I give a twirl of my drive-the-boys-wild look. "And yes, I ride."

"Well then, perhaps you'd like to join me."

The thought is horribly tempting. It's been months since I've been in the saddle (both connotations running through my head), but it's also undeniably a bad idea. Chris Cantor is a bad idea—a very attractive, very charming, very, very bad idea.

"I can't. I'm still on mom patrol," I say, proud of my restraint.

"Beth," Chris calls, and amazingly the woman materializes from the barn. "Keep an eye out for Faye's kids. If they come looking for her, tell them she'll be back in an hour and look after them until then."

"Will do," Beth says.

"Must be nice having women at your beck and call."

"Not just women. Men, children, dogs. I'm the producer. I rule the world." He gives a sadistic ruler-of-the-universe laugh then leads me into the barn.

Chris may be ruler of the universe in his make-believe world, but on our ride, I'm the one who takes the reins.

We slow to a trot after a full gallop through a flat pasture.

"That was amazing," he says, breathless. "I've never ridden full-out like that."

"And you probably shouldn't again. I'm surprised your horse didn't leave you in the pasture."

"Madame, are you making fun of my riding skills?"

"What riding skills? You told me you could ride."

"No, I said I was going riding and asked you if you ride. There's a difference."

I dismount, and Chris begins to do the same.

"Wrong side," I say, stopping him. "You need to mount and dismount from the left, otherwise it freaks out the horse."

He slithers off the other side and winces. "A little hard on the haunches."

"The way you were bumping around, I'm surprised you can walk at all."

He picks up a clod of dirt and throws it at me, pegging me on my jeans. I curl away in defense, my hands up, and when I unfurl, he is in front of me, his lips coming down on mine. I release the reins, and my horse scampers off with Chris's, and I should be concerned because we're miles from the farm, and there's a good chance we've just lost two good horses, but at the moment, Chris's breath is mingling with mine, sweet and heavy, like he ate a piece of chocolate before we started out, and I can't be concerned with runaway horses.

Pure electricity runs through my veins, my body ringing like a tuning fork. His hands are on my shoulders, mine on his chest, and when he pulls away, I'm breathless.

He smiles, brushes a hair from my eyes, and says, "I've been wanting to do that for weeks."

"So what took you so long?"

"You're a damn hard woman to get alone."

I laugh, and it causes him to kiss me again.

He's smaller than Sean, at least six inches shorter, his shoulders narrow, and I do not need to crane my neck.

His hands slide down my body to wrap around my back, and my body melts against him, my leg sliding between his knees, the bulge of his jeans swollen against my hips.

He lowers me to the ground, his tongue working its way into my mouth as his left hand slides beneath my shirt, his fingers burning against my skin and causing me to moan.

He pulls away, his lips curled in a grin. "This is going to be fun."

I nod and pull him back to kiss him again. I need more fun in my life.

As we continue to kiss, an alarm, thready and thin, blares in my brain, a warning siren screaming that this is a bad idea. But the rush of blood in my ears drowns it out. Then the horrible, wonderful spot two inches below my belly button joins in, fluttering and trilling and spreading outward until every fiber in my body is singing and cheering me on and telling me not to listen to my brain, which has no sense of fun and adventure at all.

"God, you're sexy," Chris says, coming up for air.

I pull him back down, and his tongue dives back into my mouth as his hand continues to inch up my ribs, then his fingers touch my bra, and I push him off so abruptly, he falls to the ground.

Crappy, cheap utility bra! Dishwater gray from a zillion washes! The thought blindsides me.

Chris groans and rolls onto his back, clearly in pain. "Shit. Are you trying to kill me?" The source of his agony pulses impressively from his jeans. "First with the horse and now with sexual torment and denial?"

I laugh, lean over, and peck him on the lips. "I think you'll live."

His hand wraps around the back of my head, and he pulls me into another long kiss, and when he releases me, he says, "I really do like you."

"I like you too," I say, pushing off him and standing. "But I might stop liking you if I have to walk three miles back to the barn. So get up and help me find our horses."

I hold out my hand to help him up, and he takes it and pulls me back to the ground to kiss me again. He doesn't take it further than that, but we have a grand time rolling around in the hay.

42

I wake feeling altered and wonder if others will notice. Though Chris and I were entirely alone, and I'm certain no one witnessed our romp in the pasture, I feel naughty and a little guilty as I walk onto the set.

He said he really likes me. And I think I really like him back. This could be the start of something. Could this be the start of something? I think this is the start of something.

Something.

Wow.

After tethering the horses in the barn, we went our separate ways, and since we parted, my insides have been on fire, glowing with an incandescent brightness I'm certain is visible for everyone to see.

No one seems to notice, including Chris.

We've been on the set two hours, and he has yet to even glance my way, and I realize, if Chris Cantor is going to be in my life, I'm going to need to get used to his mercurial moods.

This morning he's fit to be tied and not flirting with anyone. His body is wound tight like a rattler as he storms around the farm barking orders and snapping the heads off anyone who happens to get in his way.

An accident on the 15 has caused half the cast and crew to be late, and now the shooting schedule is behind, the first scene just getting under way.

Emily and Tom sit beside Molly and me as we watch Chris work out the details with the horse trainer. Emily lost interest in the process after about five minutes and sits reading a book. Tom is fascinated, his eyes taking it all in.

The weather isn't helping anyone's mood. It's only ten in the morning, but already it's hot as the Sahara and the wind is gusting, creating a steam bath of swirling dust that covers all of us in a sticky film of dirt. Henry and the makeup crew are beside themselves trying to tame the frizz and keep the actors' faces from melting on screen.

"What you reading?"

I glance sideways to see Caleb squatting beside Emily.

She looks up, and her eyes pulse once when she realizes the superstar teenage heartthrob Caleb Jones is talking to her. Then with incredible cool she says, "*Gregor the Overlander*. It's from Suzanne Collins's first series before she wrote *The Hunger Games*."

"I haven't read that one," Caleb says, "but I read *Gregor and the Code of Claw*."

Pause.

"Oh," Emily says. "I liked that one."

Pause.

"You read that one?"

"Yeah, I've read them all. This is my second time reading them."

Pause.

"Oh."

I nearly giggle. The two are so charmingly awkward.

"Well, maybe I'll see you tonight at the barbeque," Caleb says as he stands.

"Yeah, okay. See you."

When he's gone, she looks at me in disbelief, and we share a priceless mother-daughter moment.

Emily doesn't see it because her back is turned, but when Caleb is ten feet away, he glances back, a shy peek over his shoulder, undeniable puppy crush in his eyes.

I wish Chris would look over, give me a glance, a smile, some indication that what happened between us is on his mind at least a little. I realize it was only a kiss, but he said he really likes me. That means something. Doesn't it?

Do I want it to mean something?

Last night I was giddy with the thought, but now I'm not so sure. Watching him, I try to imagine him in my life, to insert him into a scenario that works. Us living in the burbs, him coming home after a day on the set to me and the kids. A peck on my cheek as I finish making dinner—maybe short ribs and rosemary mashed potatoes. I hand him an expensive glass of wine. He tells me about his day, and I tell him about mine and about the kids.

As much as I try, I can't see it. Yet I really want him to look my way and give me one of his trademark winks, to let me know he's considering the possibility as well.

Do I even like this man?

I think I do. Yesterday, when he was charming and sweet and saying all the right things... and *doing* all the right things... I liked him very much.

I watch as he and the horse trainer discuss the angle of the shot. Something Chris says makes the man furrow his brow and nod, the man's respect evident, the same respect Chris gets from everyone. He's Chris Cantor. I can't really be so arrogant as to think I deserve better.

Smart, funny, successful, wealthy, a good kisser. I'm a thirty-two-year-old college dropout with three kids. Let's be real here—if Chris Cantor is interested, I'm interested.

Chris walks away from the trainer, and as he heads toward his chair, he barks at one of the extras to change his shirt because it's smudged with dirt. It's not the extra's fault. We're all smudged with dirt, and a moment before, the guy was asked to carry a bale of hay into the corral.

Next he snaps at Jeremy, who stands beside the chicken coop entertaining Miles by trying to juggle three of the fake eggs. "Stop fucking up my set," he barks.

"Chill, Chris," Griff says, striding into the corral. He wears work boots, faded Levi's, and a Willie Nelson T-shirt, and by the way he walks up to the horse and smooths the mare's muzzle, I know he rides. "We'll get it done."

"About time you got here," Chris seethes.

"Can't do anything about traffic."

Griff is unaffected by Chris's temper, his voice as calm as if Chris had greeted him with, "Good morning, Griff. Great to see you."

"You could have gotten here yesterday," Chris snaps.

"It was my day off. Went fishing. Caught three trout and a bass."

"You think I give a shit..."

"Chris, simmer down. We're a couple of hours behind, and we've got a week to make it up."

Chris's nostrils flare.

Griff claps him on the shoulder. "Relax. We've got this."

With a curt nod, Chris walks back to his perch. "Let's do this," he says.

Griff shakes the trainer's hand then gives a small wave to Jeremy and Miles, and Jeremy resumes juggling his eggs.

When Griff turns to walk back toward the main camera, his gaze levels on me and turns cold, a fierce look that causes me to turn away.

I get it. I was wrong. I owe him an apology. I haven't exactly had the opportunity. He just got here. What does he want me to do, stand up in front of everyone and announce that I know it was my fault Molly got hurt and that I was an unjustified bitch and that I'm sorry?

He'll get his damn apology. First opportunity I get, I'll tell him exactly what he's waiting to hear, that he was right and I was wrong, that he's a genius and a hero and that I'm an idiot and a coward.

"Mom."

"What?" I snap at Molly, who I realize has said my name three times without me answering.

"It's time."

"Right, okay." I return my focus to the moment. "So you know what you're doing?"

"I walk up to the howrse wlike I want to pet hewr, but the howrse gets scawred and twries to stomp me, but Gwrant saves me."

Grant is a new character, the eight-year-old wiseass son of the new foreman on the farm.

"Grant is going to knock you to the ground."

Molly smiles. She and Tom rehearsed the scene half a dozen times last night and had a great time rolling around in the mud. Tom loves rehearsing with Molly. He's a perfect stand-in for Miles, and last night he did a terrific job pretending to be Grant.

"Then he puwlls me thwrough the fence," she says.

Molly and I do this with every scene, a back-and-forth dialogue of what is going to happen. It's not so much a rehearsal as a summary. Sometimes she needs more explanation and sometimes less. Like now, she says, "What do I do when I'm out of the cowrrawl?"

"Grant gets mad and says, 'Are you stupid? That horse could have killed you.' And you're going to be kind of shy because you don't know Grant."

Molly's mouth skews to the side, just like it did the first time we read the script.

"I know," I say. "It's kind of silly, but that's the way the writers wrote it."

I've taken it upon myself to memorize the scenes Molly is in, her lines as well as everyone else's. It helps me rehearse with her without having to use the script and also allows me to be in the right spot on the set to cue her if she needs it.

"Okey dokey, jokey smokey," she says.

I brush a curl from her forehead and peck her on the nose. "Break a leg."

"You bwreak a wleg too," she says, then skips toward the corral as the kid who plays Grant steps through the fence on the other side.

I'm not crazy about the actor they chose. He has serious attitude and treats his mom like crap. He was cast because he's a star. Last year he played a scrappy orphan in a postapocalyptic movie that was all the rage. In my opinion, the kid should enjoy his success while it lasts because, though he's cute now, he's not going to be cute as a man, and I can't imagine there will be too many roles for scrawny, obnoxious thirty-year-olds.

"Molly and Grant stand here and here," Chris says, pointing to two chalk marks on the ground.

I'm not nervous about this scene. The horse is a beautiful, gentle mare who wouldn't hurt a fly, and her trainer is an old horse whisperer who has complete control. Relative to the car scene, this is a piece of cake.

Chris says, "Camera one, go tight on Molly as a cutaway in case she doesn't get the emotion and we need to do it in two shots."

Molly takes her place, but Grant refuses. "That horse just shit," he says. "I'm not rolling around in horse shit."

"Baby, they're cleaning it," his mom says as he climbs back through the fence.

A crew member shovels the manure into a sack as another rakes the soil.

"The dirt is still contaminated," the kid says, marching toward the cabins. His mom races after him in a ridiculous pair of heels that sink into the dirt with each step she takes.

"Jesus fucking Christ," Chris screams as he spins in a circle and runs his hand through his hair. "What the fuck?"

"Chris, look," Griff says, causing everyone to turn their attention back to the corral.

My mouth falls open. Tom, *my Tom*, has taken Grant's spot, and Molly has taken her spot. The cast and crew instinctively quiet, Chris steps back, and the crew members who were cleaning the dirt move out of view. Beth raises her hand, and her fingers pop up one by one. "Action."

Molly takes two steps toward the horse, her hand reaching toward the mare's muzzle. The trainer blows a piercing whistle, and the horse rears up. Molly freezes, her eyes get large and her mouth opens, then she stumbles back a step. Bam! Tom tackles her to the ground, and the horse's hooves come down yards from either of them. Tom grabs Molly by the arm and yanks her under the fence.

I hold my breath. Aside from speaking inside our cabin, Tom hasn't said a word since we arrived on the farm.

"Are you stupid?" he says in a voice that is not his own, the words spitting with an accent remarkably like the kid who just stormed off the set. "That horse could have killed you."

Tears spring to my eyes, and I bite down on my knuckle to stop from crying. In front of a hundred strangers, my son, who never speaks in front of strangers, just spoke. Emily leaps to her feet beside me and hugs me around my waist, both of us jumping up and down in place.

Molly's hands go to her hips. "No, I'm not stupid. You'wre stupid."

Tom's nose flares, and he shoves Molly, and Molly shoves him back. Tom's face squints into a scowl, then he whirls and marches off toward the barn.

"Wait," Molly says, running after Tom. "Wait fowr me."

Tom keeps right on walking, his fists balled at his sides.

"And cut," Chris says, marching onto the set. "Can someone please tell me what the hell is going on? Who the hell is that? And who changed the damn script?"

"I'm sorry," I say. "That's my son. I'll keep him out of the way..."

"Does he have an actor's card?"

"Uh...I..." I'm nearly as speechless as Tom normally is.

Before I formulate a response, Tom and Molly are back, Molly grinning like a baboon, Tom shyly smirking beside her. The cast and crew burst into applause, and Tom's grin widens to fill his whole face.

"He's my bwrothewr," Molly announces proudly.

Tom is at my side now, and I wrap my arm protectively around him and drop a kiss on his head, my emotions stuck in my throat, the tears barely contained—pride, disbelief, relief.

"Fifteen-minute break," Chris says, causing the cast and crew to scamper off in search of caffeine, nicotine, and shade.

"So, Two-Bits, are you going to introduce me?"

"This is Tom," Molly says proudly. "And this is my sistewr, Emiwly."

"Hello, Emily," Chris says, shaking her hand. "You're as beautiful as your mom."

She blushes and so do I.

He turns to Tom. "Well, young man, that was quite a performance. Are you an actor?"

My heart locks up, all of us looking expectantly at Tom to see if he'll answer.

He nods.

"Well, welcome to the show," Chris says, then turns back to me. "Beth will work it out with SAG to get him his actor's card. I assume she should call Monique to deal with the contract?"

He's all business, and I'm a little stung by the brusqueness.

I nod, and he walks away, then turns back. "And you, Two-Bits, stop changing the script."

"But I would nevewr wlet someone cawll me stupid, and I'm not shy," Molly says.

He smirks and shakes his head. "Fine. I'll talk to the writers, but stop changing the script without talking to me first."

"Bossy, bossy, Chwrissy Cwrossy."

A look of pure adoration crosses Chris's face, then he turns to me and gives a smile bright as the sun. "Maybe we can all have lunch together?"

My heart warms and chills at the same time, unsure if his renewed attention is because of me or my daughter.

Without waiting for my answer, he gives his signature wink then pivots and walks away.

I kneel down so I'm eye level with Tom. "Buddy, that was awesome."

He nods, and the crooked smile I love so much fills his face. He's as amazed as I am, relief flooding from his small body and straight into my heart.

43

Tom and Molly shoot one more scene together, Tom's voice miraculously continuing to show up as Grant. Like Molly, he's a natural-born actor, and I'm stunned by how comfortable he is in front of the camera.

Chris is a no-show for lunch, which while a little disappointing is also a relief. I want to revel in Tom's breakthrough, and I can't do that with Chris Cantor around.

We eat as a family beneath the shade of an oak tree, and when we finish, Beth tells us that Molly and Tom are done for the day, which is especially good news because Emily and I have some shopping to do. Emily needs a new outfit to wear to the barbeque tonight where she is going to see Caleb, and I need a new bra.

I've made a decision. Regardless of whether Chris Cantor is a good idea, having sex with him is a good idea—a very good, very needed idea. I'm thirty-two years old and have not had sex in over eight months. It doesn't need to be meaningful. I can do meaningless. I can.

I've got three kids. Prince Charming is not going to ride in on a white horse or drive up in his black Porsche and whisk me away to his castle in Beverly Hills. Nice as that sounds, that's probably not in the cards. So unless I'm ready to commit to a life of celibacy, I need to loosen up and have a little fun.

I can do this. I want to do this. I can. I do.

I'm going to do this. Damn it, get over yourself, just do it!

44

The plum lace bra I bought itches and is digging into my flesh. The matching panties are equally uncomfortable. I try to convince myself that they are thrilling reminders of what I have to look forward to, but most of my focus is spent on resisting the urge to rip them off right here at the dinner table.

We are at the barbeque, Molly and Tom on either side of me, Jeremy across from us.

Emily left us before we even got in line for our food. Caleb waved her over to his group, which included Miles's two older sisters and Gabby.

Chris has yet to make an appearance, and I'm starting to wonder if my suffering is for naught. Everyone else is here, nearly two hundred people chowing on tri-tip, corn on the cob, potato salad, and baked beans. It feels like a celebration, which I suppose it is. This week marks the end of shooting the first three episodes of the season.

Jeremy's a great kid and seems to have adopted us as his surrogate family for the week. His own family lives in Minneapolis, and it sounds like he misses them something fierce.

Though he's twenty, he doesn't seem it; there's a guilelessness about him that makes him seem younger. He was seventeen when he got the part and still in high school. He dropped out to take the job, and his good looks and golden voice missiled him to instant superstardom.

At the moment, he is telling Tom about the perils of being famous. "Crazy stuff," he says. "You wouldn't believe the things girls'll do to get your attention. You're in it now, so you better watch out."

Tom shakes his head like Jeremy is nuts. Until this morning, Tom was a social outcast, a mute. He was not a person girls even noticed, let alone did crazy things to get the attention of.

"I'm telling you. Good-looking kid like you, the little ones, they're going to be all over it." He looks at me. "Mom, you better go through his fan mail before he does, make sure it's G-rated, if you know what I mean."

"Actually I have no idea what you mean," I say, thinking about the roses and locket sent to Molly and wondering if it gets worse. "What have people sent you?"

"You don't want to know. What they send, what they do. Some fans are serious, section-eight certifiable. Makes you kind of feel bad for them but also kind of freaks you out. This one fan, she's got thirteen tattoos dedicated to me—my face, my name, quotes I've said. She's like nineteen years old. What's her future husband going to think of that? The guy's going to need to change his name to Jeremy."

"What else?" Tom says, forgetting that normally he doesn't talk to Jeremy, his excitement trouncing his inhibition. This day just keeps getting better.

"Well, let's see. There's this one crazy bit…broad who changed her last name to my last name, then she had plastic surgery to alter her nose so it looks like mine, got a spray tan so she looks black instead of white, and got green contact lenses so our eyes match. It's totally freaky. You can Google her. She's posted all sorts of photos of herself on the internet. Her name is Jenny Schwinger. It's like looking at myself in drag."

"What's dwrag?" Molly asks.

"It's when a dude dresses up like a girl," Jeremy says. "Then there's this other girl who tweeted me over eighteen thousand times this year. That's like fifty tweets a day."

"So what do they send you?" Tom asks, clearly excited at the prospect of such devoted fans and by the idea of receiving swag in the mail.

"Oh, you don't even want to know. Love letters by the troves, gold watches, cologne, bras, panties. I even once got a love note written in menstrual blood."

"Yuck!" I squeal.

"What's that?" Molly asks.

"Men's blood," I say quickly. "Someone wrote him a note in blood."

"That's awesome," Tom says.

Jeremy shrugs. "You kind of get used to it. But you've got to remember: it's not real. Those girls, they're not really in love with you—they're in love with your character. I'm nothing like Jeremy from the show. No one's as awesome as that guy. He's badass and charming, gets all the girls, and never has a zit. Meanwhile, I'm a half-Jewish, half-black scrawny band geek from Minneapolis who never had a date before I got this gig, and if any of those girls really knew me, they wouldn't send me squat."

"You're hardly scrawny," I say.

"I was scrawny," he corrects. "But the script called for buff, so after they hired me, they whipped my body into compliance with a personal trainer who kicked the shit out of my nerd genes. I hate it and love it. I love looking good, but I hate working out."

"Well they made you gorgeous," I say.

And he is. Unlike some of the others in the cast, Jeremy looks as good in person as he does on the show. Six foot two, skin the color of molasses, moss-green eyes, and hair sheared to within a centimeter of his perfectly shaped head.

"I cheat every chance I get," he says. "Speaking of which, Molly, Tom, want to join me for some s'mores?"

I watch them go and, when I'm certain no one's watching, sneak off toward the cabins.

Chris's cabin is a row from our own. The front window flickers with orange light, and I picture him relaxing in front of a fire, enjoying a few minutes to himself.

I will knock, and he will be surprised. He will pull me through the door, and we will resume where we left off. My nerves buzz with anticipation as I climb the steps.

When I reach the porch, I stop to push my boobs up in my uncomfortable bra to give my small breasts as much boost as possible. Tiptoeing forward, I peek through the glowing window, hoping to catch a glimpse of where he is before I knock.

My face blanches in shock as I rear up, then burns in horror as I stumble back, whirl, and race toward the woods, trying to erase the image from my mind. But Rhonda riding Chris like a horse is seared on my brain like a branding iron, her blond hair whipping around, her silicone breasts bouncing—an indelible image that will be impossible to forget.

Lungs heaving, I stop, collapse to the ground, rip the ridiculous bra from my body, and hurl it into the river beside me. Then pulling my knees to my chest, I bury my face against them.

It's amazing how bad my taste is in men. If there was a competition for worst intuition when it comes to the opposite sex, I'd be the Grand Poobah.

Rhonda! Really?

At least the waitress was young and beautiful and not someone I knew. Rhonda's a beast, a forty-something, silicone-infused, brainless bitch. We work together every day. He was going to screw her then screw me. Or vice versa. I shiver with disgust, unsure if my abhorrence is from insult or hurt. I think about kissing him yesterday and desperately want to rinse my mouth out with soap.

"You lost something."

I lift my head to see a large, dark figure walking toward me. The moon is behind him, and because my eyes were buried against my knees, my vision is blurry.

He steps closer, and I tense, then when I recognize who it is, my eyes bulge. *Griff. Crap.* The last man…other than Chris or Sean…I want to see. Naked except for his shorts, his body beaded with water, he stands confident and unshy, my ridiculous plum bra dangling from his outstretched arm.

I snatch the embarrassment from him. "Thank you," I say, unable to meet his eyes, both from humiliation over him finding my slingshotted purple undergarment and because the apology I owe him is now so overdue that there's absolutely no excuse.

"You're welcome," he says, the words a declaration, letting me know my gratitude is accepted for more than his chivalrous return of my bra.

"Fine," I snap, my eyes whipping up to meet his. "Thank you. You were right, and I was wrong. Molly got hurt because of me. I'm a terrible mother and a terrible person and I shouldn't be allowed to parent anyone or make decisions regarding my welfare or anyone else's because I obviously lack all judgment regarding whether someone should be trusted or if they're just a lying jerk telling me what I want to hear so they can get what they want. So, I'm sorry. I'm sorry I was rude to you, I'm sorry I suck, I'm sorry you have to put up with me at all."

His head tilts, and my own head collapses back to my knees, and I pray he will leave.

He doesn't. Infuriatingly he continues to stand there.

"Do you need something?" I mumble.

"You're right," he says. "You do have terrible judgment, but you're also all she has, and you're the one who got her into this, so somehow you're going to need to figure it out and start protecting her."

I nod my head against my jeans because he's right. But he's also wrong. I'm not the one to protect her; I've already proven that. A good mom is a lioness who roars, bares her teeth, extends her razor-sharp claws, and bristles to twice her size to defend her cubs. I, on the other hand, buy cheap purple bras and jump into bed with the reaper.

45

I'm put to the test before dawn.

Because the weather is expected to shift this afternoon with a chance of rain, the shooting schedule has been changed again, and the river scene that was originally scheduled for tomorrow is now being shot today.

Thanks to Molly's sassy improvisation outside the corral, the writers rewrote the entire episode, inserting Molly into this scene that previously only involved Grant. Originally the plan was for Grant to sneak across the river to the neighbor's shed to steal two cases of fireworks that are stored there. Now the plan is to have Molly tag after him.

"Chris," I say, charging up to him after reading the revised script. "Molly can't do this."

It's difficult to look him in the eye.

"Faye, good morning," he says cheerily. "I looked for you last night. Where'd you run off to? I was looking forward to picking up where we left off." Wink.

My stomach turns. How was I ever attracted to this man? His nose is too big for his face, his hair thinning, his chin too small. And he sleeps with women like Rhonda!

I swallow back the acid and ignore the innuendo. "Chris, Molly can't do this. She doesn't know how to swim."

"She doesn't have to swim," he says, distracted by something behind me. He walks past, and I follow. "She just needs to wade across, and Tom will be holding her hand. Beth, move camera one downstream and tell him to start wide so we see the whole river." Beth, who is now beside us, repeats the direction into her headset.

"What if she slips or he lets go?" I say.

"It's only knee-deep. Beth, that's good. Stop right there."

"Knee-deep on you is hip-deep on Molly." Then, propelled by the lingering shame of my conversation with Griff, with great courage, I add, "She can't do it. Molly doesn't know how to swim. She's not going in the river. I won't let her."

He turns and tilts his head. "Faye, no offense, but you really don't have any say in the matter."

I'm struck speechless then, a second later, manage, "Of course I do. I'm her mom."

"Exactly," Chris says. "You're her mom, and I'm her boss. The scene requires her to cross the river, so that's what she needs to do."

"What if I say no? If I refuse to let her do it?"

His lips curl into an amused smile. "Well, my goodness, what have we here? That kiss empowered you, did it? Turned me on too, but I didn't lose my head about it."

I blanch at the implication. "This has nothing to do with that. This is about Molly. Molly doesn't know how to swim."

"Settle down." Then he leans in close, his mouth next to my ear. "You keep going like this and I might have to call for a break so we can work off some of my excitement."

I feel my hand tensing to strike him. Instead I step back, my fury barely contained. "Molly's not doing this."

The smile drops from his face as he realizes I'm serious. "She is doing it. You signed a contract."

"I'm sure I didn't sign a contract that says I'm going to endanger my daughter's life."

"She'll be fine. You're overreacting."

"I'm not. Look at the river, there's a current." I'm painfully aware that my voice has become high-pitched and squeaky and that people are watching us.

His focus shifts to look past me but not to look at the river, his eyes on the shore as he yells over my shoulder, "Camera two, I need you focused on the shed. I want a reverse shot from Grant's perspective."

"Chris," I say, irritated beyond belief that he's ignoring me.

He turns back to me. "Look, Faye, here's the deal. I like you and I like Molly, but I have a show to produce. So either Molly does the scene like a good little actress or you pull your high-and-mighty mom act and she doesn't, and tomorrow I find another little girl who will, and the studio sues you for breach of contract. Molly's cute, but she's not irreplaceable. Your choice."

The wind goes out of me like I've been sucker punched. In the blink of an eye, Chris has gone from friend to enemy, making it clear that we are dispensable, his loyalty as thin as the hair on his head.

"Exactly," he says. "Door number one as I presumed." He walks away. "Places, people."

I stand frozen, the decision paralyzing me—stop the scene and it's over or let Molly walk across the river.

"I going in the watewr?" Molly says, walking up with Tom. A clear plastic bandage has been taped over her stitches and makeup painted on top of it that perfectly matches Molly's skin, her wound now protected and invisible.

"No. I mean, they want you to, but you don't need to. We don't have to do this. We don't have to do any of this. We can just leave. I can get another job, and we can go back to the way it was. If we stay living with Grandma, maybe I can still afford to pay for Emily to go to private school next year, or maybe they'll give us a scholarship. They really like her, and the soccer coach is excited about her joining his team. Maybe they'll offer us a discount so we can make it work." My words tumble out, and both kids are looking at me like I've lost it, which I have. I don't want to do this, and I don't want to not do this. I want to do this, but I don't want Molly to go into the river. That's what I want. "We'll be fine. I can return the car and get something less expensive. Namaka might take me back, but even if they don't, there are other restaurants..."

"You towld me not to go neawr the wrivewr," Molly says, interrupting my rambling.

"Exactly. You shouldn't go near the river because you don't know how to swim. So yes, you need to stay away from the river."

"But we're just going to walk across," Tom pipes in, his voice tight. "And I'm going to be holding her hand, and *I* know how to swim. We don't need to leave. We just need to walk across the river. Nothing's going to happen to her. I'm going to be holding on."

I feel his desperation. Unlike Molly, who can take acting or leave it, Tom is already crazy about his job. He rehearsed his part a dozen times last night and read through the scripts of the last three episodes so he would be up to speed on what's going on.

"Tom, yes, baby, you're just walking across, but the river is moving. What if you slip?"

"I won't. I won't slip, and I won't let go."

"I'wll howld on wreal tight," Molly offers, clearly not wanting to let her brother down.

"Places, everyone," Beth yells.

"One take," Chris says. "Drying everyone down and reshooting will take forever, so let's get it right the first time."

Tom looks at me anxiously. He wants this so bad.

My head shakes. This isn't a good idea.

"Come on, Tom," Molly says, making the decision for me and pulling Tom away before I can react.

My small lioness voice screams at me to stop them, but it's drowned out by the rushing water and the blood pounding in my ears, and I watch paralyzed as Beth's hand rises, her fingers counting down. "Action."

Tom's and Molly's sneakers are draped around their necks as they slide on their butts down the embankment—my eight-year-old son leading my four-year-old daughter, who doesn't know how to swim, into a river. And I know, regardless of how this turns out, this moment will not be forgotten, the moment I was too much of a coward to stand up for my kid and stop this from happening.

Their feet hit the water, and they shudder from the cold. I shudder with them. *Stop this. Stop them.* Still, I do not move. They move deeper, each step tentative as they measure their footing on the rocky bottom. *I am the worst mother on the planet.* Steadily they move forward, Tom being very careful, his face intent, his hand gripping Molly's wrist tightly. Even Molly looks serious, her brow puckered in concentration as she follows, checking her balance each time before lifting her foot to take another step.

The current is five feet away.

Four.

Three.

I lunge, my feet tripping on the uneven dirt. But before my sneakers touch the water, I know I am too late, my eyes fixed on the crosscurrent that I could not see from the shore. My mouth opens to warn Tom at the exact moment it pulls him unexpectedly sideways, his momentum yanking Molly forward and off her feet.

A dozen people race with me into the water, Chris among them, all of us splashing and tripping over rocks. A cameraman is in front of me, one of Griff's guys. Young and strong, he moves faster than the rest of us, covering the distance quickly and making me believe it is going to be all right.

Tom clings to Molly's wrist, holding on with both hands as the current pulls at her. She flounders face down, the water running over her. Tom's face is twisted with effort and panic, his muscles trembling. The man sees it as well and throws himself toward Molly at the exact moment her thrashing breaks Tom's hold, sweeping her out of reach and carrying her away.

I stumble after her, slipping and falling hard against a rock. Scrabbling to my feet, I lunge forward again, but Chris grabs me and yanks me toward shore. "Faye, stop."

I writhe and kick against him.

"She's okay," he says, but I don't hear him. My hand flies across his face, snapping his head sideways.

"She's okay," he says again, tying me up in his arms to keep me from slapping him again. "Griff has her."

The words make no sense.

I turn my head in the direction Molly was carried. *Griff has her.* Twenty feet downstream, Griff walks from the water, his thick arms wrapped around Molly as she clings to him, her face nuzzled against his neck.

Chris releases me, and I limp down the bank, my hip bruised from when I fell.

"I'm sorry, baby," I say as I take her from Griff's arms. "I'm so sorry."

Softly she sobs against my shoulder, her body trembling.

Chris walks up beside us. "Hey, Two-Bits."

"Leave us alone," I scream. "Don't you come near us."

Carrying Molly, I hobble away.

Tom catches up. "I'm sorry, Mom," he says. "I tried to hold on."

"It's not your fault, baby," I say. "It's mine. Molly had no business going in that river. It's my fault, nobody else's, just mine."

I stumble into the cabin, straight into the bathroom, and turn on the spigot to the tub.

"Hang in there, Bug. A warm bath will take away the chill."

She continues to cry quietly, and her tears destroy me. Never have I hated myself more.

"Can I do something?" Tom asks, and I look over to see his face white with guilt nearly as decimating as my own. I hold out my arm, and he walks into my embrace, and for a moment, the three of us sit on the bathroom floor clinging to each other.

When he pulls away, I say, "Go to the food truck and ask if they have chocolate ice cream and bring back a bowl."

"But we haven't even had bwreakfast," Molly says.

"I know, baby, but your mom got real scared, and the only thing that makes me feel better when I get that scared is chocolate ice cream. Would you like some as well?"

"Yeah, I do," she says, her tears drying.

"I'm on it. Two bowls of chocolate ice cream coming up," Tom says, sprinting away, desperate to help.

As I put Molly in the tub, there's a knock at the door, but I ignore it.

A moment later the door opens, causing me to turn.

Silhouetted in the opening is Chris. "Hey, Two-Bits," he says. "Ready to try again?"

46

The show did not go on.

Chris left, followed by my rant that I'm sure sounded insane to anyone within listening range. I had more than a few choice words and basically told him he could take his job and shove it. After he left, I calmed down, and Molly enjoyed chocolate ice cream while soaking in a warm bath, and I had a bowl of ice cream myself and stewed in my anger.

I have no idea if we are still employed by *The Foster Band* or Fox Studios, but what I do know is that Molly is never going into a river again because Chris Cantor or anyone else tells her to. And she won't ever again be put in a wrecked car to be pulled out by a drunk actor. I meant what I said—Chris Cantor, Beth, Fox Studios, the whole damn lot of them can go to hell. My baby's not going to be put in danger again.

After I pull Molly from her bath, I call Monique Braxton. She's as livid as I am over what happened. We're not as powerless as Chris made it sound. The contract I signed goes both ways. I'm not only Molly's mom, I'm her manager, and as such, I have the power to say no if his demands are out of line.

Our conversation is wrapping up when she says, "So, on another subject, I got a call yesterday from your husband."

"Sean called you?"

"Yeah. He wants me to send him a copy of Molly's contract with the Gap. He didn't mention anything about *The Foster Band* or about Tom, and I didn't bring it up. Anything I should be concerned about?"

I don't have it in me to conceal the truth, and at this point, I have nothing to lose and need to trust someone, and Monique Braxton seems like a good person to trust.

It takes nearly twenty minutes for me to tell her about the sad state of my marriage, about Sean's abandonment, and the truth about how we ended up in LA.

She listens patiently, ignoring the buzzing of other calls in the background, not rushing or interrupting me, which I appreciate enormously since it's a difficult confession and horribly humiliating.

I finish by telling her about Sean's reappearance in our life, and she gets real quiet then mutters, "Shit."

Turns out, I screwed up. Royally. I should have pressed charges for abandonment. I should have filed for legal separation.

Now, because I'm an idiot, Molly's contract and Tom's contract will be viewed as community property. Which means Sean is entitled to manage half the money that isn't put into the kids' mandatory fifteen-percent trust funds. It gets worse. She explains that in 2000 a new law was passed that makes a child's earnings the child's property, which sounds great except for the gaping loophole that doesn't provide any recourse against a parent misspending the child's money until the kid turns eighteen, at which time the kid can sue a parent, but usually by then it's too late and the money is already gone.

The double whammy is that even though Sean will only have access to half the kids' earnings, if he doesn't pay the taxes, the kids will be liable for those taxes when they turn eighteen. With penalties and compound interest, the amount could be staggering and could easily eat up their trusts. So, in other words, Molly and Tom could end up with nothing.

The only way to avoid this is for me to take the half I'm responsible for managing and, rather than invest it for their future, use it to pay the entire tax burden. This will guarantee that the trust funds will be safe, but it won't give them anything beyond that. The result of all this is that if Sean does what I think he will, takes his share and doesn't pay the taxes, the kids and I will end up living on my management income; Molly and Tom will get to keep fifteen percent of their earnings; and meanwhile, Sean will get three times what they get to keep for doing nothing.

"There's nothing I can do?" I ask when she finishes the explanation.

"You can try and convince your husband to do the right thing, pay the taxes he's supposed to pay and get a job to support himself so he doesn't need to live off his kids."

My heart sinks into my stomach. We're screwed. Sean lives by the mantra that only fools pay taxes. The day Molly and Tom become old enough to sue him, I'll encourage them to do so, but I also know it will be too late. Sean's never had two nickels to rub together. By the time they win a lawsuit against him, there won't be anything left.

Dinner is finished, and we are playing Candy Land in the living room when there is another knock at the door. I answer it expecting to find either Beth or Chris coming to tell us either we're fired or that they're sorry. I'm surprised when I open it and find Helen Harlow dressed in jeans and a T-shirt.

Even in pedestrian clothes she looks like a movie star, her hair shinier than the rest of the world's, her eyes sparkling like emeralds, her expression full of intrigue and drama, though she's neither smiling nor frowning.

"May I come in?"

I step aside to allow her entry.

"Hi, Miss Hewlen," Molly says, leaping to her feet and running into the woman's legs.

"Why hello," Helen says, clearly taken by surprise at Molly's jubilant greeting. She pats Molly's hair.

"We'wre pwlaying Candy Wland. You want to pwlay?"

"I'd love to," she says, shocking me.

Molly grabs her by the hand and pulls her to the coffee table. Emily's eyes bulge, and I feel Tom's voice disappear.

"Let me get you a chair," I offer.

"I'm fine on the floor," she says, sitting down Indian-style beside Molly before I have a chance to move.

"We'wll stawrt ovewr," Molly announces, gathering up the cards and restacking them.

"Ms. Helen can use my piece," I say. "I'm going to wash the dinner dishes."

Emily moves the pieces back to the start, and I watch in amazement as my kids play Candy Land with one of the most famous women in the world.

When I'm done in the kitchen, I return to the living room and curl my feet beneath me on the couch.

Helen laughs when Tom sends her piece packing back to Candy Cane Square.

"Sorry," he says, making my heart sing. His voice is still odd, as though he has a Boston accent, but it's loud and surprisingly confident.

"Just my luck," Helen says with a laugh.

On the next turn, Emily wins.

"Want to pwlay again?" Molly asks.

"Perhaps in a moment. First, I need to talk with your mom."

She stands with amazing grace for a woman near fifty, and the two of us walk onto the small porch in front of the cabin. It's a beautiful night. The rainstorm from the afternoon dissolved into a cloudless sky, and the humidity cooled off to a balmy warmth that makes me want to sleep beneath the stars.

"I'm glad to see Molly's okay," she starts.

I nod but say nothing, unsure of the reason she's here, wondering if Chris sent her.

The crickets have woken along with the frogs down by the river, and their chirps and croaks fill the silence as Helen figures out how to say whatever it is she came to say.

Her eyes look past me then, after a minute, return. "Did you know I was younger than Molly when I started in this business?"

I nod. Everyone knows Helen Harlow was born in the spotlight. The Pampers commercial she did when she was an infant is still shown sometimes.

"So this life is the only life I know." She stops again, her perfect arched brows furrowing over her famous eyes. "I know I'm going to regret this."

"Regret what?" I ask, having a hard time believing anything in my life is intriguing enough to make Helen Harlow uncomfortable.

"Getting involved," she says. "The golden rule in Hollywood is mind your own business, and here I am about to break it."

I laugh. "Nice rule, very compassionate."

"That's exactly it," she yelps, like I just revealed the missing link. "That's exactly what I came to say."

I shake my head, confused. The thing I've noticed about Helen Harlow is that, when the lines aren't given to her, she actually has a hard time making herself clear. Like the Rumpelstiltskin comment, she talks in riddles and is so dramatic that it's difficult to figure out what she's actually trying to say.

"In this business, there's no compassion, eat or be eaten, fend for yourself, lion eat lion and so forth. Welcome to the dog's den."

"That's why you came here, to welcome me to the lair?"

"Well, yes," she says, sounding angry. "Because you don't seem to get it."

"Sorry," I say. "I didn't realize I was bothering you."

"Well, you are. Watching you flail against Chris is like watching a lamb baaing at a lion as he licks his chops in anticipation of his next meal, and I actually lost about five minutes of sleep the other night because of it."

"Five whole minutes. Wow."

"I'm Helen Harlow—my sleep is important."

"Of course, your majesty. So what do you suggest? Perhaps the beheading of me and my children?"

"How about just of you, and I'll let your children be managed by someone like my mother?"

"A punishment worse than death," I jest.

"My mom would be the best thing that could happen to them," she snaps, and I realize I crossed the line.

"I'm sorry," I say sincerely, knowing better than to insult someone's family. I would feel the same way if she said something about my mom. It's okay for me to criticize her, not okay for anyone else to.

"You could learn a few lessons from my mom," she says. "No one messed with her, and no one messed with her kids. My mom instilled fear in directors and producers a whole lot more menacing than Chris. She had her regrets, mostly getting us into the business in the first place, and not getting my younger brother out sooner, but all in all she did good. We're all still here, and by Hollywood standards, that's a miracle."

"You think it's a miracle that you and your brothers survived? Don't you think that's a bit dramatic?"

"I am a diva, but no, I'm not being dramatic. Surviving without serious defect in this industry is definitely the exception, not the rule. Take a look at the child stars from the past two decades and see how many of them, a, are still alive, and, b, have survived without some sort of substance abuse, psychological issue, or eating disorder. Of the dozens of kids I've performed with, I can count on a single hand those who found some sort of contentment as adults—that includes me and my brothers."

"That only leaves two fingers," I say.

"Exactly. I'm not saying it can't happen, and for me, thanks to my mom, this has been a blessed life, but I'd need to have my head in the sand not to notice it hasn't been happily ever after for most of the others. And the way you're going, Molly's not going to be landing on one of my fingers soon. You've been on the set less than a month and already she's landed in the hospital once and nearly drowned."

"So you came here to tell me I suck. Thank you. Had you not stopped by I might not have realized that."

"I came here to tell you you're annoying me," she says. "My mom might have had a reputation as a bitch, but none of us would have ended up in that river today. She was the fiercest stage mom in the business because she knew otherwise we would drown."

Her choice of words is no accident.

I close my eyes and sigh, feeling completely defeated. "I'm not cut out for this."

"No one is," she says. "This business is ruthless, and there's no training. New recruits are thrown into the deep end, and you either learn to swim with the big fish or you become fish bait. So unless you're calling it quits, you need to grow a pair of cojones."

I laugh at that expression coming out of her pretty, pink lips.

She smiles back. "Griff isn't always going to be there to save her."

I rear back. In the emotions of the day, I actually forgot about Griff and that he was the one who pulled Molly from the river.

"Shit," I say. "I mean shoot."

She smiles.

"I never thanked him. I…Today was so crazy…Molly was upset, and then…I can't believe I didn't thank him. I keep doing that, screwing up with that guy. Ugh!"

"So thank him now."

"I can't. After what happened today, I don't want to leave Molly alone."

"I'll watch them."

"You?"

She looks hurt. "I am a mom myself, you know."

Until this moment, I forgot she was a mother. Two daughters. They must be college-age now or older.

"I'm actually going to be a grandmother in a month. Talk about tough on the diva ego. I still can't decide if I'm going to let the kid call me Grandma."

She shudders, and I laugh.

"Go," she says. "We're fine. I love Candy Land."

47

In front of the crew's barracks, a two-story building that looks like a budget motel, heads lift as I approach. I recognize most of them—cameramen, grips, sound techs. They sit around a fire pit. One of them strums a guitar, another plays along on a harmonica. When I get close, the music, laughter, and conversation stop. A few offer mechanical smiles, but most don't bother. I'm on their turf after quitting time, and I'm not welcome here.

But I'm one of you, I want to say. *I love sitting around a campfire, listening to music, and roasting marshmallows.*

With a small smile of *I mean you no harm*, I move past, and the music and conversation resume.

My feet carry me to where I know Griff is, the same place he was yesterday, swimming in the wide part of the river. I round the last bend, and there he is, his back facing me—broad, bare, and spotted with drops of water.

He turns. "Took you long enough," he says loudly. He has a beer in his hand, and I realize he might be drunk.

My mouth glubs. "You've been waiting for me?"

"Well, go on, spit it out. Thank you. You're wonderful. My next child will be named in your honor, blah, blah, blah…" Belch.

"Why are you waiting out here for me?"

"You think I'm going to let you grovel in front of my crew? That's just what I need, to put on a performance for my guys."

"A performance?"

"Pretend I'm fucking pissed off because Molly almost got hurt and they think it's your fault. Those guys really like Molly."

"You don't think it's my fault?"

"Of course it's your fault. I'm just not pissed at you."

"You're not mad?"

"Livid as hell, just not at you. Damn asshole."

I figure he's talking about Chris.

"Can't blame a squid for not having a vertebrae."

Now he's talking about me.

"Or for being sliced and diced into calamari by a fucking shark. Damn, that's a hell of a metaphor. I should write that down." He swallows the remainder of the beer and drops the bottle to the dirt.

"You're drunk."

"Maybe. How many bottles are on the ground?"

I step closer. "Twelve."

"Then I'm only half-drunk," he says, looking around to locate an untouched six-pack on the dirt behind him. He pulls out one of the bottles, twists off the top, and takes a swig.

"How about I help you back to camp?" I say, hating that he's so drunk that he might not remember this conversation, which means I'll need to thank him again.

"The squid wants to help. I'll tell you how you can help. Help me out by telling me what the hell you see in that guy. I mean, really, inquiring minds want to know. That asshole puts your kid in danger, she lands in the hospital, and the next thing you know, you're trading saliva with him in the pasture."

Blood rushes to my face. "How'd you..."

"Know? Hell, everyone knows. You're lucky your little make-out session wasn't on the six o'clock news. I mean, Rhonda you expect to be doing that shit, but you almost seem normal."

"I am normal."

"Yeah, see? Almost normal." He toasts me with his half-empty beer. "Except for the lack of backbone and your fetish for assholes." He grins again. "Boy, I'm on a roll."

"What you're on is a bender," I say. "Come on, let's get you back to camp."

He chuckles. "ME go back to camp with YOU. Ha!" Then, "Ha, ha, ha, ha, ha," until he's laughing so hard that his whole body is shaking. "ME..." He points at himself and nearly falls off his rock then points at me. "With YOU."

"Okay, big boy, let's go."

Sean's been known to tie one on, and I've supported him out of plenty of bars. Griff's bigger than Sean, linebacker size, but I think I can manage. "Upsy-daisy. They're making s'mores and hot dogs back at camp, and I bet I can scrounge up some coffee."

"Show up with Chris's sloppy seconds," he slurs. "Never live that one down." Belch. "I'm drunk, but I'm not that drunk. Thanks, but I'll find my own way back."

He stumbles to his feet, takes a step forward, loses his balance, falls back, trips over the rock, and lands flat on his back in the water, his eyes closed.

Crap. The current pulls at him, turning his body and trying to tug him from shore.

I wade in, grab hold of his arm, and drag him onto the dirt. The guy weighs like seven hundred pounds, and when I'm done, I'm soaked, breathless, and pissed.

I plop onto the rock where he had been sitting, pop open a beer, and call Emily on my cell phone. She puts Helen on, and I explain what happened and that it's going to be a while and that she doesn't have to stay. She assures me that she's fine staying and that she'd rather be hanging out with my kids than babysitting Griff by the river.

"Faye," she says as I'm about to hang up.

"Yeah?"

"Take care of him. He's one of us."

48

Us.

I love being one of "us."

I sit beside the set contemplating who exactly "us" is.

Griff, who looks miserable this morning—hunkered and moving slow, sunglasses on—is a confirmed us, as is Helen and myself. Griff's cameramen along with the grips and lighting techs are tight with Griff, so I assume they're with us. Henry's too awesome not to be part of us and so is Jeremy. The ones I can't decide on are Jules, Caleb, Gabby, the sound crew, or the craft service folk.

My us-ness is comforting. Like knowing what table to sit at in the high school cafeteria, suddenly I belong. I'm nearly giddy with the inclusion, and my happiness makes me realize how lonely I've been. In Yucaipa, I had Bo, our neighbors, the ranch hands, the moms of my kids' friends, but in LA, other than my mom, I have no one.

Emily has definitely found her crowd as well. As we wait for the crew to finish setting up the next scene, she hangs out a few feet away with Caleb, Gabby, and Miles's two sisters. They're laughing and joking, and Emily seems right at home, happy and popular like she used to be in Yucaipa.

Caleb says something funny, and my eyes bulge as I watch her giggle with undeniable guile. She's working it. My twelve-year-old daughter just tittered like a temptress—her eyes looking up through her long lashes, her hair draping seductively across one eye. And Caleb is eating it up, nudging her playfully with his shoulder.

My focus instinctively shifts to Gabby and Miles's sisters. All three wear frozen expressions of fake support. Four girls and one superstar boy equals trouble. Miles's sisters are harmless. Like Emily, they are young and goofy, and though envious of the attention Emily's getting, they're fine being spectators. Gabby is another story. Though she's three years older than Caleb, her attraction is beyond that of friend. All you need to do is watch the way she looks at him to know she has feelings for him.

Emily and Caleb are oblivious to the insincere grins around them, their attention completely on each other, Caleb making lame jokes and showing off while Emily says things like, "No way," "That's so cool," and "Will you teach me how to do that?" Neither knows quite what to do with their limbs or how to position their mouths, and it's a bit like watching two baby giraffes learning to walk, both cute and excruciating at the same time.

Helen walks from the commissary with two cups of coffee and offers me one.

"I think Griff needs this more than I do," I say.

"Let him suffer. Damn fool. He knows he can't hold his alcohol."

Sensing we're talking about him, he turns, and Helen toasts him with her coffee. He flips her off, and she toasts him again. After I called Helen last night, she called his lead cameraman, and a few minutes later, four of Griff's crew arrived and carried him back to the barracks.

A moment passes in silence until I say, "Thank you again for last night."

"I should thank you. Normally I find these trips tedious, but last night was fun. Molly's a riot. There's a little naughty in that package."

I laugh. "Did double red turn into triple red?"

"More than once. Tom and Emily moved her right back in place. Then the next turn, she'd do it again, totally innocently, like she just miscounted."

"She is persistent."

"But also very entertaining as all the world will soon find out."

"I hope so, but that's not why I was thanking you. I appreciate you watching them, but I was thanking you for coming to the cabin in the first place and for this." I lift my coffee.

"You might not want to thank me after you taste it. It's awful."

"For including me," I say, not letting her sidetrack the conversation. "Really, you have no idea how much it means to me. So thank you. Really, last night..."

"Stop," she snaps, cutting me off. "Would you just stop already?"

I blink rapidly at her abruptness.

She frowns and groans, then says, "Crud, you really are a pain in my rear end."

I have no idea what I've done to piss her off, so I stay quiet.

"It wasn't even my idea. Last night I didn't even want to go to your cabin. It was Griff's idea, so stop thanking me."

"Griff?"

"Yeah, the big oaf. He called and told me he was getting shitfaced waiting for you to show up to thank him and asked if I could I give you a nudge. I told him I didn't even know you, and he told me to get off my high horse and get to know you, that you seemed like you were all right."

"But Griff hates me. He called me a squid."

She laughs. "He calls me an ice queen. Says I'm so cool I could freeze a thermal reactor."

"You are cool," I say, "but in a good way."

She gives a resigned smile at my insistence to adore her then says, "Not today. Damn it's hot out here."

As if to confirm the statement, a gust of furnace air puffs, making the already oppressive heat so warm that it stifles the conversation.

"Places, people," Beth says.

"Helen?" I say, before she can turn her back to get into character. "How did Griff get there so fast? In the river—how was he able to get to Molly before the rest of us?"

"He was waiting downstream. He knew what was going to happen before it happened. That's the way it is with Griff. He has a sixth sense for trouble."

The moment they start the rehearsal, I run to the commissary.

Fifteen minutes later I return, march up to Griff, and hold out my coffee cup. "Peace offering," I say.

"Coffee. Yes. I accept."

He takes a sip and nearly spits it out. "That's not coffee. Are you trying to poison me?"

"It will cure what ails you. Trust me."

He holds it out to hand it back. "I'd rather suffer."

"Baby." I refuse to accept it. "Drink it down like a good boy, and I promise not to tell your crew what really happened last night."

His eyes bulge, and I give a wink, pivot, and return to my seat. Today is so much more fun than yesterday.

"Why is Griff pinching his nose as he drinks his coffee?" Helen says. "And why is he guzzling it like that?"

I shrug and smile.

∽

Poor Rhonda.

I actually feel sorry for her.

Chris has an amazing ability to literally forget everything that happened before, good or bad. By the way he's behaving, you'd never know that yesterday Molly almost drowned, that he threatened to fire us, or that, for the second night in a row, he screwed Rhonda's brains out.

Today he acts like she doesn't exist, ignoring her even when she gives his butt a squeeze as she brushes past.

I'm not a fan of Rhonda's, but pangs of sympathetic understanding clench my heart as I watch her desperation grow. She thinks this might be the start of something, and as a single mom I relate to how infrequently possible somethings come along. Only two days ago, I also considered Chris as a man with future potential—reliable, caring, passionate, respectable, devoted. Ha! It's amazing how a hard wish can distort things.

Embarrassed as I am about kissing Chris, I know now that I dodged a bullet. No matter how much I tried to convince myself I was just in it for fun, I'm not wired that way. If I would have slept with him, I would have expected something to come of it. And like Rhonda, my heart would have pounded in confusion and panic if Chris went about his day as if nothing had happened.

On top of my sympathy, I'm also embarrassed for her. Everyone knows. Eyes follow her as do snickers and whispers. Their tryst might as well have been projected on the side of the barn, and I'm horribly thankful it's her and not me they're cackling about.

Griff gives me a smile and a thumbs-up, and I return the gesture, glad to see my surefire hangover cure of pickle juice and Sprite is working its magic and that he's feeling better. He returns to contemplating the angle for the next shot, and I return to contemplating him.

I find myself looking at him a lot today, surprised by what I see. It's as if I'm seeing him for the first time and am shocked I was so blind. If you would have asked me yesterday to describe him, I would have said lumberjack or mountain man—big, rugged, gruff. The beard and his size give that impression, a burly man of brute strength rather than good looks, but if you look close, he's far more refined, his posture straight, the features beneath his beard chiseled. Despite his efforts to appear otherwise, Griff is more royalty than knight, and it makes me wonder why he wears the disguise.

49

Our week at the farm is finished. Molly has a few short retakes, then we can get on the road. I'm anxious and not anxious to get home. I need to deal with the Sean issue, and I'm dreading dealing with the Sean issue.

I call Emily to tell her to finish up with her friends. She answers on the fifth ring, her voice dreamy. For the past three days, she and Caleb have been inseparable. Last night they sat on the porch whispering until nearly midnight. When they stopped whispering, I got concerned, but when I peeked outside, they were just sitting on the steps holding hands, Emily's head resting on Caleb's shoulder.

I'm nearly as happy for Caleb as I am for Emily. The kid is always on his own. Union rules say that a guardian needs to be on the set with a minor at all times, but I have yet to meet either of Caleb's parents or anyone who is looking out for him. This week I've taken him under our wing, and I can feel his relief. Like me, he's happy to be part of an "us."

"Hey, Em, we need to get going."

Emily sighs then tells me she'll be over in a minute.

I smile at her lovesickness, vaguely remembering the feeling, the blissful wonder and optimism of first love, innocently believing your devotion will last forever and carry you through anything—precious and beautiful, before reality and disappointment make you cynical.

Chris barks at a sound tech, causing me to turn my attention back to the set to find Griff looking at me. He screws up his face so he looks like Elmer Fudd, and I laugh. The guy is very funny.

Chris sees the exchange. "Griff, get your damn head in the game."

Chris is not happy that I have become an "us." Like the star high school quarterback, he is pissed off that I've chosen to hang with the outcasts instead of the cool kids.

Since the river incident, I've made it clear that the only relationship I want with him is a professional one, but he refuses to take the hint, and I actually find myself avoiding him so he won't corner me and strike up another conversation full of not-at-all-subtle innuendo.

It is not only annoying but cruel. Yesterday, while blatantly pursuing me, he was callously disregarding Rhonda. And as a result, Rhonda turned *Fatal Attraction* scary, wailing and pounding on his cabin door, demanding he let her in. The whole camp could hear her, and it was horribly humiliating. Finally Henry was able to reason with her and led her away.

This morning, Rhonda is gone, and Miles's dad is on the set instead. The guy seems okay. Ex-military, he walks with a limp and seems to always be in pain, but he takes care of Miles and Miles's sisters with a devotion I respect. He certainly doesn't seem like the bloodsucking sponge Rhonda said he was. He wears old Levi jeans, still uses a flip phone, and doesn't seem enamored in the least by the stars or glitter around him. Mostly he looks tired and worn out, and I can't decide if it's from his service in the war or his marriage to Rhonda.

Emily shuffles up and hugs me around the waist. "Hi, Mom," she says, laying her head against my ribs, and I need to stop myself from laughing at her lovesick languor.

"Want to help me pick up a few things for the trip home?"

She nods and takes my hand, swinging it between us as we walk. A few feet from the corner of the commissary, she stops and puts her finger to her lips.

Gabby's voice reaches us first. "Really, Caleb? Of all the girls in the world, that's who you choose to hook up with?"

"She's cool."

"Really?"

"Yeah, really."

"She's a hayseed who buys her clothes at Walmart and who has never seen the inside of a salon."

Emily's hand tenses in mine.

"I like her," Caleb says, but his voice lacks conviction.

"Christ, Caleb, you have supermodels giving you room keys. Have you seen your fan mail?"

"Chill, Gabs. It's not like we're a thing."

"Thank God. Could you imagine the field day *Tiger Beat* would have with that? You with Emily nobody?"

"The press isn't going to find out."

"They will if you keep seeing her. Caleb, I'm your friend. Emily isn't one of us. You get that, right?"

"Yeah, I get it."

"You sure?"

"Yeah, I said, I get it. It's not like I'm going to see her after today. She was here, and it was easy. That's all it was."

Like a fist to the solar plexus, the air goes out of me, my ribs caving inward as Emily whirls and races away.

My first instinct is to chase after her, but instead, I follow my second instinct and march forward, rounding the corner just as Gabby says, "That's good. I thought you were really losing it there for a minute. Really, Caleb, you're a star. You're way too good for that girl."

Caleb's face goes pale when he sees me. Gabby barely reacts.

I ignore her and focus on him, my nostrils flaring as I take a deep breath to light into him. But as I open my mouth, I find I can't do it. His jaw quivers, and his expression is so sad that it makes me realize that this horrible moment will define not only Emily but also this boy. And so, because I love my daughter more than I love anyone, I am cruel, and rather than yelling, I confirm his thoughts. "You just lost the best thing that ever happened to you."

I turn to Gabby. "Why don't you go stick a spoon up your nose? You look like you're running low on energy." I have no idea if the rumors of Gabby's drug use are true, but it's the first thing that comes to mind, so that's what I say. If there's one thing I've learned in the past month, it's that it actually doesn't matter if rumors are true. It only matters if they're perceived to be true. Gossip can ruin you.

She sneers at me. "I don't do drugs."

"You should," I say. "Might help you lose weight." I'm stunned by the depth of my meanness but also not. She hurt my baby, and at this moment, I want to hurt her back, which judging by the darkness of her features, I have.

Three kids decimated in a matter of minutes. And as I run back toward the cabin to pick up the pieces of my daughter's shattered heart, I wish life had a rewind button so I could turn back time and have us not walk up to the commissary when we did, to have us not listen at the exact moment that Gabby was being a jealous, catty teenager with a crush on a boy who is in love with someone else. Because I know, no matter what I say to Emily, words won't fix this. Like a fire that destroys a house, with time you can rebuild, but it will never be the same and you will never feel as secure.

50

We're halfway to the elevator, pulling our new roller suitcases, when Sean steps into the parking garage from the street. "Hey, kids."

"Daddy." Molly drops the handle of her bag and runs straight into Sean's outstretched arms. He lifts her and twirls her around.

Emily also leaves my side, shuffling over to him and burying her head against his stomach. "Hey, M&M. What's the matter, babe?"

His genuine concern makes me want to scream. He's never there when the actual calamity strikes but somehow always manages to appear after, swooping in like a superhero.

Emily sniffles and sobs. "I need new clothes," she says, shocking me.

Sean looks to me for translation.

"She doesn't need new clothes. What she needs is new friends."

Emily's head shakes against Sean's shirt. "No. I need new clothes. I'm dressed like a farm girl, and if I'm going to live here, I need to dress better."

I can't believe that is what she is taking from the experience.

"Well, luckily that's something your old man can take care of. The Galleria's right around the corner. Let's go."

"Sean, no," I say.

"You want to come with us?"

My mouth opens, then snaps shut, then opens again. "No. And they're not going either. We need to go upstairs and unpack."

"Okay, kids. It looks like it's just us. Let's go." With the girls attached to him, he walks toward the street.

Tom hesitates.

"Tom, you coming?" Sean asks with a glance back.

Tom looks at me, his loyalties torn.

"Go," I say, mustering up a fake smile. "Have fun."

He trots after them, and my smile drops, my heart thumping erratically in my chest. Something very bad is happening, a dark force creeping toward me that I feel but am powerless to stop.

I watch as they climb into a brand-new red convertible Mustang parked at the curb, and my eyes bulge at the sheer expense of it, knowing the only way Sean could afford a car like that is if he sold his rig.

"Top up or down?" he asks.

"Down," Molly squeals, and the black top collapses into the trunk.

They drive away, and I am left alone in the garage with the bags.

51

My nails are nibbled to nubs. The laundry is done, and the condo is spotless. I've baked cookies and written a list of everything that needs to be done in my life—at the top of the list, *Call Divorce Lawyer*, underscored three times. I sip a beer as I stare at the list, hoping the alcohol will settle my irritation.

I wish my mom were here. While we were gone, she took the opportunity to visit a friend in San Francisco, and she doesn't get back until tomorrow. Strange how I've grown used to her company. She still nags and annoys, but I find comfort in it. Like an irritating conscience sitting on my shoulder, her pestering is reassuring, letting me know when I'm being an idiot and when I'm doing all right. Like I know right now she'd be having a fit, screeching at me for what a mess I've made of things, but then she'd sit down and help me figure it out.

It's one of the reasons I haven't gotten us a place of our own. Though I hate to admit it, I like living with my mom, and I know she likes it too. If we move out, something precious will be lost, all the unplanned moments we share together.

She would be proud of how I stood up to Chris and blown away that Tom started talking and got himself hired as Grant. I want to tell her about Helen and Griff, and how now we're all friends.

The last thought makes me smile, and I wish I had Griff's number so I could text him something stupid like, *Silly rabbit, Trix are for kids*. He would get it because it makes no sense, and most of our jokes are like that, nonsensical randomness that somehow makes us laugh.

I could use a laugh right now, my irritation at critical mass. It pisses me off that the kids love Sean so much. Part of me feels like they should love me enough not to love him. I know that's wrong, but being here alone while they're off with him is awful. And so while I know it isn't fair to make them choose, I want them to choose, and I want them to choose me.

He left us, abandoned them. How can they forgive him so easily? Shamefully I recognize that I also considered forgiving him and taking him back.

Why? Do I think so little of myself?

The answer is instant and absolute—a simple, universal truth: *We all want to be loved and loneliness is a powerful elixir for forgiveness.* Our need to have someone care about us is as rudimentary as hunger, and it allows us to overlook faults and accept less than we want or deserve.

My thoughts are so distracted that I'm startled when the door opens and Molly walks in. "Hi, Mom," she singsongs. "We'wre back."

Tom follows, and my eyes bulge at his new getup of camo fatigues with a black T-shirt. He looks like a thug. I frown at the skull cap low on his head and the leather band with studs on his wrist—the ensemble similar to an outfit Grant would wear on the show.

"Hey," he says, the attitude and voice not my son's.

Emily is transformed as well, her heartbreak that was so gut-wrenching only hours ago manifested into a disturbing adaptation. Her long, wavy hair has been sheared to shoulder length, and her outfit—a plaid mini-skirt, tight white tank top, and knee-high black leather boots—looks like something Kira would wear. The new look is edgy and sexy, and combined with her natural height makes her look closer to seventeen than twelve.

Sean follows them in and sets at least six expensive-labeled bags beside the door.

I expect him to turn and leave, but instead, without even a glance my way, he follows Emily to the couch and sits down beside her. Leaning back, he drapes his arm over her shoulder and pulls Molly onto his lap, his body language suggesting he's settling in for a while.

"Excuse me," I say.

"Mexico versus the US is on," Emily says excitedly, clicking to a channel showing a soccer match.

"Sean," I say.

He glances back but makes no effort to move, like he belongs here, like this is his home.

"Damn, they're already down," he says, his attention turning back to the screen.

"By how much?" Tom says in his strange voice as he sits on the other side of Sean.

Unsure how to move him, I pivot from the meteor that crash-landed in the middle of my life and return to my list, underlining *Call Divorce Lawyer* three more times.

52

Molly twirls in a circle, her black skirt flaring around her thighs, the bedazzled edge winking in the light. Her denim overalls have been cast aside for our big night—her night—the night of the season premiere.

At six o'clock, the first episode of season four of *The Foster Band* will be aired to millions on the East Coast, an hour later it will be in the middle of the country, and two hours after that it will reach California. It will continue its journey around the globe until it finishes its travels fifteen hours later in Cuba, at which point an estimated forty-four million people will have been introduced to Molly.

The studio is hosting a party for all the people involved in the show and their families. Three hundred people will be there. The event is being held at the Park Plaza Hotel, and a limo is being sent to pick us up.

I've never been in a limo. I've never been to an event in a ballroom at a five-star hotel. I've never been to a premiere party. And I've never watched my daughter star in the number one show on television! My cheeks hurt from my constant smile.

My mom is my plus-one for the night, and her excitement exceeds my own. The dress she wears—a gauzy, taupe gown with a low neckline—emphasizes her proudest feature, her bodacious bust. It is the twelfth gown she's bought since I invited her to join us two weeks ago, the other eleven returned to the frustrated Nordstrom's saleswoman who was helping her. Her hair is freshly highlighted, and this afternoon she had her makeup professionally done. Sometimes I forget how beautiful my mom is, but she really is a stunner—tall and blond with curves that turn heads.

I take a final glance in the mirror to assess my own transformation, and my smile grows. My dress, a simple indigo silk slip that hugs tight at the bodice and flares at my hips, was an extravagance. But how many times in my life am I going to go to a once-in-a-lifetime event like this? I swish back and forth, admiring the way the liquid fabric opens and closes seductively around my legs.

"Em, the limo's here," I holler toward the bedroom.

I'm slightly concerned about Emily's reunion with Caleb. The two haven't seen each other since we left the farm a month ago. She assured me when we went dress shopping that it would be fine and that she was over it, but mother's intuition is telling me otherwise.

Something has changed in Emily since our return, a subversive secretiveness that concerns me. Most of her time is spent alone in her room, and when she does come out, she divulges little about her day, her friends, or her life.

School started a week ago—her first year of middle school—and I blame it on that, a new stage in which she is simply figuring out how she fits in and who she is. The private school she's enrolled in is near the studio and caters specifically to children who are either celebrities, the children of celebrities, or the siblings of celebrities. The school is safe and convenient, and Emily seems much happier than she was at public school. The school's soccer coach has taken a real shine to her, and she now plays on his club team, which keeps her busy every afternoon and on the weekends.

The school costs a small fortune, but luckily I only need to pay for Emily since Tom's role as Grant allows him to attend studio school.

Life has worked out grand for Tom. Thanks to his new career, he no longer needs to contend with the overwhelming challenge of public school with its unruly classrooms and dozens of classmates. Studio school is only three hours a day and usually only consists of him and Miles and the studio teacher.

"Em, let's go," I yell again.

She steps from the room, and I gasp.

"Em, that's not the dress we chose. What happened to…? Where's the…? You're not wearing that!"

Her dress, if you can call it that, is a narrow tube of vanilla sequins cropped at her thighs and chest. On her feet are a pair of gold platform heels at least six inches tall.

My phone buzzes. It's the limo driver texting again to let us know he's waiting.

"Get changed," I say. "Now."

"I can't. I returned the dress we bought for this one." A glimmer of a smile curls her red-painted lips. "This is the only dress I have."

Heat creeps up my chest to my face. She planned this, timing it so I'm left with the impossible decision of letting her go in a tramp outfit or telling her she can't go, which would mean either my mom or I have to stay home as well.

"She looks fine," my mom says, clearly realizing the options as well and choosing option number one. "Come on, Faye, let's go."

I glare at Emily. She is definitely her father's daughter; this is exactly the kind of stunt Sean would pull. It's possible he even put her up to it.

My divorce lawyer told me I need to let Sean see the kids. So the way it's been working between us is that the weekends are now his, an arrangement that, quite frankly, sucks. While I'm responsible for getting the kids to school and work and for rehearsing their lines and giving them baths and helping them with their homework, Sean is responsible for nothing but taking them to the beach or the movies or amusement parks and bringing them back Sunday night stumbling tired, drunk with love for their dad, and their heads filled with his off-color ideas of right and wrong and how to deal with the issues in their lives.

He probably even returned the dress with Emily, the two of them tittering with glee as they hatched the plan, identical smirks on their faces, like the one she wears now. I hate it when I see him so clearly in them, the man I hate manifested in the kids I love, confusing the notions of love and hate until they're muddled into a maddening brew that makes me want to slam a sledgehammer into a wall.

Grabbing a dishcloth from the counter, I hold it under the sink, march over to my twelve-year-old daughter, and wipe the expression from her face along with the rouge, lipstick, and mascara she caked on. There are black smudges beneath her eyes, but at least her face no longer looks like a hooker's.

If looks could kill, I'd be dead, her laser-green eyes piercing me, but luckily all her vicious glare does is make me smile.

"Now we can go," I say.

"I'll just put it on again when we get to the party," she says.

"And I'll just wipe it off again, and I'll do it in front of everyone, with Caleb front and center."

She storms past, wobbling on her ridiculous shoes, and as I follow, I wonder how it got this bad this fast. Only four short months ago, she was my little girl who didn't give a damn about clothes and who would have laughed at a girl like the one she's become.

53

There's a red carpet! An actual strip of four-foot-wide plush red walkway leads from the limousine to the entrance of the Park Plaza Hotel.

And paparazzi!

A virtual ocean of press crowds the runway, the throng kept at bay by a wedge of bodyguards that stand like tuxedo-clad pillars parting the sea to protect the passage to the promised land.

It's all very exciting.

Cameras flash, and reporters shout out, "Molly, look this way." "Over here." "Give us a smile."

A woman with a clipboard beside the entrance asks my mom, Tom, Emily, and me to step to the side so the press can get some shots of Molly alone. She looks absolutely darling, her smile radiant as she waves and twirls and curtsies for the crowd.

My mom grasps my hand and gives it a squeeze.

What a moment. I hold her hand tight to keep myself from jumping up and down with the sheer joy of it.

We are ushered into the grand ballroom, and my breath catches. It's the most glamorous room I've ever seen—marble columns, crystal chandeliers, painted cornices, a stage with a twelve-piece band playing jazz.

Centerpieces the size of cars stuffed with white roses adorn fifty black-clothed tables, and hundreds of stunning people in gorgeous gowns and tuxedos sit and mingle around them.

By the time we reach our table, I'm breathless—my eyes, ears, and nose working triple time to take it all in, my brain buzzing with disbelief that we are a part of it.

Our table is near the front, and already seated there are Miles, his two sisters, and his dad. Since her meltdown at the farm, Rhonda has vanished, and Miles's dad has taken over as Miles's manager.

Tonight he looks uncomfortable, a pinched expression of endurance on his face like he already can't wait for the night to end.

My mom sits beside him and his disposition lightens. I blush as she introduces herself with a slight bow so her assets are well presented, a gesture not lost on Miles's dad, whose eyes obediently follow her lead before self-consciously snapping back to her face.

I look around for Griff and spot him standing beside a table one row over speaking with Helen. No date. Surprise and relief wash over me. Which is very selfish. Griff treats me like his kid sister, calls me Squid, and teases me every chance he gets about kissing Chris, making it very clear that he's not romantically interested in me in the least. The problem is, the clearer he makes his disinterest, the more attractive he becomes.

Feeling my stare, he looks my way and gives his signature Elmer Fudd grin, which I ricochet back at the exact moment the band stops playing and the room grows dark, and my heart leaps in my chest as my feet leap toward my chair. Everyone around me hurries into their seats as well, chairs scraping against the floor as they maneuver for a clear view of the massive screen that has descended in front of the stage.

My pulse pounds in time with the seconds ticking down, then the room begins a unified, thunderous countdown. "Ten, nine, eight, seven, six, five, four, three, two, one." Showtime.

So quiet you can hear a pin drop, a commercial for the season premiere of *Deathfinder* finishes, then the opening credits for *The Foster Band* roll, and the crowd bursts into a short ovation before quickly quieting again, then the "previously on *The Foster Band*" segment finishes and the show begins.

The first half of the episode doesn't involve Molly, and my pulse settles as I relax into spectator mode. The show is so different from the performances that created it that I almost forget it's a product of the work we did. The music and sound effects combined with the camera angles are completely transformative. And the editors did an amazing job, each scene pieced together for maximum impact. I understand now why we did so many takes, why each line was said six times, ten times, a hundred times. The final version is the best of all those tries spliced together into seamless perfection.

Molly appears and my heart explodes with pride and awe. She's so much larger than life, so much grander than the little girl sitting beside me bouncing her legs and slurping her Sprite. The scene is the one of her and Miles arriving with their dad at Mr. Foster's office and the dad collapsing of a heart attack.

Beside me, my mom dabs her eyes with a napkin when Molly starts to cry. I look around and several other women are dabbing their eyes as well. *Way to go, Molly!*

The final scene is of Molly and Miles being driven away from the hospital with Mr. and Mrs. Foster watching. Molly looks through the car window and lifts her hand in a final good-bye, and a fraction of a second later, the car is T-boned by the ambulance, jettisoning it onto the sidewalk as the audience is thrown back in their seats by a wall of noise and blinding light.

I knew it was coming, and I still nearly jumped out of my chair. The scene, which was dramatic when shot, is now mind-blowing—the special effects and sound editing amplifying it to epic proportions.

Mr. Foster runs toward the car as Mrs. Foster screams at him to stop. Molly cries out, and the show ends. Then the audience is on their feet applauding, and I stand with them, my heart bursting with pride.

54

There is a champagne fountain for the adults and a chocolate fountain for everyone. Dinner is filet mignon or sea bass, and the bar is open.

Work hard, party harder seems to be the motto, and before the band finishes its first set, people are dancing on tables and letting loose. Tom and Miles are in a corner playing a game with bottle caps, and to my chagrin but not surprise, Emily has reunited with Caleb, the two giggling beside the caviar bar. Molly is on the dance floor and being passed around like a hot potato, twirling and bopping and sashaying her way into everyone's hearts.

My mom and Helen have struck up a conversation, and I know this will be remembered as one of the greatest moments of my mom's life, the night she hung out with the great Helen Harlow at the Park Plaza Hotel.

Funny how quickly the stardust has left my own eyes. Only two months ago, I too was awed by these people. Now they are mere humans, some exceptionally talented, but with flaws and problems like everyone else.

My dress, which I thought was so glamorous, pales in comparison to the glitter of the bedazzled designer gowns and bling sparkling around me. Diamonds, rubies, and sapphires, not the costume variety, adorn the necks and wrists and ears of most of the women and some of the men.

I wander, fascinated by the spectacle and catching glimpses of conversations. Most of the discussions are about wealth or vanity, what bargains are to be had, what investments will triple or quadruple fortunes, what new surgeries are all the rage—procedures to extend youth, the ultimate commodity in Hollywood.

The chocolate fountain is four tiers of decadence cascading to pool into a three-foot-wide bittersweet pond at its base. A woman dressed in a white uniform stands behind it with a rag in her hand to keep it clean. She is my age, perhaps a little older, a gold band on her left ring finger. I wonder if she has kids. Judging by the darkness beneath her eyes, I think she does.

I rake a strawberry through the sweet waterfall and take a bite. The chocolate is dark and smooth, the kind imported from an exotic faraway place like Belgium or Ethiopia or Venezuela. I stare at the gallons flowing like brown silk and wonder what will happen to the chocolate that isn't used.

"Dance?"

My face lights up when I turn to see Griff extending his hand. Taking his outstretched palm, I try to disguise the jolt that ignites on contact then my disappointment when his expression doesn't change at all, no reaction whatsoever to me, my touch, my dress. I might as well be his mother, his sister, or an aunt with a wart on her chin.

"You clean up well," I say, fishing for a compliment.

"Thank you," he answers, not taking the bait.

I don't let it go. "You didn't compliment my dress." Releasing his hand, I pirouette in a circle and chirp, "I feel pretty, oh so pretty," imitating Maria from *West Side Story*.

"Nice," he says, with the enthusiasm of a bailiff announcing a docket number.

"It's silk."

"And it's blue," he says.

I squint up at him, my nose flaring. "Yes, it's silk and it's blue. And. I. Look. Pretty. Why can't you give a girl a compliment?"

"Is that what you're looking for? How about my costume?" He spins around. "Do I look pretty?"

"No. You look like a high school shot-putter who was held back sixteen times and who is finally getting to go to his high school prom."

He laughs, a deep chuckle that causes his body to quake with delight. Then he takes my hand again and leads me to the dance floor.

The band is playing Madonna's "Like a Virgin," and around us people are either swing dancing, hip hopping, or grinding depending on their generation. Griff does none of these things, his beefy arms flailing wildly as he flounders around like a beached octopus, endangering anyone within a ten-foot radius. He whips me around, a goofy grin on his face, his movements having no correlation whatsoever to the music. One of his cameramen gives him grief, and Griff shoulder checks him halfway across the dance floor.

When the song ends, I am laughing hysterically and breathless.

"Evening," Chris says, stepping up beside us and looking very dapper in a tieless, all-black tuxedo. "My goodness, Faye, you are a sight to behold, a pure vision in blue."

Griff stands silent watching us, a smile still on his face.

"And you look dashing as well," I answer, feeling slightly preposterous with all the silly pretense. And I realize that, rather than return Chris's flattery, what I really want to do is make a joke about it like, "Who died?" or "Yes, Godfather, I took care of it," then kneel down and kiss his ring.

"May I cut in?" Chris asks with a slight bow to Griff, nearly making me laugh while at the same time horrifying me. I *really* don't want to dance with Chris. It's bad enough that everyone knows I tongue wrestled him at the farm; the last thing I want to do is add fuel to the fire.

Griff looks at me, sees my frozen expression, and says, "Nope, this one's mine. Go find your own piece of finery." Then he twirls me away and dips me nearly to the ground.

"You probably shouldn't have done that," I say.

He whips me back up so our faces are inches apart. "Probably not, but you looked like you'd rather eat a jar of live spiders than dance with him."

"It was that obvious?"

"Good thing Molly and Tom didn't inherit their acting genes from you."

He spins me from his arms, and we resume our flouncing.

When the song ends and the band begins to play Marvin Gaye's "Let's Get It On," the mood changes, and there's an awkward second between us until Griff takes my hand and leads me off the floor to the bar.

"What do you mean I don't know how to dance?" he says in mock defense. "You just don't recognize great style when you see it."

My laugh is cut short when I see one of the set designers pointing me out to a security guard near the door. Griff notices as well and stands with me.

"Ma'am," the guard says when he reaches us, "are you Emily Martin's mom?"

My blood turns cold as my head nods.

"You need to come with me. There's been an incident."

55

A golf cart! You took a golf cart that didn't belong to you?"

My vision is red, the hotel security office and the people in it tinted crimson as Emily stands in front of me, eyes on the ground.

"Answer me," I screech, painfully aware that the hotel security director, Caleb, and Griff are standing only a few feet away.

Emily looks up through her mascara-coated eyelashes, then her eyes slide to Caleb and she does the most awful thing—she giggles.

My muscles clench, the heat of my anger scorching, and for the first time in my life, I feel the impulse to hit my child, a physical urge nearly impossible to contain. And when Emily titters again, my hand begins to rise. Then Griff is between us, his hands pinning my arms to my side.

"Thousands of dollars," I yell, craning my neck to see around him. "Do you get that? You crashed a golf cart into a car, and it's going to cost thousands of dollars to fix. That's what you think is funny?"

"I'll pay for it," Caleb volunteers, and I actually lunge at him, Griff holding me back.

"You little shit," I scream. "You spoiled little shit."

Emily looks at him lovingly as if he is offering his right kidney, a chivalrous declaration of devotion. The kid's worth a hundred million dollars. He's throwing pennies at her, not laying down on a sword.

"Faye," Griff says, his voice a whisper close to my ear, "you need to calm down. They're drunk. Wait until they're sober and deal with it then."

I rear back like I've been struck, break away from him, and lift Emily's chin so she's forced to look at me. Her eyes are glassy, her breath coated with the sour stench of alcohol.

She laughs again like I have no power at all, and this time Griff doesn't get there in time, my hand stinging from where it slashed her across her rouged cheek and painted lips.

I stare at my hand in disbelief, my repentance instant. "Em, I'm sorry."

"It didn't hurt," she says, her insolent glare igniting my desire to strike her again.

I take hold of my right wrist with my left hand to quell the impulse, take a deep breath, and say, "Em, let's go. Of all the days to pull a stunt like this, you chose today, the day that was supposed to be Molly's day."

"Every day is Molly's day," she snaps back.

I match her stare, furious that she is trying to turn this around.

My mom appears in the doorway. "I'll take her home."

"No, Mom, you stay."

She steps forward and touches my cheek, a gesture so unexpected and gentle that it nearly unglues me. "Tonight is your night as much as it is Molly's, and I've already had the time of my life. Let me take her."

Something in my mom's words reaches Emily, the slightest shadow of remorse crossing her face, and for that reason, with incredible gratitude, I nod.

When they're gone, I give the security director my contact information, then Griff and I turn to leave. We're halfway to the door when I realize Caleb's still in the room.

"Caleb, where's your mom?" I ask.

Shrug.

My voice softens. "Would you like me to call her for you?"

"I tried," the security director says. "No answer."

Crap. Crap, crap, crap.

I walk back into the room, wrap my arm around Caleb's shoulders, and say, "Come on. Let's get you something to eat, then we'll find you a ride home."

56

We're famous.

Like a light switch...no, more like a tsunami...our life has been carried away on a roaring wave that makes it difficult to catch a breath.

We woke up the day after the premiere unaware how much our world had changed. Then we walked into the parking garage to half a dozen reporters waiting for us, cameras and microphones ready, and that's when I realized that in the span of a single night, Molly had become a full-fledged, bona fide celebrity.

"Molly, how old are you?"

Molly held up four fingers.

"How long have you been singing?"

Molly's brow crinkled, not understanding the question. Hasn't everyone been singing their whole life?

My heart pounded the whole way to the studio. *Us, celebrities. Us, famous.* I couldn't believe it. It was unbelievable.

The second week things got worse or better depending on your perspective. In the second episode, Molly and Miles sang with the band, and Molly also had a solo performance where she knelt by her bed, eyes closed, hands clasped together as she sang a prayer for her dad called "Moonbeams to Heaven." Both songs topped the music charts for a week.

Since the premiere, *The Foster Band* ratings have soared into the stratosphere, and Chris and the studio execs are happy as hyenas in a meat locker.

The result of our success is that now, wherever we go, people crowd us for autographs and snap our picture, and the paparazzi trail us from the condo to the studio and everywhere in between.

No matter where we are, a crowd surrounds us. There are websites dedicated to celebrity sightings, and since everyone in the world is connected, within minutes of us doing something as mundane as going into a Starbucks, we have an audience. Cell phones and iPads document our every move, hundreds of photos of Molly blowing on her hot chocolate or me ordering an almond biscotti posted to hundreds of Facebook pages and websites that are then viewed by tens of thousands of followers.

At first it was exciting, but now, nearly two months later, we're all kind of tired of it. Being famous is a lot of work. It takes enormous effort to constantly be upbeat and polite, and there are some days when we're tired and just not in the mood to smile and wave.

Actually most of the time we're tired. Our schedule has become grueling. The demands outside the studio have erupted into a whirlwind of obligations that suck up every spare minute—interviews, photo shoots, appearances, endorsements, and fund-raisers.

Most of it is grand. Molly is treated like a queen, and I'm treated like the queen's mother. The fans love us and are so excited to see us, and if you give them a smile or an autograph, it's as if you've handed them the moon.

Helen has told me that I need to learn to say no, and sometimes I do, but it's difficult to say no to raising money for cancer or diabetes or clean water in Africa, knowing that a few hours of our time can literally change lives. It's also equally difficult to turn down the opportunity to make tens of thousands of dollars for Molly to show up at Toys "R" Us for a few minutes to announce that her favorite game is Twister. So on and on it goes, a demanding, exhilarating merry-go-round that leaves little time for rest and even less time to slow down and smell the roses.

Because of the hullaballoo that surrounds us, the studio now provides an armored limousine to drive us all the places we need to go. This both gets us where we need to be and also provides a layer of protection between Molly and her adoring fans, many whose love borders on obsessive.

There are now dozens of John Lennons haunting our lives, and it seems like every day another inappropriate gift or solicitous letter arrives. I understand now why Monique Braxton shrugged off my concern over the flowers and why the officer was so dispassionate about pursuing John Lennon over the locket. Compared to the lewd gifts and lascivious letters we've received since the premiere, the roses and necklace are tame.

Because of this, I should be scared all the time, living in a constant state of fear, but what I've discovered is that fear is like happiness, it simply can't be sustained. The truth is my adrenaline is worn out, which in turn is terrifying, since it is fear that keeps me on guard, and I know that when I forget to be scared is when something bad is going to happen. Knowing this causes moments of extreme panic and paranoia. I'll be going about my day, totally not thinking about the letters or threats, when something will happen—a sharp movement, the flash of a camera, a loud noise—and my heart will seize up, certain we're under attack. When my pulse finally settles, I promise not to slack off again, but the vow is short-lived because it's simply impossible to maintain that kind of vigilance. So instead, I do what the others on the show do, which is not think about it, ignoring the fact that there are hundreds, possibly thousands, of weirdos infatuated with my daughter. I especially avoid thinking about the "creepers" as Jeremy calls them, the fans who, for some demented reason, are hell-bent on hurting Molly.

We've only received two of those sort of letters. The first from a religious fanatic who thinks Molly is the face of greed and materialism and therefore needs to be punished for her sins. The second from a man with a warped idea that Molly would enjoy a spanking and who has set out to detail all the ways in which he would like to give her one. Both letters were passed on to the police. Considering the number of letters we receive each day, two is a very small number, but two nutcases obsessed with hurting my four-year-old still seems like a lot.

Last week, one of Kira's creepers was caught breaking into her dressing room. It shook up everyone that he made it that far, especially Kira, and now she won't go anywhere without a bodyguard, not even to the bathroom.

Nighttime is the hardest, the time when my guard is down, my subconscious free to roam to all the dark places I don't allow it to go during the day, and lately I've been having a hard time sleeping at all.

Our limo driver's name is Mack, and he reminds me a little of Bo in that he is tough and sweet at the same time. Black as beans, he doesn't have a neck or hair or much of a chin, but he does have a great sense of humor and a heck of a voice that he uses to sing along with whatever happens to be playing on the radio. He also has a temper and no problem whatsoever running over a reporter or fan if they get in his way. He gives them fair warning with his horn, but then it's up to them to step aside so we can get through.

At first I hated the idea of a limo and driver—it felt so pretentious—but now I realize we'd never get anywhere if Mack didn't clear the way. The paparazzi are the worst. They will risk life and limb to get a shot of us. When they first started trailing us, I couldn't believe it was worth their time, but last week I heard one of them got $15,000 for a photo he took of Molly tying her shoe in the parking garage. The headline read, *Molly Martin Learns to Tie Her Shoes!* Molly's been tying her shoes for months. *Fifteen grand?* Suddenly I understood why they're so dogged in their pursuit. Part of me wants to toss them a morsel now and then so they can be successful, but a larger part of me is reluctant to give them anything, hoping they will move on to more lucrative prospects.

Each of the members of our small clan deals with the attention differently. Molly seems immune to it. Once in a while she'll wave or smile, but like squirrels in a park, there are so many that eventually you no longer notice them. Tom avoids. He stays close to my side, his eyes on the pavement. Emily engages. She loves the reporters and takes every opportunity to taunt and tease them.

Yesterday, when we returned home, one of the paparazzi yelled out, "Molly, how about you show us a new dance move?"

Molly ignored him, but Emily leaped right out in front and, to my extreme mortification, spun so her back was to the photographer, bent over, and shook her booty in an exact imitation of Miley Cyrus's VMA twerking performance. She righted herself, pivoted back around, and said, "Miley taught me that." Then with us trailing after her, she continued on to the elevator, leaving the photographers busting up laughing and with a nice gossip shot to sell to the highest bidder. It was actually a hilarious moment, very funny and not at all sexy, but I wish she wouldn't encourage them.

I'm reluctant to ask her to stop because things are so tenuous between us. Since the night of the premiere, she and I have tiptoed around each other in an attempt to mend fences. I confiscated her iPhone for a week as punishment for what she did but didn't come down any harder than that. The hangover she suffered the morning after seemed punishment enough.

Both of us feel bad about what happened. I feel terrible for slapping her, and she feels terrible for ruining my special night. She's been on her best behavior, and I've made a concerted effort to give her more of my time. I feel like we are getting there, inch by inch our relationship returning to solid ground, and I don't want to do anything to jeopardize that, so I let her continue to have fun with the reporters.

Today will be a move in the right direction. This evening is Emily's school's open house, and not only am I going to be there, but after, she and I are going to go out for a nice dinner, just the two of us. Her favorite food is lasagna, and there's a restaurant called Angelini Osteria that is supposed to have the best lasagna in the city.

Fortunately today is a table read day, the day we read the script for the next episode. It's the easiest rehearsal day and the shortest. We should be finished by two, giving me plenty of time to drop Molly and Tom at home, change, and get to Emily's school for the event.

As Mack weaves his way through the freeway traffic, I review the script with Molly and Tom. Both kids' parts seem to grow each episode while Miles's diminishes, a result of the audience polls proving that Molly is a fan favorite and that Grant is also gaining popularity.

As proud as I am that the world loves Molly, the added pressure of more scenes combined with her newfound fame is proving to be a lot, and this morning she's done, her head on my lap, her eyes blankly focused on nothing as I read her parts aloud, hoping some of it is sinking in.

Her fatigue can't be blamed entirely on her job. Today her exhaustion has more to do with her father than her fame. Sean has no regard for the demands Molly faces each week or the fact that she needs to be up at the crack of dawn. Last night he brought her home near midnight, sunburned and exhausted after a weekend of nonstop romping and fun.

I keep hoping his notorious wanderlust will kick in and that he will leave, but unfortunately it doesn't look like he's going anywhere. The financial motivation for sticking around is a powerful anchor, keeping him rooted in the role of doting dad and playing the part of a far more devoted father than he has ever been before.

Mack pulls the limo up to the door of the soundstage.

"Later, Mack," Tom says.

"Stay cool," he says back.

Molly rubs the back of Mack's bald head. I don't know why she does this, but she does it every time she gets out of the car. Mack doesn't seem to mind.

The set is always quiet on table read days; the crew either has the day off or they come in late, so I'm surprised to see the master bedroom set lit up and to see Griff positioning a camera as if preparing to shoot a scene.

We're almost to the conference room when a tickle in my brain causes me to turn back. The set is almost out of sight, only a sliver of the room still visible, just enough of a view to see Griff and the camera, the lens no longer aimed at the set but instead angled toward me. When he realizes we've stopped, he straightens, and for the briefest flicker, our eyes catch, then he blinks, his intense expression softens, and he turns away.

❧

The conference room is packed as it always is when we do a read-through. Molly and I take a spot at the table with the primary cast members, and Tom takes a seat along the perimeter with the secondary characters, guest stars, and editors.

Bradley Mitten and his wife, the dynamic writing duo, sit at one end, Chris and Beth at the other. Mitten scans the sidelines until he finds the guest star he's looking for, a girl around sixteen with chestnut hair and connect-the-dot freckles. She was cast to play the part of a groupie named

Linda who is obsessed with Jeremy, and I knew when I read the script that the part had been written to satisfy Mitten's perverse appetite for young starlets.

Every few weeks, another teenage female guest star, chosen by Mitten, appears for a role. As Henry put it, *The guy's like a horny Hemingway. If he's allowed to dip his pen in your inkwell, you get the part.* I cringed when Henry said it, and I cringe now as I watch Mitten smile at the girl and as the girl twinkles her fingers back.

Griff walks in, breaking my attention and causing my pulse to beat slightly out of rhythm, our brief encounter this morning throwing it off-kilter. He takes his seat on the other side of Chris, and I feel him not looking at me. Then I watch as he takes a deep breath, forces his body to slump in the chair, and deliberately alters his expression to one of practiced boredom.

He's acting, I think, the revelation striking like a bolt of lightning.

Chris says something funny, and Griff offers a retort that causes the room to chuckle, then he turns my way and gives his signature Elmer Fudd grin. Usually I return the smirk, but this morning my face doesn't respond, and after an eternal second, he turns away.

"I want to change that line," Chris says. "I want Molly to say it instead of Gabby."

At the mention of Molly's name, I pull my attention back to the script and scan the page to find Gabby's name.

The line he wants to give Molly is, "What a man-whore," said in response to Jeremy bringing Linda, the obsessed groupie, home for dinner only a day after he broke up with his girlfriend.

"Molly can't say that," I say.

"Good morning, Faye," Chris says, as if just noticing I'm in the room. "Why not?"

I'm surprised when my response is remarkably calm, my distraction over Griff causing me to forget my normal reticence. "Because she's only four."

"That's what makes it funny."

"That's what makes it inappropriate."

His face shifts almost imperceptibly, and the air in the room shifts with it.

For four months, I've witnessed Chris's temper and have learned that you never want it directed at you. Everyone else knows it as well, and I feel them watching now with horror and thrill, sympathetic for what's about to happen while at the same time elated that it's not happening to them.

"Are you a writer?" Chris says.

"No, but..."

"A producer? A director? No. Do you have any fucking idea what the audience wants? No. So, shut the fuck up." His voice is not so much loud as mean. "After that..." he goes on.

"Molly's not saying that," I say, interrupting him, my voice barely loud enough for anyone to hear.

Chris stops and his eyes drill into me.

Seconds tick by and no one breathes, or perhaps it's only me that is holding my breath.

"Fine," he says finally. "Gabby, you'll keep that line."

Jeremy, who sits beside me, leans over and whispers, "You shouldn't have done that."

"He's not God," I whisper back.

"But he thinks he is."

57

I think our day is done. Molly and I return from lunch and are on our way to pick up Tom from studio school when my phone buzzes.

I nearly groan when I see the sender is Beth. *Let It Shine recording session bumped to 2:00 today.*

Penance for my impunity or simply bad luck, I'm not sure. All I know for certain is that our short day has just turned long, and my only hope for making it to Emily's open house is for the rehearsal to go smoothly and for us to finish the recording in one or two takes.

We pick up Tom and walk him to the limo to be driven home by Mack, then Molly and I head off to Newman Scoring Stage on the other side of the lot. The table read this morning took four hours, technically that's an hour more than Molly's supposed to work in a day and only leaves half an hour for her to be on the lot, but it never works out that way. Now that Mack drives us, we no longer even have to leave the lot to conserve Molly's precious minutes. The union rep responsible for the studio's compliance with the child labor laws now has no way of monitoring how long we've been here. Chris and Beth are careful to keep us moving from location to location so we are never in one spot too long, and sending us to the music studio is one of their favorite tricks.

"Okay, Bug, let's do this," I say, pulling the music sheets from my bag so I can read the lyrics to her as we walk.

"I tiwred," she says, shuffling along beside me, her eyes on the sidewalk.

I put the music back in my bag and lift her into my arms. Her arms wrap around my neck, her head slumps onto my shoulder, and before I've taken ten steps, I feel her heavy snores against my neck.

I carry her to the courtyard beside the building and sit down on a bench, jostling her lightly to wake her. Her response is to nuzzle tighter against me and mumble, "Want to swleep."

I check my phone. Our call time is in an hour.

"Okay, Bug, ten more minutes of sleep then we need to rehearse."

This has become my method of mothering, pure negotiation, this for that—the line of parenting and managing blurred into a hazy relationship of compromise. The mom side of me wants to tell her to nap because she's already worked hard and deserves a break, while the manager side of me knows her day isn't over, and if she shows up unprepared, there will be hell to pay, our day indeterminately extended until it gets done, so we should rehearse and make it easy on ourselves.

I set the alarm on my phone to ring in ten minutes, lean back on the bench, and close my eyes as well. Griff looking at me through the lens fills my mind, and when the alarm bleats, I'm disoriented, my eyes darting around, searching for Griff. Then I realize I'm in the courtyard of the music studio with Molly asleep on my lap, and I close my eyes again to regain my bearings. Molly's deep rhythmic breaths pulse like a soothing metronome against my chest, and only when my phone rings do I realize I drifted to sleep again.

The call is from the studio director asking where we are. Our call time was ten minutes ago.

Molly's still half-asleep when I carry her into the room, the musicians and the director glowering at us for making them wait. And they have yet to discover the worst of it.

Molly is utterly unprepared.

58

I keep looking at my watch, a fervent wish for this day to be over.

When I'm certain there's no chance of making it to Emily's open house, I call Sean and ask him to take my place.

Life has turned out unfair for Emily, and I feel awful about it. In Yucaipa, she was the center of our universe—the oldest, the leader, the one with all the activities and friends. Now Molly and Tom are in the spotlight, and she has been relegated to the sidelines. Everywhere we go people clamber to see Molly and Tom while she is asked to step aside.

I haven't met her teachers or her friends and have yet to make it to one of her club soccer matches. Tonight was important. I needed to be there. I told her I would be there. My frustration makes my head pound. This wasn't my fault, or maybe it was. Perhaps I shouldn't have challenged Chris this morning, but I really had no idea it would lead to this. And truthfully, had Sean brought the kids home at a reasonable hour, Molly wouldn't be so exhausted and the recording session would be going better. Chris and Sean—I can't decide which one irritates me more.

"What do I get in return?" Sean asks when I get a hold of him.

"You get to meet your daughter's teachers and spend an extra night with Emily," I say, rolling my eyes.

"Besides that. After all, I'm helping *you* out."

"You know what, forget it," I say. "Let's just skip the open house altogether, disappoint Emily, make her feel like no one gives a shit about her…"

"Whoa, settle down. I'll be there. I was just messing with you."

"Thanks." I sniffle back my frustration as I watch through the glass of the music studio as Molly flubs her lines for the twentieth time.

After I hang up, I call my mom to make sure Tom got home safely. He did, and the two of them are enjoying a dinner of hot dogs and chips in front of the television while watching a DVR recording of *The Voice*, and I'm so jealous that I can barely muster a thank-you before saying good-bye.

Finally, after a dozen more tries, we've maxed out our time on this side of the lot, and the director has no choice but to release us.

It's already dark when we walk outside. The sun has begun rising later and setting sooner, so each workday seems eternally longer, and I wonder if the shortage of daylight is contributing to our chronic exhaustion, making me worry that a vitamin D deficiency or perhaps some other deficiency is causing our constant fatigue.

"I did bad today," Molly says, her face drawn and sad.

"No, baby, you were just tired," I say, resting my hand on her shoulder.

She pulls away from my consolation and folds her arms across her chest, her disappointment in herself curling her small shoulders as she shuffles forward. Because no matter what I say, she knows that she did in fact do bad, and because of that, we wasted everyone's time and now we need to come back and do it again. I want to make it better, but I can't, because sometimes you screw up and you feel bad about it, and even if you're only four, that sucks, and no one, not even your mom, can change it.

"Hey, Bugabaloo."

Molly's head snaps up. "Daddy!" She runs into Sean's open arms.

I look down at my phone to check the time, and my face goes red. Open house should still be in full swing. He stands beside our limo, Chris and Mack beside him.

"What are you doing here?" I say, trying to keep my voice level in front of our audience.

Sean bounces Molly up and down. "We are going to dinner."

"Yeah!" Molly says, hugging his neck.

"Chris and Mack, will you excuse us?" I say.

The two men walk out of earshot.

"I mean, where's Emily? And why aren't you at her open house?"

"Chris called," he says with a nod toward Chris, like I don't know who Chris is. "Asked if we could meet. Said he felt bad that he hadn't gotten to know Molly's other parent."

My skin prickles as I glance at Chris. His eyes hold mine, his message clear—challenge him again and I'll be going the path of Rhonda.

"Where's Em?" I manage.

"I asked if it was okay if we skip the school bullshit, and she said that was cool with her. And since we were coming to the set, she called that kid Caleb, and they're going to hang together while Chris and I take this one to dinner." He bounces Molly again, and she smiles.

"You sent her off with Caleb? Are you nuts? I told you what happened at the premiere."

"Yeah, but your version wasn't nearly as funny as Emily's. I swear I nearly pissed my pants when she told me about the security guard running from the restroom and chasing them with his pants still unzipped as they took off in his cart."

"Sean, it's not funny."

"Christ, Faye, where's your sense of humor? It's hilarious."

"She was drunk."

"And you've never gotten drunk?"

"Not when I was twelve."

"Man, you used to be fun. What happened?"

"I grew up."

He shakes his head. "No wonder Em doesn't like you anymore."

My heart pinches with the hurtful declaration.

"Sean, we should go," Chris says, stepping forward. "Our reservation is at seven."

Sean walks around me, loads Molly in the back of the limo, then climbs in after her.

Chris follows. Halfway in, he stops. "It was just a line, Faye. She's an actress, and it was just a line." He slides the rest of the way in and closes the door.

Just a line. And as I watch the limo drive toward the gates, my dad's voice comes back to me. *A line in the sand, Faye. At some point, we all need to draw our line and stand behind it.*

I drew my line and look what happened.

"Hey."

I look up to see Griff walking toward me, a sandwich in his hand.

"You're still here," I say. "I thought there were no shoots today."

"Exactly. The perfect time to figure out what the hell I'm doing so people think I'm spontaneously brilliant when I do it tomorrow. Where's Squidoo?" Griff's nickname for Molly. He either calls her that or Squid Junior.

"Hijacked by my ex and Chris."

Griff's eyebrows rise. "They know each other?"

"They do now."

"Scary."

"Exactly."

"So you're kidless?"

I look around me as if checking. "Looks that way."

"Perfect. Then you can help me."

Without waiting for my response, he pivots toward the soundstage, and I lope after him, perfectly happy to put off catching a cab home to face my mom and explain my latest parenting debacle.

The soundstage is eerily dark and quiet, and if Griff weren't a step ahead of me, I'd be creeped out. Cold as a coffin, my breath frosts in front of me, and the emergency lights provide only enough light to see vague shadows of discarded equipment and scaffolding that litter the corridors. We step onto the master bedroom set, and Griff flicks the breaker, blazing the room into blinding brightness.

The set is altered from its usual state, the bed set higher, the floor laid with green carpet.

"It's the dream sequence," Griff explains. "And I need the floor to disappear."

"How can I help?"

"I need you to be Helen."

"Ha! No problem, I'll simply grow a foot, get a figure and a voice, become impossibly beautiful, and learn how to act."

"You are beautiful, and I don't need you to act. I just need you to be her stand-in so I can figure this out."

You think I'm beautiful? I want to say, milking the offhand compliment for what it's worth, but I restrain myself.

He positions me beside the bed then walks behind the camera. "Say something and act it out then walk over to the mantel."

"What do you want me to say?"

"Whatever's in your heart."

"Two all-beef patties, special sauce, lettuce, cheese, pickles, onions, on a sesame seed bun," I sing as I pretend to stack all the elements into a sandwich then take a giant imaginary bite.

He laughs. "Profound."

"I'm hungry."

After several takes, Griff has the shots he needs, and I walk to where he is and watch over his shoulder as he pops the disc from the camera then slides it into his laptop.

He adds a filter, aligns the different shots so they're in sync, then says, "Ready?"

I feel his anticipation and my own heart picks up its pace.

I nod and he clicks play, and miraculously I watch as my body disappears and my shadow crosses the room to pick up the photo from the mantel.

"Whoa, that's amazing," I say as Griff swivels, his face lit up.

I reach to hug him, but my head does not tilt and neither does his, our lips coming together as my arms wrap around his neck.

He pushes away, his hands pressing on my shoulders to put distance between us, then he stands, stumbles back, and the back of his hand rises to his mouth as if blotting away the kiss.

"I'm sorry," he says.

"Sorry you kissed me, or sorry you're being a jerk?"

"Both."

"What is it? Do I smell? Am I ugly? Do you just not like women?"

"I like women."

"Just not me."

"I especially like you."

"So then, what is it? Is it because I kissed Chris?"

He snort laughs, a chortle through his nose that causes my skin to sizzle.

"I'm glad you find this amusing."

"If that were the reason, I'd have to give up women altogether. Chris has kissed at least half the women in LA, and the ones he hasn't are the ones you don't want to kiss."

I glare at him, not finding any of this the least bit funny.

He steps toward me and pulls me against his chest, then says, "I've given a lot of thought to kissing you, and it has nothing to do with Chris, but I decided it's not a good idea."

There's no meanness in his tone, but the words cut like a knife just the same, and I can barely restrain myself from reaching up and forcing him to kiss me, proving that he's wrong, that kissing me is a good idea, a very good idea—that I'm a very desirable, very kissable, very good idea indeed. Instead I mumble, "I get it. A mom with three kids, a family that's not yours, that's not what you want."

He rears back. "Where'd you come up with that? That's not it. Jesus, woman, will you at least let me say my piece? Damn it. Where was I? Damn frustrating."

"*I'm* frustrating. That's hilarious coming from you, Mr. Hot Cold, Hot Cold."

"At least I recognize that there are consequences to what I do."

"What the hell's that supposed to mean?"

"It means you can't just act on whatever impulse you feel the moment you feel it and expect it to all work out."

"So a few moments ago, when you were kissing me, that was carefully planned out?"

"No," he snaps. "That was a mistake."

"I'll say." I whirl and storm away, tripping in the darkness as I try to see through my tears, not stopping until I'm out of the soundstage, off the lot, and a block away.

Shivering with cold and rage, I pull out my phone to call for a cab, and that's when I see the five missed calls, three from my mom and two from Sean. And I know before I press play that this awful night is about to get worse.

59

Emily can't be reached. Sean tried calling her after dinner so he could take her home, but she didn't pick up. His second message told me that he had dropped Molly off at my mom's and that I still needed to get Emily before I went home. My mom's messages consist of "Where are you?" and "Your idiot ex-husband just showed up with Molly but not Emily, so I hope you know that you need to bring her home with you," and "Where the hell are you?"

I call Emily's phone. No answer.

I call Beth at home, and she is less than thrilled with having her night disrupted. "What do you want?"

I explain the situation, and her answer is, "Well, what the hell do you want me to do about it?"

"I want you to give me Caleb's number."

"It's not my place to give out cast members' numbers," she says and hangs up.

I call Helen. She doesn't have Caleb's number. Neither does Jeremy.

I consider calling Griff, but at the thought, my chin starts to tremble.

With no options left, I dial the only number that remains. He picks up on the fourth ring. "Chris, I need your help."

My knight in shining armor, Chris not only gives me Caleb's number, but he insists on picking me up so we can find the kids together.

"I've got a stake in this too," he says, as he guns it down Wilshire Boulevard toward the beach where Caleb's limo driver said he dropped the kids two hours earlier. "Caleb's got three scenes tomorrow. Lately the kid's been losing focus. Not that I don't sympathize. When you're thirteen, hormones can be very distracting." Then he looks over at me and sets his hand on my knee. "Hell, at forty-five they're very distracting."

I lift his hand from my leg and give it back to him.

"Come on, Faye," he says. "This would be so much more fun if you and I could be friends again." His hand goes back to my leg, this time an inch higher than it was the first time, and I feel the tears threatening. I want to move it, but I'm scared, the awfulness of this day that started with me challenging him at the table read fresh in my brain.

"Please, Chris," I say, my voice cracking with emotion.

He sighs through his nose and takes his hand away.

60

Only Caleb is at the beach when we get there. After Chris called Caleb and told him to stay put because we were coming to get them, Emily said she wasn't feeling well, so Caleb sent her home in a cab.

Caleb squeezes into the backseat of the Porsche, and Chris pulls back onto the road.

Tension so thick it weights the air fills the small confines of the car as Chris drives to my mom's condo. Chris is not happy with Caleb. I'm not happy with Caleb. Chris is not happy with me. I'm not happy with Chris. Caleb is simply unhappy. The kid is beloved by millions but doesn't seem to have a single person in the world who cares about him.

When we've been driving ten minutes, I try Emily's cell phone again. She picks up on the third ring, and using all my self-control to keep my voice level, I say, "How are you feeling?"

"Fine."

"We've been trying to reach you all night. Why didn't you pick up?"

"Because, *like you*," she hisses, "I was busy."

The phone goes dead.

Three paparazzi lie in wait when Chris pulls to the curb, their cameras clicking away as I step from the Porsche, and I wonder if I'll end up in the tabloids, *Molly Martin's Mom Dating Show's Producer, Chris Cantor*.

The reporters are becoming familiar to me, a rotation of about twenty different faces that pop up daily either at the condo or outside the studio gates. Tonight there is a pair who look like brothers, both swarthy and dark with grease-stained, collared shirts. Molly calls them Rat and Kale because one is massive and the other scrawny, making them look a little like the characters from *Sinbad*. The third is a guy who I call Tony on account that he always wears a Bass Pro Shops hat, and Bass Pro Shops is Tony Stewart's NASCAR sponsor.

I give them a small customary wave and smile, masking my misery until I'm past their prying eyes and safely in the building.

As I ride the elevator, I close my eyes and focus on my breathing. *I'm not going to get angry*, I tell myself. *I need to fix this, somehow make this right. Screaming at her won't help.*

When I walk into the condo, my mom frowns then points to the closed bedroom door. "She got here a few minutes ago."

I kiss Molly on her head and tousle Tom's hair as I walk past, giving them a smile I don't feel. *I'm not going to get angry.*

Emily looks up from the magazine in front of her as I walk through the door.

"You pierced your nose!" I screech, my vow detonated by my fury.

61

Emily lies propped up on her elbows, a bored look on her face. Twinkling from the middle of it is a tiny diamond stud stuck in her right nostril.

My mom runs in and spins me out of the room. "Faye, you need to calm down."

"Calm down? My daughter has a spike through her nose."

"She has a small piercing that will close up in a matter of days if you can convince her that having an earring in her nose is not a good idea," my mom says calmly as she continues to steer me into the kitchen and sits me at the table.

As soon as my butt hits the seat, I get woozy, and I realize I haven't eaten since lunch. My mom must sense this because she plops an apple in front of me then pops a frozen burrito into the microwave.

By the time the oven beeps, I've devoured the apple and my rage has settled into a dark swirling brew. My mom sits beside me as she slides the burrito onto the table. "Eat," she says.

I shovel the tasteless calories into my grateful body and mutter around it, "What am I going to do?"

"Fix it. You got yourself into this mess, so now you need to get yourself out of it. An earring in a nostril is the least of your problems. Sean's not going away, and that's a hell of a lot more dangerous than that thin sliver of silver."

"And what is it exactly you think I should do about it? He's their dad."

"Yeah, brilliant choice that was."

"Real supportive," I mumble, dropping my face onto my crossed arms on the table.

"I'm here, aren't I?"

62

I watch Emily sleeping, her body curled with the comforter wedged between her knees, her copper hair splayed on the pillow.

I've always loved her hair, bright like a new penny in the sun, the color of warm syrup when the lights are low. As I watch her, I think of her as a baby, her rolls of peach-colored skin, the way she would look at me with her big green eyes, those dazzling eyes that received so many compliments. Sean's eyes. I used to love that she inherited his best feature.

Emily has always been the most like him. In looks and personality. Both of them athletic, charming, brazen, and confident to the point of being cocky—heroic or destructive depending on whether they are living in times of war or peace. The kind of fearless that would run into a burning orphanage to save a hundred children, the kind of reckless that would have a bonfire in an abandoned church and set the whole town ablaze.

So unlike Molly, Tom, and myself.

If we were cartoons, Molly, Tom, and I would be the Looney Tunes, and Emily and Sean would be Marvel superheroes.

As I watch her, my mind trips on how to fix things. My mom is right; Sean is dangerous. Until now, I've been careful not to disclose too much to Emily about her dad, afraid of revealing the depth of my feelings. I love her with every ounce of my being and, at this point, hate her father equally so. And being that they are so much alike, I was certain this would be confusing. But in protecting her from the truth, somehow I've allowed him to become good. A terrible mistake.

I rub her shoulder to wake her, and she groans and covers her eyes, her arm catching on the stud in her nostril and causing her to yelp with the pinch. Sadistically I hope it continues to hurt, perhaps even becomes infected so she has no choice but to remove it.

"Hey, Em," I say quietly. "Come on, baby, you need to get up. You have school."

She groans again and pulls the pillow over her head.

Tom, who sleeps beside her, rolls from his side of the bed and stumbles toward the bathroom.

"Come on, two more days then you're off for a week. Get up, go to school, then tonight we'll talk."

She clenches the pillow tighter against her face.

I pull it off and toss it aside so she can't reach it.

She blinks her eyes open in a hateful squint. "Go away."

I smile with as much love as I can muster then happily do as she asks, returning to the living room where I am not so despised.

Crawling into the sleeper bed, I cuddle against Molly, and she curls into me. I breathe in her sweet smell and gently stroke her arm to wake her, and I remind myself that this isn't Emily's fault. Last night I failed her. That single night was supposed to be hers, and I didn't show up. This year has been hell for her. Her dad left us, she was uprooted from her home and her friends, and my attention was wrenched away. Emily used to be like Molly. Before everything changed, she too used to let me cuddle with her and soothe her awake.

63

Griff can barely look at me or I at him.

"What's going on with the two of you?" Helen says between takes.

"Is he married?" I ask.

"Griff?"

"Yes. Is he married?"

"Oh," she says, looking back and forth between us. "Fishing off the company pier and now your heart is stuck in the cookie jar."

"You're mixing your metaphors."

"Yes, I suppose, but you get what I'm saying."

"So is he?"

"Is he what?"

"Married?"

"No need to get snippy. No, Griff is not hooked. See, look how I brought that metaphor back around."

"Impressive," I say with a defeated exhale. "Fine. He's not married, and he's not gay, so then it's back to me simply being repulsive, even though he kissed me last night like a man discovering Niagara Falls after stumbling through the Sahara."

"We are a species of narcissists," she says.

"What's that supposed to mean?"

"It means that just because he's not gay or married, you assume it has something to do with you."

"It doesn't?"

She shrugs. "I have no idea. Maybe you're a lousy kisser."

"I am not a lousy kisser," I say too loud, causing several of the crew to look over and smirk.

"Then maybe it has nothing to do with you. Maybe it has to do with him."

I'm about to press her about it more when Tom interrupts. "Mom, can you run my lines with me again?"

Tom has his biggest scene of the season today, and he's terribly nervous. Unlike Molly, who is mostly unconcerned about her part, her scenes, or her lines, Tom takes his role very seriously, and today there is a scene that revolves entirely around Grant. But what has his stomach slick with nerves is that the script calls for him to cry, something Tom hasn't done since he was a baby. Despite being debilitatingly shy, Tom is tough as nails, his emotions buried beneath thick layers of self-consciousness, pride, and self-preservation, concealed so deep that I can't imagine them ever being unearthed.

"I can't do it," Tom says when we finish reading the scene and his eyes are still bone dry. "I don't know how to cry."

His blue eyes plead for me to help him, but he and I are too much alike. If you asked me to reveal myself in front of an audience, I would be as incapable as he is.

"I don't know," I say. "Maybe ask Molly how she does it."

"I asked her. She says she just does. That when she needs to cry, she just makes herself cry."

I shake my head, blown away by this bizarre ability and wondering how many times my sympathies have been manipulated by this prodigious, slightly disturbing talent.

"I can't do that," Tom says. "I can't."

"Can't is a long way from won't." Tom and I both turn to see Jules talking to us. He's been beside us the whole time, slouched on a stool waiting for the next take to begin, but I hadn't thought he was listening.

"You think I'm not trying?" Tom says, reverting to Grant's tough-guy attitude, his stance widening, his head cocked to one side.

Jules's watery eyes squint as he sizes Tom up. "You're trying to fake it, I'll give you that."

"Of course I'm trying to fake it," Tom shoots back. "That's what I'm supposed to do. I'm supposed to act upset."

"No," Jules says. "You're supposed to *be* upset." He sighs out through his nose while looking steadily at Tom, as if deciding whether or not it's worth the effort to continue. Then with a frown and another sigh he says, "What's the worst thing that ever happened to you?"

"Nothing," Tom says quickly. A blatant lie if he's answering for either himself or his character.

"Then I can't help you," Jules says, standing and walking away.

He's taken two steps when Tom blurts, "My dad left. I wouldn't...didn't...I couldn't talk in school, so he left."

My heart splits open, and I step forward to protest his distorted view, but *Jules* is already there.

"Okay," he says, his face a neutral mask that is not sympathetic or callous but emotionless and poker-straight. "So there it is. Now all you need to do is be brave enough to use it, to allow yourself to *be* upset and let the camera see it. No one needs to know where it comes from; they just need to feel it. If you can do that, you'll be fine."

Tom looks unsure.

"Scared?" Jules says. "You should be. It takes incredible courage to open yourself up like that. And each time you do it, you leave a little piece of yourself behind. Hell, I've been doing this so long, not much is left. But I'm good; no one can say I'm not good at what I do. A hell of a lot better than you."

Tom glares at him. "That's because I'm only eight."

"No," Jules answers. "It's because I don't *act*, and neither does your sister. Molly can cry when she wants because she knows how to feel. If something is sad, she gets sad—not her character, her. It makes her good but not great. To be great, you need to go further than that. You need to become the character, surrender that part of yourself." Jules's eyes flicker with passion as he speaks, a fervor I've never seen in him before. "Each time I'm filmed, I leave a thin layer of myself behind, apparitions of my former self captured in a billion pixels that will live on in perpetuity, hundreds of specters of my spirit inhabiting the earth, though I'm still alive.

The Native Americans understood that. They believed photos stole their souls, and they were right."

As he talks I wonder who Jules might have been had he not become a star. I imagine him as a professor teaching history or political science, a flask in his desk drawer.

"That's how you do it," Jules says. "Give them a piece of yourself and they'll eat it up every time."

64

What's going on?" I say to Henry as Molly and I walk into base camp. We just returned from being off the lot for the past two hours, and we obviously missed something important while we were gone. As we walked through the soundstage to get here, the air was electrified with hushed whispers.

Molly climbs into Henry's "torture chair" as she calls it, and Henry looks over her head and says, "Gabby," then he makes a slashing line across his throat.

"Gabby's dead?" I say, swallowing hard.

"No," he says, rolling his eyes. "She's getting the ax. Rumor has it, she's going to hang herself in the season finale."

"Why?"

"Why is Gabby the character going to hang herself or why is Gabby the person getting the ax?"

"Gabby the person."

"Mitten's had his fill."

"Gabby's one of Mitten's girls?"

"That's how she got the job."

I do the math. "But that can't be. Gabby would have only been thirteen."

Shrug. "Old enough to know what she wanted. There were a thousand girls who tried out for that part."

"Maybe she was the most talented."

"*Please.* Mitten chose her. The casting director and Chris picked everyone else, but Mitten insisted on Gabby."

"And now Mitten's writing her off because he's done with her?"

"Either that or it's because of her weight and the drugs. She's already bottom of the fan chain, so Mitten or the studio execs or Chris decided to get rid of her while the audience still gives a damn if she gets killed off. It's a good move."

"A good move? This is her livelihood." I don't particularly like Gabby, but my mom gene is rearing up in protest at the brutal disregard of a sixteen-year-old girl's welfare, feelings, and future. "If she has a drug problem, they should help her."

Shrug. "It's part of the business. Actors get fired."

Henry sprays Molly's hair, his hand protecting her eyes.

"Will she move on to another show?" I say.

"Doubt it."

As much as I want to protest, I know he's right. Gabby's not cute like Molly or beautiful like Kira. Her personality is bland. She's a little overweight and has a reputation for doing drugs. Not exactly a winning combination.

"Maybe she can do something else," I say.

"Like what? All she knows how to do is act. Best-case scenario is she moves somewhere outside of Hollywood, changes her name, lives off her trust, and takes up a hobby like painting or Tae Bo."

I shake my head. Sixteen and she's washed up. I look at Molly obliviously playing a game on my phone, her legs bouncing in the chair, and I make a vow not to let that happen to her. Acting is something she does; it's not who she is. She needs to have something else to fall back on when this ends. She needs to go to school and experience the world outside of Hollywood.

But how do I give her that when this world is so consuming? We've only been doing this four months, and already our old life is a dim memory, the world beyond the set blurred to the point where it barely seems relevant. Yucaipa, Bo, the stables, coffee shops, malls, theaters, gas stations, parks—it's all still there, but we are no longer a part of it, or rather, we're at the center of it, all of it whirling around on the periphery. That sounds horribly egocentric, but that's how it feels, like the set is the sun, the rest of the world reduced to stardust caught in its orbit, ever-present and vast but no longer important to our lives.

"No one's supposed to know about the Gabby thing," Henry says. "So keep it hush-hush."

"Does Gabby know?"

"I doubt it. Usually the actor is the last to know. But it could also all be a crock of bull...bologna. For all we know, the studio's floating the rumor because a bunch of contracts are up for renegotiation and the producers are looking to strike fear into the actors and their agents."

"Message received loud and clear," I say, my own fear striking like a bullet to the chest. If we lose this, we'll be right back where we started—me and three kids, with no job and few prospects.

65

It's Tom's turn, the last shoot of the day before everyone gets a well-earned week off for Thanksgiving.

"Ready?" I ask, feeling his nerves but also his excitement.

He nods, gives his trademark crooked smile, and my heart fills. For all the things I've done wrong, I did this right. Tom's the happiest he's ever been. Here, in this make-believe world, he's found his place, and for the first time in his life, he's thriving. The cast and crew are like an extended family, and Miles has become his best friend, something he's never had before. But mostly it is his purpose that makes him whole. Outside his role, he's still quiet, reticent to the point of taciturn, but when he's in character, he's fearless. Acting isn't just a hobby or something he does because he has to. When he's in front of the camera, he comes alive, becoming more than what he is in his own life—bold, confident, daring—a heroic version of himself.

He turns from me to face the wall, a trick Helen taught him, and I watch as his eyes close and twitch back and forth, the scene playing in his mind as he visualizes it. Then with a deep breath, he turns back and bravely takes his place on the set.

A standing ovation, everyone is on their feet clapping, and I breathe. Tom was brilliant, and I have to bite back my own tears that leaped into my eyes in response to his moving performance.

Chris claps Tom on the shoulder. "Hell of a job. One take. How about that? You can all thank Tom for starting your vacation early. That was brilliant, fucking brilliant."

Everyone breaks into applause again, and Tom's grin is so wide that I'm certain his cheeks will be stretched out when he stops, and I think this might be one of my proudest moments ever.

My phone buzzes, and I pull it out to see a text from my mom. *Meet us at the clinic on Wilshire, Em's nose is infected.*

66

My mom takes Molly and Tom home, and I take Emily out for pancakes at an all-night diner because there's something about pancakes for dinner that makes everything a little brighter, and we could use a little brightness right now.

The right side of Emily's nose is swollen, red, and slick with antibacterial ointment. The doctor assured us the hole would heal and not leave a scar. She needs to take antibiotics for the next two weeks to ensure the infection won't come back.

She sits across from me chewing on her pinky nail and staring at the white linoleum table. Silent, I wait her out, not pushing her, afraid to incite an explosion, hoping somehow a little time together will bring us back to solid ground.

"I can't even do that right," she mutters. "A stupid nose piercing, and I can't even do that."

My heart hitches. Emily's never been the kind of girl who lacks confidence.

"Em, what's going on?"

She looks up at me through her brow, not so much with shame as defeat. Then she shakes her head like I could never understand.

"Talk to me," I say. "Give me a chance."

For a long moment she says nothing, then finally she lifts her face and looks at me with her pretty green eyes. "You want to help?"

"Of course. That's all I want, a chance to help."

The server interrupts, arriving with platters of Frisbee-size pancakes two inches high, sweet deliciousness wafting off them. Emily pours the warm maple syrup over hers then hands the small pitcher to me, then both of us take a giant bite and nearly moan with pleasure.

When my first mouthful is swallowed, I say, "Tell me what I can do."

Emily leans back, her eyes steady on mine, her gaze so much like Sean's I need to check my reaction to be sure I'm not wincing.

"I want you to set up a meeting with Monique Braxton," she says. "I want to act."

67

The Thanksgiving hiatus might sound like a vacation, but for Molly and me, it's more of a weeklong publicity tour that kicks off tomorrow on the East Coast with a live interview on *Good Morning America*, an interview I'm particularly excited about because it means I get to meet my number one celebrity crush, George Stephanopoulos.

Originally, we were supposed to fly out this morning, but because I needed to follow through on my promise to Emily, I pushed our flight back to the red-eye so I would have time to take Emily to see Monique Braxton this morning.

We are in the reception area on the same suede couch Molly and I sat on five months ago, the same pretty receptionist sitting at the desk across from us.

Emily's not at all nervous. She sits beside me paging through *People* magazine, while I, on the other hand, am a wreck, both desperately wanting this for Emily and desperately not wanting it at the same time. Mostly what I want is for her not to want this, because it is all wrong for her and it feels very dangerous. Already the crazy world of show business has corrupted her, and she's only on the perimeter. I can't imagine what it will do to her if she's immersed in it. But at the same time, it feels like a horrible betrayal to root against her. She's so excited, and every mother wants for their kids what they want.

"Ms. Braxton is ready for you," the receptionist says, and we follow her down the hall.

"Faye, good to see you," Monique Braxton says, coming around her desk and taking my hand in both of hers, and again I'm struck by how tiny she is, the only adult around whom I feel tall. "And you must be Emily."

Emily limply shakes Monique Braxton's hand and says, "So I was thinking maybe movies. The television thing is cool, but it takes up a lot of time, so I'd rather do movies."

Blood rushes to my face. "Em, that's not how it works."

She ignores me. "Maybe an action flick like *Transformers*."

"Okay," Monique Braxton says, "but first things first. Let's see how you do with a quick read for a commercial." She picks up two scripts from her desk, hands one to Emily and the other to me. "Faye, would you mind reading Oliver?"

"Not at all," I say, entirely comfortable at this point with pretending to be everything from old men to little girls.

"Emily, your role is that of a teenage daughter who is trying to sweet-talk her dad into buying her her first cell phone. Begin whenever you're ready."

"When I was your age," I start in a gruff voice, then stop. Emily is supposed to interrupt me.

"Oh, right," Emily says. "Now it's my turn. Okay. When you were my age, dinosaurs still roamed the earth," she reads with zero intonation. "But just think how much better life would have been for the ancient cavemen if they could have called their daughters to check on them instead of having to leave their warm caves."

Monique Braxton interrupts. "Okay, Emily, let's try it again, but this time do it without the script and say it with personality, like you really are this girl and you really want your dad to get you that cell phone."

"When I was your age," I start again.

Long, excruciating pause.

"When you were my age, you were a caveman," she says. "But get me a cell phone and you won't need to leave your cave."

It takes all my willpower not to cringe.

Monique Braxton gives a weak smile. "Emily, why don't you go back to the reception area while I talk to your mom for a minute."

"Okay," Emily says, handing back the script. "But remember, I want to do movies. Molly and Tom work like *way* too much."

When the door closes behind her, I apologize.

Monique Braxton waves me off. "I can see why she might have the wrong idea that this business is easy to break into. After all, look at Molly and Tom. She is a pretty girl."

I nod, hope flashing with the compliment until she quickly dashes it. "Faye, she doesn't have it."

"But maybe if she works at it…"

"I'm sorry, but no. In good faith, I can't represent her. It's not fair to her, and it's not fair to the casting directors who count on me to send them talent. Like I said, she's pretty, maybe steer her toward modeling."

I close my eyes for an extended blink as I nod.

"Do you want me to tell her?" Monique Braxton offers.

"No. She'll blame me regardless, so I might as well be the one to break it to her."

"It's the worst part of this job," Monique Braxton says. "Destroying dreams."

68

Molly and I are at the airport, both of us nervous and excited. Neither of us has ever been on an airplane. Molly's nose is pressed against the glass as she watches the planes taxi and land in the darkness.

The audition fiasco with Monique Braxton is a hazy memory, like the lingering aftertaste of an early breakfast of garlic bagels, salmon, and red onions. Emily hates me, and she hates Monique Braxton, and as soon as we left Monique Braxton's office, she called Sean and asked if she could stay with him instead of my mom while Molly and I were in New York. As I predicted, she blames me. She thinks I sabotaged her by telling Monique Braxton I didn't want her to act. I didn't sabotage her, but I am relieved.

Accompanying us on the trip is our publicist, Patrick. Patrick's okay, a bit annoying but efficient. At the moment, he stands a few feet away pecking on his phone.

Publicists are sort of like babysitters. They schedule interviews and appearances, make sure you show up to them on time, and make sure all the parties behave themselves.

Patrick is what my dad would call a glad-hander, one of those guys who slaps backs and throws his head back when he laughs. His face is ruddy and round like a slab of bologna and he talks a lot, which is why he's a bit irritating. But the thing I like least about him is that, though he's on our "team," I trust him about as far as I can throw him, which, considering how beefy he is, isn't an inch. When he's around, I feel like it's half to watch out for us and half to watch us, like the studio is keeping tabs on us, afraid of something, though I'm not certain exactly what that something is.

As we wait, a few people ask for Molly's autograph, and she obliges, scrawling a curly "M" that has become her signature, but then a crowd starts to form causing Patrick to grow concerned, and he shuttles us from the waiting area to a private lounge.

Three minutes before our boarding time, a flight attendant arrives and escorts us onto the plane before the other passengers. We stop at the cockpit to be introduced to the pilots who also ask for Molly's autograph.

The plane takes off with Molly and me gripping each other's hands, my heart in my throat. It feels so unnatural for a giant machine of steel to be flying through the air, and it takes a while for my brain to get used to the idea and to convince my pulse that we are not going to fall out of the sky.

Molly and I should sleep. We need to be on the set at six for hair and makeup, which won't allow any time for us to stop at the hotel and rest. But we're both far too excited to close our eyes.

In the seat in front of us is a little girl perhaps a year older than Molly, and before you know it, the dad has traded rows, and Molly and the girl are lost in endless games of Crazy Eights and Go Fish.

I now have Molly's window seat, and I stare through the tiny pane of glass at the kazillion lights of LA spread out like a Christmas blanket below. An hour later we are floating over rural countryside, the moon reflecting off a patchwork of farms sliced with roads and rivers and spotted with houses and barns.

There's so much and so little to see. Living in LA makes you believe the world is a crowded place, but flying across the country makes me realize how empty it actually is. There's so much land, space, and sky that I feel utterly small, while at the same time, when we fly over a city, I'm struck by how much has been created—both the crammed and the empty resonating overwhelming greatness—man's and God's. At certain moments, I'm inspired, and at others, I'm struck with a profound sadness, a sense of irrelevance that leaves me feeling fragile and empty and anxious for the trip to be over so I can feel grounded again.

An hour before we're scheduled to land, Molly returns to her seat and falls asleep on my lap, and when the plane stops outside the gate and I wake her, she's not ready to be woken.

"Come on, Bug, we're here. You need to get up."

"Don't want to."

"I know, baby, but you've got to. We're in New York."

"Don't want to."

Patrick relieves me of my carry-on bag so I can lift Molly in my arms. Her head flops onto my shoulder, and she falls back to sleep. I carry her through the airport to the baggage claim area as dozens of people pursue us with their phones, documenting the momentous occasion of Molly snoring on my shoulder.

By the time we get in our limo, it's four in the morning and already I regret my decision not to spend the trip sleeping, my eyes so heavy that I feel them closing as we drive into the city.

Molly continues to sleep, missing the entire amazing journey. LA has a few tall buildings but nothing like the skyscrapers of New York. My neck hurts, and my head is dizzy from looking up at them.

We pull up to Times Square Studios at 5:45 and step onto the busy street. It's not yet dawn, but already the sidewalk is bustling with businesspeople dressed in beautiful wool suits and furs and vendors bundled in parkas and sweatshirts selling pretzels, knishes, hot dogs, and handbags.

Molly is scheduled as the fourth guest. She gets her hair and makeup done, and we are waiting backstage for her turn when the show cuts to a commercial and George Stephanopoulos walks off the set to greet us.

The sight of him coming toward us causes my pulse rate to triple. George. Freaking. Stephanopoulos!

He shakes my hand then turns from my mouth-gaping starstruckedness to Molly.

"It's a pleasure to meet you, Molly. I watch your show every week."

"My mom watches youwr show awll the time too," Molly says. "And she has a huge cwrush on you, and befowre she and my dad got a divowrce, she said that, if she wasn't mawrried to my dad, she'd mawrry you."

I nearly drop my coffee, unable to believe she just said that. I want to die. Seriously. Curl up into a little ball and disintegrate.

"Did she now?" George Stephanopoulos says with a wry smile as he turns to face me and my mortification.

"Hey," Molly says, causing him to turn back. "She's not mawrried now. So now she can mawrry you."

George Stephanopoulos raises his left hand. "Except I'm already married."

"Oh. Okay." Molly looks past him to me. "Sowrry, Mom, he's awl-wready mawrried, so you need to mawrry Gwriff instead."

This time the coffee does drop from my hand; luckily the lid is on and there's only a sip left, so it doesn't spill, but it clunks to the floor, and I need to scramble to my knees to retrieve it.

It always amazes me how much more attuned my kids are than I give them credit for. I think they're oblivious, lost in their egocentric worlds, then they go and say something like that, and I realize they're paying a lot more attention than I imagined.

"See you on the set in a few minutes," George Stephanopoulos says as the AD signals to him that the commercial is about to end.

"In a few, good as new," Molly yells after him.

69

Molly does a marvelous job answering George Stephanopoulos's questions, the same rote questions she's grown accustomed to.

"Have you always known you wanted to be a singer?"

"I'm onwly fouwr, so I haven't had a wlot of time to think about it."

Audience laughter.

"Who is your favorite Foster sibling?"

"It depends. Mostwly Jewremy, but sometimes Miwles. Evewryone's wreawlly nice to me."

On and on the questions go until finally, "Will you sing for us?"

Molly slides from her chair and walks to the stage beside the interview set where a band is already set up and waiting. She sings her hit single, "Moonbeams to Heaven," and the audience goes wild with applause, then the show cuts to a commercial and Molly is shuttled from the stage.

A quick shower for me and a bath for Molly at our hotel and we're back in the limo and on our way to FAO Schwarz for the unveiling of a new line of gourmet lollypops being introduced by Hershey called Molly Pops. Huge posters of Molly holding a Molly Pop wallpaper the windows, and a horde of hundreds stand behind ropes as the limo drops us in front of the giant toy store.

"That me?" Molly asks, her brow pinched as she studies the larger-than-life photos of herself.

I can understand her confusion. Between the makeup and the Photoshopping, the posters barely look like her. She looks like a smoothed-out version of herself without a mole, a vein, or a flyaway hair.

Girls squeal and mothers and fathers press forward against the three police officers who part the crowd so we can pass. I hold Molly tight as Patrick shuttles us into the store. Though we've grown accustomed to fans swarming around us, it's still disconcerting, especially at moments like these, when the line that protects us is so thin and the crowd is so large, when the smallest fissure would crumble our defenses and leave us at the mercy of a stampede.

Dealing with this kind of fanfare is the most difficult part of Molly's success. It's so frenetic and at times so desperate. Hands reach to touch us, and voices clamor for our attention. People throw things at us—flowers, stuffed animals, chocolate, compliments, overtures of love. Girls scream Molly's name and hold out pens and paper and skin for her autograph. Many have their hair curled like Molly's and a lot wear overalls. Sometimes the excitement overtakes one of them, and they will faint or break down and cry.

It's strangely surreal and slightly disturbing, and when we are in the moment, like now, it's as if I am viewing it through a lens, my brain disconnecting from what's going on so it feels as if I'm not actually experiencing it but rather observing it from outside my body.

A Hershey's representative escorts us to a spot between the two escalators, and after a brief introduction and lots of applause, Molly cuts a large red ribbon with a pair of scissors nearly as large as she is, and a twenty-foot-tall acrylic display with a molded image of Molly holding a Molly Pop is unveiled. The bubble over Molly's acrylic face reads, "Molly Pop, Molly Pop, Oh Molly, Molly Pop."

For the next two hours, we sign autographs for the fans with a wristband, how or why they are the ones with the privilege to meet Molly a mystery. A crowd of others press forward against the velvet ropes to take photos of us.

Above us, on the second floor, is the famous floor piano—a giant electronic keyboard that kids can dance on to make music. As we work, the laughter and discordant notes of the kids playing float down to us.

"Can I do that?" Molly asks at one point, looking up from her autographing.

"Sure, baby," I say, though I can't imagine that she can, since the moment she steps on the platform, the world will stop, and everyone will be watching, and she'll be left alone to play the music by herself, and it will no longer be fun.

It's after three when we finish.

"Now can I pwlay the piano?" she asks.

I look at Patrick, who looks at his watch and shakes his head. "We're fifteen minutes behind schedule already, and we can't be late."

I squat down to Molly's level and look her in the eye. "How about you and I come back tomorrow and we wear disguises so no one will recognize us and we dance on the piano then?"

Molly's mouth curls into a knowing grin as she nods. She also knows it will be more fun if no one knows who she is.

"Pwromise?" she asks.

"Promise," I say, and already I'm thinking of ways to disguise her trademark curls.

Patrick herds us into the limousine where a lunch of burgers and fries awaits, and we pull away with a tail of paparazzi behind us—a few scooters and half a dozen beat-up, colorful little cars with their windows down and cameras balanced on the door frames. They weave in and out of the thick New York traffic, sticking dangerously close as we race to Yankee stadium.

Patrick lights up at the sight of them, and I have the feeling that our itinerary was sent to the media ahead of time by our delighted publicist. It is not unusual for the pack to be tipped off by a publicist, an agent, or the star themselves. All press is good press, and free press is the best press.

The mayor and his family meet us in front of the statue of Mickey Mantle for a photo shoot, then we are ushered onto the field for Molly to sing the national anthem, a song she fortunately has memorized because *The Foster Band* performed it in one of the episodes.

We watch the ball game until the seventh inning, then Molly sings "Take Me Out to the Ball Game" and almost gets the words right. The crowd roars in laughter when she bumbles a few of them, then they help her out on the final verse.

We leave before the applause has even settled to race back across town for a dreary dinner at a fancy French restaurant called Jean-Georges. The Hershey executives are attempting to show us a good time but fall short, partly because we're exhausted and partly because caviar and escargots prepared by a top-notch French chef don't do much for a four-year-old.

We arrive back at the hotel at ten, Molly falling asleep before her head even hits the pillow.

I long to collapse as well, but first I need to attend to the dozen urgent emails and texts that arrived during the day. Most are requests for Molly to do this or that, and the others have to do with real-life issues like overdue dental cleanings and the dry cleaning that needs to be picked up.

I save the message from Sean for last then, with a deep sigh, press play.

"Hey, Faye, great news. I called Chris, and he got Emily an audition. I guess the writer for the show, Bradley Mitten, has been looking for a new love interest for Caleb and Emily's the perfect age. So I need you to call your mom because she's being a bitch and telling me we can't stop by to pick up the jeans Emily wants to wear for the audition."

My hair sticks up all over my body, my fingers fumbling to hit the callback button.

"You can't take her to see Mitten," I say when he answers.

"Christ, Faye, calm down. What the hell's wrong with you? It's all set."

"Well, unset it. Mitten's a sick son of a bitch."

"Maybe, but he's a sick son of a bitch with a lot of power. Did you know that he's the one who discovered Gabby?"

"Yes, I know that! And I know why he chose her. The guy's a pedophile."

Sean laughs. "You always have had a flair for the dramatic."

"I'm not being dramatic. I'm telling you how it is."

"Yeah, right. And you, Faye Martin, are the only one who knows."

"Everyone knows."

"Everyone knows that the writer of *The Foster Band* is a pedophile, and yet no one has said a word about it? Faye, I get that you feel high and mighty in your new role, but you're not the only one with connections anymore. Face it, I succeeded where you failed. Em's stoked about this. So I know I'm stealing your thunder, but you need to get over it."

"Sean, this isn't about me..."

"You're right, it's about Em. Do you realize how hard this has been on her? Tom and Molly being stars and her being a nobody?"

"She's not a nobody."

"That's how she feels."

"Sean, please, listen to me. I know Em wants to be an actress, but it's really not her thing. She's good at other things..."

"She's going to be good at this," he says. "Christ, Faye, Em is right, you really do play favorites. I know Molly's cute, but Christ, you should hear yourself. Em's your daughter too, you know."

My jaw clenches, and my nose pinches against his hurtful words. "It's not about favorites. Em can't act."

"You memorize your lines and say them when it's your turn. It's not rocket science."

I rub my temple, my head throbbing. "Okay, fine. If she really wants to do this, I'll look into other agents..."

"She doesn't need another goddamn agent. I told you, I got her a private audition. I thought you'd be happy. The three of them can be on the same show, and you and me, we can manage them, be a team again, like we used to be."

My breath catches with his suggestion of reconciliation, time slowing as the silence pulses, percolating then sizzling across the three thousand miles between us.

"Sean," I say finally, with as much compassion as I can muster, "it's not going to happen. There's no new role for a love interest for Caleb. Mitten just uses that as bait. You need to believe me. This isn't real."

"Go to hell, Faye. Go to fucking hell!"

The line goes dead and I turn off my phone, feeling like I'm already there, the fires of damnation burning a hole in my exhausted brain.

70

My eyes fly open, my breath heaving, the dream dissolving before I can catch it. My dad...no, Tom...one or the other, one first that became the other. Muddled the way lost dreams are. Panic. Something to do with water. Them, but I was the one drowning. I sit up and look at the clock. Five thirty. I rub Molly's shoulder. "Come on, Bug, time to wake up."

"Don't want to."

"I know, baby, but people are waiting."

At six, we're on the move again, our paparazzi tail still in place, making me wonder if they work in shifts or simply don't sleep.

First stop is the St. Regis Hotel where we do a press circuit, which is kind of like media musical chairs—six consecutive interviews in six different luxury suites with six different publications—same questions, different faces.

When we're done, so is Molly. She needs sleep and so do I. No such luck. Lunch is with a mucky-muck from Mattel who wants to discuss the possibility of an exclusive endorsement deal for their Little Mommy line.

Molly practically falls asleep in her soup. She doesn't even like dolls, but the deal is for a lot of money and Fox loves the idea of a Molly/Mattel partnership that will generate advertising dollars for the studio.

"Now can we go to the piano?" she asks when we climb back in the limo.

Patrick shakes his head, and my heart pounds. We need to make it back to FAO Schwarz. I promised. On the limo drive to lunch, Molly and I devised a plan. If I tightly braid Molly's hair and we wear hats and glasses, and if we don't stay too long, and if Molly is careful not to laugh her signature gravelly giggle, and if we don't pull up in the limo, we might just get away with dancing on the piano undetected. All the supplies for the ruse are in the limo and ready to go; now we just need the time.

At two o'clock, we're on the set for a taped segment of *The Today Show*. Molly tries, but the enthusiasm just isn't there. She perks up when she sings but then barely responds when Matt Lauer high-fives her after.

"When do I get to dance on the piano?" she asks when we're done.

I turn to Patrick. "We *need* to get to FAO Schwarz."

He nods. The man is a wheeler-dealer without a paternal bone in his body, but even he realizes how important dancing on the piano has become to Molly.

"Three more interviews and there might be time," he says.

"No," I say. "Cancel one if you have to or cancel them all."

"Cancel? We can't cancel. It's *Teen Vogue*, *Rolling Stone*, and *Highlights*."

"Then combine them or shorten them. Molly's done her part, and she needs to dance on that piano."

He nods and scurries away to figure out how to condense the next three hours into two, and Molly hugs me around the waist, as pleased with me as I am with myself for standing up to him.

The interviews fly by thanks to Patrick telling each reporter precisely how much time they have, and by setting his phone on the table with the stopwatch displaying a countdown to detonation.

We're halfway through the final interview with *Rolling Stone*, and I'm getting excited because it looks like we'll not only have enough time to dance on the piano but also be able to visit the giant candy shop and enjoy our treat across the street in Central Park.

"How do you feel about the accusations that your costar Gabby has a drug problem?"

I step forward, but Patrick is already there. "This interview is over," he says, literally pulling the plug on the microphone that is connected to the man's recorder.

His severity surprises and pleases me, though I'm uncertain if his fierceness is out of loyalty to Molly or the show. Boundaries for interviews are set ahead of time—what can be asked and what's off-limits—but it doesn't stop some reporters from crossing the line. They usually wait until the end of the interview, when they know they have their story locked up, then they throw in a zinger, hoping to catch Molly off-guard and to incite a reaction that will score a "hot" interview. In the past two months, Molly's been asked about sex, drugs, alcohol, gay rights, and abortion—things she knows nothing about.

"That's not fair," the reporter whines. "It's a legit question."

Patrick rolls his eyes. "Molly, you're done. Stomp on a few of those piano keys for me."

And I decide Patrick's not so bad after all, and that maybe he has more of a paternal gene than I gave him credit for. Molly high-fives him, and we skip out of the hotel suite and down to the limo. Patrick will be staying in New York to spend Thanksgiving with family, so finally, for the first time in two days, Molly and I are on our own.

"FAO Schwarz," I say to the limo driver. "And step on it."

We're thrown back against the seat as the driver guns it out of the hotel's driveway. Thirty seconds later, he slams on the brakes. Half an hour after that, we've only traveled five blocks in the halting afternoon traffic, and Molly has conked out on my lap.

I keep looking at my watch as the limo continues to inch along at a crawl. Our candy store/Central Park time is gone, and our piano time is dwindling. I will the traffic to move faster. I close my eyes and pray. I make promises to God that I will be a better person if He will just part the sea of cars and let us get to FAO Schwarz.

When the driver's phone rings, my heart sinks. Though I can't hear the conversation, I hear the turn signal go on at the next intersection, and I realize what's been said. The driver has been told to take us to the airport so we don't miss our flight.

71

You pwromised."

Molly and I stand on the sidewalk of the departures terminal. Our limo driver pulls our bags from the trunk and sets them beside us. I hand him a tip, and he climbs back into the car and pulls away.

"I know, Bug, but we ran out of time."

In my peripheral vision, I see a flash, and suddenly I'm painfully aware that we are being watched. I turn my head to see at least a dozen paparazzi with their lenses trained on us.

"You said," Molly says. "You said aftewr we did evewrything we had to do, we would go back."

"I know and I tried, Bug, I really did, but it wasn't up to me."

"Molly, over here," a reporter says.

Another calls, "Molly, look this way."

"Molly, tell us how you liked New York?"

Molly sticks her tongue out at the reporter.

"Molly," I gasp.

"Molly, give us a wave."

"How about a smile?"

"Molly, look this way."

Molly sinks to the ground and puts her face in her hands.

I signal to a skycap, who hustles over, scans our tickets, and puts tags on our bags. Cameras continue to flash, each flare like a grenade exploding in my brain.

"Come on, Bug, let's go," I say, holding out my hand.

She ignores me. She's done, her disappointment on top of the exhaustion too much to take, and I feel the meltdown mounting.

"Baby, we have to."

Her head shakes side to side, and suddenly the reporters are very quiet, all of them captivated by my predicament, salivating at being present to witness how I deal with my famous four-year-old refusing to budge.

I handle it the only way I can. I trigger the explosion. Molly writhes and kicks and screams as I pick her up from the pavement, her fists pounding my back, her feet leaving welts on my thighs. "You pwromised," she screams. "You said we'd go back to the piano."

Our carry-on bag dangles from my arm and drags behind me as I wrestle her into the terminal, the reporters following us, their cameras blazing.

"She didn't tip the skycap," one of them says with glee. A dozen pens scrawl the juicy oversight in their notebooks, and I feel my tears threatening. Molly is now in full hysteric mode, her face red with fury, her back arching as she pushes with all her might to break my hold.

"You pwromised. You said. You pwromised," she screams.

Every person we pass watches, half of them pulling out their phones to record the spectacle.

I run to the restroom and into the handicap stall then collapse on the toilet with my sobbing bundle, my whole body convulsing as my tears escape.

People have followed us in, and I need to bite my knuckle to keep my sobs from being heard through the thin barrier that protects us.

"Which one is she in?" a nasally voice says.

A moment later, a woman's frizzy head pops over the wall of the stall beside us. Ruthlessly she snaps photo after photo of Molly and I clinging to each other, and I don't think I've ever hated a person so much.

"I'm sorry, baby," I whisper as I kiss Molly's head, my eyes glaring at the woman.

Molly sniffles, her tantrum spent as the woman continues to take photos.

"Out," a man's voice bellows, causing the woman to disappear. "Now," he barks again.

"I'm going," her nasally voice says.

A moment later, the man says gently, "Ma'am."

I pinch my nose, unable to respond, Molly and I trembling, though both of us are hot and sweating.

"Ma'am," he says again. "I'm with airport security."

I do not trust him. I no longer trust anyone. He could be an imposter. He is an imposter, I'm sure of it. We are in hell surrounded by devils. Me and my baby, alone.

My hand shakes as I pull out my cell phone.

"Griff," I whimper, my voice a strangled whisper.

"Faye? Faye, is that you? Where are you?"

I hold the phone beneath the door, and a cocoa-colored hand takes it from me.

"Hello, who am I speaking with?" the man says, then I listen as he tries to explain to Griff as best he can what happened and why Molly and I are hiding in a stall in the restroom of the airport. He doesn't get the story completely right—he misses the part about Molly sticking her tongue out at the reporter and having a tantrum—but he gets across the basic gist that something happened outside the terminal that caused us to be pursued by a pack of paparazzi, and that we are now huddled in a stall extremely distressed.

"Ms. Martin," he says when the explanation is finished, "Griff says you can trust me. I'm here to escort you to your gate."

And I have no idea if it's true, but just hearing the man use Griff's name gives me faith, and I lift Molly in my arms and open the door.

The man is short and round with a kind face and a badge that says Gomez. He hands me back my phone, which is still lit up with Griff's name.

"Griff," I croak into it.

"Yeah, I'm here."

My lungs release, and air seeps in.

"Hang in there, Squid," he says. "Officer Gomez is going to get you on your plane."

"Stay on the line, please," I say.

"I'm not going anywhere."

72

We'll be landing in LA in approximately thirty minutes," the pilot announces. "Los Angeles has partly cloudy skies, and it's an unseasonably warm eighty-two degrees…"

I open the shade to look at the world below, midnight black except the weak starlight casting shadows on the miles of tract homes, farmland, and mountains below—a place like Yucaipa, maybe Simi Valley or Thousand Oaks. How I want to strap on a parachute, take Molly in my arms, leap from the plane, and float back to that place.

We are escorted off the plane before the other passengers, and a security guard meets us at the gate. He ushers us to a private waiting room, where we're told we will stay until our bags have been retrieved and loaded into the car that's been sent to pick us up.

"Hey," Molly says from the couch beside me. "That's us."

She points to the television mounted in the corner of the room, and my blood freezes, then I scramble frantically to shut it off, hitting every button until finally the horrible report that shows Molly sticking her tongue at a reporter then having a fit as I carry her off is silenced.

Molly's face is gaunt and horrified. "They show that on tewlevision?" she says. "That woman said you hit me. You hit me?"

"She said I hit you?" I say, trying to recall what I saw as I was trying to turn it off, and like instant replay, the report spirals in slow motion through my mind.

Pretty blond reporter, impossible white teeth. *Superstar Molly Martin and her mother, Faye Martin, were spotted earlier this evening at JFK*

Airport, where it appears there was an altercation that led Faye Martin to slap the four-year-old for sticking her tongue out at a reporter…

"No, Bug, I didn't hit you. You know I didn't. You were there."

"Why they show that?"

At that moment, the door opens and Griff steps in. I blink several times to make sure I'm not imagining it then leap into his arms, my head buried against his chest as he wraps his arms around me.

"Trouble," he says. "With a capital 'T.' That's what the two of you are."

I nod against him, never so happy to see anyone in my life.

"Hey, Squidoo," he says over my head.

"Hey, Gwriff," Molly says. "Did you see the tewlevision? They say Mom hit me."

He lets go of me and sits beside Molly. "First of all, Squidoo, as an actress you should know that what they show on television isn't real, and second, you should know that you should never watch anything about yourself on television."

"But they showed me cwrying."

"You're a little girl. Sometimes little girls cry."

She still looks sad.

"Come on, time to get you girls out of here." He stands, puts on a baseball hat and a pair of sunglasses, then turns his back to Molly. "Walk or piggyback ride?"

She leaps on board.

"What's with the disguise?" I ask, stung by the idea that he's embarrassed to be seen with us in light of our recent headlines.

"Best to keep a low profile when you're around trouble," he says.

"I didn't hit her."

"I know. There are like seventeen other shots of what happened on the internet, and all of them show that your hand never came close to Molly, that you were just trying to keep your bag from slipping off your arm."

"So why are they showing that one?"

"Better story," he says as he gallops out the door with Molly on his back.

I trail behind, mortified, angry, and stunned that the press can be so ruthless.

"Shit," Griff says.

Through the exit doors, a horde of paparazzi press up against the glass, a crush of people with their cameras and microphones ready. It looks like hundreds, and I can't believe it's worth it for them to stand out there waiting for hours just to get a photo and a sound bite of me and Molly. Aren't there more important stories to cover than a kid having a tantrum and her mother carting her away?

Griff hesitates, gauging the situation, then swings Molly around in front of him so he's holding her like a football. "We need to rush them. Faye, you go first, and I'll follow with Molly. The limo is straight through the second door."

My heart pounds like a cattle stampede in my chest as the doors open and I charge through the crowd. Mack sees us, runs forward, and hunches over me, pushing me toward the limo as arms and phones and cameras and words are slung at us. I turn my head to look for Molly and see Griff right behind me, Molly tight against him.

The reporters press in on us more and more until finally we reach the car and Mack is pushing me into the backseat, then Molly is being thrown into my arms and the door is being slammed. The limo lurches forward, and I crane my head over my shoulder, watching in horror as Griff holds back the crowd so we can move forward, his hat and glasses gone.

Reporters run after us, risking life and limb to sprint through the airport traffic with their cameras raised like swords, flashes erupting on either side of us, until finally, one by one, they give up, several of them flipping us off. Mack keeps an almost constant hand on the horn as he bulldozes his way forward, his message clear—get out of our damn way or I'll run you over.

Griff is still on the sidewalk. A lone reporter, a woman with red hair, stands beside him, her lens not following us but instead trained on Griff, and something about the way she's smiling sends a chill down my spine.

"What about Griff?" I croak.

"He'll find his way," Mack says.

"That was fun!" Molly says.

73

When we reach the freeway, my phone buzzes, and I pull it from my back pocket, consider not answering when I see who is calling, then reluctantly press the answer button. "Hey, Sean."

"Faye, the phone is ringing off the hook," he says excitedly.

"We're fine."

"Yeah, I know you're fine. So *Extra* is offering the most..."

"I didn't hit her."

"Really? Looks like you did. Not that anyone can blame you—looks like she was being a little shit. But I'm thinking if we don't do an exclusive..."

I hang up.

"Was that Daddy?" Molly asks.

"Yes, baby. He wanted to make sure you were all right."

"Is he coming to see me?"

"No, baby. He's taking care of Em."

My phone buzzes again and I ignore it, but when it continues to buzz, I pull it from my pocket to turn it off and am shocked when I see it is Chris who is calling.

"Chris?"

"Faye, you okay? How's Molly?"

Tears spring to my eyes with his concern.

"We're okay. Griff came and got us. We're in the limo and on our way home."

"Thank God. Damn buzzards. Where the hell was Patrick?"

"He stayed in New York to spend the holiday with family."

"He left you on your own? Are you kidding me? Well, rest assured, he's done for. I'll make sure of it."

Patrick sending us off to the piano with a high-five flashes in my mind. "No, Chris, that's not necessary. It wasn't his fault. It was all...It was just too much. I didn't hit her. You know that, don't you? I didn't hit Molly. My bag slipped. I was just reaching up to catch it. They made it look like I hit her, but I didn't."

"I know you didn't hit her, but that's irrelevant."

"Irrelevant? It's not irrelevant. You need to tell them. We need to have a press conference or something and tell them I didn't hit her."

"Faye, calm down. The last thing we need to do is call more attention to this. What we need is for you to lay low for a few days and let this all blow over."

"But everyone's going to think I'm a horrible mother, that I hit my kids."

He laughs. "Yeah, you look like a real bruiser."

"Chris, it's not funny. I don't hit my kids, and I didn't hit Molly."

"Welcome to the crazy world of celebrity, where fiction becomes fact. You don't hit your kids and Helen isn't sleeping with Jeremy and Jules isn't Gabby's father. It's all part of the game. You just need to go with it."

"But there's a limit."

"There's not."

"There should be."

"Faye, you chose this life and the exposure that goes with it. Fortunately Americans have a very short attention span. Take the rest of the week off, and by the time you come back to work, another story about another famous somebody will be in the news, and everyone will have forgotten all about this. Now can I talk to Molly? I want to make sure she's okay."

I hand the phone to Molly, who lights up when she finds out it's Chris. "Hey, Chwrissy Cwrossy," she says, and my heart swells with gratitude at how much Chris cares.

74

Where are we going?" I ask when I realize we're not heading in the direction of my mom's condo.

"Can't take you home," Mack says. "There's a media mob waiting there worse than the one at the airport. Griff says to take you to his place."

The words send a new tremor down my spine with the thought of my mom and Tom being at the condo alone with the piranhas below.

My mom picks up on the first ring. "We're fine," she says, knowing my panic before I can even ask. "We have plenty of supplies and plan on just holing up until the reporters get tired or bored."

"Griff called you?" I ask.

"Yeah. A good guy that one. Why can't you date a nice guy like that?"

I nearly groan in annoyance. I've avoided telling my mom about my unkissable status with Griff, not able to bear her nodding along in agreement.

"We're just friends," I say, the statement sounding as adolescent and lame as it is.

"Yeah, I know you're just friends. That's the problem. The nice guy is who you decide to make your friend; the jerk, you marry."

An hour later, we're in the city of Pasadena, a hillside community of rolling hills, old orange orchards, and quaint neighborhoods. We thread our way through the town and onto a quiet street with ranch-style homes like the ones I used to dream of living in when we lived in Yucaipa.

I press my head against the glass and let the coolness seep into my head. Anonymous people living anonymous, worthwhile lives. I wouldn't mind being anonymous again. As a matter of fact, the idea is beginning to appeal to me greatly.

The limo pulls to a stop in front of a gable-roofed bungalow with natural wood shingles and dark green trim. A taxi pulls up behind us. Griff pays the driver and steps from the backseat, his jaw clenched, his face blanched white.

"You okay?" I ask.

He ignores the question, marches to the stoop where Mack has set our bags, and leads us inside.

Whoa! Appearances can be deceiving. What looked modest on the outside is mind-blowing on the inside. The house is a sprawling chalet with leather couches, a grand piano, and an expanse of glass that looks out on a courtyard flanked by two wings.

"Come on, Squidoo, I'll show you your room."

Molly shuffles after him.

Through the window of one of the bedrooms, I watch Griff help Molly into her pajamas then tuck her beneath the covers. He sits beside her, and by the way she's smiling and the way his hands are moving, I'm guessing she asked him to tell her a story.

I wander the living room, admiring the beautiful furniture and Griff's amazing collection of artifacts from around the world. I don't know where the masks, strange wooden board games, and terra-cotta bowls came from, but I know they didn't come from anywhere nearby. There's nothing Ikea or Target about anything in the room.

I stop beside the piano. On the wall above it is a collage of at least forty photographs that chronicle a remarkable life. Griff can't be more than five years older than me, but he's done so much more with his time on this earth. There are photos of him holding snakes, riding elephants, and standing atop mountains. He's been to places where there's only snow and places where there's only sand. He's hauled in swordfish from the ocean and trout from jungle-laden streams. He's ridden rapids and jumped from airplanes. The man's lived more adventures in a third of his life than I could imagine living in all of mine. In a few photos, he poses alone, but in most he is surrounded by others—friends, foreigners, women—all of them grinning at the lens, sharing the amazing moment.

I'm filled with envy. I can only dream of having a life so full and am jealous that so many have already laid claim to his heart.

Griff is back.

"You didn't have to do that," I say.

"Which part, tuck Molly into bed or rescue you at the airport?"

"Well, you kind of had to rescue us. After all, the show must go on."

His face loses its humor. "That's not why I did it."

I look away.

"Come on," he says. "I need a drink."

I follow him into the kitchen, and he pulls two Heinekens from the fridge.

"Glass?" he asks.

I shake my head.

"A low-maintenance girl. I like that."

"Yeah, real low maintenance—you only need to leap into a pond of poisonous snakes and fight them off so my daughter and I can get to our limousine, and I won't demand that you provide me with a chilled glass for my beer."

He smirks, but it's low wattage, and again I wonder what's wrong, but this time I don't ask. Silently I drink my beer, waiting for the alcohol to seep into my bloodstream and take the edge off. Over and over my mind catches on the reporter's bright white teeth and her pink lips telling the world I slapped Molly, my memory replaying the fuzzy video that showed my carry-on bag falling from my shoulder as I reached to lift Molly from the sidewalk, my hand flying up to keep it on my arm and the vague appearance it gave of me hitting her.

"People are so cruel," I say. "At the airport, no one helped us. Everyone just gaped and took pictures, like seeing Molly break down and me struggling to get her away from the reporters was entertainment."

"It was," Griff says with a sigh, then he drains the rest of his beer and grabs another. "The public is used to seeing headlines about celebrity meltdowns. Personal issues are fair game."

"This wasn't that," I say. "This was an exhausted little girl who needed a moment to calm down."

"Exactly, but that doesn't sell commercials or pay salaries, so they spun it for maximum impact, and the masses took to it like pigs to mud."

He tosses our empties in the trash then grabs two more beers from the fridge, and when he shifts sideways to reach the bottle opener below the sink, I see it, a photo not with the others in the living room. It is a black-and-white shot framed in thick ebony wood. In it, a tall white-haired man smiles at the camera, his arms draped over the shoulders of a little girl with blond hair and a good-looking, darker-haired boy. The man registers first—Trent Hemsley, one of the most famous actors of his time, best known for the cowboy series *Arroyo*, which he directed and produced. My focus shifts to the girl, catching on her dazzling eyes—*Helen!* I snap to the boy—exotic eyes, dark at the rims, high cheekbones—*Griff? Griffin Wade? Megastar, teenage heartthrob?*

"You're famous?" I stutter.

Griff's eyes follow mine to the photo, and he sighs. "Was," he corrects. "A long time ago."

Griffin Wade—his disappearance was legendary. There were even bumper stickers that said *Where's Griffin Wade?* that became all the rage for years after he vanished.

My eyes fix on the picture. With the exception of the eyes and cheekbones, the boy in the photo and the man he turned into look nothing alike. As a matter of fact, it's hard to imagine Griff as a boy at all; with his linebacker size, deep voice, and abundance of facial hair, it seems like he must have hatched that way, fully grown, burly and tough.

It's no wonder no one recognizes him. I pride myself on being observant, and I was a religious watcher of *Arroyo*, and until this moment, I had no idea Griff and Griffin Wade were the same person. And even sitting here, the evidence in front of me, it's difficult to believe.

My eyes flick back and forth from the photo to the man, trying to make sense of it, until finally the puzzle clicks into place. "You don't want to be famous?" It's half question, half realization.

His head shakes. "Being good at something and recognized for it is great. It's all the other stuff that sucks."

I lean against the kitchen island, and he sits on a stool, making his famous eyes level with mine. *Griffin Wade is sitting beside me sharing a beer. That's crazy.*

"So you changed your name?" I ask.

"My name, my country, my personality."

"And then you came back?"

"Ten years later. I assumed it was safe. I didn't look like I did. I had this kick-ass beard." He strokes his furry chin.

And more of the world aligns itself as I realize why he wore the hat and sunglasses at the airport, a wave of horror washing over me as I remember the red-haired woman with her camera aimed at him.

"That reporter recognized you," I say.

He finishes his beer and sets it down. "Figures I would fall for the one girl in the world with a kid even more famous than me."

And the last piece of the puzzle clicks—the reason kissing me was not a good idea—then, just as quickly, the revelation is blown to smithereens with the realization of what he just said. "You've fallen for me?"

He answers by wrapping his hands around my hips, pulling me between his legs, and pressing his lips to mine.

"Are you sure about this?" I say.

"Very sure. Only good thing about tonight is that I no longer need to worry about it. Might as well do as I damn please, and at the moment, the only damn thing I want to do is you."

75

We are in his bed, our frantic lovemaking over. His eyes are closed, his right arm draped over me, his fingers caressing my shoulder.

Thirteen years. It's been thirteen years since I was with a man other than Sean. Thank goodness Griff and I both have a sense of humor and that we're both a little drunk. Even with the lubricant of alcohol, I was extremely self-conscious and Griff was a bit too enthusiastic, both of us awkward and clumsy and making a less-than-graceful holy mess of the whole condom thing and who does what.

It doesn't help that Griff is Griffin Wade. The entire time we were having sex, I kept thinking about it. *I'm having sex with Griffin Wade—teen idol, superstar. He's probably slept with hundreds of women, maybe even thousands.*

Now we're lying together in what is supposed to be postcoital bliss, but instead my feelings are all over the place, tangled between wanting to flee in extreme mortification over how bad I was and the desperate desire to have a do-over.

When I can't take my tortured thoughts a second longer, I push up onto my elbow and say, "You're Griffin Wade."

"Was," he says, his hand unwrapping from my shoulder as his eyes open and his mouth tightens into a frown.

"But tomorrow you're going to be him again because that woman recognized you."

He says nothing, only the flare of his nose revealing his concern.

"I'm sorry," I mumble, the superstar dissolved instantly into the man

I've grown to love. "I've ruined everything for you. Everything you've fought so hard to protect is going to..." I search for the words. "It's not going to be what it was anymore."

"Nope," he says, sitting up and pushing me back to the bed, his hands on my shoulders, his body hovering over me. "Starting at this moment, nothing is the same as it was." Then his lips are coming down on mine, and the comforter is being pulled away.

I want to pull it back, to cover myself, because I'm acutely aware of the fact that my body has had three children and should not be scrutinized so closely. But he is merciless. Sitting up, he runs me over head to toe, first with his eyes then his touch, his fingers traveling down my sternum to my rib cage then tracing the thin scar that smiles between my hips, his caress so gentle it makes the skin tremble.

"Molly," I say. "Stubborn even then."

He kisses the sacred spot, his lips lingering a second before moving south and traveling to a less sacred spot that causes me to writhe in torment and ecstasy, awed that such pleasure and pain can come from the same wonderful, horrible sliver of flesh.

76

Mom, I hungwry," Molly says, appearing in the doorway and finding Griff and I tangled together in the sheets as if it's the most natural thing in the world.

"I've got it," Griff says, pecking me on the nose before he slides from the covers, and I'm relieved to see that at some point in the night he pulled on pajama bottoms. "You rest. Squidoo, you ready to have the best waffles on the planet?"

"Wready, Fwreddy," she answers, grabbing Griff by the hand and pulling him from the room.

I try to close my eyes to savor the extra moments of sleep, but their laughter from the kitchen keeps distracting me, and I hate not being a part of it. So after less than two minutes, I hop out of bed, pull on my clothes, and join them.

"Do you get the paper?" I ask as I settle at the table beside Molly.

"Trust me, Squid, you don't want to look at the paper, not today. As a matter of fact, for the next week you should avoid newspapers, television, and the radio. It's better if you don't hear what they're saying."

I know he's right and try not to think about the entire nation thinking of me as a woman who slaps her children, instead trying to focus on sitting in Griff's bright kitchen as the best waffle on the planet is placed in front of me.

My phone buzzes on the counter, and he hands it to me.

"Faye, I swear I'm going to kill the bastard," my mom says when I answer. "If he comes anywhere near me, I'm going to slice off his balls and shove them down his throat until he chokes on them."

"Mom, calm down. What's going on?"

"Haven't you seen the news?"

"The airport thing?"

"No. Sean."

"Sean's in the news?"

"Yeah, he's in the news. The bastard's ranting and raving about how he won't rest until his children are safe, that in light of you hitting Molly and Emily..."

"Emily? What's Emily got to do with this? Em wasn't even with us."

"Not yesterday, from before, when you slapped Emily at the Park Plaza Hotel. The security director came forward yesterday and has been on every news channel going off about how you whacked Emily in front of him."

"Whacked? That's what he said? He said I whacked her?"

Griff takes the phone from my trembling hand and carries it to the living room, out of earshot of Molly, who is staring wide-eyed at me.

"Sorry, Bug," I mutter, my body quivering with panic, mortification, and guilt.

"You whacked me?"

"No, baby, not you, Emily."

"You whacked Em?"

I shake my head. "No, Bug, I didn't *whack* Em. Eat your waffle."

But she doesn't eat her waffle. Instead she sits quietly staring at it, wondering why the world is saying I slapped her and whacked her sister, probably wondering if maybe I did and if maybe she just forgot or doesn't realize it.

Griff is back. He hands me my phone. "We need to go," he says. "Your husband's on his way to the condo with Emily, and it's probably best if we don't let him face the press alone."

"I thought you said I needed to avoid the press."

"That was until I found out your husband is going to use them to try to get custody of your kids."

77

We arrive too late.

A block away from my mom's condo, we see Sean standing on the top step of the building's entrance, his arm draped over Emily's shoulder as he talks to the dozens of reporters around them.

"Duck down," Griff says as he pulls on a baseball hat and puts on his sunglasses.

Molly and I curl so we're below the dashboard, and a moment later the truck bounces from the road to the ramp of the parking garage.

"Okay," he says. "Let's go quickly while your husband's got them distracted."

"But shouldn't we stop him? Who knows what he's saying?"

"Too late," Griff says. "We needed to stop it before it started, or get there first to present your side of the story. Now it will look defensive if you jump in, so we need to let it play out. Come on, the stairs are closer." I feel his tension, his fervent desire not to be seen, and again I'm reminded how much this is costing him.

"I'm sorry," I say as I punch in the security code to the stairwell.

He gives a weak, brave smile. "My life was starting to get dull."

We reach the landing of the sixth floor at the exact moment the elevator dings open and Sean and Emily step off it.

I carry one of our suitcases and the now infamous carry-on bag. Griff carries the larger suitcase and Molly.

For a moment, we all just stand there looking at each other.

"Em, go get those damn jeans you want," Sean says.

"Take your sister with you," I say.

Griff sets Molly down, and Emily takes her by the hand and leads her into the condo. "Hey, Itch, how was the Big Apple?"

"Thewre was a big appwle somewhewre?"

Emily giggles and drops a kiss onto Molly's curls then closes the door, locking out the tension in the hallway that is so thick the air feels liquid. Griff and Sean size each other up, their postures fake relaxed, their muscles coiled.

"Sean," I say. "This is Griff. He works with us."

"I know who the hell he is," Sean says. "He's all over the fucking paper, along with you and Molly. Griffin Wade, back from the dead, Faye's knight in fucking armor. So tell me, *Griffin*..." He nearly spits the name. "Is this..." He gestures to the two of us. "...love or are the two of you just fucking?"

Griff says nothing, the vein in his neck pulsing.

"She is a good fuck," Sean continues. "She'll fuck you until your balls shrivel off. Has she fucked you that good yet, *Griffin*?"

Griff steps toward him, causing Sean to laugh and my blood to turn cold. Griff is big, but Sean is mean. I step between them, my hands on Griff's chest, his heart thumping against my fingers as I shake my head, my eyes pleading for him to let it go.

He swallows and takes a step back, a move that I can tell takes every ounce of his will.

I turn to Sean. "You need to stop talking to the press. I didn't hit Molly. I told you that."

He smiles a toothless grin. "Doesn't really matter if you did or didn't. That's the beauty of it. All that matters is that the world thinks you did. Now don't it? You don't want to share. Well, neither do I. You can't have it both ways, Faye. You're either with me or you're against me, and you made it pretty damn clear where you stand, so I'm coming at you. I'm going to get full custody, and I'm going to make Em as famous as the other two. A fucking trifecta."

I ignore the threat and focus on the immediate danger. "Sean, please, listen to me. Don't take Em to this audition. I know you think this is an opportunity, but it's not. Mitten does this, he lures young girls in with promises..."

"It got Gabby the part."

"For a price," I say, struggling to keep my voice level. "She paid a price and so will Em. You don't want that."

"Don't tell me what the hell I want."

I lower my eyes, my heart spitfiring with panic, and in a voice as deferential as I can make it, I say, "Please, Sean. I know how much you love her. Don't do this to get back at me. This isn't who you are. You're a good man..."

"Ha!" He throws his head back and laughs then levels his gaze on mine. "Only you, Faye, would still not realize I'm not the man I was. Hell, I don't even know if I ever was that man."

Emily walks out the door. "I'm ready," she announces, her backpack slung over her shoulder.

"Sean, please."

"Em, go on down," he says. "I'll be there in a minute."

Emily steps onto the elevator, and when the door closes, he turns back to me. "You know what they say about the green-eyed ones...no, green ones...maybe the same thing. Makes men horny. Mitten's going to love her."

Griff charges, sidestepping me and throwing a haymaker at Sean's head. Sean ducks it easily, rolling beneath it before rising back up to throw his entire body into a punch that he drives into Griff's solar plexus. Griff drops to his knees, the air knocked clean out of him, then Sean finishes him with a blow to the temple, and Griff is on the ground and unconscious before I can move an inch.

Sean steps over Griff's body and glares down at me as I squat beside him. "Keep him away from me, Faye. Next time I'll kill the bastard." Then in no great hurry, he saunters to the stairwell.

Griff groans, and I look down at him, his left eye already beginning to swell.

"Does it hurt?" I ask, helping him sit up.

"The eye? Not so much. My pride? Hell, yeah. I can't believe I didn't even land a punch."

"Sean's a fighter," I say, trying to be reassuring.

"My Viking and Cherokee ancestors are groaning in their graves. I got pummeled in less than ten seconds by a man half my size."

"He's not half your size, maybe three-quarters your size."

"You're not helping."

I lean in and kiss him, and his arms wrap around me as he mumbles against my lips, "Now you're helping."

When he pulls away, I'm breathless. He might not be much of a fighter, but he's a hell of a kisser.

"I need to stop Mitten from auditioning Emily," I say.

"You know those rumors about Bradley aren't true. He lost his daughter, and it screwed him up, makes him sappy and nostalgic, which causes him to get overinvolved with the teenage actresses, but he's not having sex with them."

"You know that for sure?"

His brow furrows as he thinks about it, then he says, "Fine, I'll call Chris and make sure Bradley's not alone with her, but I still think you've got it wrong." He takes out his phone. "Trouble. I knew it the moment I saw you. With a capital 'T.' "

"You said your life was dull."

"And now, thanks to you, it's full of peril."

"Don't worry, Sean's gone."

"It's not Sean I'm worried about. Only one heart, and it's in the hands of a Squid."

78

Thanksgiving was spent divided, and when Sean came Friday night to get Molly and Tom, I refused to give them up. In turn, he kept Emily. He continues to threaten filing for full custody, and I threaten the same. He's bluffing. I'm not. Taking care of three kids full time would crimp his style; I would like nothing more than to have Sean out of my life for good.

I called my lawyer, and she is looking into what grounds we might have to petition for full custody, but she has yet to come up with anything. The health, safety, and welfare of the kids is all that matters, and Sean's not a danger to them, at least the court won't see him as one.

The stress of everything that happened this week and Emily's absence is battering Molly emotionally, and for the past two days, she's had a tough time sleeping and has reverted to sucking her thumb, a habit she gave up when she was two.

Tom is weathering things better. He might have even been relieved that he didn't need to spend the weekend with his dad. Unlike the girls, Tom's relationship with Sean has not been fully repaired since Sean's return. Tom internalizes things more than Molly and Emily and has always been more aware, and despite my efforts to protect the kids from Sean's deceit, I think Tom sees it and doesn't fully trust him.

The best part of our time off was Griff. Three of the past five nights my mom volunteered to watch the kids, and every blissful moment of that time was spent in his arms.

Now our time off is over and we're on our way to the studio, my stomach in knots. Molly hasn't run her lines and lies listless on the seat beside me, her thumb in her mouth. We've had ten days to rehearse, and yet she's completely unprepared, and I'm worried she might be coming down with the flu.

The media frenzy over the incident at the airport has died down and been replaced by an equally disturbing outpouring of support, our social media sites and fan mail blowing up with an outcry of anger, sympathy, and dismay over either the injustice of the accusations or in advocacy of corporal punishment for children. In the past week, so many stuffed animals, flowers, and gifts have been sent to Monique Braxton's office that we could open our own store. Molly knows about none of this—the letters and goods dispensed to either the trash or the Salvation Army, without Molly being the wiser. The intimacy of it all is very disturbing, so many people who have never met us weighing in with an opinion about our life, as if they have a say.

And of course, the new attention has rustled the "creepers," adding several unsettling letters and gifts to Molly's stalker file with the police.

"Bug, we need to read the script," I say.

She doesn't answer.

I smooth her hair and look out the window. We are stopped at a red light, and in the lane beside us is a bright blue BMW convertible. My eyes fix on the three girls in the backseat with their made-up faces, crop tops, and diamond belly button rings.

Emily is going to be one of them. The thought pops in my head before I can stop it.

The car squeals away, and the girl on the right stands on the backseat and lifts her shirt to flash the truck beside them. The driver honks in appreciation, and the girl falls back against her friends, the three of them cracking up as if that was the funniest thing in the world.

❧

The day is going about as bad as I expected, everyone irritated with Molly because she doesn't know her part. The scene, which should have been done in an hour, has already taken twice that, and she still hasn't gotten it right.

Chris calls cut again then marches across the set to lean in close to her. "Two-Bits, did you not memorize your lines?"

Molly looks at the ground, her shoulders slumped, then she loses it, tears running down her cheeks as she stammers and searches for an explanation, nothing coming out but a grief-stricken sob.

"She's tired," I say. "This week was..."

He waves me off and bends down, his hands on his knees. "Okay, Two-Bits, calm down. Take a deep breath." He looks over his shoulder to the crew. "Break for fifteen."

The crew scampers off, Griff leading the way, literally racing off the set without even a glance at me. This morning has been hell, not just for us but for him—his revealed identity as an ex-superstar wreaking havoc on his life.

After getting pummeled by Sean, he left my mom's condo to find a swarm of press lying in wait beside his truck, his freshly swollen eye adding fuel to the feeding frenzy and inciting all sorts of new speculation on the juicy soap opera of our lives that is unfolding in the news for the whole world to see.

Then this morning, he arrived to a hostile crew, his guys pissed off by what they see as a betrayal. Us versus them, crew versus cast, the camps as divided as union versus nonunion. You're one or the other; you can't be both. They thought he was one of them, when in fact, he's an imposter who belongs to the enemy camp.

To top it off, Chris was awful to him when he showed up this morning for the first scene. *Well, well, look who's joining us. Griffin fucking Wade, gracing us with his legendary presence after making us all look like idiots for not having a fucking clue that Griffin fucking Wade was our director of photography.*

Heat crept up Griff's face, but he said nothing, just took his usual place to wait for the shoot to begin, and his expression has remained blank since, making it hard for me to breathe, a tanker of guilt rolling over my chest and parking there.

"Okay, Two-Bits, let's learn this," Chris says, taking Molly by the hand and leading her to his director's chair. "Beth, I need a Red Bull."

Beth scurries off, and I watch with appreciation as Chris patiently goes over the scene with Molly line by line.

Beth returns a minute later and holds out the can to Chris.

"It's not for me," Chris says. "It's for Molly."

I leap from my seat and snatch it away. "Thanks, but that's okay. We don't drink energy drinks."

"You said she was tired," Chris says.

"Yeah. She's tired because she's not feeling well."

"And this will pep her up."

"I'm not drugging my kid."

"It's not a drug. It's caffeine."

"She's tired, Chris. She needs rest, not caffeine."

He frowns at me. "Fine." Then he turns back to Molly. "Okay, Two-Bits, you've got it now?"

Molly nods and starts to walk back onto the set, but Chris grabs her arm before she takes her first step and spins her to look at him, his eyes locking on hers. "Two-Bits, this can't happen again."

Molly bites her lip to hold off another downpour and nods.

∞

We finally got through the scene and are now eating lunch in our limo with Helen. She picks at her undressed salad—hold the croutons, hold the cheese, hold the calories and taste. Staying immaculately starved is grueling work.

Molly and Tom are in the front seat with Mack eating Happy Meals from McDonald's as he teaches them how to play poker. Every once in a while we hear giggles and yelps of excitement through the glass.

"It's just so much pressure," I say. "Molly's not going to be perfect every day. You should have heard Chris this morning. He was so harsh, and his opinion means so much to her. With everything that's going on with Sean, I just wish he would be a little more understanding, like he actually cares instead of pretending he does."

"Chris does care," she says. "Don't confuse what happened on the set this morning with not caring. He was seriously upset about what happened at the airport. Did you know he fired the whole publicity company, not just Ham-Face?"

My stomach knots with more guilt. What happened wasn't Patrick's fault. Zero tolerance is exactly my point. Chris might care, but he expects too much.

Helen continues, "I've known Chris a long time. He's a good guy. Outside the show, a very good guy. But it's tough. He's responsible for keeping *The Foster Band* on top, and that requires a bit of brutality. His hubris versus his humanity, it's a constant struggle for him. But make no mistake, he cares. He lives, eats, and breathes this show. Sometimes his temper blows and he doesn't use kid gloves, but he does it because he cares, not just about the show but about us. He does it so we will all still have jobs to wake up to in the morning."

My phone buzzes. Though we've already logged six hours, we're needed at the music studio for a recording session that will probably last the entire afternoon.

79

It wasn't planned. It wasn't like I dropped Molly at the music studio then walked back to the soundstage thinking this was what I was going to do. I didn't even realize I was doing it until I found myself knocking on Chris's door.

Now I'm in front of him, my heart pounding as I take the seat across from him.

Stay calm and explain the situation rationally. There's no need for emotion.

"Chris, we're done," I blurt. "Molly…me…we can't take it anymore. My family is falling apart. My older daughter, Emily…"

"Whoa," he says, holding up his hand. "Calm down. Start again."

I take a deep breath, fold my hands in my lap to quell the shake, chew the inside of my cheek until the panic passes, and when I'm in control say, "Chris, we can't do this anymore."

He smiles, and relief washes over me. Helen was right. Chris isn't a bad guy, and I remember the first time I stood in this office on our first day when Molly and I were late and lost and he showed us to the wardrobe room.

"That's better," he says. "Now tell me what's going on."

I explain as best I can about how overwhelming everything has become, how difficult this week was, how unhappy we are and that I just want to go back to being a normal family, and how I want Molly to have a normal childhood without so much pressure. I tell him about Emily deciding to live with Sean and how little time I've been able to spend with her.

When I finish, he rocks back in his chair and sighs. "I understand," he says. "Being a stage mom is tough. It can be extremely demanding and sometimes overwhelming, and you're right, it takes its toll. And you have both Molly and Tom to deal with, plus Emily at home. I can see where it could get to be too much."

I nod, so glad he understands.

"Sean and I talked about it," he continues, bristling the hair on my neck. "He was concerned you were reaching your breaking point."

"I'm not breaking," I squeal. "I'm telling you we don't want to do this anymore, that it's too much for Molly. She's not having a normal childhood."

"No, she's having a childhood most girls dream about. I admit the New York trip should have been handled better. Damn incompetence, that fool leaving you alone. It makes me furious every time I think about it. Does that idiot have a clue how fucking dangerous that was? Maybe a bodyguard."

"I don't want a bodyguard! That's exactly what I don't want. More separation between us and the real world. What I want is to go back to being normal."

Chris blinks several times in confusion as if I'm speaking a foreign language, so I clarify. "We quit."

He laughs. "Faye, I like you. As a matter of fact, for a time I *really* liked you, and you know how I feel about Molly, but you realize that's not how this works, right? You can't just quit. That's cute though, very cute."

Heat floods into my cheeks. "I'm not being cute. I'm being serious. We're done. Write us off the show."

He shakes his head. "First of all, it's not up to me. Second, even if it was, I wouldn't do that because Molly's the greatest thing that's happened to the show since it started. And third, like I said, I like you, so I want to stop you from doing something you'll regret. Your daughter is a commodity, at the moment, a hot commodity. There's no telling how long that will last, but at the moment, it's a gold mine."

"She's not an it."

"That's where you're wrong. Molly is an it. Gap has invested in her as well as Mattel and Hershey's. Fox, RCA Records. This is bigger than you and me. It's not about Molly the person but Molly the brand, a brand worth hundreds of millions of dollars."

"She's a kid," I roar. "My kid, and everyone seems to be forgetting that. She's my kid, and I decide what she does and what she doesn't do."

The smile drops from his face, and he shakes his head. "Faye, she is your kid, and you do make the decisions, but your choices are more limited than you seem to understand. One, you can buck up, get back to work, and reap the rewards, or two, you can continue to go postal, and someone else will step in to take over managing Molly's career, and they will reap the rewards."

"I'm not going postal," I scream like a lunatic. "I'm trying to save my family!"

"Then I suggest you choose option one," he answers calmly. Then he stands, walks around me, and opens the door, showing me the way out.

80

I walk from Chris's office back to the music studio and sit on the bench outside the building, my thoughts muddled in confusion over how things got this out of control.

The sun breaks through the thick cover of clouds, and I lift my face to soak up its warmth, looking up through the branches of the oaks that line the courtyard. The trees remind me of the apricot trees in Yucaipa, dark skeletons barren of leaves and fruit, but if you look closely, you can find a small bud, a sprig of green, the promise of spring.

I think of Molly playing with the little girl on the airplane, nothing special, two girls lost in a game of cards, yet it was miraculous. For months, Molly hasn't had a friend, hasn't held hands, run, skipped, or jumped with a kid her age.

Childhood is a fleeting blink, a momentary bridge of time that shapes who you are and your life to come. It's incredibly precious and brief, and you can't get it back. Chris is right. Girls dream of what Molly has but only because they don't really understand it. Ever since we hopped on this crazy ride, it's as if time has sped up, and I'm suddenly horribly aware of the passage of it. Next month Molly will be five, and the month after that, Tom turns nine. Warp speed, Emily leaping right past her youth altogether.

In the distance, a hawk circles, gaming its prey, perhaps a mouse or a squirrel. I watch, my compassion split between the hunger of the bird and the fate of its next meal. There's something beautiful in the simplicity of it, hunt or starve. My life used to be simple like that, difficult but simple. I worked hard to care for my family. We didn't have a lot of money, but we got by. I took pride in holding it all together and making it work, as much pride as I take now in managing Molly and Tom, perhaps more because the challenge was wholly mine and I was more in control.

My ambitions have always been modest. When asked by my third grade teacher what I wanted to be when I grew up, I proudly answered a wife and mother. The snickers that followed taught me not to be so honest again, but those humble aspirations never changed. Is it so shameful to make a life out of caring for those you love?

This wasn't what I signed up for, or maybe it was, but I didn't know what I was signing up for at the time. Ignorance is my defense…and greed. I admit that I saw dollar signs, a chance to be more than just a worker bee struggling at the bottom. And yes, fame. Who doesn't want to be famous? On some level, all of us thirst for acknowledgment, affirmation that we are special in some way—talented, good, worthy. And the power that comes with it. People revering you, wanting to do things to please you. Power to make a difference as well. Our appearance able to raise tens of thousands of dollars for a needy cause. The ability to sway opinion, knowing that if I dress Molly in a particular shirt or if Tom carries a particular book, they will become instant bestsellers. There's a headiness in being so important.

But also a price. We earn money, but we also generate it, so much of it that it is a vital source of income for hundreds, even thousands. So we are expected to work to maximize our output, our lives filled with obligations and demands too much for one person to meet.

Molly's life is no longer her own, and as a result, none of the rest of us have lives either, our world reduced to managing and maintaining her celebrity. Like a parasite, her fame consumes us, invading and devouring everything beyond it.

This is my fault, but I did not see it coming; the glitter and glamour blinded me. In some ways, it still does. Though I'm reluctant to admit it, part of me is relieved we are being forced to stay. Chris's refusal to let us quit lets me off the hook, takes the responsibility out of my hands, and spares me from making a decision I would need to defend to the world and that I might regret.

And I would, in some ways, undoubtedly regret it. Tom is thriving. It's easy to forget about Tom, to not include him in the equation. He doesn't demand attention the way Molly and Emily do. But the truth is, this world suits him, and he is doing better than he's ever done before. Here, in the land of make-believe, he has found his place, his purpose, and his voice.

As have I. The past is not so distant that I have forgotten how difficult my life was before all this. I was husbandless, jobless, and penniless, my prospects dismal. Now I exist in a world where I am important, where my ego is fed daily, where money rolls in like the waves, and where I am in love.

Yes, Molly and Emily are in trouble, but in a sense, Tom and I have been spared.

Our contract is for three seasons. We've made it through half of one, which leaves two and a half to go. I shudder at the math, unable to imagine what six times what we've already been through will do to us—to Molly and Emily.

The clouds close rank, sending shadows across the trees, and I watch as the hawk dives then rises back into the sky with something in its beak, its hunger staved off for another day. And my sympathy is undeniably for its prey, its life over simply because, when it woke today, it chose the wrong path.

Jeremy comes out of the studio with Molly on his back. She bounces up and down and shouts, "Giddy up, gawllop."

Jeremy does as she asks, rearing up then skipping across the sidewalk to dump her at my feet.

"Good howrsey," Molly says, patting his head as Jeremy bows to her, then he scampers off to play with people his own age.

Taking Molly by the hand, I lead her to the limo, watching as my feet move in and out of the glimpses of sunlight. We reach the parking lot, and I lift my head, and that's when I see it, parked a row from our waiting limo, red as a candy apple, its black convertible top up.

I whirl around and pull Molly back toward the soundstage.

"Mom, whewre we going?" Molly says, scrambling to keep up.

"Your dad is here," I say, my panic mounting. "Your dad and Emily."

"Why awre we wrunning?"

We're running because I'm praying that I'm not too late.

81

Where is she?" I scream at Sean when I find him behind the living room set engaged in conversation with the woman who plays the social worker. Since Sean decided to settle in LA, he's been working a rotating circuit of women, so I'm thinking Regina of Albuquerque is now out of the picture.

He swivels to look at me. "Hey, Bugabaloo," he says to Molly, patting his leg for her to hop on board, which she happily does. His eyes narrow as he looks at me, but his face remains a composed mask of coolness for his audience.

"Where's Em?" I ask.

"Mitten called her back for a second audition," he says triumphantly.

"Where?"

"I don't know."

"What do you mean you don't know?"

"I mean, I don't know. He said something about needing to record her voice."

"Molly, stay with your dad," I say as I race toward the sound lab, a room tucked away at the back of the soundstage that is used for recording voice-overs and mixing sound effects.

I hear Sean attempting to follow with Molly, but I lose him by cutting through two of the sets then doubling back so he's heading the opposite direction of where I'm going.

The red light above the sound lab's door signals "In session." I ignore it and storm in.

Emily and Mitten are in the soundproof vocal booth, a space with foam walls, a stool, and a microphone. Emily has on a pair of headphones, and Mitten is adjusting a camera so it's directed toward her.

"Stop," I say as I throw open the door from the recording bay to the booth.

Both turn to look at me.

"Emily, go," I say.

She stares but doesn't move.

"Now!"

"I'm in the middle of my audition," she says.

"No, you're not. This is not an audition, and you are not going to get the part of Caleb's girlfriend."

"Why not? Molly and Tom are doing it."

"That's because they have talent," I blurt before I can stop myself.

Her eyes squint, full of fury and hate.

"I'm sorry, Em," I say.

She pulls off the headphones and flees.

I turn to Mitten. "Stay away from her. Go near her again, and so help me, I'll call a press conference and announce to the world what a sick bastard you are."

His beady eyes narrow, his pale lips puckering. "If you are referring to the vile rumors about me, there's nothing you can say that has not already been said. I auditioned your daughter as a favor to Chris and called her back again because I didn't want to callously dismiss her as you just did. You're right, she has no talent. My hope was to give her the opportunity to discover that for herself."

My eyes narrow in distrust, and he returns my glare.

"Just stay away from her," I say. "I mean it. The press doesn't know about Gabby. Go near Emily again, and I'll tell them exactly why you insisted Gabby get the part."

His face pinches. "It's probably not the best idea to threaten someone who can destroy you."

"Destroy me? As in write Molly and Tom off the show? Please, if only I should be so lucky. That's all I want. As a matter of fact, I'll make a deal with you: write us off this show and I promise to never speak your name to anyone ever."

His mouth curls into a toothless grin. "Tell me, Faye, who do you think is more important, you or me?"

"You," I acknowledge. "But as important as you are, Molly's got you trumped."

"We don't need you to keep her."

82

I am in Griff's bed in his home.

He does not hate me or blame me for his anonymity being obliterated, which causes me to hate myself and blame myself intensely for the damage I've done to his life. The media is having a field day with his reappearance, and now, like us, he can no longer go anywhere without his presence making news and a horde of reporters slinging questions at him.

He says it's worth it, that I'm worth it, but it does little to lessen my guilt, and I can't help but wonder if he was right, if kissing me was a bad idea indeed, and if he wouldn't have been better off steering clear altogether.

He caresses my shoulder, and I roll toward him to rest my hand on his cheek. My mom offered to watch the kids, so I sent Molly and Tom home in the limo. Like Cinderella, I need to leave by midnight and mutate back into the person I really am, the mother of two child stars who both need to be on the set at dawn. But at the moment, I'm a childless princess lying in the bed of my handsome prince.

"Favorite movie?" I ask.

"*Sleepless in Seattle*," he says without a blink.

"Nice try."

"Works on most girls."

He kisses my nose then readjusts himself so he is on his back, my head on his shoulder. "Let's see, favorite movie? When I was a kid, it was *Jaws*, but now I think I'd have to say *Forrest Gump*. I watched it again a couple nights ago. It's my go-to movie. It's just so damn hopeful in light of so much crap, and Forrest has to be the most brilliant character of all time, not the sharpest tool in the shed but the most chivalrous and romantic character ever."

And I know I'm done for. *Forrest Gump* is my go-to movie as well, though I never rewatch it. It's too sacred for that. I simply remember it. Forrest asking Jenny to marry him. *I'm not a smart man, but I know what love is.* And even when Jenny doesn't love him back, he continues to love her because that's exactly the point. He *knows* what love is. Thinking about Forrest and his mom and Jenny and Lieutenant Dan and Bubba lights up my heart every time.

I kiss him, and he kisses me back, then we're going at it again, like refugees starved for food, frantic and hungry, limbs bumping and getting tangled. This is how it's been between us, moments of tenderness and moments of panic, both of us terrified that what we have isn't real or that, for some reason, time is running out and it's going to disappear.

After, when we're done and lying beside each other breathless, both of us slightly self-conscious of our clawing, frantic performance, I say, "Tell me what you're thinking."

"I'm thinking that was insane, and that I need to start going to the gym or running if you're going to be so demanding."

"Ha ha," I say. "But really, tell me your thoughts."

"My thoughts are that I want to recover my breath and do that again."

"That's your desire not your thoughts."

"I'm a man. The two are pretty much the same."

I smile but refuse to let him off so easy. "Just a peek at what's turning inside that brain of yours, please. Today was rough, and I want to know what you think about it."

It's only a flicker but a realignment of his thoughts just the same as he alters the truth, and I feel a chill of betrayal ice my spine. He feels it too and doesn't allow me to pull away, which I am trying to do, my hands braced against his chest as he holds firm.

"Stop," he says. "It's just not my place."

"Your place?" I ask, confused but only for a second. He thinks I'm asking his opinion about my life, when I was actually asking his opinion about his own.

"This business with Emily is between you and Sean."

I purposely didn't tell Griff about my conversations with Chris or Mitten. He loves me, but he also loves the show and his crew, and it would upset him to hear I tried to quit. Besides, there's no point. Chris made it clear we're stuck, and Mitten made it clear that I have no power over him. But it was silly for me to think Griff wouldn't have heard about Sean chasing me through the set as I searched for Emily.

"But you have an opinion?" I say, while wishing I'd never asked him to tell me what he was thinking and that we could go back to postcoital, conversation-less cuddling.

"My dad used to say there are two kinds of people," he starts, and already I know I'm going to be lumped into the wrong group. I try to kiss him to shut him up, but he rolls away and looks at the ceiling, his arm behind his head. "Those who lead their lives and those whose lives lead them." I jerk away from him and stand abruptly as he props himself up on his elbow. "You asked," he says.

"Shut up." I pull my shirt over my head. It's inside out, but I don't care. What is it with these people? My mom, Griff? I'm doing the best I can. I'm working my ass off and raising three kids while dealing with a manipulative, asshole ex-husband who, by law, has the right to half parent the aforementioned kids and who has turned my daughter against me while at the same time endangering her. So excuse me if I'm not in total control of the situation.

I pull on my jeans and shove my panties in the pocket.

"Faye, stop," he says. "Come back and lie down. I'm just saying..."

"I know exactly what you're saying," I snap. "You're saying I'm a fuck-up who married the wrong guy because she stupidly got pregnant when she was nineteen and has been fucking up ever since. And you're right, look at me now, sleeping with you. Knowing my luck, I'll end up pregnant again. I seem to have a knack for that, not planning for condoms to break. Don't worry, I'll text you in a few months and let you know if you're going to be a daddy."

I storm off, but after three steps I need to turn back because I left my keys on the table. I pivot, spinning right into his arms, which are reaching for me. I wriggle to free myself, but it's a halfhearted effort.

He whispers into my hair. "I'm sorry." And the thing is, I know he is, but I also know as I relent and allow him to lead me back to the bed that he believes what he said and that he's right—there are people who lead their lives and those who are yanked around like a yo-yo.

Today I tried to take control. I talked to Chris and tried to quit. I stormed in on Mitten and threatened him if he went near Emily. But as usual, rather than making things better, I feel like I only made them worse.

83

I stare at the papers in my hand. I've been staring at them for a full day now, since they were given to me last night as Molly, Tom, and I walked to the elevator after our day at the studio. The emergency change of custody order gives me twenty-four hours to refute the evidence Sean presented to the court proving I am a danger to my kids. The evidence includes:

1. A sworn affidavit from Elizabeth Glenn, the social worker from Yucaipa, attesting to my negligent behavior both in sending my children to the car unattended during our first meeting and in not getting Tom the therapy he needed for his disability, despite multiple counseling sessions in which I was advised to do so.

2. Two sworn affidavits from two street vendors from the Third Street Promenade testifying that I left Molly unattended on the promenade and subsequently lost her.

3. A sworn affidavit from the nurse at Methodist Hospital testifying that the gash on Molly's arm was inconsistent with the explanation I gave of her cutting her arm on a slide, and that the injury was more consistent with that of a knife wound.

4. A sworn affidavit from Beth that I allowed Molly to do a river scene without warning her that Molly couldn't swim, a scene in which Molly subsequently almost drowned, my lack of concern showing blatant disregard for Molly's welfare.

5. A sworn affidavit from the security director at the Park Plaza Hotel attesting to me slapping Emily across the face.

6. Video footage of me slapping Molly at JFK airport.

7. A written letter to the judge from Emily:

 Dear Judge,

 Please help us. My mom is not a good mom. She is mean and she doesn't care about us. All she cares about is my sister being famous. She leaves my little sister who is only four alone a lot and also leaves my brother who is eight alone. She also hits us when she gets angry. I have already left to live with my dad, but I am worried about my brother and sister. It would be better if we were all together and my dad was taking care us. Thank you.

 Sincerely,
 Emily Martin

I called my lawyer immediately, but with so little time, there was nothing she could do. The problem with trying to refute the evidence is that there's nothing to refute. It is all either the truth, a version of the truth, or a lie I can't disprove. So today I sit on the couch staring at the letter from Emily as a social worker and my mom pack up the kids' things so they can move in with Sean.

In a month, there will be a hearing to determine whether the order should be extended beyond the temporary period. I have until then to figure out how to turn this around or to beg forgiveness, leniency, and mercy from the court and pray I don't lose them forever. My lawyer is hopeful that by then we will have a counterargument and evidence to discredit the testimony against me.

I stare at Emily's letter so hard that the ink blurs. Is it possible to love and hate your child at the same time? My hurt is so deep that I feel like my organs are turning black. Sean put her up to it, but still, the writing is hers. She wrote those horrible, wounding words.

My mind is having a hard time processing what is happening, my life unraveling so quickly that it makes no sense. How did Sean know about Ms. Glenn? Or the hospital? The answer comes in disconnected waves. *He didn't. He couldn't have. Someone told him. No one could have told him. I was the only one who knew about both. More than one person told him. He has been planning this. That's not like Sean. Sean doesn't plan things.* Mitten's words come back to me. *It's probably not the best idea to threaten someone who can destroy you. We don't need you to keep her.*

My palm presses against my chest to push back the pain. Life needs an undo, a magic button that can turn back time so I can fix this, a rewind switch to return me to the moment before I threatened Mitten, or further back, to the moment on the promenade when Molly was singing and dancing with Leroy.

84

The kids are gone. I've had a week to get used to the idea, but the shock has still not worn off. I am numb except for the pulsing ache beneath my rib cage, each breath agonizing as though the air is made of shards of glass.

My mom hovers, afraid of what I might do—collapse from despair or act out and do something crazy like kidnap the kids and flee. She's right to worry, my thoughts vacillate between the two.

I wait for the complete breakdown, to lose it and go insane. It seems the least I can do. I lost them, misplaced them, didn't pay close enough attention, and now they're gone. But despite my synapses exploding with everything I've done to cause this, cruelly my brain remains intact, completely, horribly aware of what has happened, and it is only my heart that is cleaved in two.

Griff calls constantly and has tried to visit. I refuse to talk to him or see him. I cannot face him. He was right. There are those who lead their lives, and those whose lives lead them, and I am the latter, my life snatched away without even a fight.

I do not rant or rave, my emotions strangely quiet, a deadness, as if a winter chill has sent my feelings into hibernation. Perhaps for self-preservation, knowing that to allow them out would incite a storm, a tornado of madness that once released won't be contained.

It is an eerie calm as I sit day after day unmoving on the couch, my feet curled beneath me, the television blinking. A small itch buzzes in my brain like there's something to be done, perhaps someone I should call or somewhere I should go—a vibration of disbelief, the pulsating refusal to accept the truth, that there is *nothing* for me to do.

The shadows shift, and I watch them grow long on the carpet. My stomach rumbles. There are apples in the bowl on the coffee table in front of me, put there so the kids would be reminded of the healthy snack, the stone bowl keeping them cool. I make no move to take one, though they are large Rome apples—expensive apples—the kind I've become accustomed to buying.

Such stillness. Quiet I craved a week ago, now it chokes me, the emptiness pressurized like a pneumatic chamber until I feel like I might implode…or perhaps the opposite, burst from my skin into a fireball of destruction running naked through the streets, murdering anything in my path until I get to my kids, which of course I would never do. I am a coward. It has been proven again and again that I would never do anything so bold.

If I sit here long enough, I wonder if I will turn to stone like the bowl. The thought comforts me—cold, impenetrable stone.

85

When there's a knock at the door, I ignore it. There's no one I want to see.

"Helen, thank you for coming," my mom says behind me, causing my head to spin around so fast that I'm in danger of whiplash. Kiss-kiss, the two women greet like French royalty.

I smooth my disheveled hair, wipe the crusts of sleep from my eyes, shove the sweats I've been sleeping in for the past week beneath the couch, and push to my feet.

"Helen? What are you doing here?"

As always she looks radiant—her skin, hair, clothes so flawless that everything around her looks duller and more dilapidated.

"I heard you were wallowing in your wounds," she says, almost causing me to smile. The woman is really too much when it comes to mixing clichés.

"Yes," my mom says, "she certainly is. I'll leave you two to work it out."

My mom grabs her purse and leaves us as Helen glides across the room to sit down on the couch, ankles crossed, hands folded on her lap. "Well, aren't you going to offer me a drink?"

I look at the clock on the television. It's ten thirty in the morning. "All I have is wine or vodka."

She frowns. "I meant coffee."

I shuffle to the kitchen and manage to start a pot, my hands shaking from the sudden burst of activity after a week of barely moving.

While the coffee brews, I search the fridge and pantry for something to eat and find a half-empty bag of Oreo cookies that nearly causes a meltdown. I steady myself against the counter, rein in the thoughts of Molly licking off the creamy centers, and carry the bag to the coffee table. I set it in front of Helen, hoping she'll eat the rest of the reminder and purge it from the condo.

She takes a cookie and nibbles the edges like a bird, and I return to the kitchen to retrieve her coffee.

When I sit down beside her, she says, "Chris will be calling this afternoon, and you need to be prepared."

I blink several times. "Chris? Why?"

"Because Molly and Tom have more power than you think, and Chris was a fool to think he could just shove you out the way he did with that birdbrain Rhonda."

"Chris did this?" I say. "No, he didn't. It was Mitten."

"Mitten? Oh, darling, you really don't have a clue, do you? Mitten's harmless. He's a writer. He writes stories and pokes his head out once in a while to act important, and the producers tolerate his eccentricities because without him there would be no show, but he has no real power."

"But Chris is on my side. He told me so."

"Faye, you've been doing this long enough that you should know, believing what people tell you in this business is both foolish and dangerous."

I shake my head. "I wasn't cut out for this."

"No one's cut out for this. You think I was born the way I am, or Jules, or even Chris for that matter? This business changes you. It makes you stronger or weaker, better or worse, but one thing it doesn't do is leave you the same. As I told you before, Chris isn't evil, only ambitious. The show and its success are all that matter to him, threaten either of those and he'll cut you out like a cancer, which is what he thought he was doing by getting rid of you..."

"How was I threatening the show? He had already convinced me that quitting wasn't an option."

"He knows you threatened Mitten..."

"How?"

"The walls have ears."

I close my eyes and for the millionth time wish I could rewind time, go back and do it different, instead of threatening to expose Mitten, just do it. Set up a hidden camera in his office to catch him with some young starlet and send it off to *Star Gazer* or one of the other tabloids anonymously.

"Between that and threatening to quit, you were a loose gun…"

"A loose cannon," I correct.

She frowns at me. "A loose whatever. The point is, he was worried and figured it was better to get rid of you before it got out of control. And of course, the whole Griff thing isn't helping matters."

"He's mad at me because Griff is famous?"

She rolls her eyes like I'm an idiot. "No. He's mad at you because he's a man and you chose Griff over him. It's the whole alpha-male thing. Griff's always been his rival in terms of power, and now it turns out that not only is Griff the super alpha because he's mega-famous, but he also gets the girl. I'm not saying that's the reason Chris did what he did, but it probably didn't help."

I drop my face into my hands.

"You should call him," she says.

"Who, Chris? You said he was calling me."

"Griff."

The thought causes my heart to close in on itself, my head shaking back and forth. I can't face him knowing that once again life steamrolled over me and that I let it happen. I can't do it. I won't ever be able to face him.

"Well, like it or not, you're going to have to face him at some point," she says.

"No, I won't," I mumble into my hands.

"Yes, you will. I told you, Chris is going to call. He needs you to come back, and when you do, Griff is going to be there."

"You just got done telling me I'm a cancer. Why would he ask me to come back? You're crazy."

"Yes, certifiable, but that has nothing to do with this. He needs you to come back because your children…well, two of your children…are brilliant little thespians."

"What are you talking about?"

"I'm talking about the fact that Molly and Tom seem absolutely incapable of performing without you." She gives a naughty smile. "Ever since you've been gone, no matter who works with them, neither is able to remember their lines, and the show is terribly behind because of it. And I have no idea what's gotten into Molly, but she won't even crack a smile for Hershey's or Mattel. It's downright catastrophic." Her voice is full of glee.

"And whose idea was it for them to suddenly become incompetent?"

"Let's just say you have friends in low places," she says, her grin widening, and my heart cracks open an inch with overwhelming affection for this beautiful, wonderful woman who has become my friend.

"So Chris is going to ask me to come back as their manager?" I say, barely able to whisper the wish out loud for fear it will jinx it from coming true.

"Yes, so you need to be prepared."

"Prepared for what? Yes, yes, I'll come back. Can I come back today?"

"Today is Sunday."

"Then tomorrow."

"See, this is why I needed to talk to you. You're terrible at this. You can't say yes."

My eyes bulge. "Of course I'm going to say yes."

"Eventually you're going to say yes," she corrects. "But first you're going to negotiate."

The light bulb goes on. "I'm going to force him to give me my kids back."

"You're going to ask him to undo what he's done," she corrects.

I nod, a glimmer of hope igniting.

"Then you're going to figure out how to get yourself and those darling kids of yours out of this mess," she continues.

I shake my head. "I tried that. That's how I ended up here. From now on, I just need to play by the rules and not rock the boat."

"To hell you do," she says, her temper flaring. "You need to get them out. That older one of yours is already going down a dangerous path, and Molly's going to be right behind her."

"You don't know that."

"It's a pretty good guess. Child stars end up miserable. It's a fact."

"You're not miserable."

"I'm the exception, and make no mistake, I've had my share of misery. I'm tired of going to funerals, and I'm not standing at Molly's or Tom's."

"You're being dramatic."

"Normally I would say guilty as charged, but there's no need for theatrics here. It's the simple truth, child stars end up screwed up. Being famous when you're young messes with you, and a lot of us end up dead. We struggle, and when the struggle gets to be too much, we throw in the white flag."

"You didn't struggle," I defend, irritated with her tale of woe as she sits on my couch in her designer jeans and Prada boots with her limo waiting downstairs to drive her to her mansion. If I do what she's suggesting and break Molly's contract, the studio is going to sue me, and I'll lose every penny I have and won't have a pot to piss in, or worse they'll take the kids away from me permanently. That's struggling.

"Of course I struggled," she snaps. "I'm better now, but I struggled like hell. I lost two husbands, nearly my daughters, and I still struggle with eating and with looking at myself in the mirror. I'm still standing, but I struggle."

"If it's so damn awful, get out. You're Helen Harlow. If you want to quit, quit." I realize I'm being rude, but my patience is used up for Hollywood royalty, the despots of Tinseltown like Helen and Chris, who can do as they please; write their own tickets; decide what they do or don't want to do—who, with the snap of their fingers, can make or break lives; who have no idea what it's like to be a mere mortal, a nobody with no power at all.

"I don't want to quit. This is what I do. It's the only thing I know how to do and the only thing I do well. Plus I'm treated like a queen and I make a shitload of money."

"You're contradicting yourself."

"No. I'm telling you how it is. That's why Griff came back also. He's great at what he does. Even when he was a kid, he could visualize a scene, see it in his head then recreate it. This town nearly killed him, and he shouldn't have come back, but he did because, like me, this is what he knows and it's what he's good at. I can't believe he pulled it off as long as he did, nearly ten years without anyone realizing who he was until you came along."

"If you're here to make me feel better, you're doing a lousy job of it."

"I'm here to tell you that Chris is going to call and that you need to be ready, and that you then need to figure out a plan to get yourself out of this mess without getting yourself fired again."

"Yeah, okay, I'll get right on that."

"Rumpelstiltskin," she says.

"Really? That again? I thought we were over the whole intimidate-the-new-stage-mom thing."

She laughs, a high, lilting giggle. "I did have fun meeting you that first day, like a cat toying with a lamb. But this isn't about that, it's about the actual story. You're kind of like the maiden. You're stuck and your children are going to be taken from you if you don't figure a way out."

"Yeah, okay. So?"

"So, do you remember how it ends?"

I recall the story. Rumpelstiltskin turned a room full of straw into gold for a young maiden in exchange for the promise that she would give him her firstborn. When the promise came due, she begged him not to take her baby, and out of pity, he gave her one chance to save her child—she had three days to guess his name. If she did, she could keep her baby. It was an impossible task, except Rumpelstiltskin was cocky and foolishly sang a song around his campfire, giving away his secret, and the maiden's child was spared.

"My mom really liked that story," Helen says.

"So you're saying I should be like your mom. Thanks, I'll keep that in mind." I shake my head and drop my face back into my hands. I'm not Helen Harlow, and I'm certainly not her mom.

"I'm not saying you should be like my mom. I'm saying you should be like the maiden. The story is about the reversal of power, about using the arrogance of the person who thinks they're in control against them. The studio thinks they're untouchable, that the show is invincible."

I lift my face to look at her. "And it's not?"

"I'm saying there's more than one way to skin a dragon, and sometimes charging straight at it with a knife isn't the best approach. Television shows are like Jenga, pull out the right brick and the whole thing comes tumbling down."

My head tilts, and silence pulses between us as what she's suggesting registers in slow motion like a sunrise, glowing warm at the edges then growing brighter until it blazes white and fills my whole brain. "You're telling me to sabotage the show?"

"I'm not telling you to do anything," she says, a small smile playing on her lips. "Though if the show were cancelled, your problems would be solved."

"Helen, if the show is cancelled, you'll be out of a job."

"Please," she says as she stands, "I'm Helen Harlow."

86

Sabotage the show. The notion is unsettling and perversely attractive.

Grabbing my purse and phone, I follow Helen out the door, for the first time in a week, certain of what I need to do. If there's a person who will know how to bring down a show it's Bo. Home. I need to go home.

Too impatient to wait for the elevator, I take the stairs. Because the kids are no longer around, neither is the paparazzi, so as I walk toward the Pathfinder, I am unconcerned that my hair hasn't been washed in days or that I am wearing stained sweats and an old T-shirt of Sean's that says, "C.S.A., Can't Stand Idiots."

I am ten feet from the car and clicking open the locks when a man steps from the shadows, startling me and causing the keys to drop from my hands.

"Where is she?" he says.

It takes a second for me to recognize him, and if it weren't for the round glasses, I might not know him at all—John Lennon. But he doesn't look like the clean-shaven young man who used to wave at us from the corner. This morning his face is shadowed with beard, his hair is long and unclean, and his expression is anything but friendly. In his left hand is a folded sheet of paper, in his right, a small gun.

My heart clatters around in my chest. The gun is not pointed at me. It hangs loose by his side. But regardless of its aim, there is a man with a gun standing two feet in front of me demanding to know where my daughter is.

"Where is she?" he says again.

I want to answer, but I can't, my voice lost in my fear.

"I need to see her." Despite being in his twenties, the man sounds oddly like a little boy.

My head shakes back and forth, and my strange waitress voice emerges to say, "She's not here."

"When's she coming home?"

"I...I don't know," I stutter. "She doesn't live with me anymore."

"She lives with the man with the red car?"

I don't answer, my eyes fixed on the gun.

"I don't like him. He isn't nice."

I don't mean to, but my head moves up and down.

"She's with him because you hit her? You shouldn't have done that. That made me mad."

I wait for the gun to rise and shoot me because I made him mad, but surprisingly it is his other hand that rises.

"You need to give this to her," he says, thrusting the paper toward me.

My hand trembles as I take it. Then he bends, picks up my keys, and holds them out, dangling them by my keychain that says "World's Greatest Mom," a gift from Emily two Mother's Days ago.

"You'll give the letter to Molly?" he asks as I take the keys from his extended hand.

I nod.

"Thank you," he says with bizarre politeness, then he walks past me, shoves his hands and the gun into his jacket pockets, and walks out of the parking garage.

I whirl and race back to the stairs. My fingers fumble with the code, and my feet trip up the risers, but I manage to make it up the six flights.

My first call is to my mom, warning her not to come home. She tries to ask questions, but I cut her off. There's no time; I have other calls to make.

My second call is to the police. I explain who I am and what happened, and the operator instructs me to stay on the line, but like I did with my mom, I don't have time and hang up before she finishes the request.

The third call is to Sean.

"Calling to grovel," he answers by way of greeting. "Tough being on the other side of the custody fence."

"Sean, there's a man with a gun, and he's looking for Molly."

It takes nearly ten minutes for me to sputter out what happened, and with each word, I feel Sean's anger rising. "Christ, Faye, you need to get the fuck out of there. I'm coming to get you."

"No, Sean. I'm fine. The police are on their way then I'm leaving. I'm going to Bo's for a couple days."

"That's good. Bo's is a good idea." His tension and fear for me resonates through the line. "Did you bolt the door?"

"Yes."

"And the chain?"

"Yes, and the chain. Sean, he's not coming up here. I don't know why he had the gun, but he wasn't threatening me with it. It's like he wanted me to see it so I would know he was serious, but he wasn't trying to scare me with it. He was just showing it to convince me that I needed to give the letter to Molly."

"What's the letter say?"

I sit down at the table and, my hands still shaking, unfold it in front of me. The paper is plain white and unlined, the lettering rudimentary and sloppy:

> Dear Molly,
>
> I hope you get this before it is to late. As you no by now I love you very much. I have left you dozens of pomes letters and gifts hoping that you wood relize how much I love you and wood start to love me back. I wanted to talk to you but there are always to many people around.
>
> I no your mom is scared of me and that is why she told you not to wave at me anymore. I don't want to scare her I just want you to no how much I love you. I want to spend the rest of my life with you. We cood run away together and be alone without anyone else around.
>
> I can't wait any longer for you to notice me. I've got to do something to proove my love! By sacrificing my freedom and

possibly my life, I hope you will relize how deeply I love you. You can save me. I will be at the Hilton when the president arrives. If you are not there I will no you didn't give me a chance. This is the greatest overture of love I can give. I am doing this for you.

I love you forever,
Ethan W. Howell

"Holy shit," Sean says, just as sirens pull up outside the building.

"The police are here."

"Molly's not going anywhere fucking near that goddamn hotel," Sean says, fury in his voice.

The letter sends the police into a tizzy, and the condo looks like a squad room, and I've been interrogated by at least a dozen different people from half a dozen different agencies. The president's staff has been put on alert and the itinerary for his visit changed so he will no longer be staying at the Hilton when he arrives next week.

Stakeouts are now in place at the hotel, at the condo, at Ethan's apartment, and at Sean's apartment, and an APB has been put out on Ethan W. Howell.

It's nearly two thirty, and my head is throbbing.

My mom has returned and sits with me on the couch as the whirl of activity spins around us. The current debate seems to be whether Molly should be used as bait to flush him out if they are not able to apprehend him before the president arrives.

Sean's answer is an adamant no. And for the first time in her life, my mom agrees with my ex-husband. I should be relieved that the decision is not up to me since custody at the moment solely belongs to Sean, but I'm not. Ethan's sad, troubled eyes keep piercing my brain. If he sees Molly, he might not hurt anyone, and he might not hurt himself.

At three o'clock, I call Sean. "Sean, please listen to me. This guy, he won't hurt Molly. He's just confused and a little off..."

"Confused and a little off with a goddamn fucking gun. I told you, Faye, Molly's not going anywhere near him. I hope the police take him out with a sniper bullet."

"Sean, don't..."

"One less fucking nutcase in the world." He hangs up.

I'm thinking of calling him back when the phone buzzes in my hand. Chris is calling.

87

Chris huffed and puffed, swore up and down that he had nothing to do with the custody hearing, acted furious when I refused to come back unless the court order was reversed, then hung up on me.

An hour later, the police and FBI finally gone, he called back. At first he tried to be cajoling and sweet, and when that didn't work, he tried bribing me with more money. When I refused to budge, he rattled off a litany of expletives and threatened to sue me, and that's when I hung up on him.

The next morning, while I was having breakfast with Bo, he called and said he would see what he could do. And that afternoon, as I was driving home, my lawyer called to tell me the judge had reversed the order. The reversal was based on affidavits she received from both the nurse and Beth recanting their earlier statements as well as from two street vendors who witnessed Molly being looked after by Emily only a few feet from where I was applying for jobs. The new evidence also included a video of the airport incident from a different angle, showing clearly that I did not hit Molly.

The only evidence that remained was Ms. Glenn's report, the security director's testimony about me slapping Emily, and Emily's letter. The judge dismissed Ms. Glenn's report as irrelevant because it wasn't current and because I did get Tom into therapy, and she interviewed the security director and Emily and must not have found their testimony compelling enough because she rescinded her judgment immediately, declaring me fit as a mother and admonishing Sean for fabricating evidence against me.

88

When Molly and Tom walk into the condo, I can't stop hugging them, and within an hour, they are completely sick of me. But I can't help myself. I can't believe they're really back.

Emily refuses to return, court order or not, and there's nothing I can do but hope to figure out a way to get us out of this mess and back to Yucaipa, hoping when the gravy train dries up, Sean will move on, leaving Emily no choice but to come home.

I make a nice dinner, give the kids their baths, read the script to them for tomorrow, then leave to drive across town to Burbank.

I park in front of a large Mediterranean house that is unremarkable from its neighbors—pale stucco, a brick driveway, neat hedges lining a manicured lawn. Surprisingly there's no security gate and no paparazzi. My eyes scan in my rearview mirror, searching for lurking predators, and when I see no one, I step from the car and walk unencumbered to the front door, realizing that, though Gabby is famous, she is less adored than the other Foster family cast members, none of whom could ever live in a home so unguarded.

"Faye," Gabby's mom says, surprised when she sees me. "What are you doing here?"

"I'm sorry to disturb you, Graciela, but there's something I want to discuss with you, and it needs to be said in private."

"Please, come in," she says, a shadow of distrust crossing her face.

I follow her into the house, through the living room, and into the kitchen, passing two boys sitting on a couch playing video games.

"Is Gabby home?" I ask as I settle on a stool at the granite-topped kitchen island.

"She's in her room. Would you like some coffee?"

"No, *gracias,*" I say, immediately regretting the use of my limited Spanish.

She goes about making the coffee anyway, perhaps for herself, perhaps to bide time.

I watch her as she works. She is an unremarkable woman—her hair flat black, her skin brown, her weight somewhere between thick and heavy—and even though we've met several times, it's possible, if I were not in her home, I might not recognize her. We don't know each other well. Gabby is sixteen and therefore no longer needs a guardian on the set. So, other than to say hello, we've barely said two words.

The coffee begins to drip, and she takes the stool across from me, her fingers laced on the counter in front of her. Her hands are older than the rest of her—chafed and scarred from a life of hard work. The nails, however, are freshly manicured, painted a pretty blush pink. It's an odd juxtaposition of the two lives she's led, one as a poor Mexican migrant worker and the other as the stage mom of Gabby Rodriguez, famous actress and singer.

"You're here about Mitten," she says, catching me by surprise and rendering me speechless. "I heard about your older daughter. Emily, is it?"

I nod.

"I will save you time," she says. "We have no intention of saying anything about Mitten."

"So the rumors are true? Gabby... he and Gabby..." I get stuck on how to word it.

She helps me out. "Had sex? I have no idea."

I swallow, and my face blanches with her directness. My plan is simple—take out Mitten. As Helen said, without him there is no show. Bo confirmed it. Actors are only as good as their lines. If Mitten goes, the good actors like Jules and Helen and Kira and Jeremy will follow, and the show will collapse. Jenga.

"But if they had sex, that's rape," I say.

"Only in America would you call it that," Graciela says. "Where I come from, girls have sex when they are ten for a loaf of bread."

She is not emotional, quite the opposite, her face as dispassionate as if we were discussing Gabby having been stung by a bee three years ago, and my skin crawls with her coolness.

"Gabby got much more than a loaf of bread," she continues. "Sex. Puh. I heard the rumors—that bitch, Kira, telling people that Gabby was cast because Mitten has a thing for fat girls. I did not ask Gabby. I do not care. Gabby is not so special. There are many girls as pretty and who sing as well. If it was for sex with that little man, so what?"

I cringe, and her mouth curls into a cruel smile. "You think you are better than me, but you are not. We both sold our daughters for a price, to live a better life, to have a future, the only difference is I am willing to admit it."

I stumble to my feet, mutter something about being sorry to have disturbed her, and as I flee, her words follow me. "You come to my house with your judgment and ask me to jeopardize what we have to help you. *No gracias. Prefiero montar un burro a través de una alcantarilla.*"

My Spanish is limited, but I'm fairly certain she said, *No thank you. I'd sooner ride a donkey through a sewer.*

I drive home defeated. It was ludicrous for me to think I could take down the show. Preposterous and foolish. And dangerous. I squeeze my eyes and pray Graciela does not tell Chris about my visit.

I just got the kids back and already I have jeopardized keeping them. No more stupidity. From here on out, I toe the line. Until our contract is done, I will lay low and play by the rules. We have two and a half years to go. Molly will be seven, Tom eleven, and Emily fourteen. Tears fill my eyes.

89

Driving to the studio, I'm nervous. Like a leper returning from exile, I'm self-conscious and ashamed over what has happened. Yes, I've been exonerated, but only after my dirty laundry was aired for everyone to see.

Anxious as I am about facing the cast and crew, it is the thought of facing Griff that has my stomach in knots. He called at least two dozen times over the past two weeks, none of his calls returned. He must hate me. I deserve to be hated.

I drop Molly at base camp and Tom at studio school then make my way to the set. At the edge, I stop, my heart hammering as I brace myself against the dozens of eyes I feel watching me, then with a deep breath, I lift my head to face them.

Surprise. No one is looking at me, not a soul, everyone going about their business as if I was never gone or as if my return is no big deal.

Except Griff. Sensing my arrival, he turns.

I wait for his wrath, but instead of the anger I expect, the ache in his expression nearly wrenches my heart from my chest, and I lower my eyes, unable to stand my shame.

"Morning, Faye," Chris says brightly, stepping up beside me. "Glad to have you back, and let's hope the amazing one-take Molly is back as well."

He walks past without a care in the world, and I marvel at his ability to forget the past so easily, the epitome of a water-under-the-bridge attitude. And as I watch him continue onto the set, I'm envious, wishing I could do the same.

Or maybe it's not as easy for him as it seems. Something *is* different. I watch as he and Griff discuss the lighting, friction between them that wasn't there before, and I think Helen might be right, two alphas is one too many for Chris to have on his show.

Back and forth they volley until finally Chris pulls his producer card, and Griff has no choice but to back down. It's a childish display of feather ruffling, Chris showing off that he has the biggest plumes.

Chris walks back to his chair, his eyes sliding my way, his chest puffed out in superiority, and I must be a defective hen because I couldn't care less who has more power. My attraction is only for Griff, my body warming as I watch him direct his crew with the new orders.

∞

"Break," Beth announces. "Kira and Jeremy, music session. Everyone else, be on the office set in an hour."

Everyone scurries from the set except for Griff, who sits on the scaffold that holds the main camera.

"All right, Mr. DeMille, I'm ready for my close-up," I say, attempting to keep the moment light as I walk in dramatic Gloria Swanson fashion toward him, my heart pounding as I force myself to look him in the eye. My plan is to tell him how sorry I am for everything then to explain that I need some time to work things out, thereby letting him off the hook.

When I'm two feet away, someone flicks the breaker and the lights go out, dimming the stage to shadows. Then Griff is swooping off his perch, and before I can open my mouth to say a word, he has swung me around and backed me against the scaffold, my shoulders pressed to the cool metal as his lips come down on mine.

"Don't do that again," he says when he pulls away.

To avoid getting upset, I turn the emotion around. "Really? I thought that was kind of fun."

He doesn't return my smile, his face a fierce mask. "Shut me out. Don't do that again."

My chin starts to quiver, my composure teetering on the brink of rupture until his lips graze mine, quashing the tremble. "Please," he says, his voice so gentle that it cuts me to the core. "Please, Faye, don't do that again."

90

Griff and I are in Molly's dressing room, curled together, naked and breathless. Henry has taken Molly for ice cream and Tom is still at school.

I've confessed everything about the past two weeks except for Helen's suggestion to sabotage the show and my visit with Graciela to try to pull it off. Instinct cautions me against it. Griff loves me, but he also cares about *The Foster Band* nearly as much as Chris, and telling him I was thinking of betraying the show would be like telling him I was thinking of betraying him.

"So this guy Ethan is still out there?" he asks when I finish.

I nod against his chest. "He's just a kid, a messed-up kid. It was scary at the time, especially because he had a gun, but it's not like they show in the movies. He wasn't some evil-eyed bad guy. He's just a young mixed-up guy who thinks he's in love with Molly, and when I think back on it, it mostly makes me sad."

"Faye, you get that he's dangerous? He might be messed up and pitiful, but that doesn't make him any less of a threat."

"I know, but..."

"No buts. The guy is dangerous. Dangerous to you. Dangerous to Molly. Period."

I nod again. I know Griff is right, but I also do pity Ethan. Love can make you crazy. I know that better than anyone.

"I tried to quit," I say, changing the subject. "That's part of the reason Chris did what he did. It was the day we got back from Thanksgiving break. Molly wasn't feeling well, and I didn't want to do this anymore. I still don't..."

His arms stiffen. "You can't quit."

My own muscles flinch at his abrupt intractable response. "That's what Chris said."

Griff rolls onto his side so he is looking at me. "Faye, I get that sometimes this is hard, but this isn't a game. Making a show is serious business; a lot of people are counting on you, and you can't just quit."

"You quit," I defend. "Of all people, you should understand. It's not just hard—sometimes it's horrible. You know that. You were at the airport. You saw how bad it was. You told me yourself that being famous sucks. That's why you got out."

"After the show was done. I would have never left during it."

And I realize my instinct that cautioned me against telling Griff my plan was right. Griff's been breathing stardust his whole life, and as such, he is a blind follower of the Hollywood religion—the show before everything else—and asking him to choose between me and the show would be like asking him to choose between me and his god.

"You get that, right?" he says when it's been a minute and I haven't responded.

You get that my life is being torn apart? You get that my kids are the most important thing in the world to me, more important than any show? "I'm losing Emily," I say. "If I don't get us out, I might never get her back."

His face tenses, and I watch as he literally bites back his thoughts, taming them into a more diplomatic response. "You and Sean are going through some pretty rough stuff, and Emily's a bit of a wild kid. The show has nothing to do with that." Translated, what he is saying is *Your life is fucked up and you've totally fucked up your daughter, and you can't blame that on the show.* He continues, "The show is counting on Molly and Tom. Hundreds of people, the cast, my crew, my crew's families. This show is their livelihood. This isn't just about you. When you're involved in a show, the personal stuff needs to be set aside."

His loyalties revealed, he pulls me back into his arms. *Screw family, the show must go on.* Until this moment, I wouldn't have believed that's how he really felt. But now I know, and if it comes down to him being with me or against me, I know exactly where he stands.

91

Mrs. Martin, we need your help."

I carry the phone out the door of the condo into the hallway so the kids won't hear my conversation with the detective. Molly and Tom know nothing about Ethan showing up with a gun, about his threat to the president, or about his letter to Molly, and I don't intend for them to find out.

I listen as the detective tells me that Ethan was spotted an hour ago by a surveillance team who then followed him into an apartment building across from the Hilton. When they tried to apprehend him, he climbed out the window of a seventh-story apartment and is now standing on a ledge threatening to jump unless he gets to see Molly.

"I know it's a lot to ask," the detective says, "but I assure you she won't be in any danger."

My mom has joined me in the hallway and is listening in. She backs away from the earpiece and shakes her head.

"He has a gun," I say in my waitress voice, my throat closed up in panic.

"He doesn't. The gun is in the apartment. He purposely left it so we wouldn't shoot him. This guy doesn't want to die. This is a cry for help. And that's what we want to do. We want to get him to come inside so we can help him. I wouldn't be calling if I didn't think it was safe. I believe if he sees Molly, he'll come in peacefully."

My mom pulls back and shakes her head harder, her eyes bulging.

"Molly's only four. She... This won't make sense to her... Seeing a man standing on a ledge claiming to be in love with her... It's... I can't."

Silence pulses between us for an eternal minute until finally the detective sighs and says, "I understand. Sorry to have bothered you. I needed to at least try."

I squeeze my eyes shut, and the image of Ethan holding out my keys and saying thank you fills my brain. "Wait. Okay. Tell him we're on our way."

My mom follows me into the apartment screaming, "Faye, have you lost your mind? You can't do this. You're not really going to do this?"

Despite my mother's rant, Molly doesn't hear her. She sits totally engrossed in watching *The Backyardigans*, her mouth suspended open in complete zoned-out mode. Tom sits beside her with his music headphones on, both blissfully oblivious to everything around them, the way a four-year-old and an eight-year-old should be.

Griff's voice plays in my head: *No buts. The guy is dangerous. Dangerous to you. Dangerous to Molly. Period.*

Sean screams at me: *I told you, Faye, Molly's not going anywhere near him. I hope the police take him out with a sniper bullet. One less fucking nutcase in the world.*

Helen: *Sometimes you need to say no.*

My dad: *A line in the sand, Faye. At some point, we all need to draw our line and stand behind it.*

I return to the hallway and hit the callback button. "I'm sorry, Detective. I've changed my mind."

92

Ethan is dead. Moments after I told the detective we weren't coming, Ethan stepped off the ledge and died. His last words were *I love you, Molly. This is for you.*

I found out almost immediately after it happened because, within minutes of his death, the media stormed our condo, screaming questions up at our window and buzzing the intercom.

Now, two hours later—the shades down, the intercom disconnected, my phone muted—a dozen police officers surround the building attempting to keep the peace, a task about as easy as herding a swarm of bloodthirsty locusts.

Like a lump of burning coal sitting in the pit of my stomach, the news has decimated me, charring my insides and making me hollow. There are no tears or hysterics, only the sick, empty feeling of knowing I am responsible, that I was the one who could have stopped it.

Since finding out the news, I have tortured myself by reading every shred of information I can find on Ethan W. Howell.

Twenty-three. He was only twenty-three.

The son of a wealthy businessman, he had a brother he was not close with and a sister who died when he was a toddler. The sister passed away from leukemia when she was five, and a photo of her shows a little girl with curly blond hair who looks a little like Molly.

Over and over, I watch the YouTube video of Ethan's death, recorded by a spectator who stood behind the police tape. Twenty seconds long, it shows Ethan crying and shaking, his hands spread out against the brick of the building to hold him in place as he made his overture of unrequited love. Then the awful irretraceable step, the panic when he realized what he had done, and the video cuts out. It does not show him hitting the ground, but I do not need a visual to flinch in horror each time I watch it.

Robotically I go through the evening routine, giving the kids their baths, reading their lines to them, tucking them into bed. I am pulling the covers up around Tom when he asks, "Who's Ethan?"

"No one you need to worry about," I reassure him.

He looks unconvinced, and I know at some point I will need to explain why the press has descended on our home and is shouting questions about someone named Ethan. But at the moment, I am at a loss as to exactly what to say, the truth too gruesome for an eight-year-old to handle. The truth too gruesome for a thirty-two-year-old to handle. *Ethan is that guy who used to wave to us on the corner, the guy with the sweet smile who would do a fist pump if he saw us. Well, he's dead now because he became infatuated with your sister and decided he couldn't live without her, so he threatened to kill the president to prove his love, and when the police found out, they tried to arrest him, and he got scared, so he stepped onto the ledge of a building and threatened to kill himself, and I could have saved him by letting him see Molly, but I didn't and so he died.*

"Mom, you okay?"

"Yeah, baby, I'm fine." I kiss him on the head then go to the living room to lie down with Molly. I crawl in beside her and smooth her hair from her face, her forehead damp from the heat radiating from her small body. Outside, on the street, the press still prowls. I hear their voices and occasional laughter, vultures circling, waiting for us to emerge so they can pick our bones.

As time ticks by, the charred emptiness that consumes me begins to glow, an ember burning and growing hotter until it rages like an inferno. *He's dead, but I didn't mean to kill him. I didn't want to kill him. I didn't ask for this. I don't want this.* Sorrow to anger, disbelief to outrage. Unable to lie still another minute, I throw back the covers and begin to pace. Molly's blue elephant, won for her by Sean when she was a toddler, lies on the table beside the door. Emily's cleats sit on the floor below it where she dropped them after her last game. Remnants of who we were before Ethan, before the show, before my life was taken from me. *Graciela is wrong. I did not sell my daughter. I will not sell my daughter. This is not a better life. I am not like her. She and I, we are not the same.*

Wandering silently through the dimness, I scan the relics, and by the time I peek in on Tom, asleep in the room Emily used to sleep in, my skin is on fire. And when I see the rainbow-colored bag sitting open on Emily's desk, the bright blue "Sugar-Free" banner above the Life Savers logo, my lips curl into a smile that holds no joy. As Helen says, there's more than one way to skin a dragon.

93

This morning, in order for our limo to get through the studio gates, the Fox security force needed to form a brigade to keep the media at bay. As we drove through the swarm, Molly and Tom stared out the tinted windows, confused over what had changed between yesterday and today.

I am immune to the media frenzy, completely inoculated to their prying, needy greed. Let them say what they want, let the public think what they want. I no longer care. My only concern is getting out. My single goal is to put this behind us and find a way back to normalcy.

Griff and Sean have both called incessantly since the story broke. I have ignored both of them. This is *my* problem and mine alone. I love one, hate the other, and trust neither of them.

I drop Molly at base camp, drop Tom at studio school, and continue on to the staging area.

"Good morning, Beth," I say with a smile.

The woman squints at me with her beady eyes. "Where's Molly?"

"With Henry."

She grunts then returns to her cell phone, punching in the schedule for the day. Despite my hate for the woman, she is incredibly good at what she does. Beth is the woman behind the man—the one who makes Chris Cantor look amazing.

"Beth," Chris bellows, "let's get this going."

She springs off her stool and into action, and so do I.

Beth's choice of candy is Werther's caramels, and she goes through them like Tic Tacs. Lucky for me they make a sugar-free version known to cause explosive gas and diarrhea. The satchel Beth carries from set to set sits open on the table.

Out with the old and in with the new. I pull out the half-full bag of candy from the satchel, empty half the bag I brought with me into it, then place the new bag where the old bag had been. The exchange takes less than a minute.

I turn with the confiscated candies in my hand and freeze. Kira stands a few feet away, watching me from the shadows. Her eyes move to the Werther's bag, and her head tilts in curiosity.

"How long have you been standing there?" I ask, my heart ricocheting in my chest.

"Long enough."

I eye her warily as she sips her Starbucks, thoughts of tabloid headlines and lawsuits flashing through my mind.

"You do a nice little kitten routine," she says, her lips curling. "Playing with the big cats now. Better retract those claws before someone else notices."

"You're not going to tell?" I stammer.

"And ruin all the fun? Why would I do that?" Her wicked smile widens, and she pivots and walks away.

My heart thumping crazily, I run to the craft services station, dump the evidence, then hurry to the set to watch the show.

94

Where the hell is Beth?" Chris barks, and it's all I can do to suppress a smile, my vengeance caramel-sweet.

"She's in the restroom," someone says.

"Again? Fuck."

I offer to check on her.

"Thanks, Faye. Good to have you back."

Kira smiles at me, her grin making me feel both ashamed and a little proud.

I rush to the restroom where Beth has spent most of the last two hours. "Beth," I say sweetly through the partition of the bathroom stall.

"What the fuck do you want?"

"Chris needs the schedule."

"I'll be there in a minute."

"He needs it now."

"Fine. Fuck." She holds her phone beneath the door, and I nearly cheer with how easy that was. "Password is *lights*," she says.

"Thanks."

"Fuck."

Fuck you too! I think as I skip away, my thumbs moving lightning fast over the tiny keyboard.

The first text is to Mitten. *Please go to the sound lab for voice over edits.* I nearly press send then remember the text is coming from Beth and backspace to delete the "please."

The second text is to Gabby. *Sound lab now.*

I camp in the storage closet across the hall from the sound lab with the door cracked open. Gabby arrives first, followed a few minutes later by Mitten.

I count to a hundred then text *Cancel* to both of them.

If they leave right away, my plan failed. If they leave after ten minutes, there's a good chance it worked.

Gabby races out somewhere in the middle, after about five minutes, her face upset as she hurries away. A minute later Mitten shuffles out, his eyes on the ground, a frown on his face.

When a safe amount of time has passed, I race into the sound lab and straight into the vocal booth. The lens of the camera is directed through the glass into the editing booth, the green light on. I turn off the camera, eject the disc as I saw Griff do, then run from the room and back to the set, erasing the texts I sent from Beth's phone as I go.

"Where the hell have you been?" Beth snaps. "Give me my damn phone."

I hand the phone back to her. "Sorry, Tom needed me," I lie.

"Goddamn it, Beth, where the hell is the present for this scene?" Chris yells, his patience used up.

Beth turns to look for the prop, her expression flustered, then she runs from the set and back toward the restroom.

"Fuck!" Chris yells. "Somebody get me the damn present."

95

Shocked.

I stare at my mom's laptop, my heart thumping wildly as I watch the video for the second time.

Crap. Crap, crap, crap!

My plan is in shambles, or it should be, but it's not. It's actually entirely intact, making what I'm seeing that much more horrible.

Six minutes, one second shy—five minutes and fifty-nine seconds. The image isn't perfect, Gabby is off-center as she waits in the editing booth by herself, then Mitten arrives. Mitten says a few words to which Gabby shrugs. Silence while they wait together, then both look at their cell phones as the *Cancel* message comes through.

Mitten turns to leave, but Gabby says something to make him stay. Her gestures become animated as she talks. She is angry. I watch as Mitten nods, his face screwed up in what looks like sympathy. Gabby swallows, her shoulders fold forward, and her expression drops from anger to hurt. Mitten touches her shoulder to console her, then, his mouth still moving, she lurches at him and presses her lips against his. He stumbles back, his eyes wide, his head shaking as he protests her advance. Gabby isn't listening. She starts to lift her shirt. Mitten steps forward and puts his hand on her arm to stop her, then he raises his left hand to show her his simple gold wedding band.

I read his lips. *I'm married.*

I read hers. *I need this job.*

His head shakes as he says, *I'm sorry.*

She runs from the room, and a minute later, with a deep sigh, Mitten follows.

I press the pause button and stare at the empty room on the screen. The truth. It's not what I expected, but it's damning just the same. I rewind to the spot where Gabby kissed him and pause. It's impossible to know in that second that he is protesting her advance. I forward the frame of Gabby lifting her shirt while Mitten touches her arm. The rolls of Gabby's stomach over her jeans are visible beneath her hideous bright pink bra, and I'm not sure which the media would exploit more, Gabby's grotesqueness or Mitten's.

Griff was right. Mitten's not a predator. He's the opposite, a pious man trying to do right by these young girls.

I look at Molly asleep on the sleeper bed, her thumb in her mouth, then at the photo of Emily on the mantel.

The truth is in my hands, but I'm not sure what to do with it. Pressing the heels of my hands against my eyes, I sit unmoving for a long moment.

Mommy, what's suicide? Molly asked during our lunch break as I unwrapped her turkey sandwich. Tom looked at me, curious as well.

It's nothing, baby. Eat your lunch.

Taking a deep breath, I straighten in my chair, wiggle the mouse to rewake the computer, then screen capture the two damning frames from the video and save them to a thumb drive. I put the hoodoo in an envelope and address it to *Star Gazer* then walk from the condo toward the mailbox down the street. As I walk, an old nursery rhyme plays in my head: *Hickory dickory dock, the mouse ran up the clock…*

My hand trembles as I open the drop slot.

Sliding doors, a stoplight turning red, an unexpected detour that causes the world to pivot in a way you didn't expect. This is not like that. This is the opposite. This is like pulling a lever that will change the course of a train, steering it toward a cliff that will kill everyone on board.

The steel flap clunks closed, the smallest thud of metal against metal. I stare at the closed slot then at the envelope still in my hand.

The clock struck one, the mouse ran down, hickory, dickory, dock.

Putting the envelope in the pocket of my jacket, I shuffle back toward the condo, my eyes studying the cracks in the sidewalk. As I walk, I pray I did not just make the biggest mistake of my life, that by not pulling the lever, I didn't just spare everyone else while sending our own train hurtling toward that very same cliff.

96

We are on the holiday break, and I am in heaven. This morning, Christmas morning, I woke up in Griff's arms. The kids spent Christmas Eve with Sean and Emily. Mack dropped them off an hour ago, just in time for lunch.

I am in Griff's amazing kitchen cooking an amazing feast for my amazing man and my amazing family, while the aforementioned amazing man is in the living room putting the training wheels on Molly's new bike. After it is assembled, he is going to take the kids on the trails behind his house in search of wildflowers.

My mom stands beside me, sipping wine and keeping me company, and Bo and Jeremy are both on their way and will be here by dinnertime. Heaven. Peaceful and blissful and perfect.

We've been off from work for nearly a week, and this vacation actually feels like a vacation. Because of the Ethan incident and the media storm surrounding it, Molly no longer gives interviews or makes appearances. Even Chris agrees that she needs to be buffered from the insanity.

The only downside is that Emily is not with us. I sent the gift I bought for her—a new soccer bag, cleats, and an autographed Mia Hamm jersey—with Tom and Molly last night, but the kids brought it back unopened. I will keep it in hopes that, at some point, she will change her mind.

Pulling the turkey from the oven, I inhale its wonderful smell, baste it, then slide it back in the oven. Giggles erupt from the living room, Molly cracking up over something Griff said. Tom pipes in, making a wiseass remark that causes Griff to belly laugh like Santa Claus.

A small glimpse of what my life might be like if we continue on as we are. Heaven. Perfect blissful heaven.

97

It's been four weeks since I chose to do nothing, and every day I thank my lucky stars that I did not drop that envelope into that mailbox. As if Christmas never ended, our life has settled into an exquisite rhythm that is almost normal. Molly, Tom, and I work hard during the week, spend our evenings with Griff, either at his house or at the condo, and on the weekends, Molly and Tom go to Sean's, giving Griff and me some alone time.

There's talk of Molly being nominated for an Emmy. An Emmy! The thought fills me with incredible pride. She would be the youngest actress ever to be nominated for the honor. Tom is also doing amazing and is now the third most popular character on the show, right behind Molly and Jeremy. Kira did not take the bump well. Caleb didn't care. Each week, Tom's part grows, and with it, his confidence.

We are, aside from the Emily factor, happy—really, really happy.

Especially me. It's almost ridiculous how happy I am. It sounds cliché, but in the English language, there's only one worn out, overused way to say it: *I am in love*, and I am incredibly grateful I didn't ruin it.

Though Griff and I have only been together a couple of months, already we are thinking of a future together, which is the main reason I've stayed living with my mom. Though I can now afford a home of my own, a fact that is utterly astonishing, I have not begun looking for a house because I'm not sure if I should be looking for a home for just us, for a home for an "us" that includes Griff, or not looking at all because we will be moving into Griff's house and will become an "us" there.

These wonderful, distracting thoughts swirl constantly in my brain, making it difficult to focus on anything else. Like, at the moment, I am supposed to be reviewing Tom's homework because he has his state tests on Monday, but instead of reading over his math worksheets, I sit at the table sipping a glass of wine and daydreaming about getting married in Griff's backyard, Bo walking me down the aisle, Helen being my reluctant, stunning maid of honor.

The dream is so wonderful that when the phone rings, I ignore it, reaching to hit the off button so I can silence it. Then I see the caller ID and my heart lurches.

"Em?"

Tears tremble through her tiny voice, driving instant panic into my heart. "Mom?"

"Baby? What's the matter?"

"Will you come get me?"

I'm already pulling my shoes on. "Of course, baby. Where are you?"

"I don't know," she sniffles.

"Okay, baby, deep breath, look around you. Tell me what you see."

98

The thirty minutes it takes me to get to her are the longest of my life, my heart racing at such a frantic rate that it nearly collapses when I finally spot her sitting on the curb in front of a club called The Vault, loud music thundering from its walls.

She wears the sparkly dress and stilettos from the premiere, her eyes streaked with makeup, her lips bruised. Gingerly she climbs into the car, and a wave of nausea washes over me with the realization that more than her lips were violated.

"Baby?" I say.

"Please go," she rasps, not looking at me, her body curling into itself as she leans her head against the glass.

I drive away, her silent tears and trembling body wrecking me, the putrid smell of alcohol and vomit filling the car.

"You're going to be okay. I'm just going to find a place to pull over so I can call the police."

"NO!" she screams.

"Baby, we have to."

Her mortified sobs and hysterics trump my civic duty and I drive on. "Okay, baby. It's okay. You're okay. I'll take you home."

"Not Grandma's," she croaks. "I don't…please…Molly can't see me… don't take me…" Her voice is swallowed by her shame.

"Where's your dad?" I manage, my own voice a hair trigger away from breakdown.

"Out with his girlfriend."

I feel the pulse of blood throbbing behind my eyes, a seizure of anger so strong that it's difficult to see straight.

"Just take me home," she mumbles.

"So you do want to go home?"

"Dad's house," she clarifies.

Over my dead body.

99

Griff looks in on us, his face worn with worry. We are in the same room Molly slept in after the airport fiasco. I sit beside Emily on the bed, stroking her hair. She is showered now, but soap and water could not wash away the redness around her mouth or the sausage-size finger marks on her arms from where she was held down, and each time I look at them, sickness like a fist rises in my throat. Twelve years spent protecting her dissolved in this single night of failure, and my hatred for myself—my selfishness, my cowardice, my weakness—is so overwhelming it's a struggle to draw breath.

When she was a baby, I used to watch her sleep like I am doing now. I would lie beside her and breathe her in, dewy and pink, marveling that this tiny person was mine. I could not believe how much I loved her, and at the same time how much a stranger she was, this small alien being with emerald-green eyes not at all like my own—the mystical oneness of pregnancy cleaved into two separate beings the moment she took her first breath, a new bond forged by her utter dependence on me to care for her and my overwhelming desire to do just that, knowing I would give her my last breath.

Kissing her gently on the temple, I walk into the living room and fall into Griff's arms.

"We need to leave," I say.

"Not tonight," he says, pulling me close.

"LA," I clarify. "We need to leave LA."

His muscles tense, his arms wrapping a little tighter, holding me in place. "You can't leave, that will only make things worse."

"Worse? How can it be worse? Did you see my little girl?"

He kisses the side of my head and rubs my shoulder. "We'll figure it out. Somehow we'll get through this, but leaving isn't the answer. I know you're upset, I'm upset too, but what happened isn't the show's fault..."

"How can you say that?" I pull away, putting space between us. "She was with Caleb and Gabby. Caleb invited her, and Gabby got them into the club."

His nose flares slightly though his voice remains calm. "They forced her at gunpoint to dress the way she did and sneak out to go with them? They poured alcohol down her throat?"

"You're saying this was her fault?" I hiss, my skin burning.

"I'm saying you can't blame the show."

"Maybe not directly but indirectly. If we weren't on the show, none of this would have happened. She would have never even gotten into that club. She's twelve. Caleb is only thirteen. Gabby sixteen. But because they're famous, no one blinked an eye at the three of them hanging out and drinking at a club that's supposed to be for people over twenty-one. This world is warped, don't you see that?" But even as the words leave my mouth, I know he doesn't, and I soften my tone. "I need to save them."

"Then save them, but not by quitting the show. That's not the answer."

"Tell me another way."

He holds out his arms for me to return his embrace, but instead I stand. "I need to go."

"Please, Faye, don't."

"I mean I need to go for a walk, clear my head."

He stands. "I'll go with you."

"No, you stay. One of us needs to be here in case Em wakes up."

He pulls me into a gentle kiss then releases me. "I'll be here. I'm always going to be here."

∞

The night is cool and clear, my steps certain. I open the mailbox and drop the envelope inside.

100

Sean called this morning frantic, entirely unaware that Emily had been missing from her bed since last night.

I told him what happened then told him to go to hell.

He called again. I didn't answer.

Last night was one of the hardest of my life, guilt and worry making sleep impossible, my exhausted brain plagued with so much regret that nothing else existed. Several times during the night, Emily startled awake beside me, bolting upright with a cry before looking around, realizing where she was, then curling back into a ball, shivering until she slipped back into unconsciousness. I tried to comfort her, but each time she pulled away from my touch and my words, making it clear that, through it all, she still hates me.

This morning she agreed to let me take her back to the condo under the condition that we didn't tell Molly and Tom the truth. Our story was that Emily's mouth was bruised from getting hit with a soccer ball. Molly believed the story but Tom didn't, and throughout the day, his eyes have repeatedly slid to the closed door of the bedroom where Emily hides.

It is evening now, and we are having dinner. Emily didn't want to come out, so I brought her a plate and set it on the table beside her. She did not look at me or the food. She lay curled on her side, her eyes staring at the wall. I did not force her. Nothing will be forced on her.

The door pounds, causing all of us to look up from our meal.

"Damn it, Faye, open up," Sean bellows through the wood.

"Daddy," Molly says, climbing from her chair.

I leap up and pull her back.

"Mom, please take them to your room."

My mom herds Molly and Tom away, and with a deep breath, I go to face their father.

His eyes are wild, the stench of alcohol and sweat rising from his skin, his jaw clenched and his nose flared. I watch him inhale—pot roast and potatoes, one of his favorites—and for a flicker, I wonder if the girlfriend he was out with last night while Emily's life was being destroyed cooks, and I decide, based on his pained expression, that she doesn't.

Stepping toward him, I force him back into the hallway, then close the door.

"I'm here for the kids," he says. "The weekends are mine."

I shake my head.

"Get the hell out of my way, Faye."

My pulse kicks up a notch. Sean's never hit me, but impulse control has never been his strong suit, and considering the state he's in, I don't put it past him to lash out now.

"Sean, please," I say, forcing my voice to stay calm, needing him to hear my words, not my emotions. "You don't have to do this. You want the money, that's fine. I'll send you half each month, no strings attached. I'll even pay the taxes. I don't care about any of that anymore."

"What the hell are you talking about? You think this is about money? They're my fucking kids, Faye. What happened to Em isn't my fault."

I feel his desperation to believe it, the same desperation I feel when I think about what happened, an intense need to off-load the guilt to Caleb or Gabby or rotten luck or bad circumstances. But regardless of how hard we wish it, the fault is ours—she's our baby, it was our job to protect her, and last night we failed.

"Sean, you need to go. The kids aren't going with you tonight." *Or any other night.* I don't add the last part.

"Bullshit. You can't put this on me. I should be able to leave a goddamn twelve-year-old to watch out for herself without thinking she's going to go to a bar to get laid."

My fury hits like a cyclone, my hand flying toward his face.

He catches it, his grip clenching my wrist so tight that it hurts. "Watch it, Faye."

Emily walks from the condo. “Daddy?” she says, her voice small.

He releases me. “Hey, baby,” he says, his expression transforming from rabid to devoted in a heartbeat. “You ready to come home?”

She nods.

“Em, no,” I say.

“I just need to grab my things,” she says, her eyes on the ground as she pretends she doesn’t see me.

“Get your brother and sister too,” Sean says.

With her shoulders rolled forward, her body curved protectively around her heart, she shuffles back into the condo.

“Please, Sean, don’t do this,” I plead, my anger wiped out by my desperation to stop what is happening. “She needs to stay here. She needs to heal. You know that. I know you do. You’re her father, a good father.”

His eyes flicker, the smallest glimmer of the man I used to love flashing for an instant until he shakes it away. “That’s right, Faye. I am their father, and it would be best if you remember that.”

“This is ruining her.”

“She’s already ruined.”

My temper flares again. “She’s not. Don’t you dare give up on her. A single mistake does not define a person.”

“It defined me,” he shoots back, his eyes locking on mine.

“You didn’t have to marry me.”

He blinks rapidly like I’ve stunned him. “My mistake was leaving,” he says. “That was my mistake. The best thing I ever did was marry you.”

And like a pin puncturing a balloon, his words destroy me. So much has been lost so quickly. A year ago, we were together living in Yucaipa, struggling but getting by, our kids healthy, our family whole, Emily unharmed.

Our broken dreams between us, the tears I’ve held for the past twenty-four hours flood from my eyes and my chin drops to my chest. Too much. It’s all too much. Everything Emily was, everything I was, everything we were…gone, the loss overwhelming.

“I’m ready,” Emily says, appearing with a shopping bag of her things over her shoulder, her eyes still cast on the floor. “Grandma won’t let Molly and Tom go with us.”

Sean's voice cracks, a hitch in his words as he says, "Yeah, change of plans, M&M. I need to cut out of town for a while, so you need to stay with your mom."

My face snaps up to look at him, but it's too late. Already he's walking toward the stairwell, his posture relaxed except for his hands, which are clenched in fists at his side, revealing the courage it is taking for him to walk away. And in this moment, he is the man I loved, the man I knew that no one else saw.

101

We are on the red carpet, walking toward the theater where the premiere of Jeremy's new movie is about to be shown. I take comfort in the fact that Jeremy's career is soaring, knowing that, like Helen, Kira, and Jules, if *The Foster Band* fails, he will be fine.

Molly walks on my left and Tom on my right. We smile politely at the cameras and wave to the reporters we recognize. When we reach the middle of the walkway, Tom and I step aside so the photographers can get a few shots of Molly alone.

Molly looks adorable. She wears a yellow satin dress with small daisies embroidered at the waist. She still prefers overalls, but on big nights out, her girly side has started to emerge, and already I can see the last remnants of baby leaving her.

As I watch, I think about the headline in this morning's paper, *Gabby Rodriguez Joins Sexual Harassment Class Action Lawsuit Against Fox*. The headline was printed above the photo of Gabby lifting her shirt as Mitten touched her arm. It is a very incriminating shot. It looks as though Mitten is encouraging her, and his smile, that only I know is consoling, appears lecherous.

It's been a week since the story broke. The first headline, which was printed over the photo of Gabby and Mitten kissing, read, *Sex Scandal on the Set of The Foster Band*. A day after the story ran, four young actresses came forward accusing Mitten of sexual harassment, claiming he threatened to have them fired if they refused his advances. Mitten adamantly denied the allegations, but Fox terminated his contract anyway, and his wife, stalwartly loyal, left with him.

I feel bad for what I've done to him but do not care as much as I should. Helen is right. This business changes you. It makes you stronger or weaker, better or worse, but it doesn't leave you the same. I am not the same. I am one of them now, as ruthless as Kira, Chris, or Beth. My only concern is for my family. Emily is not doing well. She has not returned to school, rarely comes out of her room, and refuses to talk about what happened.

Life has been cruel to her, and we need to return to Yucaipa where she can heal. Along with what happened to her physically, she has been battered emotionally. Since that fateful night, Caleb has cut off contact with her. Either out of shame or anger, he refuses to talk to her and has blocked her number. He avoids us on the set and is rarely seen outside his dressing room. More than one kid was destroyed that night, and there is little to be done but hope that both can find a way to move past it.

Sean's absence is also destroying her. She feels like she has been abandoned. Perhaps someday I will be able to explain it to her and she will find a way to forgive him, but at the moment, his desertion cuts like a knife, and she feels betrayed, helpless, and alone.

In six months after, I have filed for sole parental control based on legal abandonment, I might contact him, see if he would like to have a role in the kids' lives, but it will be on my terms and he will never again be in charge of their welfare or the decisions that dictate their lives.

One of the reporters asks Molly to spin for them to show how her dress flares, and she does a ballerina pirouette that causes a united "aw" from the audience at her adorableness. I suppress a yawn, and beside me, Tom sighs. It's the same pirouette she's done to the same "aw" a thousand times before.

I hope Chris is right, that the public has a short attention span and that, in time, they will forget what Mitten has been accused of. I will always regret that I was the one who did this to him. But it was the only way. Just as Bo said, the cast and crew know that without the Mittens the show won't be the same. The remaining shows for this season have already been written and the junior writers can manage the rewrites. It's next year people are worried about. The number one show on television is no longer a sure bet, possibly even a sinking ship, depending on who you talk to. The lead sound tech quit this morning. He's the fourth crew member to leave this week. More are certain to follow. Panic has set in and paranoia is spreading, eyes furtively slide to one another throughout the day and hushed whispers fill the corridors between takes, each cast and crew member attempting to divine what the others are thinking.

Despite the exodus, the lawsuit, the bad press, and losing the Mittens, Griff, Chris, and Beth are doing a remarkable job forging forward, each day somehow managing to get it all done. Griff holds the crew together, Chris, the cast, and Beth juggles it all with superhuman strength, efficiency, and stamina that boggles my mind.

Molly curtsies, and I step forward and take her by the hand, smiling sweetly for the cameras as we walk toward the theater and as I contemplate my next move.

102

I glance over the top of the script I'm studying at the woman about to be destroyed and offer a smile. As always, my friendly greeting isn't returned, Beth's beady eyes blinking once before returning to her phone.

She never apologized for lying to the judge, for unjustly sabotaging me and nearly causing me to lose my kids, never felt me worthy of that sort of consideration. Yet I am the one who will cause her ruin.

Of all the things I feel bad about, this isn't one of them. She thinks she is immune. While everyone else scurries around in panic, Beth studies the day's schedule unconcerned. I watch as she unwraps another Werther's, then pops the candy in her mouth, and I am fascinated by how oblivious she is to the fact that her day of reckoning is upon her.

"Beth, I need to speak with you," Chris says, appearing from the hallway that leads to the executive offices.

Beth looks up, her face tilting in surprise at Chris's civil tone. Then she stands and follows him toward his office, and when I'm certain they can't see me, I smile.

My comment to Henry was offhand and casual, a simple, "Who do you think set Mitten and Gabby up to take those photos?"

And for the rest of the day, Henry was off to his beloved gossip races, speculating with everyone who sat in his chair about the whodunit. *It had to be an inside job. It was definitely the sound lab. They must have been lying in wait. Someone who hated Mitten. Gabby was just an innocent victim.*

I'm not certain how they figured it out, perhaps someone called

Mitten and asked him, perhaps someone called Gabby, but by the time lunch rolled around, eyes were sliding toward Beth and jetting away when she returned the glances, and I knew she had been nailed to the cross. This is my kill move, planned over a month ago and set up bit by bit so, when I used it, the show would be at its most vulnerable.

Beth returns, and my pulse quickens. Her face is ghostly pale like she might be sick, her eyes darting side to side.

Gathering up her belongings, she turns to leave then pauses. Turning back, she looks at me then down at her phone, and I watch as she pieces it together, her expression changing from question to shock to fury.

"You goddamn bitch."

❧

When I walk into Chris's office, his head is in his hands. He looks up, his eyes weary as a field surgeon's.

"Hi, Faye." He musters a small smile. "What's up?"

"We quit."

He blinks once but says nothing, already the conversation so different from the one we had two months ago, the day we returned from Thanksgiving break, when I explained I wanted Molly to have a normal life, when I knew Emily was in trouble, when I told him I wanted to quit, and when he told me it wasn't up to me.

"When we quit is up to you," I say. "The choices are simple. One, you can release Molly and Tom from their contracts, and we stay to shoot the last three episodes of the season, allowing the show to become syndicated and getting you to the dark season, which will allow you to regroup, get a new writing team, hire a new AD, and resume next year. Or two, you can refuse, and I will leave with Molly and Tom tonight, and you'll never see us again."

His eyes narrow as he assimilates the threat, and as I look at him, I think, *Rumpelstiltskin, I know your name*. The balance of powers has shifted, the show no longer invincible. Losing Mitten was crippling, losing Beth a near-fatal blow. Losing Molly at this point, with three episodes to go and no one to rewrite them, would be the proverbial last straw that breaks the camel's back.

He leans forward like he'd like to tear my throat out but continues to hold his tongue.

"I suggest you choose option one," I say, pivoting and walking out the door.

103

I walk to the commissary to pick up Molly. In my purse are the release contracts for Molly and Tom. I feel like a gladiator returning from the Colosseum triumphant, not so much euphoric as relieved to still be standing, battle worn and exhausted, ready to leave the arena behind and never raise a sword again.

Henry and Molly sit with Mack playing cards at a picnic table. Each has a pile of Sweeties candies in front of them that look like they are being used as poker chips. Molly's stack is the largest by at least twice.

"Ready to go?" Mack says, standing.

"Now can I eat them?" Molly asks Henry, looking longingly at her winnings.

"Yep. You won them—now you can eat them." He grabs a handful of his own winnings and fills his mouth, then around the candy, he says to me, "Hey girl, crazy news about Beth, don't you think?"

My skin flushes with guilt as I nod.

"Good thing that camera in the sound lab has a backup drive. Chris would never have believed it if she hadn't been caught red-handed. Of course Mitten and Gabby confirmed it. Both said Beth was the one who set them up."

I swallow. "What backup drive?"

"Those shots of Mitten and Gabby, the camera they were taken from has a backup drive. Griff pulled the footage, and he said that clear as day, it showed Beth taking the memory card. Craziest part of it all is that it turns out Mitten is innocent. Gabby was coming on to him, not the other way around. Gabby caved as soon as Chris confronted her, and now she's saying she's dropping the lawsuit, that it was all a lie. She's been posting on Facebook and tweeting all afternoon saying how sorry she is for not coming out and telling the truth. Some sort of come-to-Jesus moment, saying how she owes Mitten her life, that he was the only one willing to give a Mexican migrant worker a chance, the only one who saw past her weight to her talent. She's getting serious props about it, like it's so brave for her to be so honest. There's even buzz about her being asked to be on the next *Dancing with the Stars*." Henry stops then cocks his head. "You okay?"

I manage a nod and a strangled, "I left something on the set." I whirl and race back toward the soundstage, tears flooding my eyes. He chose us. It came down to a choice between the show and us, and he chose us.

Ten feet from the building, a voice stops me. "I should never have trusted my heart to a squid."

I turn to see Griff standing in the alley between the buildings. I start to move toward him but stop before I've taken a step, my shame overwhelming me. My eyes drop to the ground, and I wrap my arms across my chest. I want to say I'm sorry, then I want to thank him for what he did, then I want to tell him how much I love him, but I can't form words.

"Wasn't right what you did," he says.

I nod and my chin quivers.

He steps toward me, closing the distance between us in a stride, then he lifts my chin, and his eyes lance me with his anger and his hurt.

"I needed to get them out," I mumble.

"That wasn't the way."

"There was no other way."

"Bradley didn't deserve that."

I nod, and again my shame decimates me, the tears I've been holding back leaking from my eyes. "Or Beth," I say.

"No. Beth deserves what she got. Nobody messes with my family."

It takes a minute for the words "my family" to register, and when they do, my eyes blink rapidly, refocusing on his to see the devotion piercing through the anger.

"What about the show?" I say.

"It will go on. They need a new AD, a couple new kids, a new director of photography, and possibly a new writer, but they'll regroup and be fine. Chris is very good at what he does."

"A new director of photography? You're leaving?"

"I have some personal business to take care of."

"What kind of personal business?"

His right eyebrow rises, he gives an Elmer Fudd grin, then his lips come down on mine.

NOTE FROM AUTHOR

Dear Reader,

One hour before John Hinckley shot President Reagan in a desperate act to get the attention of Jodie Foster, he wrote a letter that began:

> Dear Jodie:
>
> There is definitely a possibility that I will be killed in my attempt to get Reagan.

He went on to say how much he loved her and the ways in which he had tried to prove it:

> Over the past seven months I've left you dozens of poems, letters and love messages in the faint hope that you could develop an interest in me...I know the many messages left at your door and in your mailbox were a nuisance, but I felt that it was the most painless way for me to express my love for you.

He ended it with a final overture of his unrequited love:

> I would abandon the idea of getting Reagan in a second if I could only win your heart and live out the rest of my life with you...By sacrificing my freedom and possibly my life, I hope to change your mind about me...I'm asking, with this historical deed, to gain your love and respect.
>
> I love you forever,
> John W. Hinckley

Hinckley got off six shots before he was tackled by police. He wounded the president, two security officers, and President Reagan's press secretary. The letter was used as evidence in the trial against Hinckley, and everything about it is so disturbing that I thought it perfectly illustrated how obsessive fans can become and how scary it would be to be the object of such twisted devotion.

The world of celebrity is fascinating. It is the topic of thousands of magazines, talk shows, news shows, reality shows, and websites. But what would it be like to be swept up into that world? Or to have your child swept up into that world? Thrilling? Terrifying?

We've all heard the train wreck stories. Headlines about Disney stars' tragic downfalls, miraculous recoveries, and outrageous antics plaster the covers of magazines on every newsstand. That story didn't need to be told. And I had no interest in rehashing a *Mommie Dearest* tale about an overzealous stage mom. The story I wanted to tell was about someone real who finds themselves catapulted into superstardom and what that does to them.

I struggled figuring out who that person was, but then I read Pattie Mallette's autobiography, *Nowhere but Up: The Story of Justin Bieber's Mom*, and was struck by the idea of writing a story about a woman similar to her—the story of a young, struggling single mom whose child is discovered on YouTube and becomes an overnight sensation.

Other autobiographies and biographies inspired me as well, but none more than Melissa Francis's story, *Diary of a Stage Mother's Daughter*. What struck me about Melissa's book was that the story wasn't about her. It is a tragic memoir about the damage Melissa's celebrity did to her family, especially her older sister, Tiffany, who died a young death from drug-related heart failure. The story struck a visceral chord, and after reading it, I knew the story I wanted to tell—the story about the destruction a child star's celebrity causes not just to her but to those around her. I wanted it to be Faye's story, Emily's story, Tom's story, and Sean's story as much as Molly's and for Molly's fame to be the catalyst for what happens to each of them.

No Ordinary Life is not meant to be a statement on the entertainment industry or a generalization about young actors. It is fiction, designed to be dramatic and fraught with trials and tribulations. So though this story was inspired in part by real stories, it is not real. Many young stars not only survive their young celebrity; they thrive because of it, going on to live happy, fruitful adult lives both in and out of the spotlight. Molly is a figment of my imagination as is every other character.

I hope you enjoyed reading the story as much as I enjoyed writing it.

Sincerely,

Suzanne

DISCUSSION QUESTIONS

1. Do you think Faye is a good mother, a good person? Do you think she failed Emily? Do you think some of her decisions were selfish?

2. Faye was Molly's manager, and sometimes the line between doing what was right for Molly her daughter and doing what was right for Molly the star became blurred. Do you think Faye handled the double role well?

3. Sean was an opportunist who returned to ride the coattails of Molly's success. Faye protected the kids from the truth of why he came back as well as the truth about why he left in the first place. Do you think this was the right thing to do? Do children see themselves as a reflection of their parents? If so, is it better for them to view their parents in the best light?

4. What do you think of Sean? Do you sympathize with him at all? Were his motives entirely selfish or do you think he returned hoping for reconciliation? Did he redeem himself by walking away? Do you think he is out of their lives forever?

5. Was Faye to blame for Emily's rape? Sean? If Emily had not been raped, how do you think the story would have played out?

6. Everyone wanted something from Molly. How much is too much?

Should Faye have brought Molly to the suicide scene to save Ethan? Is Faye to blame for his death?

7. By sabotaging the show, Faye betrayed Tom, who had found his place in the world and was thriving. Do you think Tom will revert back into his shell or continue to thrive? Did Faye choose the welfare of Emily over the welfare of Tom? If Tom discovers what Faye did, how will it affect him? Will he be able to forgive her?
8. What do you think lies ahead for Molly? Will her celebrity follow her or will she be able to return to a "normal" life?
9. As Faye discovers, celebrity is more than just fame. With it comes money, power, privilege, enormous responsibility, lack of privacy, danger, and stress. Do you think, had Faye realized what she was signing up for, she would have been more equipped to protect her family? Or do you think, regardless of how aware she was of the perils, celebrity by its very nature is corruptive?
10. The media played a significant role in the story. How do you feel about the way the media pursues celebrities? Do you think there should be boundaries? What about those celebrities who are under eighteen or those who are famous by association but who didn't choose to be famous—siblings, parents, the children of celebrities?
11. A disproportionate number of child stars have issues. Do you think their celebrity causes them to struggle or are people who choose to be celebrities predisposed to having difficulties? If you believe it is the first, what do you think can be done to protect child actors and their families from the dangers of stardom?
12. Does it affect your impression of the story to know that much of it is semibiographical—based on the stories of real child stars? Has your perception of child stardom changed?
13. How do you feel about Faye implicating Mitten for something he

didn't do? Do you think the end justified the means? Do you think there was another way?

14. Faye frames Beth for leaking the images of Mitten and Gabby. Do you have sympathy for Beth or do you think she got what she deserved?

15. Graciela (Gabby's mom) admitted she sold her daughter for a better life. Is there some validity to this? Is it okay for a child to sacrifice some or all of their childhood to provide better circumstances and a more promising future for the family? How would you feel about your child being the provider of the family? How would it change the family dynamic? How much sacrifice is too much—free time, friends, sports, education, innocence?

16. The way the laws are currently written, a child star can end up with little or none of the money they earn. The Coogan Law requires that fifteen percent of a minor's earnings be set aside in a trust until they turn eighteen. Do you think this is enough? Should parents be able to manage the remainder of the money or should an independent party be responsible? Should parents/siblings be compensated because the child actor's celebrity affects them as well?

17. Molly is discovered through a YouTube video. Do you think there should be regulations on posting images of someone without their consent?

18. The waitress from the steak house slept with Chris hoping Chris would help her get her foot in the door, and Chris called it "a fair exchange." Do you think sex for opportunity is a fair exchange or is it a form of prostitution? Faye almost slept with Chris because she needed "a little fun" in her life, convincing herself that she could have "meaningless" sex. Do you think sex can be that uncomplicated or does it always come with expectation?

19. Have you ever experienced celebrity? If so, how did it affect you and those around you? Most of us want to be acknowledged as special or for doing something well, but do you crave fame? Would you rather have constant recognition or anonymity?
20. After reading this story, do you feel differently about celebrities? Who is the most famous person you've met? What was the experience like? How do you think the experience was for them?
21. Who was your favorite character? Why?
22. Movie time: Who would you like to see play each part?

ACKNOWLEDGMENTS

Special thanks to the incomparable Nick Ellison, whose sage counsel, unrelenting faith, and much-needed humor keeps me optimistically pecking away at the keys. Thanks also to everyone at the Nick Ellison Literary Agency, especially Blair Beusman, Danielle Zuckerman, and Chloe Walker.

Thanks to my editor, Alex Logan, who stuck with the story through its many twists and turns and to the entire team at Grand Central, particularly Beth DeGuzman, Julie Paulauski, and Kristin Vorce.

Also thank you to Lindsey Boyd for her insight into the world of Hollywood. To Paul Peterson for his input and for his advocacy for young stars through his organization, A Minor Consideration. To Regina Szal for sharing her expertise on selective mutism. To Sally Eastwood for always reading my stories before they're ready and giving invaluable feedback. To Anne Emigh, Kari Larsen, and Tami Cahill for their early reads and encouragement. To Wieke, Amy, Bettina, and Jenny for always being there to toast in the joyous moments of our journey together. To Suzy Missirlian for always having my back and for her relentless support. To April Brian for her talent and generous spirit. To Russell Pierce for sharing his expertise. To my daughter Halle for her incredible attention to detail and unwavering honesty.

To the rest of my remarkable family, without whom none of this would be possible.

And finally, thank you to Jodie Foster, Melissa Gilbert, Melissa Francis, Shirley Temple, Pattie Mallette, Mary-Kate and Ashley Olsen, Jodie Sweetin, Maureen McCormick, Barbara Cameron, and Miley Cyrus for sharing their stories, which allowed me a glimpse into their remarkable lives.

ABOUT THE AUTHOR

Suzanne Redfearn is a summa cum laude graduate from California Polytechnic University and is an architect, in addition to an author. She is also an avid surfer, golfer, skier, and Angels fan. She lives with her husband and children in California.

To learn more about the author, visit her website at SuzanneRedfearn.com.

Suzanne Redfearn tells another riveting story about a devoted mother fighting to protect her young children in *Hush Little Baby*.

Please turn the page for an excerpt.

3

Eat," Gordon says. "You need to be out the door in half an hour."

My body protests as I push to sit up against the pillow. He hands me a plate with a slice of whole-wheat toast and a soft-boiled egg.

He doesn't mention the reason I'm in the guest bedroom and neither do I.

It's moments like these I wonder if I'm the one who's crazy and if maybe the nightmare didn't actually happen.

He pats the comforter over my abdomen, and my battered ribs flinch at his touch, reminding me with no uncertainty that the nightmare was, in fact, real.

"Morning, son," he says with a celebratory grin, as though his earlier performance were a glorious triumph of baby-making to be rejoiced. On his cheek is a red scratch barely an inch long, a pitiful testament to my lack of resistance.

This is how it goes, an unexpected explosion after months of calm. Always, just as I start to relax and believe I'm safe, just as life resumes its hum and I'm lulled into believing it wasn't as bad as I remember or that it isn't going to happen again—that he's changed, I've changed, we're good now—bam! It happens again, worse than I remember, always scarier and worse.

Addie bursts into the room. "Daddy, youw're home!"

Gordon scoops the galloping four-year-old into his arms, plants a kiss on top of her red curls, then twirls her back to the ground.

Addie's feet touch the carpet, and she spins to me. "Mowrning," she says as she jumps onto the bed and wraps a hug around my neck, then pulls back, her freckled face widening into a huge grin. "I got you a be-wrthday pwresent." And as quickly as she appeared, she vanishes.

Gordon sits on the bed beside me and places his hand on my belly. "I'd be happy with another girl as well," he says, and I will myself not to tremble.

Addie's back. In her hands is a lump wrapped in taped-together magazine pages.

"Open it. Open it," she says, her energy buzzing like a hornet in heat.

I peel off the wrapping.

"I made it myself."

I hold up the long strip of yellow-and-blue-plaid flannel. It's about five feet long and varies in width from a few inches to a foot. I recognize it as a piece of one of Addie's baby blankets.

"It's beautiful."

"It's a scawrf."

"Oh."

"For in case you get smudges again."

Addie's eyes sparkle, Gordon's recede, and mine fill as I swallow the emotions back inside. I didn't think she remembered. I hoped she'd forgotten.

Scotch tape patches the edges of the scarf where it frayed.

If I speak, the tears will escape, so instead I nod and wrap the soft gift around my neck as the memory replays—almost exactly a year ago, my life darkening as Gordon strangled me. Then after, the "smudges"—swollen red, bruised blue, vermilion green, then jaundice yellow—a month of color changes ringing my throat before they disappeared.

"How you get smudges?" Addie asks.

Gordon pats his thigh, and Addie climbs on board and wraps her pink arms around his neck.

"Sometimes, Ad, someone gets real mad or real sad," he says, "and by accident they hurt themselves. And that's what happened to your mommy, but then your daddy showed up and stopped her, and she got all better."

A thousand jolts of electricity couldn't shock me more.

I stare at my husband as he spins his horrible tale, my fear and shame teaming up to squelch the pride and outrage that rise like a fist in my throat.

Your father strangled me. Your father tried to kill me. Your father is insane. The smudges are from his arm wrapping around my neck and squeezing so hard I couldn't breathe.

My mouth doesn't move.

Addie sits on his knee, her left hand on his massive shoulder. Her right pokes the dimple on his chin, and she studies him with a hero worship that can't be shattered with the truth.

Dragging footsteps, then the shaggy head of Drew appears, followed by his spindly body.

He plops himself onto the foot of the bed.

"Mowrning, Dwrew," Addie says. "You see what I got Mom for hewr bewrthday?" She points to the scarf as I start to unwrap it.

"Youw're not gonna weawr it?"

"Of course I am." I rewrap the boa, my neck sweating in protest.

"It's a cut-up blanket," Drew says.

"It's a scawrf."

"It's stupid."

"At least I got hewr something."

Drew sneers at her, his muscles tensing.

"Time to get dressed," I announce, shifting the tides. Addie trots off, and Drew shuffles behind her.

"Eat," Gordon says. "Eating for two."

With another kiss to my belly, he follows them out.

This is how it goes, the initial shock absorbed like a wave, disappearing in the chaos of the day—ignored, pushed aside—remembered in every breath and bruised movement, but overwhelmed by the responsibilities of life, buzzing in the shadows of my mind and creating a cloudy numbness that, by day's end, will progress into paralyzing fear.

The pattern's so familiar it's like déjà vu before it's happened.

For the next few weeks, I'll obsess on preventing another attack, catering to Gordon like he's a king—loving him and worshipping him with abject devotion. I will work out, wear sexy lingerie, attempt to be more beautiful than I am. I will smile and purr, forsaking my dignity, my pride, and any sense of self that remains, all in a vain attempt to prevent it from happening again.

Like now, though I'm nauseous, my system wrecked, and in no condition for food, I force the breakfast Gordon's given me down my bruised throat in an effort to please him.

This will go on for a while, perhaps a few weeks, until exhausted, I give up in despair, slipping into an antipathy so deep that a chill shudders my spine to remember it. Waking up, breathing, existing becomes a chore—bathing, grooming, eating out of the question.

It is a dangerous time—a time of feeling nothing, wanting nothing—a time when I'm no longer afraid. So I tempt fate, taunt Gordon and my mortality with sloven disregard, inviting and inciting my own destruction.

Two years ago, I accidently-purposely left the stove on and nearly burned down the house. Another time, I half-intentionally released my parking brake, taking out a parking meter and the trunk of my car. And a year ago, I had an affair—Russian roulette with five bullets in the chamber.

I choke down the last piece of toast, closing my eyes and willing it to stay put.

If I survive, if I don't destroy myself, eventually Addie and Drew will bring me back from the ledge, and thoughts beyond the present will begin to break through as I think of their future and what will happen to them if I don't pull it together and figure out how to make things right. And as the bruises fade, my resolve will grow, and I will become determined to reclaim my life.

Gordon senses this, instinctively knowing when I begin to regain my strength.

As we lie in bed, my head spinning with thoughts of escape, he will turn to me. "Jill, you know how much I love you."

I will nod.

"And if I ever lost you…" His voice will trail off and he will shake his head, then he will look at me fully so I can witness the veracity in his eyes. "…I'd go crazy."

He is crazy. I already know this.

"You won't leave me," he will say. "You wouldn't do that? Do that to me and the kids?"

And my heart will twist in terror for Addie and Drew.

This is how it will happen. This is why I have stayed.

I set the empty plate on the nightstand and, numb and sore, hobble toward our bedroom.

I limp as I walk and try to force my left leg to bend, but the battered muscles refuse to cooperate.

Each step aches. My pelvis is bruised, and my ribs pulse so acutely I wonder if they're broken. Halfway there, I stumble into a gimpy run, lunging for the bathroom and getting there just in time to vomit my efforts into the bowl.

I flush away the evidence and, my head spinning, pull myself to the seat. I rest my forehead against the cool edge of the vanity. Below me, the trash can holds the empty tampon box, and the pain intensifies as my breaths deepen with despair. I can't be pregnant. I'm already at my breaking point.

Gordon's hand on my neck was a warning, its loosening, a show of mercy. I close my eyes and feel his fingers tightening, the thin stream of air whistling to my lungs.

If I stay, he will kill me. If I leave, he'll destroy Addie and Drew. This is the impossible catch-22 I'm left with.

There's a third possibility, but I pretend I don't recognize it. Like an itch I'm afraid to scratch for fear it will fester and grow, I turn from it, close my ears to it, drape it in a sheet, but like an elephant in the room, it cannot be disguised—it smells, it bellows, it takes up too much space.

NO! I scream. I refuse to acknowledge it, consider it. I push it back. It doesn't budge.

I pull on my clothes and turn on the faucet to drown it out.

Run, it whispers.

I apply my makeup, a heavy coat of foundation and a deep shade of lipstick to conceal the truth.

Take the kids and run. Hide where he can't find you.

Leave my job, my home, my parents?

I can't...I won't...

He'll kill you; he'll destroy them.

"Jill, let's go." A holler from downstairs.

Mercifully, the choice will have to wait. Like all the times before, at this moment, my focus is on survival—survive this moment, this hour, this day.

"Jill!"

On shaky legs I stand; my time to decide is up.

∽

Drew's lunch is packed and sits on the counter above his Angels backpack, which sits on the floor.

Gordon walks from the hallway wearing the off-duty uniform worn by most of the cops in the department—white T-shirt, dark Levi's 501s, and a blue windbreaker that conceals his Glock.

He pulls a banana from the stainless steel banana hanger and walks to the door. He's going to work out, then he'll return to sleep a few hours before spending the rest of the day with Addie. And this afternoon, he'll coach Drew and the Laguna Beach Indians.

"Game's at six," he reminds me, his tone laced with warning.

I nod.

The door closes behind him, and I breathe.

I comb Addie's red curls, though they spring instantly back to an unruly mop, and finish just as the front door opens, letting in the crisp morning air along with my mom.

"Morning," my mom says, and that's all it takes.

Addie bolts to my leg, and the tremor before the eruption begins. The quivering starts with her lip, then moves outward to her chin and cheeks, culminating in a bloodcurdling wail as she clings to my skirt to prevent my departure.

Drew pulls on his backpack and watches unimpressed. When we get in the car, he'll rate it on the Addie Richter scale. Friday was mild, only a six. Today's revving up to be a nine.

My mom walks past us and pours herself a glass of orange juice. Tantrum consoling isn't in her job description nor in her skill set. She sits at the counter sipping her juice and paging through the latest edition of *Redbook*.

I pry Addie's hands from my skirt and almost escape, but she lunges back, sending a jolt of pain through my injured ribs.

"Damn it," I snap.

My mom scowls, annoyed that my expletive interrupted her reading.

"Addie, honey, you know Mommy needs to go to work." I try, though my stressed voice hardly conveys the sympathetic plea I was going for. My ribs throb, and the clock ticks.

Addie latches on tighter and screams louder, and I don't have time for this. Drew's going to be late; I'm going to be late. I wrench myself free from my sobbing daughter, grab Drew by the hand, and drag him out the door.

As we drive, the stress ebbs, and I glance in the mirror to see Drew sitting quietly in the backseat. His mop of sandy hair hangs past his forehead and curls around his ears. His blue eyes are like Gordon's, his long eyelashes are mine. Since he turned eight, he no longer sits in his car seat, so my view of him is limited to his eyes, which stare solemnly forward toward the road and the reluctant destination of school.

"Morning," I say.

He smiles for the first time of the day, an anemic grin with no teeth.

"Red or blue?" I ask.

"Red."

He always picks red, because red almost always wins.

We start to count. This morning blue cars are in fashion and I pull to an early lead, but then I miss a few, and when we pull into the drop-off lane of his school, we are even. He unbuckles his seat belt as a teacher drives past in a small red Mini Cooper.

"You win," I say.